Praise for Anne Emery

Praise for *Blood on a Saint*

"As intelligent as it is entertaining . . . The writing bustles with energy, and with smart, wry dialogue and astute observations about crime and religion."   — *Ellery Queen*

"Emery skilfully blends homicide with wit, music, theology, quirky characters."   — *Kirkus Reviews*

Praise for *Death at Christy Burke's*

"Emery's sixth mystery (after 2010's *Children in the Morning*) makes excellent use of its early 1990s Dublin setting and the period's endemic violence between Protestants and Catholics."

— *Publishers Weekly*, starred review

"Halifax lawyer Anne Emery's terrific series featuring lawyer Monty Collins and priest Brennan Burke gets better with every book."

— *Globe and Mail*

Praise for *Children in the Morning*

"This [fifth] Monty Collins book by Halifax lawyer Emery is the best of the series. It has a solid plot, good characters, and a very strange child who has visions."   — *Globe and Mail*

"Not since Robert K. Tanenbaum's Lucy Karp, a young woman who talks with saints, have we seen a more poignant rendering of a female child with unusual powers."   — *Library Journal*

THE COLLINS-BURKE MYSTERY SERIES

Ruined Abbey

Ruined Abbey

A MYSTERY

ANNE EMERY

ECW Press

Published by ECW Press
665 Gerrard Street East, Toronto, ON M4M 1Y2
416-694-3348 / info@ecwpress.com

LIBRARY AND ARCHIVES CANADA CATALOGUING IN PUBLICATION

Emery, Anne, author
Ruined abbey / Anne Emery.
(The Collins-Burke mystery series)

ISBN 978-1-77041-167-8 (bound)
Also issued as: 978-1-77090-691-4 (PDF); 978-1-77090-692-1 (EPUB)

I. Title II. Series: Emery, Anne. Collins-Burke mystery series.
PS8609.M47R85 2015   C813'.6   C2014-907600-2   C2014-907601-0

Cover and text design: Tania Craan
Cover image: © Photopat/Veer
Author photo: Precision Photo
Printing: Friesens   5   4   3   2   1

The publication of *Ruined Abbey* has been generously supported by the Canada Council for the Arts which last
year invested $157 million to bring the arts to Canadians throughout the country, and by the Ontario Arts Council
(OAC), an agency of the Government of Ontario, which last year funded 1,793 individual artists and 1,076
organizations in 232 communities across Ontario, for a total of $52.1 million. We also acknowledge the financial
support of the Government of Canada through the Canada Book Fund for our publishing activities, and the
contribution of the Government of Ontario through the Ontario Book Publishing Tax Credit and the Ontario
Media Development Corporation.

PRINTED AND BOUND IN CANADA

Chapter I

April 29, 1989

Father Brennan X. Burke was just about to vest for his early Saturday Mass at St. Kieran's church in New York City when his telephone rang. By the time the call was over, Mass was all but forgotten, and Brennan was scrambling for the next flight out of the country.

"Brennan!"

"Molly, my darling! *Conas atá tú?*"

"Níl mé go maith." Not good.

"What is it?"

Brennan did not like the sound of his sister's voice. As faint as it was coming down the line from London to New York, it was a guarded voice, and there was clearly something amiss.

He felt a pang of fear. Was she hurt? Ill? "Are you all right, Molly?"

The silence stretched across the transatlantic line.

Finally, she answered him. "I'm in the nick, Brennan. Holloway Prison in London."

There was no point in asking whether he had heard her right and whether she was serious. He had and she was. Riotous images assailed his mind, but natural caution prevailed when he spoke again. "What can you tell me?"

"They picked me up for being a member of a proscribed organization—*allegedly* a member. I'm not going to say anything more about it on the phone."

Jesus, Mary, and Joseph. Was she going to leave him with that? But she was right to keep silent; the Brits were probably listening in. Prison guards, the police, spies, who knew?

"I just wanted the family to know, Brennan, in case you don't hear from me for a while. Mam's birthday's coming up, and if I don't call . . ."

That was his sister all over, God be good to her. There she was in an English jail, facing who knew what fate, and she was worried about their mother missing a call on her birthday.

"I'm going over there."

"To Mam and Da's, you mean? This will blow the head off Da."

"He's not going to hear about it, at least for now. Going over to London is what I meant, Mol. I'll be on the next flight out."

"No, no, don't do that."

"I said I'm going, and I'm going. How long have you been in there?"

"Last night. Or this morning, I should say. Half-twelve, they came by my flat."

The knock on the door at midnight, an event feared around the world.

"How long do you expect . . . well, they're hardly going to tell you how long they plan to keep you in."

"Normally, they could detain me for two days, but they told me they're applying to keep me in for five more. Some special provision. So it . . ." Her voice wavered. "It could be a week."

Brennan was terrified for her, but he knew he couldn't show it, and he knew he couldn't ask for details.

"Do you have a lawyer?"

"Yes, I called a solicitor this morning. Can't say any more than that."

"That's right. Don't. I'll see you as soon as I can. The blessings of God on you, Molly."

Brennan felt he was abandoning her by putting down the phone, but there was nothing he could do for her at a distance of 3,500 miles. The sooner he got airborne, the better. It was seven in the morning New York time, twelve noon in London. He picked up the phone again and called his brother, a commercial airline pilot.

"Yo."

"Terry."

"Bren, I was going to call you. See if you wanted to head over to O'Malley's this aft. Lift a few jars."

"How fast can I get to London?"

"London? Are you serious?"

"Serious. Got a call from Molly. They've banged her up in jail on some kind of trumped-up charge."

"I can't be hearing this."

"I just heard it myself."

"Jaysus, don't be telling the old man she's in an English prison. All we need is him launching a missile across the Atlantic."

"I won't be telling him."

"There's obviously been a mistake. Molly would no more—"

"Presumably. Now, about a flight."

"Leave it with me. Pack your things and wait to hear. And as soon as I can get over to Heathrow myself, I'll join you. What kind of charges are you talking about? Is it what I think it is?"

"She's accused of being a member of a banned organization. Terrorist organization." Click.

†

Brennan arranged for one of the other priests to take over his parish duties for the next few days, and he packed a bag. Terry called with the time and flight number, and Brennan headed to the airport. His plane took off at ten that morning and touched down at Heathrow seven hours later, seven hours that seemed like seventy, so anxious was Brennan to get on the ground in England. With the time difference, that made it ten at night in London, and he still had an hour's ride on the tube into the city. He knew there was no chance of seeing his sister in the lockup at that time of night, but he called from the arrivals lounge anyway. All he could do was leave a message. He would be at the prison gate first thing the next morning. He found a cheap hotel near King's Cross station, but he may as well have sat up all night in the station as go to a hotel; he lay awake for hours, anxious and fearful about what was in store for his sister.

Then, in the morning, he may as well have been nowhere near the station because he was so impatient to see Molly he didn't even bother with the London Underground; he hailed the first taxi he saw and told the driver to make haste to Holloway Prison in the borough of Islington. The driver, with the reserve for which the English are renowned, withheld comment on their destination but made friendly conversation all the way there. Brennan did his best to respond in kind, but his mind was elsewhere. His anxiety was compounded when the taxi dropped him off outside the complex of red-brick buildings where his sister was incarcerated.

Molly was older by just under two years; the resemblance between them was striking. They both had black hair going silver at the temples; they had the same aquiline nose; her eyes were a dark blue and his black. Right now, though, sitting across from him in the visiting area, she was pale and red-eyed with exhaustion.

"How are you holding up? You look as if you've spent two years looking into the abyss."

"You know what they say, Brennan. When you look into the abyss, the abyss looks into you."

"Yes." He peered around him at the hard-looking inmates, their hard-looking visitors, and their equally hard-looking guardians, some of whom were men. "How am I going to get you out of here?"

"Your powers as a priest of the Roman Catholic Church are not recognized by the authorities in this place."

"Or in this country, which is why I'm not here in my clerical suit and collar."

"Yes, well . . . My solicitor is working on it, trying to get me released."

"And?"

"She'll be in later this morning. It's so good to see you, Bren. You have no idea. The place is filthy. It has rats. I've heard the squeaks coming out of them, and I saw one scurrying across the floor. I'm afraid to close my eyes in case one of them . . . And some of the people in here have me terrorized; that includes the staff as well as the inmates. But now that you're in England, I'll feel a little . . ." She cleared her throat and made an attempt at a smile. She couldn't carry it off.

He reached for her hand and was barked at by someone in authority. Male. "No contact, please, sir." Please didn't sound like please; sir didn't sound like sir.

"Terry's coming over too, as soon as he can arrange his days off."

"Terry, God love him! I'd better be clear of this place before he turns up. He'll eat the head off somebody in charge here, and next thing he knows, he'll be under arrest himself. But I can't wait to see him. What would I do without my little brothers?"

"I don't know how much use we'll be to you."

"Just having you here is enough, darling."

"Now what in the hell have they charged you with?"

"They say I assisted in the arrangement of a meeting to further the activities of a proscribed organization."

"That organization being . . ." As if he didn't know.

"The Irish Republican Army."

Brennan looked over at the guard on duty; the man's eyes were directly on him. Brennan was not about to ask his sister whether she had in fact been involved in such a meeting.

"If convicted," she said, "I could be facing anything from a fine—"

"The family will come through with that."

"—to ten years in prison."

"Jesus the Christ and Son of God! That can't happen!"

"It has happened, and could again."

†

Consumed by what he had seen and heard, Brennan could barely concentrate enough to follow his sister's directions for the tube to her place in Kilburn, in the northwest of London. But, after a couple of false starts, he found it. It was a terrace of houses with a narrow, paved laneway between it and a much larger, blander, and more modern block of flats. The first storey of Molly's terrace was done in white stone, with the upper two storeys in red brick. Each house in the row had a demi-lune fanlight over the door. Her upstairs flat had three small bedrooms, a kitchen, and a sitting room painted a cheerful golden yellow with white trim. There was a dark wood dining table with four chairs at one end of the room; at the other end was a pull-out sofa. Pictures of maps and ancient buildings adorned the walls, and her bookshelves were stuffed to capacity. Brennan knew that Molly's daughter was away studying at Oxford, and her son divided his time between Molly's and his father's place somewhere else in London.

Brennan spent the day wandering aimlessly around Kilburn and neighbouring areas of the city, too exhausted and distracted to take anything in. He had an early supper at a local chipper, then returned to Molly's and threw himself down on one of the beds. But, for the second night in a row, he needn't have lain down at all, so little sleep did he get. The few times he did drift off, his mind presented him with harrowing images of a show trial in which Molly could not be heard, and a jail cell in which she cowered in fear of vermin, her fellow inmates, and the prison warders.

Chapter II

We are the boys of Wexford
Who fought with heart and hand
To burst in twain the galling chain
And free our native land.

Patrick Joseph McCall, "The Boys of Wexford"

A call the next morning sent relief flooding through Brennan. It turned out that Molly would not have to serve up to ten years in prison, or even the full seven days allowable under the Prevention of Terrorism Act. She was less than exuberant that afternoon, though, when she was back in her own home, showered and dressed, with a cup of tea in front of her on the table and BBC Radio chattering away in the background. Any time Brennan had visited his sister in London, BBC was always the soundtrack.

"The fact that I'm out of their jail does not mean I'm out of their sight, Brennan. I can expect to be watched, harassed, interrogated, and God knows what else."

"Why?"

"They think I know something about this."

She got up, fetched her handbag, and returned to the table. She withdrew a piece of paper from the bag and placed it in front of Brennan. It was the front page of the April 26, 1989, *Daily Telegraph*. He read aloud. "Policeman murdered in line of duty. Scotland Yard, officer's family, in shock." Brennan felt the breath go out of him. He read the story. "'Detective Sergeant Richard Heath, a twenty-two-year veteran of the Metropolitan Police Service, was shot to death in his police car on Elverton Street yesterday afternoon.' A police officer murdered. What—"

"Read on."

Brennan returned to the paper. "Close to the time the shooting occurred, police received a warning call from someone using a code word known to the authorities as a code unique to the IRA, the Provisional Irish Republican Army. The caller warned of several large explosive devices that had been planted at Westminster Abbey. Emergency teams responded and people were cleared from the abbey and the Houses of Parliament . . ." He looked up at his sister. "Westminster Abbey! Please tell me they have it wrong here."

"They have it right."

"No!" Brennan could not contain himself. Even if no lives were lost, this was an unconscionable act. Westminster Abbey was one of the most magnificent Gothic buildings in the world. The great church belonged to the ages. That anyone could even consider destroying it . . . He snapped back to the present and his sister's woes. He continued reading. "Scotland Yard is remaining tight-lipped as to whether the two events were connected. 'We are following several leads in our investigation,' a Yard press officer said last evening.

"Detective Sergeant Heath was married, the father of two sons. He was an avid cricketer, volunteer rugby coach, and a dedicated member of several charitable organisations. Tributes poured in from fellow officers, people who had volunteered with him . . ." Brennan looked up at his sister. "You wouldn't be involved in anything like this, obviously."

"No."

"Well then, why are they claiming you were?"

"They seem to believe, or they purport to believe, that I am acquainted with the kind of people who would do this. The thinking, presumably, is that they could intimidate me into giving them information."

"What led them to believe you would know the kind of people who would do this?"

"It seems that my attitude towards Oliver Cromwell set them off."

"Cromwell! How could your attitude towards Cromwell land you in prison more than three hundred years after his death?"

"Well, let me tell you about a conference I attended a few weeks ago, where I presented a paper."

"I'm all ears. But, em, have you got any . . ."

"I'm all out. My local's just around the corner. We'll leave a note for Terry."

She scribbled a note, "Terry, we're at Hannigan's," and taped it to the outside door of the building. Less than two minutes later they were walking into Hannigan's bar in the Kilburn High Road. The walls of the bar were dedicated to the sport of hurling; the colours of every Irish county were on display, along with photos of teams and star hurlers.

"Molly, *conas atá tú?*"

"*Tá mé go maith*, Seamus."

The barman had cropped black hair, deep blue eyes, and wore a black shirt. He could have been behind the counter of any bar in Ireland. He put his hand to the Guinness tap and began the pour. "For you, sir?"

"I'll have a Jameson. Double it for me, would you?"

The man nodded. Didn't ask about ice.

"Anybody in the back, Seamus?"

"It's all yours, Molly."

"Seamus, my brother Brennan."

The two men greeted each other. When the Jameson had been poured, and the Guinness was settling, Brennan tuned in to a discussion going on beside him at the bar. One man, who sounded as if he might have been from Limerick, was doing his duty to educate a couple of new arrivals about the ways of the world. The world of the London Irish bar.

"You'll find the Guinness doesn't travel well, Matty. It's got a crusty head on it over here. I only drink it from the bottles here in London."

Seamus appeared to be deaf to this commentary as he commenced the second part of the two-part pour of Molly's pint.

"And whatever you do," the Guinness expert said to his pals, "don't be going up to Mickey McConachy's bar, expecting anything close to what you're used to at home. High water rates in that place, if you know what I'm saying."

"You're not saying he waters the stuff down! I was going to head up there later to meet my sister."

"He waters it, or he doesn't water it, depending on which tap he uses when he has a look at you. If he knows you and likes you, you'll get the beer or the stout as God meant it to be. Otherwise it's so watery you might as well be drinking the River Shannon. You see the smiley head on yer man and all the while he's pouring you a pint of Haitch-Two-O. Go into Mickey McConachy's drunk and you come out sober."

"This tastes fine to me," one of the new fellows said, and the pintman conceded that Hannigan's would give you a good pint, and Seamus was a fine barman.

When Molly's pint was properly settled, Seamus pushed the glasses towards them with a smile, and Brennan produced a ten-pound note.

Seamus waved it away. "Later," he said. "No entrance fee for the Burkes in here."

Molly laughed. "They know I never walk out without paying my tab. I'm afraid they'd cut me off."

They thanked the barman and walked to the back, where they found a snug and sat down, screened from view. Brennan lit a cigarette and inhaled the smoke deep into his lungs. Then he lifted his glass, Molly lifted hers, and they said in unison, *"Sláinte!"* Each of them took a good, sustaining sip.

"Now, Brennan, back to Oliver Cromwell. I'm thinking somebody grassed on me after my presentation at the 'Lord Protector' conference."

"Lord Protector. Right," Brennan muttered.

"As we know, Cromwell made quite a name for himself during the civil war years here in England. And when it was time to fight Parliament's enemies in Ireland, it was Cromwell who led the charge. He massacred thousands of people in Drogheda and Wexford and then, back in England, he received his new title. He was named, with cruel irony, Lord Protector of the Commonwealth of England, Scotland, and Ireland. Lord Protector for life. What does it tell you that there is a statue of him at Westminster, outside the Houses of Parliament? True, he was an early parliamentarian. Maybe his admirers were blind to the other things he got up to. We can't be sure. Anyway, there was a scholarly conference on him, a symposium titled 'Lord Protector of the Commonwealth: Contemporary and Current Perspectives.' A highly academic affair, with historians and graduate students presenting papers. As a professor of history at the University of London, with several publications to my credit, I got my name on the list of presenters."

"Hard to picture you there, Molly."

"I didn't submit the title of my essay until I stood up in the packed hall to present it. At that point I announced that my paper was 'Lord Protector, Me Arse.'"

Brennan let out a roar of appreciative laughter and raised his glass to her.

"And I proceeded to give them the Irish view of the oul murdherin' bastard!"

"Good girl yourself!"

"Cromwell himself wrote that, at Drogheda, there were three thousand military casualties 'and many inhabitants.' Catholic sources at the time of the Restoration said four thousand civilians had been killed. Men, women, and children. As for Wexford, Cromwell admitted to two thousand military and civilian casualties. Survivors in Wexford said only a few men, women, and children managed to get out alive. Then he smashed his way through many of the other towns in Ireland as well, all the while claiming he was doing God's work against the Catholic Irish, whom he called 'barbarous wretches.' He did this under cover of taking revenge for the uprising of 1641. The native Irish did rise and kill many of the Protestant settlers who had taken Irish lands, no question, but Cromwell's actions were against people who had nothing whatsoever to do with that.

"Then came the clearances. Irish landowners in Ulster, Leinster, and Munster were to be stripped of their lands and sent west to Connacht, leaving the three more fertile provinces for the invaders. And if you didn't go, you were killed. Hence the phrase 'To hell or Connacht.' But it didn't end there." His sister was seated across from him in Hannigan's bar but Brennan could easily picture her in the lecture hall, her presentation becoming more and more fiery as she got herself wound up.

"Now we come to the human trafficking. Thousands more Irish men, women, and children were sent by Cromwell to work as slaves on the tobacco and sugar plantations in the Caribbean. Some were sent as indentured servants, who did forced labour for a specified number of years. This had started before the Cromwell period. Others were slaves, pure and simple. Captured, branded, and sold in Barbados. All of them, servants and slaves, were transported on slave ships and flogged if they didn't do their work or if they got uppity. A new verb was coined at the time: to be *barbadoed*. Desiring to rid Ireland of unruly Irish males and surplus Irish females, Cromwell found it convenient to support the slave traders operating out of Bristol. And the great Puritan was more than happy to oblige the English plantation owners who expressed a hankering for white women. So I had a section in my paper titled 'Cromwell as Pimp' right after 'Cromwell as Slave Trader.' Oh, I said my piece, to be sure."

As his sister gave voice to her feelings about the seventeenth-century atrocities, Brennan noticed that the little English inflections she had picked up during her years here dropped away, and her speech returned to its Dublin roots. Her teenage years in New York had had little effect on her accent, and Brennan had been told the same was true of him.

"How did 'Lord Protector, Me Arse' go over with the Cromwell scholars?"

"What could they say? I stayed entirely with facts that are widely agreed upon by reputable historians and gave the conflicting accounts where there is disagreement. They couldn't dispute me on the facts. But my attitude towards the subject was not well received."

"A badge of honour, to be on the enemy list of that crowd."

"And they were academics, people who are supposed to welcome a free exchange of ideas. We all know what a farce that is. You know as well as I do, Brennan, that the herd instinct is alive and well in the ivory towers of independent thought, and woe to anyone who holds a position that is outside the bounds of fashionable opinion.

"But I've strayed from the subject of my discourse. Oliver Cromwell. You'll be interested to hear that there is a Cromwell Association that holds a commemoration every year on September third. But they decided to meet at the statue in April this year, gathering on the anniversary of his birth instead of his death, for whatever reason."

"And?" His sister said nothing more but picked up her pint and finished it off. "You were going to greet this association and offer them a different perspective on Cromwell's role in history?"

"Something along those lines."

"That hardly constitutes an offence against the state. Right, Molly?" Brennan butted his cigarette out in the ashtray.

"Correct."

"So in order for them to arrest you under the Prevention of Terrorism Act, they must have thought you were more than just an outspoken critic of the *bête noire* of seventeenth-century Ireland."

"They must have."

"Are you a member of an organization banned under the laws of England?"

"I'm not a joiner."

"Am I to take that as a no?"

"You are. By the way, Brennan, do you know how many organizations are proscribed under the law here?"

"No idea. Heaps of them, I suppose."

She laughed. "Two."

"Two banned groups, in a country of fifty million people?"

"Yes. The Irish Republican Army and the Irish National Liberation Army."

"I see."

"Both of these organizations have caused a lot of trouble in this country."

"No question. I'm just surprised that there are no other trouble-makers blacklisted."

"Well," she said, "with immigration patterns the way they are, maybe there will be others on the list someday. For now, we're it."

"We?"

"Em, not *we*. *Them*, the 'RA and the INLA."

"That kind of talk can get you in trouble, didn't yez know that?"

"Terry, my darling, it's so good to see you!" Molly got up and took her brother into her embrace.

"Seamus told me where to find you. I told him I'd have to kneecap him for being an informer."

"You didn't!"

"Of course not."

"Not the sort of thing to say in this place, Ter."

"I'll remember that."

"I mean it."

"I'll go back for drinks."

He returned shortly with pints of Guinness for himself and Molly, and a double Jameson for Brennan. There had been no need to inquire beforehand.

He sat down and raised his glass to his sister. "So, you've been sprung, Molly. Are you out on bail or what?"

"No, I'm out. Period."

"Well, then," he said, getting up, "you're sorted, and we can all go home. Coming, Brennan?"

"Oh, I think we can stay on for a few days now that we've come all this way."

"Okay, I'm easy." He sat down again and drank deeply of his pint.

"But now that I've come to the attention of the authorities, now that I'm within their sights," Molly said, "I can expect to stay within them for the foreseeable future. So you two hooligans will have to behave yourselves."

"Should I even inquire how you came into their sights in the first place?" Terry asked.

Molly filled him in on her Cromwell rant, the shooting of Detective Sergeant Heath, the explosives planted in Westminster Abbey, and the police suspicion that she might have information pertinent to the investigation.

"They came for you in the middle of the night because you gave a talk against Oliver Cromwell and were going to make a speech in front of his statue?" Terry sounded incredulous. "Has England turned into a police state or what?"

"I'll have to lead you down a long and twisty road to explain the background here. Do you remember, Brennan, that trip we took to Wexford when we were little?"

Of course he remembered. He was nine years old at the time, Molly nearly eleven. She had not yet acquired the nickname Molly and was known by Máire.

"Was I there?" Terry asked.

"You were, darling," his sister replied, "but *in utero*. Mam was pregnant with you when we took the trip. It was the year before we emigrated from Ireland to New York."

Brennan couldn't wait. Sure, sure he was loving the tour through the countryside in his da's 1946 Ford Prefect, gazing out the windows as the bright green fields flashed past him. The fields were divided by white stone walls, and there was the occasional big brown horse grazing and swishing his tail about, and there were loads of sheep. One of the sheep wandered out into the road, and Da had to stop. So did all the other cars. The great woolly creature stared in through the windscreen at the family sitting in the car. Nobody seemed in a hurry to move him out of the way.

Brennan's little brother Patrick was going mental beside him in the back seat, wiggling and squealing for Mam and Da to let him out. Patrick made a dive to the right, where their sister, Máire, was sitting, but she gave him a little shove and set him back on his arse in the seat. Brennan had seen enough of the wool and the grass, so he opened the book he had on his knees, a book all about the beautiful abbeys in Ireland. Someone had drawn pictures of them in colour and collected them in a book. An abbey was like a castle and a church mixed up together, made of stone with pointy tops and crosses, and his mother had told him about the lovely chanting the monks did. They were on their way to Wexford town, and one of the abbeys in the book was in Wexford. And they were going to see it. If they ever got themselves moving again. Mam had told him it wouldn't look the way it did in the picture. Well, of course not. Brennan knew it was nearly eight hundred years old.

Patrick squirmed his way underneath the book and sat himself on Brennan's knee. "Let me see," he said, and Brennan moved the book out a bit so the little lad could see it better.

Then, before anybody knew it, Patrick banged himself against the door and got it open and he was out of the car. He took himself off at a run and went straight for the sheep. There he was, throwing his arms around the creature and petting and kissing it. Da let out an ungodly roar and said things that would have earned Brennan a smack on the arse if he had even whispered them, and his ma said, "Declan! Your language in front of the children!" This caused the baby on her knee to start wailing. The baby, Francis, was always wailing. Brennan hoped the baby Mam had in her belly would turn out to be less like Fran and more like Pat.

Da got out of the car really fast and grabbed Pat, dug him out of the wool of the sheep, and hauled him back inside the car. Pat wasn't even scared; he looked as if he had just made the winning goal for the Dubs in the All-Ireland hurling final. Waterford, more like; they beat Dublin last year. Patrick sat there hugging himself and smiling for the rest of the trip, once the sheep moved off and the car moved on.

"How much more do we have to go?" Brennan asked.

"If you'd get your head out of the book about abbeys, you'd have seen the sign that says Wexford is five miles away," his sister replied.

That made sense so he didn't put up an argument.

And before he knew it, they were coming into the town. It was on the River Slaney where the river flowed into the ocean. His father told them pirates had been sailing out of Wexford and raiding English ships three hundred years ago. Brennan formed a picture of the sailing ships and their swashbuckling crews in this very harbour. And Da also said this was a rebel town. The boys of Wexford had fought in the Rebellion of 1798, and then other famous men had made speeches here. Daniel O'Connell, Charles Stewart Parnell, Jim Larkin. As the car made its way along the narrow streets of Wexford, Brennan saw a tall church spire rising above the town, and there was another to the left of it, to the south, he supposed it was. Another tower, shorter and square, reminded him of an Italian church he'd seen in the calendar his family had for last year; Brennan had kept it for the pictures. Then there was a castle! Or part of one anyway. He'd have to make sure he got to see that. And he did, because it turned out to be right next to the abbey.

But wait a minute, what was going on here? This was the abbey, his mam said, but there was no roof on it and no glass in the windows. It was just the pointy walls, open to the air. Brennan was gutted at the sight of it. He cried out—he couldn't stop himself—"What happened to it? It's fuckin' half-destroyed!" He felt he was going to burst into tears.

Nobody thumped him on the side of the head because of his language; it was that dire a sight.

Máire was the same way. He could tell by looking at her face that she was heart-scalded. Brennan hoped she wouldn't cry because then he might too, might not be able to stop it.

They all walked towards it, Da in the front, Mam with the baby in her arms, Máire and Brennan each holding one of Patrick's hands. Pat stared up at the place with huge eyes, blue as the sky above their heads. "Somebody's going to be in the soup for this, right Da?"

And that's when Brennan felt the anger creeping into himself. "Who did this?" he demanded to know. "And where are all the monks that are supposed to be living here and singing all day long? They can't stay here now!"

His mam put her arms around him. "I told you, pet, that it wasn't going to look the way it looked in the drawings." Well, no, he knew that. Old things looked old. Dirty or a bit crumbling down. But not this! "Some of the abbeys and the churches are even worse, *acushla*. Some are just heaps of rubble on the ground."

"Cromwell's men did this!" Da said. "This and other churches here. And they torched the Franciscan Friary up the hill, burning the brothers and priests to death." Da's voice wasn't loud, but Brennan knew he was in a ferocious temper about this man Cromwell.

Brennan had heard about Cromwell. None of it was good.

✝

Forty years later in Hannigan's bar, Brennan said to his sister, "The sight of the destruction, knowing what had been there, upset me so much I scarpered. Took off at a clip. I got lost in the town, didn't I? The rest of you had to come looking for me. Found me, I guess." He laughed and hoisted his glass.

"And then?" his sister prompted him.

"I remember giving out at length to everyone in the car on the way back to Dublin. I went on and on about Cromwell, and commended him to the care of the divil in hell. And Da muttered something, and I asked him what he'd said, and Mam said never mind. But he told us anyway that Cromwell had led an army from England into Ireland and killed thousands of people. And it was all about Cromwell fighting supporters of the deposed king. I didn't understand why there would be supporters of the king in Ireland. Weren't we always fighting the British Crown? Didn't make sense to me, at least at the age of nine."

"No wonder," Molly-nee-Máire said. "This phase of our unfortunate history arose out of the civil war in England, between those loyal to King Charles the First and those who supported the Parliament. The parliamentary forces overthrew and executed the king. Meanwhile, over in Ireland, there was an uneasy alliance of Old Irish and Old English Catholics, trying to fight off any more expansion of Protestant power in the country. Sounds strange to us today, but they were royalists, loyal to the king of England, who was king of Ireland as well. They were fooled into thinking a restored monarchy would give them back the freedom to worship as Catholics. They must have been on the drink, if they believed that. "

"Mindless with drink," Brennan agreed.

"Do you remember anything else about that day, Brennan?" Molly asked. "Sorry to be leaving you out of things, Terry."

"That's all right. Not much I can contribute to the conversation, given that I wasn't even born yet. I'll have to be content to listen and learn."

"We had tea somewhere. That, I recall," said Brennan. "And was Grandda there? No, that must have been another occasion."

"Same occasion. You had let fly with some language that would have burned the ears off the monks had they still been present. Then you ran away. You headed down into the town centre. And knowing you, you probably got fascinated by all the sights and the buildings and embarked on a little tour of your own. Meanwhile we were at the abbey, Mam pregnant with Terry, and Francis fussing, and Patrick wanting to climb the ruined walls, and it took us a while to get sorted and go looking for you."

"Right. It's coming back to me now. I slowed down after a bit and began wandering through the winding streets down to the quays and up again. Then I remember seeing the monument to '98, the Pikeman statue. I must have covered the entire town before yez caught me."

"You did. And that's how Grandfather Christy's plan to slip in and out of Wexford unnoticed came apart. Little Brennan spots Christy's old beater of a car parked in a side street. You would have noticed our grandfather's car wherever he'd parked it in town, because of the bullet holes in the boot and the back window! The way we heard it, you saw the car and no doubt got all excited, and you tried to wrench the driver's door open, but it was locked. You were spotted from inside the Cape Bar, which is right across from the Pikeman statue. One of the fellas meeting with Christy looked out and saw you banging on the car door. So Christy had little choice then but to exclaim, "Jaysus, isn't that my grandson! My boy Declan's little lad. The family came along to see the town." He went out to get you and bring you into the pub. Da had been planning to meet Christy and the other men there once he had deposited the rest of us somewhere. I don't know what all he had in mind for us while he attended this clandestine meeting but, whatever the plan was, it was off the rails by then, and we all ended up in the Cape Bar."

"A clandestine meeting, was it? All I remember now is the crowd of us in the pub. Wasn't Finn there as well?"

"He was. He came down with Christy. They were in town to talk to the boys of Wexford. After the crowd of us showed up, the men took themselves off to a separate table. The place was L-shaped, so around the corner they went. I couldn't hear much of what they were saying, and what I did hear made no sense to my young ears. I heard something about a boat and *Sasana*. Which, as you know, means England. It was all a jumble. But I knew this much: they were having a row, and tempers were high. Christy at one point thumped the table and roared, 'Never mind what year we're in; the timing has to be right!' There was silence after that, and they all drank their porter. The publican's wife came out and offered us tea and sandwiches, which we gladly accepted.

"By that time, some more children had appeared, a couple of really little girls, and a boy around our age. Their name was Delaney, I think. Their parents must have been keeping them occupied in a back room. But once we made our noisy entrance, with Patrick gabbing and Francis howling, the other children wanted to join the party. I remember the boy had a game with him, checkers or something, and he kept looking at me as if he wanted to invite me to play. And I was stealing glances at him, because I wanted to play with him, too. But I stayed put and helped Mam with the baby.

"Anyway, the men were talking about a boat. Somebody's boat or, more likely, the ferry from Rosslare to Wales. And England. Not hard to see a direct line there."

"And the reference to the year?" Brennan said. "It was 1949."

"Exactly three hundred years after Cromwell's attacks on Wexford and Drogheda, in 1649. I could only hear snatches of the conversation between the kids whooping it up and Francis bawling. But it seemed that the fellows in Wexford wanted to conduct an operation against 'revenge targets' in England, and there was a tie-in with Cromwell. Do in England what he had done in Ireland. I pictured them taking a wrecking ball to churches and abbeys and city walls, the kinds of structures smashed to rubble by Cromwell. Hard to believe there was anything left for Cromwell to smash, after the destruction of so many monasteries by Henry the Eighth the century before. Anyway, that was the way my mind was working, after seeing Selskar Abbey and you, Brennan, being so upset. Whatever it was, Christy knew it would be a failure. It would be purely symbolic, and there would be severe retribution from the British in return for very little gain. It would be a distraction from the larger purpose, which was to get the Brits out of the Six Counties of the North, get the Six Counties out of the U.K. and unite them with the rest of Ireland. So Christy used his considerable powers of persuasion to convince them to desist. But then he owed them support for something else. I don't know what actions they took, if any, between then and now. Couldn't have been very effective if we never heard anything."

She took a few moments to enjoy her pint, then said, "Here we are, forty years later. Could it be that the old plan had been revived, and Westminster Abbey was chosen as the big symbolic action? We'll take out your greatest abbey in return for the ruination of so many of ours? I don't know."

"I'm not sure I want to know," Brennan replied.

Molly turned to her youngest brother. "Sorry you missed it all, Terry!"

"Oh, don't be so sure I've missed it all," he said, smiling and taking a sip of Guinness.

"What are we to take from that?" she asked.

"Oh, nothing. I'm just a blathering bullshitter on a barstool enjoying a bit of porter. Pay me no mind."

There was something in that; Terry Burke could often be heard spinning a jocular tale just before last call at the local shebeen.

Molly opened her mouth to respond, but a television broadcast intruded on the conversation. The TV was mounted on the wall across from the snug. Up to this point it had been only background noise. Now its volume increased; someone was following the news. Brennan did not turn to watch it, but he joined the others as they listened in.

". . . condolences from police officers and organizations around the world. Mrs. Heath says she is overwhelmed with gratitude for the support shown to her and the detective's colleagues after his death.

"Meanwhile, an Essex County woman says another murder victim is being ignored. Essex police confirm that there was another suspicious death around the same time Detective Sergeant Richard Heath was killed. The body of a man was found in Colchester, Essex County, on the morning of the twenty-sixth of April. Babs Mundle of Colchester came upon his body when she was out walking her dog. Mrs. Mundle said she shares the feeling of shock and horror at the murder of the policeman in London, and his family has her complete sympathy. But . . ."

A new voice, not as polished as that of the presenter, came on. "The other bloke died, too, didn't he? I'm the one that found him. You don't forget something like that, especially the condition he was in. He'd been roughed up, like. Plain to see. You wouldn't treat an animal like that, would you? This was a fellow I'd seen about the place from time to time before I found him lying there. I'd be out walking my little dachshund, Frankie, and I'd see him. He always had a nice smile. Always had a camera round his neck. A tourist, I suppose. Lots to see round here, first Roman city and all that. No camera on him when I saw him on the ground. And the talk is that his wallet was missing, too. What's wrong with the world today? Nice chap like that, probably never hurt a soul."

"A police spokesman told this reporter that 'every suspicious death gets the same meticulous investigation. Every person, every victim, is important.' The police have not been able to identify the man yet, but they are checking missing persons reports from all over the country. They would not comment on the cause of death."

Brennan spoke over the television. "Another murder around the same time as the police killing."

"There's no reason to think they're connected, right?" said Terry. "Not when you think of how many murders there must be."

"Last I heard," Molly said, "the number was around six hundred."

"Six hundred what?" Terry asked.

"Homicides."

"Over what period of time?"

"One year, in England and Wales."

"Six hundred a *year*?!" Terry exclaimed. "What's the population?"

"England and Wales, around fifty million. Why?"

"Do you know what the numbers are in the United States?"

"Do we want to hear this?"

"I recently saw the figures for 1988, so last year there were something like twenty thousand six hundred homicides. Population is around two hundred forty-five million, so that means . . ."

Brennan did a quick calculation. "The U.S. has roughly five times the population and well over thirty times the number of homicides." He thought for a few more seconds. "Thirty-four times more."

"Somebody should tell the Americans the death penalty doesn't discourage crime," his sister remarked.

"Sets a bad example, I'd say, being murder in and of itself." Brennan took a long, comforting sip of his whiskey.

"But back to Old Blighty," Molly said. "Six hundred murders a year means fewer than two a day. So two killings the same day, or within a day of each other, is unusual."

"But the other didn't happen in London and, even if it had, this is a huge city," Brennan said. "Where's Essex?" *East Saxons*, the name meant, but how far east?

"Next county over, to the east or northeast. On the coast. A different world, I'm sure, from London. But then, what isn't?"

"How long a drive is it?"

"For you in a 747, Terry? Couple of minutes, I suppose. For the rest of us, by car, about an hour."

"So this place was a Roman city before London was?" Brennan asked.

"Apparently. But for present purposes, probably not relevant to our inquiries. The killing there sounds like a beating death, with wallet and camera stolen, and the victim here in London was a police officer shot in circumstances related to an IRA bomb plot." She polished off the last of her pint and picked up her handbag. "Time, gentlemen?"

They paid their bar bill, thanked Seamus, and stepped out into the night. People were spilling out of other bars in the Kilburn High Road, and there was an amorous couple approaching from a place up the street. Brennan could hear them trying to negotiate whose flat they would go to and how they would get there. Bus? Tube? Cab? Walk? The man was nearly legless with drink; the woman was tottering along on a pair of spike-heeled shoes. They just managed to stop themselves from falling over the bonnet of a car that was parked with its engine off. Brennan saw two men inside the car and prepared himself for a scene between them and the drunken pair. But the men did not give the hapless lovers a glance. Both of them had their eyes trained on Molly Burke and her brothers.

Chapter III

The following evening, after Molly had put in her teaching day at the University of London, and they had eaten at a local chip shop, Brennan and Terry decided that they wanted to see for themselves the infamous statue of Oliver Cromwell outside the Houses of Parliament. Their sister agreed to accompany them to the scene. The three of them opted for the bus rather than the tube, so they could take in the sights of London on the way. For Brennan, it was sufficient to admire the miles and miles of lovely residential buildings that lined the streets, many of them red brick, some a brilliant white with multi-paned windows and beautiful proportions. Brennan had been on the path to a career in architecture before being called to the priesthood. Even if London had nothing else to commend it (though of course it did), the architecture alone would be enough to have him in awe.

When they got to the river, they walked across Westminster Bridge so they could view the Palace of Westminster from the water. Brennan had always been overwhelmed by the scale and the glory of the perpendicular Gothic complex with its soaring vertical lines, its towers, turrets, and pinnacles. Now, with the sun low in the sky, the golden Houses of Parliament were reflected in the shining water of the Thames. Beautiful.

His sister read his mind. "'Dull would he be of soul who could pass by a sight so touching in its majesty.'"

"Well said."

"That's because I didn't say it. Or, at least, I didn't write it. Wordsworth, 'Upon Westminster Bridge.'"

"A brilliant civilization, no two ways about it," Terry commented.

"No question," agreed Molly. "Bask in this for a bit before we head over."

After a few more minutes of contemplation, they walked back across the bridge and around to the rear of the palace.

"There he is," Molly said, pointing ahead.

Cromwell, sculpted in bronze, stood atop a white pedestal. He was holding a sword and a Bible. Reclining on a plinth at the foot of the pedestal was a lion.

"Just gobbled up the lamb," Brennan muttered.

"Who did, the lion or Cromwell?" asked Terry.

"That will be the subject of my next paper," said Molly.

"Spare yourself the effort," Brennan advised her. "You won't be invited to make a presentation again."

"Good thing I said my piece the first time round. Go stand beside it, and I'll record the moment on film." She pulled a small camera out of her bag.

"I don't want to be immortalized with that," said Brennan. "Terry will probably paste the photo on my gravestone for a bit of posthumous humour."

"Take me then," Terry offered. He moved in beside the figure and extended the middle finger of his left hand towards Cromwell's face.

"Lovely, Terry." She pointed her camera and clicked. "Got it. You've made your statement, and it's been recorded for posterity."

"So, Molly," Brennan asked, "what exactly were *you* going to do here?"

"Splash a bucket of blood-red paint on that thing."

"Were you going to do this publicly or under cover of darkness?"

"It was intended to be a public spectacle, to be carried out while Cromwell's admirers were gathered to pay their respects. We would read a short statement about Cromwell's crimes against our people, and that would be that."

"We?"

"Me and a few like-minded proponents of non-violent civil disobedience."

"Presumably you would be arrested? Taken to jail? Good thing that didn't happen."

"I would have been arrested for vandalism, Brennan, perhaps fined or required to pay damages. Not picked up and imprisoned without charge under the Prevention of Terrorism Act."

"The peelers say you attended a meeting with a—"

"They say I assisted in the arrangement of a meeting to further the activities of a proscribed organization. Which I did not. The people involved in the red paint conspiracy were not Provisional IRA. And splashing a bit of paint on a statue would not further the activities of the Provos."

"But it gave the police the excuse to terrorize you."

"Right."

"Well, what happened?" Terry asked, looking at the statue. "There's no blood on his hands."

"I take it you are referring only to the facsimile of Cromwell, which we see before us, and not to the man himself."

"Correct."

"The mission was aborted. We were warned off."

"Who warned you off?" asked Brennan. Molly avoided his eyes. "Well?"

"There was a note in my post box. 'Cancel Tuesday's paint job. Cancel and stay away.' There was a coded signature."

"Coded signature!" both brothers exclaimed.

"I shall conclude my statement now, gentlemen."

"If you're receiving coded warnings, I'd say you'd best be prepared for another spell in the nick."

"I am not a member, Brennan."

"Well, then, who sent you the warning?"

"At the risk of boring you with unnecessary repetition, I am not a member of a proscribed organization. I am merely a law-abiding resident of London. And as such, I direct your attention to another feature of this great city, which may be of interest. In case you hadn't noticed it. Let's go across the street and have a look at Westminster Abbey, shall we?"

Brennan knew his sister well enough to know that she would not be taking any more questions. He followed her and Terry across the road behind the Parliament Buildings. Seconds later he found himself in Gothic heaven. Benedictine monks had come to the site in the tenth century; the current building was begun in the thirteenth.

"The Thirteenth: Greatest of Centuries," he said to Molly. "Architecture like this is one of many reasons for its greatness."

"If they ever invent a time machine, we all know where you'll be going."

"Don't need a time machine. I'll just stay beneath the vaulted ceiling of this spectacular building and wait for somebody to start up a Gregorian chant. If nobody does, I will. But I was not merely giving my opinion; I was citing a book by that title, *The Thirteenth: Greatest of Centuries*, written by a fellow named James J. Walsh. Walsh did not share the uninformed prejudice of those who know nothing of the mediaeval period."

"I'll grant you, the architecture was wonderful. And the chant."

"And the great Latin hymns. He writes about those. And about the organization of the hospitals, law, the universities. And, just for you, Professor Burke, women professors on the faculties of the Italian universities."

"Oh yeah? Name one."

"You're playing right into my hands. Maria di Novella, professor of mathematics at the University of Bologna. And she was not alone."

"Okay, you win. I'm intrigued. I'll track down a copy of the book. Shouldn't be hard to find in the university library."

"What are you two geeks on about?" Terry asked.

"Brennan wants me to sponsor him so he can become a citizen of this country. That way, as a Brit, he can be buried with the other great men here in the abbey."

"Well, I wouldn't go that far. Transport me back to the thirteenth century, sure, but don't do something that would earn me a thumpin' from our dear oul Irish Republican da."

Molly looked at her watch and said, "I have to get going. Now, can I trust you children not to get into trouble?"

"As long as we stay away from you with your conspiracies and coded warnings, we should be all right."

"May ravens gnaw on your neck, Terrence Burke! Woe to the men of Ireland if they show me disrespect again!"

"Yes, sister."

"You may want to stop by Hannigan's later. There's a session tonight."

"Good. See you there?"

"See you there."

†

Brennan and Terry did some more sightseeing, strolling past the buildings of Whitehall and Number 10 Downing Street, and then they detected the presence of the Sherlock Holmes pub and decided to stop in for a drink. It was a fascinating place filled with Holmes and Watson memorabilia. Someone had left a couple of newspapers on their table, so they each picked one up and skimmed the contents until their food arrived. Terry had grabbed the *Sun*, so he got to ogle the Page 3 girl. Scantily dressed females were a regular feature of the English tabloid press. Like a good brother after lights out in the double bedroom at home, he shared his findings with Brennan.

"Not the most suitable thing to be showing you, I guess, Father Burke."

"She is a child of God like you and me, Captain Burke; who am I to avert my eyes from His creations?"

"Oh, and it says Gordon Strachan has left Manchester United for Leeds. Which leads me to suggest we take in a football match while we're here."

"Sounds good."

Brennan was reading the *Independent*, catching up on what had been happening in the world since he'd embarked on his trip. Something familiar caught his eye. "Here's more on that other killing, the one that happened around the same time as the police shooting."

POLICE FOLLOWING ALL LEADS IN ESSEX KILLING

Essex police are still seeking possible witnesses who may have seen something out of the ordinary on April 25 or 26 last or who may have information regarding the identity of the man who was found dead in Colchester on the morning of April 26. A police spokesman said the man's injuries made it unlikely that anyone would recognise him, so they put together the composite sketch shown above. Police estimated his age at between 30 and 35; he was 5'9" in height and weighed around 12 stone. Babs Mundle, who discovered the man's remains, says it is a shame that no progress has been made. "This man has a family somewhere, but they don't even know he's dead, because whoever did this took his wallet with his I.D. in it. Pretty low when you beat a man to death for a few quid and a camera full of holiday pictures. That's what he was taking, is what I heard. The killer took his camera, but word is he had a little folder full of other pictures he had taken. In his jacket pocket. You know, the envelope of photos you get from the photo shop, six by fours or whatever they are. Just nice pictures of the old buildings here, so the story goes. St. John's Gatehouse, St. Botolph's, that kind of place. And old buildings from other towns around the south here as well. Must have had an interest in architecture. Or religion maybe. That might spark something in somebody's mind about who he is. You know, 'That sounds like our Bill, always taking pictures of old buildings, churches and all.' Shame, it is. You never expect that sort of thing round here, do you?"

Brennan looked up from the paper and took in his surroundings. "Crime solving is not what it used to be, since the demise of Mr. Holmes. He'd have the Essex murder solved quicker than a seven percent solution could be absorbed into his bloodstream."

"What was it he used to inject?"

"Cocaine."

"Worked for him."

"So he claimed."

"So we should see if we can make a buy out there on the street, give ourselves a hit, and offer our services to Scotland Yard."

"Or we could go to Hannigan's, have a few scoops there, and mind our own business."

"Yes, Father." Terry peered over Brennan's shoulder at the news story. "Who in God's name is St. Botolph?"

"No idea," Father Burke had to concede. "I'll have to look him up next time I find myself in a diocesan library. I'm just glad Mam and Da gave me the second name Xavier and not Botolph."

✝

Hannigan's was jammed when Terry and Brennan arrived, and their sister was in full flight giving a performance at the far end of the room. This was something you might see any night of the week in Ireland, a *seanchaí*—a traditional storyteller—holding forth in a bar for the entertainment of the patrons. A younger man, in his early thirties, accompanied her words by beating time on a bodhran. He had a mop of auburn hair, a couple of days' growth of beard, and lively brown eyes.

"That's Conn!" Terry exclaimed.

"Is it? I think you're right."

Conn Burke was the youngest son of their uncle Finn in Dublin. It had been years since Brennan had seen the young fellow. Brennan and Terry quietly placed orders for pints of Guinness and watched the performance.

"And this was when the Morrigan came on the scene." Molly Burke glanced suddenly at the window and raised her hands as if to ward something off. Several people followed her glance. She then leaned forward and whispered to her audience, "The *Morrrrigan*! Goddess of war and death. She has always been with us. She is a shape-changer who can take many forms: she might appear as a seductive young woman or an ancient crone. She might turn herself into an eel!" She wriggled and shuddered, and the drinkers laughed. "Or a cow or a wolf. She often swooped down in the form of a crow, that deadly and knowing bird of death." Conn's beating on the bodhran matched the menacing image. "And on the day I am telling yez about in ancient times, she appeared to the warriors of Ulster and Connacht on the battlefield. As the story goes . . .

"Conchobar—like him," she said, pointing to Conn. "Don't even ask how we spell it. Just say 'Connor.' He arrived with his armies of men from Ulster and had a word with Ailill about a truce. Ailill said yes for the men of Ireland and the exiles—that's you fellows!" she said, her hands taking in the assembled London Irish, and a few raised their glasses, "and Conchobar agreed for the men of Ulster."

"There's a wee gathering of us here too!" came a strong Belfast accent from the corner of the room.

Molly waved in the voice's direction and resumed her tale. "The ground between the Ulster and the Connacht armies lay bare. And 'twas not the only thing that was bare, I can tell you. The men of Ireland fight as men, naked in battle. Take a moment to savour the image, girls! Anyway, as I was saying, in the spooky half-light between the warriors' camps, the Morrigan spoke out:

> Ravens shall gnaw on the necks of men!
> And blood shall spurt in battle.
> Flesh shall be hacked, and pierced with blades.
> O the madness of battle, the acts of war!
> Hail Ulster!
> Woe to the men of Ireland!
> Woe to Ulster!
> Hail the men of Ireland!

"Woe indeed. On this night the wives of Net, called Badb and Nemain—harbingers of death, the pair of them—shrieked above the men of Ireland. The shriek of panic and alarm, a shriek so terrifying that a hundred of the warriors died of fright. It was, the storyteller informs us with considerable understatement, 'a bad night for them.'"

Molly nodded her head, her tale complete, and took a sip of her pint.

She was rewarded with raucous applause. Hands were clapped, glasses raised, drink taken.

Conn rose then, as Molly made her way to Brennan and Terry. "*Go raibh mile maith agat* to my fellow *seanchaí* and cousin, Molly," Conn said. "Thank you for that brilliant recital from the *Táin Bó Cúailnge*, the *Cattle Raid of Cooley*, a bloodcurdling piece of our history. I have to ask meself if you're the Morrigan yerself, you had so much enjoyment of that macabre bit of reportage. Now I'll tone things down a bit so as not to put our friends here in Hannigan's off their drink. Oh," he said, taking a look around the place, "I see they're still able for it. But I'll soothe yez all with a lullaby nonetheless. Will you help me out here, Dáithí?" Dáithí got up from his table with a set of uilleann pipes and joined Conn.

With the plaintive accompaniment of the pipes, Conn proceeded to sing "Rock-a-bye, Baby" to the assembled drinkers, in a heartbreakingly sweet voice.

> Rock-a-bye, baby, on the treetop
> When the wind blows, the cradle will rock.
> When the bough breaks, the cradle will fall,
> Down will come baby, cradle and all.

He stopped and took a bow to warm applause. "I'll bet yez all thought I'd be singing something political up here. Didn't yez now? Come on, admit it." Knowing laughter around the room. "Well, it *was* a political song, which may be news to some. That creepy lullaby, with the unhappy ending for the poor wee child, comes to us from the 1600s. It was about killing a Catholic baby. Sorry now, but that's the way it was. The song arose out of the fears here in England about the birth of a Catholic heir to James the Second, the Catholic king. The last Catholic king, as it turned out. There was," Conn said, having switched from his native Dublin tones to that of an English gentleman, "a bit of bother during that time in history. The Glorious Revolution, so called, the arrival of William of Orange, all of that. Anyway, here's a more literal version of the lullaby." He sang in the same sweet voice:

Rock-a-bye, baby, King Jimmy's wee heir,
The Pope's little soldier, you're not wanted here.
When the wind blows, in off the high seas,
From Holland it comes, good Protestant breeze.

Great William of Orange, sail in on the tides.
From papists and priests, please come save our hides.
The house of the Stuarts is ripe for a fall.
So down will come baby, cradle and all.

After that performance, he ceded the field to Dáithí and his pipes, went to the bar for a pint, and came over to join his cousins.

"Conn, it's been awhile since you've laid eyes on them," Molly said. "But here are Brennan and Terry. Lads, reacquaint yourselves with Conn."

They rose and embraced their young relation, and the three exchanged How've-you-beens and It's-been-too-longs.

When they stood back from each other Terry spoke to Conn in a low voice. "You're looking well." Why wouldn't he be, Brennan wondered, at such a young age? Terry spoke again, still *sotto voce*, "Whatever became . . ." But he didn't finish the question and was it just Brennan's imagination at work, or did Conn give Terry a quick shake of the head? Well, Terry flew into London from time to time and perhaps saw their cousin on the occasional visit.

Conn turned to Brennan and said, "You should come and say a Mass at our church while you're here, Brennan."

"Or to mine," said a man passing by with three pints in his hands.

"Not yours, Denny. He's from Liverpool," Conn said to Brennan, "and his church is the cathedral. Have you seen it, Father?"

"I have. I've been trying to repress the memory ever since."

"Bad, is it?" Terry asked. "Not one of Brennan's beloved Gothic cathedrals?"

Conn let out a bark of laughter. "Paddy's Wigwam, they call it.

And that's exactly what it looks like. But can't blame the Paddies for it. It was an Englishman who designed it."

"One of many architectural horrors from the sixties," Brennan said.

"Started falling apart as soon as they slapped it up. Wouldn't have happened on my watch."

"Conn's in the building trade," Molly explained.

"Aren't we all?" he said, looking around at the clientele of Hannigan's. "But really. I come down here to Sacred Heart, and it looks the way a church is supposed to look, and I'd love to have a cousin of mine say a Mass for us."

"You can count on it," Brennan assured him.

"And I'll expect perfect attendance from all of yez here." His gaze swept the crowd of drinkers.

There were grumbles from some, and references to the drink disabling them from their Sunday duties. Conn was having none of it. "There were times when the English outlawed our Mass, and our people had to worship at Mass rocks out in the fields. What would those people think now of a bunch of Catholics who won't even roll out of the cot on Sunday mornings to go to Mass? You should be excommunicated, the lot of yez."

He turned to Terry then. "Now you, Terry, you can fly me and my pals all over London. This city is jammed with traffic on the ground; quicker to fly over it, amn't I right?"

"I couldn't agree more. I don't have much patience for sitting in traffic on the ground, when I'm used to being above it all."

"Who's this that's above it all, Conn?"

Conn turned to face the new arrival and sang out, "She is the belle of Belfast City!" He got up and wrapped his arms around the young one who had just come in. She appeared to be in her mid or late twenties, with lustrous red hair piled on the top of her head in a clip. Her skin was ivory, and her eyes hazel. A lovely girl. "Evening, pet. How are you? Feeling better?"

"A bit better now." *A but batter nye.*

She saw Molly and smiled broadly. "'Bout ye, Mol."

"Tess, good to see you!"

"Lads, meet my girlfriend, my love, my darling girl, Tess Rooney. Tess, these are my cousins, Brennan and Terry Burke, Molly's brothers." They all said their hellos.

Conn kept one arm around her and squeezed. "Will you be having a pint with us now, Tessie?"

She looked at him uncertainly. "I don't know now. Maybe I'll wait."

"That's not like you, Tess. Wait how long, like?"

She whispered something in his ear. He reared back and exclaimed, "Seven months! That's a long time to be going on the dry. You're not on a weight loss kick, are you, like so many of the girls now? Because you're perfect just as you are. Now let me get you . . ."

She bent forward to him again and whispered. He replied, "Can't we just talk here? We're all family at this table."

She turned to his family at the table and said, "He does my head in." Then to her boyfriend, "All right, Connie, you asked for it. I'm two months gone, and I'll be having your wain next December!"

Her man was struck speechless. He stared at her, gobsmacked. But only for about three seconds, then a smile spread across his face. He wrapped her in his arms again, gave her a prolonged kiss, then dropped to his knees, lifted her shirt and kissed her on the belly. Rising to his feet, he took her hand in his and raised it. "Listen up, lads!" He spoke to everyone in the bar, male and female, young and old, known and unknown. "Your next jar is on me. Seamus, set them up. I'm going to be a father. And a married man. Not in that order. When, Tess? Would you like a summer wedding?"

"I, well, I . . . We might get some sun in June maybe, even in Belfast."

"You name the date, darling, and tell me what time to show up at the church and what shoes to wear. God in heaven, how I love this woman! Drink up and celebrate with me, won't yez?"

Everyone caught the mood and raised glasses to the dazzled young couple. Those whose glasses were running low rushed to the bar to take advantage of the free drinks coupon.

There weren't many people about by the time the Burkes emerged from Hannigan's into the Kilburn High Road. They began walking to Molly's flat, from where Conn and Tess would call a taxi for his place in Cricklewood. Brennan noticed a car parked not far from Hannigan's. The lights were off, and two men were inside in the dark. Just like the night before.

"The Gestapo," Conn remarked.

"Ignore them, Conn," Tess advised him. "Don't let on you've seen them."

"Who are they?" Terry asked.

"Special Branch," Conn told him.

"Just walk on past them," Tess urged him again.

"Ah, now, they know I'm all talk. All song. I'm nothing but a minstrel boy."

He raised his voice a notch and spoke to the men in the car. "On yer bike, lads. Off you go now. Nothing to see here."

There was no response from the stony-faced men inside.

†

When they were back in Molly's flat, and Conn and Tess had left in a cab, Brennan inquired of his sister, "So Hannigan's and its punters are of interest to Special Branch."

Molly's silence was not entirely unexpected. But Terry's was.

"I think the oul ears must be goin' on me," Brennan said. "I can't hear a word you're saying."

"They've been here," his sister said then.

Terry made for the drinks cupboard and brought them all a shot of whiskey.

"They were waiting for me one day when I got home."

"When was this?"

"A day or two before my arrest."

April 27, 1989

Molly got off the number sixteen bus after her shopping excursion and walked to her flat with the two carrier bags. She shifted her groceries to her left hand and fumbled for her keys. When she finally had them in hand, she looked around and noticed two men sitting in a car across the street. After she got inside she heard car doors opening and she looked out the window. Was Finbarr home for a visit? He was staying at Neville's this term—maybe one of his mates was dropping him off. But no, the two men she had seen were out of their car and walking towards her building. A few seconds later there was a knock on the door. She opened it and there they were. Coppers. No mistaking them for anything else.

One was tall and quite smart looking, handsome and well dressed in a lovely tweed jacket, shirt, and tie. Beautifully cut dark, greying hair. It seemed to Molly she had seen him somewhere before—on the street or in a café or a bar. She laughed to herself; was she so notorious that she had been under surveillance? As for the other fellow, he looked as if he had wandered too close to the bells of St. Mary-le-Bow and got them full in the face. A Cockney who'd been in a few too many scraps.

"Excuse me, Miss Burke," the taller fellow said. "I was wondering if we might have a word. I am Detective Sergeant Chambers and this is Detective Constable Peck." Chambers had what Molly thought of as an "educated" English voice. He flipped a badge at her, his warrant card, identifying him as John Chambers of the Metropolitan Police.

He was eyeing her place, which had nothing criminal or subversive on display. What were they doing here?

"Word about what?"

Chambers did the talking. "As you are no doubt aware, this city narrowly avoided a terrorist attack two days ago. To be more precise, explosives were planted but were fortunately disarmed before they could kill and maim hundreds of innocent people."

"How could you possibly think I'd know anything about that?"

"We are not suggesting that you do."

"What exactly are you suggesting, Detective?"

"Are you aware of a plan to cause disruption on the green behind the Houses of Parliament on that same day, the twenty-fifth of April?"

"I occasionally hear of demonstrations planned for the area behind the Houses of Parliament. People exercising their freedom of speech, that sort of thing. But I'm sure that wouldn't trouble the officers of the Special Branch."

"How many people besides yourself were in on the plot to damage the statue of Oliver Cromwell?"

"You people are frittering away your time hounding people who might have planned to raise their voices at a gathering of Cromwell fans?"

"At the meeting of your organization on April nineteenth, was there also a discussion of going considerably farther than raising your voices?" Chambers took out a notebook and opened it. "If it will assist you, I'm referring to a meeting you attended with Sheila O'Hanrahan, Fiona Connolly, Paddy McCann, and Tommy Dolan."

Molly didn't say anything to that. The idea that they knew everyone involved gave her the shivers. She wondered if the little painting circle had been infiltrated, or if Special Branch had bugged the room. But her silence didn't put them off one bit. The constable, Peck, gave her such a smirk that she wanted to pound the face off him.

Then Chambers said, "Did you see your cousin Conn Burke on Tuesday, April the twenty-fifth?"

"Conn!"

"Right."

Molly blurted out "No!" And that brought a smile to both their faces, and Chambers slapped his notebook shut, thanked her for her time, and they both left. She sat down and started shaking. She wondered how long they had been watching her. They must have known she wouldn't name anyone. They wanted to get her rattled. And get a foot inside her door. But what really upset her was the question about Conn. And her answer. Had Conn been up to something that day and given her as an alibi? If so, she had just blown it for him. My God!

†

So, Brennan reflected after hearing about the episode, Molly's little cadre of anti-Cromwell activists was not the only one of her associations that raised suspicion in the eyes of the police.

"Well, you've seen Conn," Terry said. "Have you asked him about it?"

"Not bloody likely."

Brennan got to the point. "Was Conn up to something that day?"

"I just told you, Brennan, I didn't ask."

Chapter IV

Be not afeard; the isle is full of noises,
Sounds and sweet airs, that give delight and hurt not.

William Shakespeare, *The Tempest*

The following day, Brennan and Terry headed for their sister's flat after enjoying the afternoon at the RAF Museum in Hendon. Terry, who spent most of his working life in the sky, was floating on air again today, as he reminisced about the Flying Fortresses, Lancasters, Messerschmitts, and other iconic aircraft they had seen. Brennan was caught up in it too; he understood completely why his brother had a passion for planes and flight.

Passing a news agent's on the way back to Molly's place, they glanced at the papers on display and saw that the composite sketch put out by the police in Essex had resulted in the identification of the Colchester murder victim. The police now had a name for him but were withholding it until they were able to notify the family.

Conn was at Molly's when Brennan and Terry arrived. He was seated at the table, writing something on a pad of paper. "Invitation list for the wedding," he said, waving the paper in their direction. "Tess said we should suss out how many will be on the guest list, so we can plan accordingly. I figured Molly would be the best person to ask about family. I'd ask my da but, if Tess wants the wedding in Belfast, he may not even be allowed to cross the border. So it might be a bit insensitive to get into this with him."

"Ah," said Brennan. Conn's mother had died of a heart attack a few years before, so it would be the mother of the bride who would be charged with most of the planning. But that was the case usually anyway, was it not? Brennan knew the Burkes would pitch in and help however they could. But Conn was right: Finn might have had some history in the North, so who knew whether he would even make the ceremony.

"Hi, Mum!"

Everyone turned to the door. A tall, slim young woman came in. She had short blond hair with bangs, a fringe in English parlance, which accentuated her huge blue eyes. She had the look of the British girl singers of the 1960s; Brennan had always admired that look. This would be Shelmalier, Molly's daughter. She must be twenty by now.

"Shelley, sweetheart, come in and see your uncles. It's been a few years."

They all embraced and said how good it was to be together again.

Conn made an elaborate bow and said, "Shelmalier, you have no peer."

"Conn, my son, are you still on the run?"

"Story of my life, *acushla*."

She spoke to her mother. "I've brought the prodigal brat home to you, Mum. He's right behind me. Or at least he was. Stopped to chat up some bird on the pavement.

"Get anywhere with her, you cad?" Shelmalier said to her brother when he entered the room.

"I had to let her go. She told me I'd only ruin her for any other man. Hi, Ma."

"Finbarr, darling, good to see you, even if I'd rather not hear half of the blather that comes out of your mouth."

He was around seventeen, Brennan knew. He was dark like his mother, with the same deep blue eyes. Thin, almost skinny, he was a couple of inches shorter than his sister.

The young lad gave his mother a hug and a quick kiss on the cheek. "The old man has been getting on my nerves so I scarpered after school. Came here instead."

"Now, Finbarr, you know your dad does his best."

"Does his best for himself, you mean. God helps those who help themselves. And our Neville does that. Hey, Conn! How goes the battle?"

Conn gave a noncommittal shrug.

"Conn has news. Tell them, Conn!" Molly urged him.

"Tess and I are getting married! June sometime. All of yez are invited."

"'Like Ares comes the bridegroom, taller far than a tall man,'" said Shelmalier. "Congratulations, Conn. I adore Tess; always have done. Bring her round to see me so we can all celebrate."

"Thanks, Shel, I will." He turned to Brennan. "Start turning water into wine for us, will you, Father? We'll be needing vats of it."

"*Fiat voluntas tua*, my son."

"Got her up the pole, have you?" was Finbarr's contribution.

"*Starting a family* is the expression, Finbarr. We're starting a family. And I'm over the moon about it!"

Finbarr actually blushed. "I'm sorry, man, me and my mouth. I didn't think . . . Sorry for being an arsewipe. It's wonderful news. Tess is a brilliant girl." He got up and shook Conn's hand.

"I was just heading out with my old friend Jane for a drink and a bite to eat," Molly told them. "Any and all of you are welcome to join me."

"I've got my course tonight," her son said.

"Oh, that's right."

"What course are you taking?" Brennan asked him.

"Auto mechanics. You know, something in the real world, to

balance out all the useless 'Henry the Eighth did this or that, murdered this wife, that wife' kinds of courses I have to sit through in school all day. The gifts bestowed by the Empire on those less fortunate round the world. All the victories claimed by the British military machine. Sorry, Shel. I don't mean to offend anyone we know."

"Off with you and be hanged, Finbarr." His sister's cheery tone belied her words.

"Could happen," he replied. "Kevin Barry wasn't much older than me when he was hanged by the British authorities in Ireland for his part in the Tan War. So don't say it too loud. Oh, wait," he said then, craning his neck and looking around the room, "I guess there are no members of Her Majesty's forces here, so maybe I'm safe for a bit longer."

"Oh, give it a rest, why don't you." There was no good cheer in Shelmalier's tone this time round.

Whatever that was about, Brennan decided to return the conversation to neutral ground.

"How do you like the night course, Finbarr?"

"It's all right. I'd like it more if my dear old mum and dad would spend a few quid and get me an old banger of a car to work on. But I'll keep after them."

"One more year of school, darling," his mother said, "and then we'll talk about cars. Though you'll notice I get around just fine on the tube, the buses, and the trains."

"I know, I know," he conceded.

"Where are you going this evening, Mum?" asked Shelmalier.

"My usual spot, the Warrington."

"You and Jane, going out on the pull! Don't drag your brothers along. We'll see them fed someplace else. Heaps of nice-looking gentlemen at the Warrington, I expect. But you're not going out in that, are you, Mother?" She pointed to the bulky brown wool sweater her mother was wearing.

"I'm nearly perished with the cold today."

"Well, I can't let you out of the house with that on. Sorry."

"Even the tide wouldn't take you out looking like that, Molly," Conn slagged her.

"Not even a sniper would take you out," Finbarr said. "Eh, Conn?"

No rejoinder from Conn, but Brennan thought he lip-read "Fuck off."

"Shelley, come in and advise me on my wardrobe. Something warm but . . ."

"But not a brown wool jumper, Mother, for an evening out. Good heavens."

"Just for the record, my darling, and all of you out there," Molly called from the entrance to her room, "I am not going out on the pull. Jane and I are going for a nice meal and a chinwag. I am still married to your father."

"Tell him that, why don't you?" Finbarr said. "He's not quite as particular as you are about his marital status. Why don't you draw up the papers and have done with it?"

"Now isn't the time for that discussion, love. I know you have only my best interests at heart, even if you're a bit obnoxious about it."

"Sorry, Mum. I do have your interests at heart. But you should hear what he says about you. Pretends to be joking in that arch way he has, but he's not joking at all. It's not about you, actually, but about, well, your side of the family. I guess that includes you lot." His eyes took in the men of the Burke family assembled in the room. "Calls you the 'Irish Problem.'" Affecting a snooty demeanour, Finbarr said, "'Spending a weekend with the Irish Problem, is she?' Or, 'The Irish Problem are coming by to drink themselves silly, are they?' And that's before he even gets started on the political side of things. He's convinced you're all out to blow up—"

"Not now, dear."

"Yes, Mother." He turned to his mother's cousin. "Conn, can I have a word?"

"You heard your mother. Not now, dear."

"Piss off. Come in here. I want to ask you something."

"Precocious brat," Shelley said equably. "You might as well hear him out, Conn. He won't let it drop. Whatever it is."

"All right, all right," Conn said.

The two younger fellows took themselves off to the kitchen. Brennan could hear them conversing in low voices but could not make out what they were saying. Whatever it was, the meeting concluded with the two of them saying their goodbyes and heading out the door together.

"What about you, Shelmalier?" Brennan asked. "Terry and I will be going out for some nourishment before I head off to St. Paul's Cathedral for a concert. You're more than welcome to join us for dinner, and accompany me to the concert as well, if you like."

"Thank you, Brennan. I appreciate the invitation, but I'm going to do some studying here. I have a paper due in a couple of days up at Oxford."

"What's the subject of your paper?" Brennan asked.

"Dante's *De Vulgari Eloquentia.*"

"*On the Eloquence of the Vernacular,*" Brennan translated.

"Do you know it?"

"Nope. Just translated the title. Otherwise it's a blank."

"He wrote about the European languages and the dialects of Italy. He was searching for the 'illustrious vernacular,' which was found potentially in all the vernaculars in Italy at the time, but which could only be brought out by the great poets, divinely inspired poets."

"You must be near the end of your academic year, are you?" Terry asked.

"Oh, no, nearly two months left. Seven weeks or so. The university term here goes to late June."

"That must be why you're so much more intelligent than I am, Shelmalier," said Terry. "You don't want to hear my vernacular!"

"On the contrary. I look forward to it, Terry!"

"He's no Dante," said Brennan. "More of a barstool *seanchaí.* But I'm no poet myself. I'm sure you're able for it, though, Shelley. So we'll let you get on with it."

"Where to, Bren?" Terry asked when they had left the flat. "Our local?"

"How about the city centre, since I'm going to St. Paul's?"

"Righto."

They went to the tube station and rode into the centre of London and walked along the city streets until they found themselves in front of what was probably the most famous criminal court in the world, the Old Bailey. The enormous Baroque building was capped by a dome and on top of that was a gold-leaf statue of a "lady of justice." From a distance you might think you were seeing a crucifix: the lady held her arms straight out from her sides, with the scales of justice in her left hand and a sword in her right.

"Both have been used in the pursuit of justice here," Brennan remarked.

"If you want some sword-based history, we should take in the Tower of London."

"No, they might throw us in and cut the heads off us."

"Got a thirst on you?"

"I could stand a drink and some solid food as well."

"Let's head over to Fleet Street. Not only is it home to press barons and muckrakers, but it is also known as a 'tippling street,'" Terry informed his brother.

They liked the look of the Bell Tavern and went inside, where they were informed that the place had been built by Sir Christopher Wren, the same man who built St. Paul's Cathedral.

"He sounds like a seventeenth-century version of yourself, Bren: an architect with a passion for great churches and great drinking holes."

"A man after my own heart," Brennan agreed.

The tavern had an old stone floor and stained glass and served a fine pint of ale. The brothers discussed its qualities and pronounced themselves pleased. They ordered a pub supper.

The talk then turned to family matters. Terry said, "He wasn't all that tactful about it, but I have to side with Finbarr on the Neville question. I think our Molly should give him his walking papers, wouldn't you say? For their first few years, he seemed to be sound. But he's given her a lot of guff in recent times. They've been separated for over a year now. Make it official and get it over with. Of course the Church doesn't exactly promote divorce, so maybe I shouldn't be annoying you about it, Father."

"She's my sister. I don't want to see her wasting any more of her time on a man who treats her like household waste. I'll help her navigate the corridors of the Church."

"Shelmalier's a bright little star."

"Nothing gets by her, was my impression."

"For sure."

"And young Finbarr. Quite a character in the making," Brennan observed.

"Bit of a hot-head but a good lad underneath, I'm thinking. He's Molly's son, after all. He usually lives with her but Neville kicked up a fuss, so the kid has been slotted for a couple of months with him. Doesn't like it much, obviously."

"Sounds as if nobody's happy with the arrangement. Par for the course in these situations."

"True."

Brennan took a sip of his ale, then said, "I was wondering about something he said. Finbarr."

"Oh?"

"He made a little jest about Molly's clothing. 'Not even a sniper would take you out looking like that,' and then 'Eh, Conn.' And Conn didn't look overly amused. What are we to make of that? Anything?"

"Who knows? Probably just the two lads blackguarding one another." Terry said. "So, you're off to hear a choir of angels."

"I am."

When they finished their meal, Brennan took his leave. Terry was more than happy to stay on in the tavern. Brennan made the short walk to St. Paul's Cathedral. It would be glorious enough to experience the building in silence, to be under its great dome, which dominated the skyline of London. Brennan recalled seeing pictures of the dome and the cross wreathed in smoke amid the fire and destruction of the Blitz. The landmark cathedral had been specifically targeted, if his memory served him, and somebody was awarded the George Cross for dismantling a massive bomb that would have destroyed the building. The English Baroque masterpiece survived the war, no doubt boosting the morale of Londoners during that harrowing time.

Now, as the concert got underway, the great cathedral was filled with the clear, ringing tones of the boys and men of the choir. They sang William Byrd's *Mass for Four Voices*, which, in Brennan's opinion and that of many others, contained some of the most beautiful lines of music ever written. Then they sang a selection of motets by Byrd and Tallis and other renowned English Renaissance composers. There were pieces by Palestrina and Victoria as well. All done to perfection. Brennan was a choir director himself, and this was the sound he tried to produce in his choirs: the straight English sound, the bell-like tone of an English boy choir. So much effort and technique went into creating that sound: perfectly synchronized vowels among the singers, the banishment of any vibrato in the individual voices, the perfect intonation, the crisp diction. England was the summit of choral achievement, always had been. Brennan often wondered what he sounded like back in New York, a Dublin-accented Irishman exhorting his choristers to sound more English, for Jaysus' sake.

After the last exquisite note faded away, Brennan stayed on until he saw the choristers and choirmaster filing out in their street clothes. He stepped forward and held out his hand, congratulating the director on such a fine performance. The man, who could have been haughty and full of himself and smug about his talent, was none of those things and engaged in a friendly, informative conversation with a fellow musician from across the pond. Brennan emerged into the hectic streets of the city with the sounds of heaven in his head.

Chapter V

The fools, the fools, the fools!
They have left us our Fenian dead.
And while Ireland holds these graves,
Ireland unfree shall never be at peace.

Pádraig Pearse, at the grave of Jeremiah O'Donovan Rossa, 1915

Janey Mack's bar in Cricklewood, where Brennan found himself on Thursday, was no cathedral. It didn't look like much from the outside, but many bars were like that in Ireland itself and in places across the seas where the Irish diaspora met to drink and socialize. Inside, the walls were covered with posters and photos celebrating the GAA, the Gaelic Athletic Association, and cartoons with captions in the Irish language. Janey Mack's had everything on tap and in a bottle that one could find in Ireland, and the offerings on the menu were familiar fare as well: bacon and cabbage, shepherd's pie, lamb stew, boxties, spuds in every conceivable form — floury, waxy, boiled, baked, champ, colcannon — and everything came with a side order of mushy peas.

The plan for the evening was a family dinner, and Brennan, Molly, and Terry were the advance party; they arrived early enough to grab a table for six. The younger relations were expected within the hour; then they would all eat, lift a jar, and enjoy the craic. No point in waiting for the lifting of a jar. They ordered their drinks of choice and returned to their table.

"I'd love to have a place like this," said Terry.

"Give you something to do when you're on the ground between flights, I suppose," his sister said. "Never mind that you have a wife and children to attend to. How are Sheila and the kids? I'd love to get over to New York and see everybody."

"They're grand altogether. I talked to them this afternoon. They wish they could be here. I like to think they miss me, but I suspect it's London shopping they're pining for. Anyway, I told them about all the sights I've seen, and the ones I intend to cram in while I'm here."

"Tell me this, Terrence: do you ever just sit around and read a book? Listen to music? Gaze at the moon?"

"Those activities, if they can be called activities, Molly, don't account for a large portion of my time, I'd have to say."

"That kind of activity accounts for most of my free time, I'm happy to report."

"But seriously, I'd love to have a bar. Brennan, you could work the place for me when I'm thirty-five thousand feet up and unavailable to pour the pints. Can't you see him working a bar, Molly?"

"I have no trouble with that. After all, they call barmen 'curates' in Ireland. There's got to be something in that. I could design the place for you."

"No need. It would look exactly like Christy Burke's in Dublin." Their grandfather's pub was a landmark on Dublin's north side. Finn, their uncle, had taken it over after Christy's death. "I'd move from Queens to the mainland just so I could call it Christy Burke's in the Bronx."

"Grandda would be smiling down on you from above," said Molly.

"If," Brennan put in, "he made it that far up. I'll have to read up on the theology of the Irish struggle."

"Oul Christy got quite the send-off," Terry remarked. "I sat with Conn at the funeral. He was just a kid then."

Dublin
November 5, 1970

Christy Burke lived to be seventy-seven years of age. Nobody expected that. And the cause of death was unexpected too: natural causes. But the throngs of people who jammed Our Lady of the Rosary church and the grounds outside weren't there to send off the kindly publican who had died quietly at home following a stroke. To be sure, there were many in the crowd who knew and loved him in his role as the owner and barman of Christy Burke's bar. But most of the two thousand souls in attendance were there to remember him for the battles he had fought for the Republican cause, beginning with the Easter Rising of 1916.

Terry was in the U.S. Air Force; he viewed his military service as a training program for a future career in civil aviation. His brother Brennan was a priest, four years out of the seminary in New York. They had flown in to Dublin two days ago. Now, on a grey day in November, Brennan would soon be up on the altar, concelebrating his grandfather's funeral at the invitation of the other two priests, and Terry was sitting in the church waiting for the funeral to begin. All around him were members of his extended family: his sister, Molly, and brother Patrick, his uncles, aunts, greats, and cousins. Notably absent was Terry's father, Declan, and his mother, Teresa. Twenty years earlier, they had bundled up the children and hustled them out of their house on the Rathmines Road, stuffed them into the family's Cork-manufactured Ford Prefect, roared down the motorway to Cobh, abandoned the car in the county of its birth, and boarded a midnight ship out of Ireland. Declan had never again set foot on Irish soil. There was a story behind that, but it was a book that lay closed to Terry, perhaps for all time. Declan Burke was a man well able to keep his own counsel.

Beside Terry in the second row of pews was a young cousin, Conn Burke, son of Declan's brother, Finn. The young fellow appeared to be around thirteen, with auburn hair and brown eyes; his eyes were rimmed with red. Not one to remain silent when there was the possibility of conversation, Terry said to him, almost in a whisper, "I wish I'd known our grandfather better. Not much chance of that after we immigrated to New York."

That was all it took. Terry soon recognized a kindred spirit, another fellow in the family with the gift of gab.

"Grandda and I were really close," Conn said. "I was just after seeing him the day he died. I liked to walk over to his place and pay him a visit. He told me I put him in mind of himself when he was a lad. And you know the bar. You've been there."

It would not occur to anyone that a member of the Burke family had not spent time in Christy Burke's bar, and they'd be right enough.

"Well," said Terry's young cousin, "that place was a hideout for our boys in the time of the Tan War, when we booted the Brits out of the Twenty-Six Counties. There's a tunnel under there, where the fellows used to hide and make their escape from the Brits and their toadies in the police force. Michael Collins himself used Christy's as one of his hiding places."

"That's right," Terry said. "Collins was a legend. A man with a ten-thousand-quid price on his head, riding around the city on his bicycle. One of the most successful guerrilla fighters in the history of the world."

"'Bollocks of steel, had Mick,' that's what Grandda said to me about Collins. And Grandda knew him well. They were together in the prison camp in Wales. The Brits fecked all our lads into the same camp together in '16 after the Rising. So they all came out determined to fight even more. And that's what they did. Three years later, they went at it again."

"Yeah, they took on the mighty British Empire. But then Collins signed the Treaty. The Brits would pull out of the Twenty-Six Counties, which would now be the Irish Free State, but the North remained in British hands. We all know how that worked out!"

The expression on young Conn's face spoke volumes about how that worked out. "Right," he said. "Irishmen still had to swear an oath to the English king! Well, the IRA weren't buying that, after all the shite they'd been through." The young fellow seemed to remember where he was and made a hasty sign of the cross. "So then it was the Civil War, the new Free State government against their old comrades in the IRA. Can you imagine what that was like, Terry?" Conn twisted around and looked at the crowd gathered in Our Lady of the Rosary church, men and women, young and old, all togged out in their Sunday best. "It would be like half the people in this church getting up and killing the other half. Brother against brother, friend against friend. I'm going to study history when I get to the university."

The lad would ace his history courses, Terry predicted. And if he was this good a talker at thirteen, he might be head of the history department at thirty.

"But I know a lot of this stuff already," Conn was saying, "from my father and from Grandda. Republicans believe we have to keep up the fight for a united Ireland, completely independent of the Brits. Otherwise, all those fellows died for nothing."

Terry added another career to his imagined future for Conn Burke: politician.

"Back in the early twenties, when I'm telling you about, it was hellish."

"Right," Terry said, "you had IRA men attacking soldiers of the first Irish national army in eight hundred years. And you had the Free State government fighting and jailing its old friends in the IRA. Christy was one of those who ended up making war against Collins and the Free State."

"Yeah, and Christy got sent to jail again, this time in Kilmainham, along with hundreds of other Republicans. Some of them probably here today." Conn turned again to the mourners pouring into the church to honour his grandfather, who had lived the history his grandson intended to study. "Grandda spent hours with me, telling me all about those days, when I'd go over to his house, or I'd sit up at the bar in the off hours. And do you know what he told me about the day Collins died? It was August in 1922. The news came into Kilmainham Gaol that Michael Collins, *General* Collins, had been assassinated in County Cork. And Christy told me he came out of his cell and what he saw was seven or eight hundred men, enemies of the state, fellows who were in there because they were on the other side from Michael Collins. And those very men were all down on their knees, saying the rosary for Collins."

Conn looked away from Terry then, as if to compose himself. Terry found himself unable to speak, a rare event indeed for him.

After a long moment of silence, Conn returned to his story. "You've heard of Tom Barry, yeah? He's one of the most famous men from the Old IRA. Well, he was there and he tells the story too. I don't think I'll ever get that picture out of my head, but I guess I wouldn't want to: the man's former brothers, now his sworn enemies, down on their knees when they heard he died."

That is when a lone piper at the back of the church began to play a lament on the uilleann pipes. Terry remembered what Brennan had said when discussing the funeral arrangements: "There is no instrument in the world that can evoke loneliness and loss like the uilleann pipes."

Everyone stood and turned as the pallbearers brought the body of Christy Burke into the church. In the usual course of things Terry's brother, Father Brennan Burke, considered any language other than Latin a travesty for the Mass. But he had been perfectly happy with the plan to have Christy Burke's funeral Mass *As Gaeilge*, in the ancient language of Ireland. This was the way the old man would have wanted it, so that was fine with Brennan. The two senior priests were obviously fluent in Irish, Brennan less so, but he had been learning some of the old tongue in his spare time in New York. Terry found himself deeply moved by the sound of the old language resonating throughout the church.

The sermon, given by Father Sean Murphy, was not supposed to be a eulogy; liturgical rules forbade it, apparently. But Father Murphy ignored the rule, and the sermon was all about Christy Burke. About his fighting at the age of twenty-three in the General Post Office during the Rising in 1916, his incarceration in a prison camp in Wales, the execution of sixteen of his brothers in arms, executions that turned the tide of Irish opinion against the British after long years of complacency on the part of the Irish people. The priest then spoke of how Christy fought during the Old Troubles in 1919 to 1921, the War of Independence. And then there was the horror of the Irish Civil War, which many could not bear to speak of even to this day. There were oblique references to Christy's activities over the ensuing decades, the priest careful to place the dead man's actions on behalf of the IRA in the context of a Catholic's dedication to a Catholic Ireland. There were a few references to the new Troubles in the North, the sectarian and political violence in Belfast and Derry and other centres, and the return of the British Army to Irish soil. Father Murphy hinted, without saying as much, that Christy had played a role in the recent struggle not long before his death.

When the Mass ended, and the priests and the family began their procession down the aisle with the coffin, a woman Terry recognized as a second cousin rose to sing a solo in Irish. No, it was not singing; it was keening, and the powerful lament seemed to go beyond the church, to fill the whole world. Many of the mourners in the churchyard and the street outside were in tears. If ever there was a cry to heaven, this was it.

The mourners got into their cars for the funeral procession along the Harold's Cross Road and over to Mount Jerome Cemetery. The gate to the graveyard was flanked by grey stone pinnacles looking like miniature spires. Dozens of gardaí, police officers, stood by, watching the crowd as it arrived. When the people got out of their cars and started walking towards the grave, the guards went with them, walking along on both sides of the funeral cortege. A new element emerged then from the back of the throng, a group of men and women in tunics, berets, and dark glasses. Some had their faces covered by scarves, a few were in balaclavas. Civilians stood aside and made room as the IRA honour guard, under the watchful eyes of the police, formed behind the coffin.

The procession went on with stately dignity, except for a small interruption by a young auburn-haired boy who tore himself from his mother's grasp and made a beeline for the honour guard. Conn Burke. His mother started after him, looking dismayed. Terry followed her gaze and found himself looking at Conn's father, Uncle Finn, whose expression was unreadable behind a pair of sunglasses like those of the paramilitary contingent. Finn made no move to stop his son from wriggling into the honour guard and marching with the Irish Republican Army. The marchers made room for the boy without missing a step.

When they reached the graveside, the crowd shuffled into place, the honour guard stood at attention, and the pallbearers made ready to commend Christy's body to the earth. Father Murphy said the requisite prayers and the coffin was lowered into the ground. Then everyone's attention was caught by something on the other side of the cemetery. A white van was approaching slowly along a pathway, its engine nearly silent. There were no markings on it. This was not out of the ordinary, Terry knew, given that the Burke family ran its own transport company. On occasion, unmarked vehicles came in handy for reasons not always noted in the company's paperwork. The eyes of the gardaí locked onto the vehicle, and several of the police officers began to move towards it. The van then reversed, turned, and approached the grave from the opposite direction. As soon as it came to a stop, six men hopped out. They wore camouflage tunics, berets, sunglasses, and heavy scarves covering their mouths and noses. Each held a rifle down by his side. The men walked up to Christy's grave, stood side by side, raised their rifles, and fired a volley of shots into the air.

✝

Now, in Janey Mack's bar, Molly was nodding her head, remembering it all. "Conn falling in step with the honour guard. His mother didn't look too happy. My boy would have done the same thing. Finbarr. What a handful he is! He thinks the sun rises, shines, and sets on Conn Burke. Boys! What can you do? Why do you suppose the guards let it go, the volley of shots?"

"Thought it best not to aggravate things, maybe," Terry said. "I've heard of that before. And they probably had more than enough people to lean on in the future, given all the pictures they snapped of the mourners, civilian and otherwise. And, remember, a lot of the guards shared Christy's politics."

"Or were dedicated drinkers at Christy Burke's bar," she smiled, "allowing the man to be honoured."

"Maybe that too."

"That was the funeral. But I'm thinking about the night before. Do you fellows remember the wake?"

"I recall being there at the house," said Brennan. "Spent a lot of time catching up with the family." Terry nodded. That was his experience as well.

"Of course," said Molly, "but there was something else going on." She took a leisurely sip of her pint and sent her mind back in time.

Dublin
November 4, 1970

Molly's grandfather, Christy Burke, lay in his coffin by the front window of his sitting room on Dublin's north side, and the room was jammed with mourners. It had been a long day for Molly, who had travelled from London with her one-year-old baby, Shelmalier. Brennan, Patrick, and Terry were here from New York. Brennan, the family's unlikely priest, was in deep conversation with their grand-mother, Sadie. Molly immediately chastised herself for thinking of Brennan as an unlikely priest. He was a wonderfully dedicated priest; it's just that he was a holy terror in his younger years, and he always had a woman hanging off of him. He was the last person anyone would have expected to see wearing a collar and living a life of celi-bacy. Now, at thirty, he cut a dashing figure in his sister's opinion, with his black hair and black eyes, and his air of self-possession. The two younger brothers had the lighter colouring and sky blue eyes of their father. Patrick had recently finished medical school and intended to go into psychiatry. Molly could see that. Even in his mid-twenties, Pat was able to console the members of the family, young and old, without any of the stiffness that sometimes marred such efforts. Her youngest brother, Terry, was standing by the coffin, uncharacteristi-cally silent. Molly did not want to intrude on whatever her normally gregarious brother was feeling.

Shelmalier, nicknamed Shelley, was just starting to walk, and Molly decided to take her for a tour around the house. The child was delighted and grinned up at everyone who watched her toddling through the crowd. There was a group of men standing in the hallway smoking and chatting. One of them looked towards the front door of the house, which had just opened to admit a priest in collar and coat; he removed his fedora upon entering the house. Molly thought a couple of the men looked familiar.

One of them began to sing, "Father Murphy from the County Wexford sweeps o'er the land like a mighty wave."

That was it. She had seen their much younger selves, a couple of them at least, on the trip to Wexford, the visit to the ruined abbey, in 1949. Now several of the men raised their voices in song, and it was a song well known to Molly. She often sang "Boolavogue" to her daughter at bedtime, because her name was in it: "the bright May meadows of Shelmalier." The little girl's eyes were gleaming, recognizing the piece. The boys of Wexford wound it up with a flourish:

> God grant you glory, brave Father Murphy,
> and open heaven to all your men.
> For the cause that calls you may call tomorrow
> in another fight for the green again!

"May God bless all who gather here," the priest said. "And I thank you for that kind tribute."

"Did yeh come in on the train, Father?"

"I did. Thought I'd be here before now but there was a delay."

"Ah but sure, you should have rung me. I came up in my car. I'll give you a spin home afterwards."

"Thank you, Geroid. I'll be happy to take you up on it."

"Go on in, Father. We've all paid our respects. The man is nicely laid out. They did a good job on him. Looks as if he wasn't sick a day in his life."

"He wasn't. Stroke felled him, just like that."

Shelley toddled after Father Murphy into the sitting room, then plunked herself down just inside the door. Molly gently eased her over to the side a bit and took an empty chair beside her. She reached into her bag and pulled out a bright yellow rubber duck and handed it down. Shelley grabbed it and stuffed its head into her mouth, then marched around the room, looking for all the world like a self-satisfied little cat carrying her prey from the field. Everything the child desired in the world at that moment was right there.

The crowd from Wexford, who had been quite boisterous up to now, began speaking in hushed tones out in the hall. If there is anything guaranteed to attract attention, it is a shift from a shout to a whisper. Molly saw her uncle Finn get up from his seat near the coffin and go out to join the visitors. She tuned in to the conversation, straining her ears to catch what she could. "Things have changed over the last twenty years."

Since the plotting in 1949? They had indeed.

"The more things change, the more they stay the same. British troops are on our soil again."

"So we have to take them on here. And we have to do a better job than we did in the border campaign!"

"Kind of hard to do a good job when our lads were lifted and dumped in internment camps on both sides of the border."

That campaign was a series of attacks by the IRA operating out of the South, Molly remembered. Flying columns—units of IRA men—conducted arms raids and hit police barracks in the Northern towns in the late 1950s and early '60s. But the governments on both sides of the border interned so many of the men that the campaign fell apart.

"And," another fellow said, "it's time to go into action against the Brits on their own turf."

"Fight them on two fronts, you're saying."

"If we don't, they won't give a fuck. So what if people die in the streets of Belfast or Derry? As long as things are cheerio in London, the British people won't care and won't make their politicians care. Only way to get their attention is to hit them where it hurts."

"By doing what?" That was Uncle Finn. "Are we going to commandeer the Rosslare ferry? Land an army on the coast of Wales and march in and occupy Great Britain? What have they got? Three or four hundred thousand men in uniform—land, sea, and sky? And even if they didn't, they could nuke the entire lot of us!"

"So what do we do, Finn, sit on our arses and let them keep sending more and more battalions into the North?"

"I'm not saying we don't operate on English soil. All I'm saying is that we stick with what we decided all those years ago. That is going to hold us in good stead now that the Brits are directly involved again."

"Ah but sure, we need to do more. We saw your oul fellow at Bodenstown in June." The annual gathering of Republicans at the grave of Wolfe Tone, a martyr to the cause in 1798; Molly had attended a few times herself. "And Christy was asking us what we were going to do about the new situation."

"Oh, I can tell you my father and I had lots to say about the new situation. And I'm not telling tales out of school when I say he and I both saw it firsthand on more than one occasion. But as for the Wexford plan, Christy was satisfied that the scheme was a good one. He knew its time would come. And that time is now."

"Good to hear, as I know we'd all agree. But I still say it's time for some fireworks over there. Time for a new campaign in England. But only the kinds of places we talked about back then."

"Will you keep your voice down, Geroid. Don't be listening to him, Finn. He hasn't seemed to grasp the fact that innocent people die in . . . that sort of campaign. If we end up killing non-combatants we're just as bad as Cromwell himself, when he slaughtered women and children in my town and in Drogheda."

"So you're saying, Fergus, that I want to go over there and kill innocent women and children, is that what I just heard?"

"That's not what you want, Geroid, but it's what you'll get. I say we fight this war like the soldiers we're supposed to be. Our targets are military targets, and I know Finn agrees."

"Anything else is unacceptable." Finn's voice was clipped in reply.

"So we need soldiers and we need intelligence," Fergus added.

"No thicks need apply, you're saying," another man chimed in. "Don't bother applying, Geroid."

"Fuck the lot of ye."

"Show some respect, would you, Ger? A man's lying dead out there, and we've a priest in our midst."

"Begging your pardon, Finn. And yours, Father Murphy."

"*Te absolvo*, Geroid."

Father Murphy's next few words, sacramental or otherwise, were lost to Molly as her daughter emitted peals of laughter over some kind of in-joke between child and rubber duck.

When Molly tuned in to the priest's conversation again, she heard, "And I see I'm not the only *sagart* in the house. Young Brennan in there would be Declan's son, if I'm not mistaken."

"That's right," said Finn. "He has a parish in New York."

"Seems to me I met him when he was just a boy. Didn't we see him somewhere, Dermot?"

"Not that I remember. But then again, some of my recollections have been dimmed by drink!"

"No, you're right. You weren't there. I was thinking of that little council of war we had, us and the Delaneys. And you, Finn. You, Declan, and Christy in Wexford town. That's where I first saw Brennan Burke. Declan had brought the family to Wexford for a visit. Thought he'd leave them to a bit of sightseeing while he joined us for our meeting in the Cape Bar. But young Brennan banjaxed it for him. Saw Christy's old auto parked in the street outside the bar. Christy looked out and spotted him, and what could he do but bring the little lad inside?"

"Kind of hard to hide a bullet-riddled car with Dublin plates on the streets of Wexford."

"True enough. The poor little fellow was wicked cross about what Cromwell and his men had done to Selskar Abbey. 'Where are the monks doing their chanting now? Are they hiding somewhere?' Just as if it had happened that very day."

"Are the monks hiding somewhere?" one of the men said. "Remember how that got us thinking? Easier for them to hide than the rest of us, wearing a robe and a hood. What do they call that, Father? It covers the monk's head."

"A cowl."

"Right," one of the other men said. "Delaney told us he'd ask the wife to run a dozen of them up on her sewing machine, that they would come in handy for our —"

"Dry up, for fuck's sake, Dermot. Consider yourself under a vow of silence starting now."

The hushed tones hushed completely then. Molly entertained herself with a vision of·a group of her countrymen, talkative by nature, forced to spend hours in a cold, dark monastery, peering at each other under their cowls, the faces just about exploding off of them from the effort to stay quiet.

But silent they were at present, so Shelmalier decided to fill the void by singing out at the top of her lungs. Then Molly heard Geroid, or maybe Fergus, exhort his comrades to return to the wake and pay respect to the dead.

✝

"That's all I heard," Molly told the family table in Janey Mack's, "so I never did figure out what was going on, aside from some loose talk about a campaign, which I took to mean another in a series of bombing campaigns that have been launched in England over the last century. We all know that came to pass, but whether these fellows had something to do with it or not is anyone's guess."

"Well, if they've had something to do with the sort of bombings that started up three years later, it was without Finn's blessing, thanks be to God," said Brennan.

"The fellow said 'only the kinds of places' they had discussed before. I remember thinking they were going to target old churches and abbeys and the like. But, as I said to you earlier, that may just have been my own interpretation. Whatever it was, they didn't elaborate on it at Christy's wake."

"But it sounds as if they had something else going on, dating back to that same meeting in '49, the one I crashed into after spotting Christy's car."

"They certainly didn't go into details about that, whatever it might have been."

Brennan had just got up for a fresh round of drinks when Shelmalier and Finbarr arrived, so he took their orders as well. They were all raising their glasses in a toast when Conn appeared, so they waited for him to be seated with his pint and then the six of them toasted each other and drank deep.

"How's the Dante paper coming along, Shelley?" Brennan asked.

"Slowly, Brennan. I'm getting bogged down in the various dialects of mediaeval Italy."

"Don't get him started on mediaeval Italy, Shel," her mother warned her. "You'll never hear the end of it."

"I stole one of Shel's papers once," said Finbarr, "and it took me years to hear the end of it. Not a paper, actually, a music assignment. I love music, always have done, but anything other than punk or hard rock was beyond me back then. We had regular assignments in composition and this time it was a hymn. I put it off till the night before, as usual, and didn't have a clue what I was going to do. So I rooted through Shelley's assignments and found one she had done for her course years before. It was called 'All God's Creatures Today.' It was for several instruments, and all the voices did was 'oooooooo.' The master had given her top marks and had written on it 'Strikes exactly the right note, Shelmalier—bravo!' So I couldn't lose. I spent all night transposing the notes onto my own music sheets and passed the thing in. The school band and choir performed all our pieces. I could hardly wait to hear what 'mine' sounded like. Could hardly wait for the applause.

"Turned out it sounded like a bunch of barnyard animals. Grunts from the tuba, quacking noises from something else, and the choir part, when I looked at Shel's original later, was really 'mooo.'"

"That's right," said Shelmalier, enjoying the memory, "I'd written a parody of modern dissonant music and song cycles. My music master was of the old school and hated all that, so he loved my composition."

Brennan could identify with that. One of the things he detested most in the world was a "choir having fun," singing jolly work songs and making all kinds of goofy noises. Same for bands having fun.

"But," Finbarr said, "my music master was a modernist. He'd actually composed rubbish like this himself. I was fucked and nearly failed the course!"

Everyone laughed at his tale, and he raised his glass to them in acknowledgement.

"I wrote a paper once," Terry said, "about ants. Flying ants. I called it 'Pissmires on the Wing.' The teacher said it's p-i-s and I'd spelled it wrong because I had a dirty mind. And it was worse when she got to the part where I added in brackets that the males existed only to breed with the females and were so dumb they couldn't even feed themselves. Molly read it and said that sounded like half the guys she knew."

"That sounds like you, Mum!" Shelley laughed.

"But anyway your mum said the paper was good. My teacher didn't like it, though, and said she didn't want to read anything about bugs from me ever again. She gave me a forty-nine on it."

"He wrote about the physics of flight, using the flying ant and other insects as examples," Brennan explained, "and the school principal intervened and gave him a grade of ninety-eight percent."

"I went to the Christian Brothers," said Conn. "They marked me down because I wrote on a test that Eamon de Valera was a towering figure in our history but had always been self-serving and a bit of an arsehole personally. Well! Brother Canavan gave out to me in front of the class. What would my father say if he were shown that disgraceful document? I was not Republican enough to be a true son of Finn Burke, and not Republican enough for the Brothers! Canavan declared, 'A man is not an arsehole until I say he's an arsehole. And Dev was not an arsehole until 1936.'"

"What happened in 1936?" Terry inquired.

"De Valera outlawed the IRA and started throwing them in prison. Years later I saw Brother Canavan at the annual commemoration at Wolfe Tone's grave, and Canavan said that would earn me time off Purgatory. And he . . ."

Conn picked up his pint, drank from it and did not resume the tale. All Brennan heard him say under his breath was "shower of shites!"

Glasses were raised and stayed in the air. Conversations were abruptly concluded; the place fell silent. Three young men had come in the door and walked to the middle of the pub. They stood, looking around. Brennan saw a party of four quietly rise from their table and move off. The new arrivals took the table without comment. Two of the new lads had longish dark hair; one had a beard. One wore a jersey bearing the insignia of the Celtics football club; the other wore blue for the Dubs. Their attention was focused on the third member of the group, an intense-looking man of around thirty with cropped, light brown hair and high cheekbones topped by narrow grey-blue eyes.

Finbarr watched the newcomers make their entrance, then leaned towards Conn and whispered something in his ear. There was no response from Conn; he had all his attention on the men who had just arrived and altered the temperature of the room.

The youngest of the three went to the bar and put in the order, "Three pints for Mr. Kane's party," and returned shortly afterwards with the goods. He put them on the table, then picked one up and placed it before the fellow with the cheekbones, so that must have been Kane. The lad stood and waited while Kane took a leisurely sip. Kane put his glass down and glanced up at the cup-bearer, who returned to his seat and pushed one of the pints to the other fellow, and brought the third to his lips and downed half of it in one go. This brought a disapproving look from Kane, but the drinker missed it.

Kane eyed the television set on the wall, then turned to his side-kicks, and whispered something Brennan couldn't hear. The young man in the Celtics jersey called out to the barman, "D'yez get Ulster TV on that? Put it on, would yeh? Something me and the lads want to look at."

The request was for Ulster news, but the voice was pure Dublin. Well, "pure" might not be the word; Kane's companion spoke with a skanger accent that would have you looking about for the nearest peeler, just in case. But you wouldn't want to be caught looking.

The barman switched the channel, and everybody in the bar stared at the screen, waiting for the news, expecting it to be bad. And it was. Two members of a Loyalist paramilitary group and an off-duty British soldier had been killed by a remote-controlled bomb detonated by the Provisional IRA.

The scene switched to Government Buildings in Dublin, where reporters had cornered a number of politicians from the governing party, Fianna Fáil, emerging from their business in the house. A member of the cabinet decried the violence committed by both sides and called for a negotiated settlement to the Troubles in the North.

Contrary views were given expression at the Kane table. "Fuckin' Free Staters. What do they know about it? Get off your arse and go up there and take a UVF bullet in the face, and then give out to us about 'both sides'! Fuckin' maggots!"

The Irish Free State had become the Republic of Ireland forty years ago, Kane's native land, and Fianna Fáil was still known not as the Free State party but as the Republican party, but things were not quite Republican enough for the true Republican.

Then it was a member of the Fine Gael party who was asked for a statement. "There is no justification for violence, for bombings, for terrorism. By any side in the conflict. Period."

"Go and burn in hell, you and the rest of the Blue Shirts! Go up and take your message to the boys in the Shankill Road. See how much justification you'll find when the Loyalists shove a grenade up your hole!"

The newscast turned to other matters, and Janey Mack's bar was quiet once again. The only conversations were whispers at the tables; there was none of the cross-room banter that had been going on only minutes before.

Terry took up the slack with an amusing tale about a dustup between the Italian and German members of a flight crew en route from Frankfurt to Rome, but even he was subdued in his presentation. Brennan tried to catch Molly's eye but she seemed intent on doing the same with her son, and Finbarr was ignoring her and trying not to look as if he were doing it.

Then Kane rose from his seat and his two sidekicks did the same. Kane gazed around the room and said, "Lads?" His gaze had taken in Conn, and Conn, looking none too happy, got up from his chair. Finbarr did the same, and Brennan saw Conn's hand go down to Finbarr's knee and press. Finbarr sat down hard, and his face was red with anger.

Conn and a handful of other men followed Kane and his group to the rear of the building, and they headed down a set of stairs. Finbarr remained at the table, seething.

Chapter VI

He that is taken and put into prison or in chains is not conquered, though overcome; for he is still an enemy.

Thomas Hobbes, *Leviathan*

Brennan was enjoying a leisurely Friday morning. Molly had left for the university, and Terry had gone out to see some sights. Probably back to the RAF Museum, Brennan guessed. So Brennan had some contemplative time to himself. He would say his daily Mass, and then give some thought to the trip back to New York. He had been here nearly a week and, with Molly free from captivity, he could hardly justify prolonging his holiday in London. Terry said he would book a flight for the two of them. Someone in the next flat had BBC Radio on, but Brennan tuned that out when he turned his mind to prayer and his tongue to Latin. He took some bread and some red wine from Molly's cupboard and offered Mass for his sister and her family. He had just completed the *Agnus Dei, dona nobis pacem* when he tuned back in to the BBC coming from the other side of the wall. There was a new development in the police murder. Brennan said a quick *mea culpa* for interrupting his worship and listened to the news.

"At a news conference this morning, Metropolitan Police Assistant Commissioner Alfred Norton spoke for Scotland Yard."

"As all of you know, there was a terrorist attack planned for that day. Bombs were placed to cause maximum death and injury to Londoners and visitors to Westminster Abbey. Innocent lives, all of them. There was enough explosive matter to cause severe damage to one of our most important, most cherished institutions, perhaps even destroy it completely. It appears that Detective Sergeant Richard Heath received information about the bomb plot and was heading towards that area. He had not even had the time to radio the information to our headquarters when he was intercepted by one of the terrorists. We believe the terrorist realized that Detective Sergeant Heath had discovered the plot, and he shot the officer in cold blood there in his car.

"We have laid a murder charge against thirty-two-year-old Conchobar, known as Conn, Burke, formerly of Dublin, recently residing in Cricklewood, who is known to be an active member of the Provisional IRA. More charges may be laid, against Mr. Burke and possibly against others, as the investigation proceeds."

Brennan stood staring at the wall between himself and the radio. He was vaguely aware that there was something he wanted to do, but he could not formulate the thought. Turn on Molly's radio? Get more news? Consecrate the host? He was in the middle of Mass, wasn't he? Maybe the radio. But he just stood there in the middle of the room, poleaxed by the news.

He wasn't much better later in the afternoon when he, Molly, and Terry were in the London Underground station, tickets in hand, looking for the Victoria line to Brixton Prison, where their cousin had been sent on remand. They walked to the platform like shell-shocked soldiers, not sure they would be able to endure whatever was coming at them next.

Brennan spoke up eventually. "If we're not able for this, we can change trains for Tooting Bec and head there instead. Where but in England could you have a place called Tooting Bec? I heard of another place called Biggleswade. What can those words possibly mean?"

But Molly was not to be distracted from the dire business at hand, namely that their cousin was charged with the murder of a police officer. "He's being held in a special unit. The IRA men are Category A prisoners — those whose escape would be highly dangerous to the public or to national security."

"I'm with Brennan," said Terry. "Let's talk about Tooting Bec and Cockfosters. And Piccadilly Circus, when you think of it. We hear that so much we tend to forget how odd a name it is. The newspapers should run an art contest for children, get them to draw the images that come to their minds when they hear these place names."

Molly ignored her brothers' desperate frivolity. "Surely this is all a horrible mistake. Pray to God it will get sorted before there is a trial. What will happen if . . . Here's the train."

They made the journey and emerged at the Brixton tube station. It wasn't long before they were facing the fortress known as Her Majesty's Prison Brixton, where their Category A cousin was on remand. The squat brown complex with its square towers could not be anything other than a prison built in the nineteenth century. They were let in to the visiting area one at a time. Brennan went first, after being thoroughly patted down in the searching area. Conn was seated at a table, waiting. He was dressed in brown prison clothing with a broad yellow stripe. Brennan was shocked at the appearance of his young cousin. The affable Conn Burke he had come to know over the past few days was nowhere to be seen. This Conn was subdued and pale. Pale except for bruising on his left cheek and around his eye. There was a raw-looking cut on his cheekbone.

"What happened to you?" were the first words from Brennan to the prisoner.

"Fuckers" was the first from Conn.

"The police did this?"

"Others have fared worse." Then he surprised Brennan with a philosophical outlook on the situation. "When I look at it from their point of view, they think I offed one of their own. I didn't."

Brennan caught his gaze and held it. Conn stared back, unperturbed. Brennan had no idea where to begin.

"Like my banana suit?" his cousin asked, pointing to the yellow stripe. "Hope it doesn't make me look fat, though I'll probably lose a stone or two if they keep me in here."

"Can you talk to me, Conn?"

"They claim the conversations in here are private, but I wouldn't put my faith in anything the screws tell me. So I hope you've got good ears and can hear over the humming you're going to do and the tapping from me."

"My hearing is excellent."

"Good."

Conn began a low hum and gestured with his head that Brennan should do the same. Brennan typically wondered what piece he should perform, then quickly reminded himself that this was not the time or the place to uphold his accustomed standards of musicianship. He began humming the largo from Dvorak's *New World Symphony*. He had no idea why, but this was not about him. Conn started knocking on the table with his knuckles.

"What's the story, Conn?" Brennan asked in a voice just above the threshold of audibility.

"They're fitting me up for this. I didn't kill any peeler."

Brennan saw no need to ask the rhetorical question "Why would they want to frame you?" The answer was obvious. The young fellow's IRA involvement was enough to put him in a frame flexible enough to be employed over and over for the rest of his life. Instead, Brennan wanted confirmation that his cousin really had not murdered the police officer. If indeed he had not.

"You didn't do it," he whispered over the other man's hums and knocks.

"I swear to you on the holy name of Jesus Christ that I did not." Conn made the sign of the cross.

That Brennan took to be a truthful denial from the fiercely

Catholic young man. He recalled his cousin's cajoling of other less-devout Irish Republicans to attend Mass at Sacred Heart church. But, just in case, a test question: "Have you ever caused the death of any other person?"

Conn looked at the priest and then looked away. After several seconds, he mouthed a reluctant "Yes."

Brennan had no desire to dwell on that. Back to the current crisis. "Do you know who killed the cop?"

Conn gave an impatient shake of his head.

"Do you know anything about it at all?"

Another shake.

"What do they think they have against you?"

"They say I was in the area."

The area of the murder and of the great building packed with explosives.

"Were you?"

A shrug, as if this detail was of no importance.

"What were you doing?"

"Enjoying the city like six and a half million other people."

"Well, then, why you? They must think they have evidence . . ."

"I don't know anything about it, Brennan," he replied without the benefit of any noise to mask his voice.

Brennan left the prison grounds with his sister and brother after they had their visits, and they headed straight for the tube. There was someone they had to see in central London.

†

Lorna MacIntyre looked like the chairman of the board, the board of any large corporation with a suite of swanky offices, like the one they were in now. The job description likely contained a requirement to woo clients and customers on the golf course and in the more exclusive clubs of London. Conn Burke's solicitor wore a dark grey suit with a crisp white shirt and a delicate gold necklace. Her black wavy hair was cut short and she wore just enough makeup to mask the freckles that dotted her face. You couldn't see them from a distance, but you could up close. She could have been a member of the Conservative Party. A framed picture on a side table told a different story. The woman with the freckled face, the long black hair bunched into a ponytail, and a multi-coloured sundress, was the same person, or had been.

Lorna laughed when she saw her guests eyeing the photo. She spoke with a Scottish burr. "Law is largely theatre. I have to deal with other solicitors, barristers, judges, and law lords, and I've found it best to look the part. You've seen it yourselves, I'm sure, marches or demonstrations in favour of progressive politics, left-wing causes, liberalization of drug laws. And what do you see? Long hair and clothing from the hippy era. My advice to them is 'You've already convinced your own. Stop preaching to the choir. It's time to show the men in suits that you're serious. Dress like them, talk like them, fool them, even for a day.' It shouldn't have to be like that, but sometimes you do better if you play the game."

"Like golf," Terry said.

"Ach, mon, there's nothing wrrrong with a game of golf. I grew up just outside St. Andrew's."

"Point taken," said Terry.

"But that's not why you're here. Let's all have a seat and I'll tell you what I know."

They took seats facing Lorna at her desk, and she got on with the meeting. "You're asking yourselves what evidence the police have, or claim to have, against your cousin." She had a folder open on the desk but she did not consult it. She folded her hands over it and said, "They have two witnesses who say they saw Conn on Horseferry Road. That road intersects with Elverton Street, where Sergeant Heath was shot in his car."

This was just the beginning of the bad news, Brennan knew.

"I imagine there were a lot of people on Horseferry Road," Terry responded. "Major street in a city with a huge population."

If the lawyer was put off by the interruption, she didn't show it. "The bullets found in the body were fired from a nine millimetre Hi-Power Browning pistol. This kind of weapon has come into the country, and into Ireland, in considerable numbers recently, and is known to be favoured by members of the Provisional IRA here."

Nobody opened up to concede that young Conn Burke was, or had ever been, associated with the afore-named organization.

"There is an ASU of the IRA, that is, an active service unit, operating out of Cricklewood, in the northwest of London, and Special Branch believe Conn is a member of it."

Nobody tried to tell the lawyer how to do her job, by pointing out that those two facts did not add up to a connection with the murder. She was well aware of that.

"That's not enough to convict him. Well, probably not, depending on what kind of jury the prosecutor can get. But it's enough to hold him for now. Doesn't take much these days, as you know yourself, Molly." Lorna paused for a few seconds before she continued. "Then there are the phone calls. As everyone knows, there was a plan to blow up Westminster Abbey."

Brennan experienced all over again the sick feeling he had when he learned of the plan to bomb the magnificent Gothic abbey. Even if there wasn't a soul within two miles of it, the bombing would be an unforgivable crime.

"And the statue of Oliver Cromwell."

Brennan willed himself not to react, not to turn and see how his sister was reacting beside him. All he had heard was that there was a plan to vandalize the statue. Now he was hearing it was going to be blown up.

"There was a less drastic plan afoot as well, conceived by a different group, to deface the statue." Lorna did not look at Molly as she said this. "The timing was chosen to coincide with a gathering of the Cromwell Association. This is an organization that was formed in the 1930s to commemorate Cromwell and promote the study of his life and work. They usually have their ceremony on the third of September each year, that being the real Cromwell Day. He had two major military victories on September the third, one over Scotland in 1650 and the next year over royalist forces at Worcester. He died on September the third, 1658. Anyway, that's the big day. But this time round they decided to have an event on his birthday, April the twenty-fifth. I heard somewhere that one of the members is near death, and that may account for the early ceremony this year. Who knows?

"These events are frequently closed to the public, but this time it was to be a gathering at the statue. Word got round, and a group opposed to Cromwell decided to protest at the site and throw red paint on the statue. But the organizers of that demonstration were apparently advised by someone or other not to proceed that day."

Brennan finally risked a glance at his sister. Her attention was focused on the window behind the lawyer's head.

"So, that was the plan: a bombing of the statue by those who took the position that vandalism was not a severe enough sanction against the . . . *Lord Protector.* And Westminster Abbey is one of the most potent symbols of Britain's history and accomplishment. Scotland Yard—the Metropolitan Police—received two telephone calls giving coded warnings about the bombs. I say 'coded' because, as you are probably aware, certain words are used by militant organizations when they call in these warnings, codes known to police, so that there is no doubt about the authenticity of the call. The first call came in to Scotland Yard at three ten p.m. The caller said the abbey was being targeted in revenge for what Cromwell and his army had done to the abbey in Wexford, Ireland, three hundred and forty years ago. He said Cromwell had destroyed the abbey and massacred the people of the town, and it was payback time. But not a true payback; there would not be a massacre of thousands of people in London. The police could spare lives if they got on the hop. They had sixty minutes to evacuate. The caller ended by saying, 'This message is brought to you by the Boys of Wexford.'"

Was this the same Wexford revenge scheme that had been plotted all those years ago? Brennan wondered.

"The police had already started to mobilize when they received the second call, again coded, this time warning of the bomb planted at the statue of Cromwell. 'Get those Cromwellian lickspittles away from the obscene thing behind the Houses of Parliament. And let them reflect on the fact that they're being shown the mercy that Cromwell never showed the Irish.' So, apparently, the Cromwell Association members were to be spared along with the tourists and other innocent bystanders. The caller stressed that the people should be evacuated away from the statue but not towards the abbey across the road to the west of it. Send the people north or south. Again the police had little choice but to go along, even though they no doubt wondered whether they were being set up for a larger attack away from the grounds. The caller again gave the authorities sixty minutes. Which threw them off because they were already well into the first hour, and now they had a second evacuation. Was this an extra hour? Or, as they began to suspect, did it mean the devices were not on a timer, but would be detonated remotely at a time chosen by the bombers?"

Brennan could feel the tension, only a minute fraction of the real thing of course, the tension of having to make life-and-death decisions in a short, frantic time, with information that could not necessarily be trusted.

"There was a mad scramble to get everyone away from the statue and out of the abbey and St. Margaret's church next door to it, out of that whole area. Then the bomb disposal units were sent in. The bombs were found and disposed of. There was a small explosive dug in beside the statue, and several larger ones inside Westminster Abbey. The damage to the abbey would have been horrendous. As it turned out, they were not fitted with timing devices but were to be set off with remote triggers. As we know, that didn't happen."

Brennan shuddered at what could have happened. He noted that Lorna MacIntyre had made no comment on the destruction of the monument to Oliver Cromwell.

"Thank Christ they were able to get everyone away," Terry said, "and the bombs dismantled."

"Yes, all's well that ends well in that regard. But that leaves us with the phone calls." The lawyer had their full attention. "The police claim it was Conn Burke who made the calls."

Jesus Christ, who died on the cross for our sins, save us from harm. How was Brennan going to process this information? The idea that his personable young cousin was capable of this sort of terrorism nearly took the very heart out of Brennan.

Nobody spoke for a full minute, until Terry asked the question nobody else wanted to ask. "What made them think it was Conn?"

The answer was simple. "His voice is well familiar to them."

Of course. He was a regular performer at Hannigan's in the Kilburn High Road, singing and telling stories. And it could even be that . . .

"There is no doubt in my mind that the Branch has been listening to his phone calls at home," Lorna said. "I've assisted Conn in various difficulties over the past couple of years—nothing like *this*, I hasten to add—and every time he has rung me it's been from a call box or another person's phone. He has always given me other numbers to use, never his flat. So there you have it."

"And the police are going on the assumption that there is a link between the bomb plot and the shooting of the officer." Brennan framed it as a statement, not a question.

"Yes, given the timing and the location. It appears that the man was shot just before or just after the phone calls; the sequence is not clear. The shooting occurred in Elverton Street, a few short blocks from Westminster Abbey. And the statue is just across the road from the abbey, towards the river. The Met's theory is that IRA men were in the area and saw Sergeant Heath in his car, heading in the direction of Westminster. They may have been afraid he had been tipped off somehow about the bomb plot, or his death may have come after the first warning call was made."

"And the phone call came from where?" Brennan asked. He could hear the resignation in his voice.

"Phone box on Horseferry Road about a two-minute sprint from the murder scene."

Chapter VII

Since knowledge is but sorrow's spy, it is not safe to know.

William Davenant, "To a Mistress Dying"

Brennan attended early Mass at Sacred Heart the next morning, prayed fervently for his cousin and the murdered policeman, and then headed to the city centre in search of distractions from the family troubles. Terry had gone out to Heathrow to hop on a flight back to New York. He would see his wife and kids and try to make an arrangement with the airline to base himself in London for the next couple of weeks, taking on some short-haul flights to and from the capitals of Europe. If Conn's problems somehow got resolved, he would return to New York and resume his regular schedule. Molly was putting in some Saturday overtime, trying to catch up on work she had missed. So Brennan was on his own.

It was not hard to find distractions in the vast city of London. He saw a double decker bus giving a tour and he bought a ticket and hopped on. Once again, he got to admire miles of great avenues and buildings. And he heard some amusing commentary as well. As they passed a statue of Queen Anne in front of St. Paul's, the tour guide gave voice to the rumour circulating back in the day that the queen had been fond of the drink. People used to say the statue was appropriate; she had her back to the church and was facing the gin shops. And when the bus drove past a gentlemen's club, Brennan learned a few things about manners that he had not been taught at his mother's knee: men had been ejected from the club for committing such faux pas as whistling or raising an umbrella. Well, Brennan would make sure he did not behave in such a boorish fashion whilst trespassing on British soil.

He headed to Bloomsbury after that to see if he could meet up with Molly at the university but she was not in her office, so he decided instead to have a look around the enormous British Library. It was a warm, muggy day. Brennan was not a man for the heat, let alone the humidity, and was happy to be heading into a cool public building. It was easy to be overwhelmed in there, particularly after learning that the library contained over one hundred fifty million items, some dating back two thousand years. There was something he had meant to look up, something that was in his mind a few days ago. What was it? Something old? England had been occupied by the Romans way back in history, and he had heard something about that recently. But he thought it was something more specific. A famous figure of history? A saint, that was it. But the name wouldn't come. It was something strange, and he remembered expressing relief that he hadn't been saddled with it.

"May I help you, sir?"

Brennan turned to the librarian or assistant who had spoken and was about to say, *Only if you can get into my mind and tell me what it is I don't know.* But instead he came out with "St. Botolph."

"All right. Now, how much do you want to know about him? We have a biography section, a religious section, and plain old encyclopaedias in our reference section, if you just want a few quick facts."

"That's probably all I need. I heard his name somewhere. A church named for him, I think it was."

"Oh, there are scads of them, believe it or not. There is St. Botolph

Without Aldgate and St. Botolph Without Bishopsgate, both here in London. I believe there's an Orthodox church here named after the same fellow. There is St. Botolph's in Colchester, what's left of it, and another in Cambridge. Others as well, but I'm not sure where they all are. And you may not need that much information."

"Sounds as if there are as many churches for St. Botolph here as there are for St. Patrick in Ireland."

"Almost seems that way, doesn't it?"

"It was the Colchester church I heard about." It had all come back to him at last, from the news story about the man who was found dead in Colchester, Essex County. The woman who was interviewed said something about St. Botolph's. He turned his attention back to his helper at the British Library. "What did you mean when you said 'what's left of it'?"

"Oh, it's in ruins now, a couple of walls left. Here, let me show you. We don't have to go far. We have some tourist bumpf near our front desk, and I know there's a book about Essex. The ruins are shown in there."

He followed her to a display case containing various illustrated books and brochures about London and the British Isles. She reached in and retrieved the one on Essex. She thumbed through it until she came to a picture of an ancient stone wall and another wall perpendicular to it, consisting of a row of round Roman arches. She handed the book to him.

"I'll leave you to it."

"I appreciate your help. I'm a priest and I should know more about the saints than I do. Never even heard of Botolph."

"You've come to the right place, Father. And I assure you we keep all inquiries confidential, so nobody need ever know of your . . . lapse in that regard."

"For that, I am grateful."

Brennan took the book to a table and sat down. He read that the building had been constructed around the year 1100, of flint and reused Roman brick, and that Colchester billed itself as England's first Roman city. The write-up said Botolph was a seventh century abbot, whose name had several spellings, including Botwulf. And that Botwulf's Town, shortened, became Boston. But that is not what struck Brennan as significant. The interesting thing was that the building in Colchester was not a church but St. Botolph's Priory, the first Augustinian priory in England. There were differences between a priory and an abbey, including the fact that a priory was lower in rank, with the prior reporting to an abbot. But anyone could be forgiven for thinking of St. Botolph's as an abbey.

And it was not the only one in town. St. John's Abbey had been founded a few years before St. Botolph's; the book said 1095, with the gatehouse added around 1400. And the place had a bloody history. This was one of eight hundred monasteries Henry VIII had set out to dissolve in the 1500s. Brennan's blood went on the boil just thinking about it, the king making a grab for the wealth tied up in the monasteries and their lands, and causing so much destruction in this country and in Ireland.

But the abbot in Colchester, Thomas Marshall, was having none of it. He was one of those who refused to go along. As a result, he was tried for treason and hanged outside the gates of the abbey. The place ended up in the hands of a family called Lucas, who were royalists when Oliver Cromwell was in power, and the abbey was bombarded by the Cromwell crowd in 1648, during the siege of Colchester. There were atrocities during that siege, as there were in other events of its kind. Brennan did not want to dwell on the deaths and the starvation. Anyway, the gatehouse was all that was left after the battle.

St. Botolph's Priory managed to survive the dissolution of the monasteries, but it enjoyed only a hundred more years before it too was destroyed during the siege in 1648. Now, in 1989, there were only two walls still standing.

Two monasteries. One a priory, one an abbey, both in ruins. Both destroyed in Cromwellian times. And a man murdered near them just around the time Detective Sergeant Richard Heath was murdered in the vicinity of Westminster Abbey, where people Brennan did not want to think about had planted explosives. Were the two deaths connected? Only by timing and architecture. And, one could argue, by the low murder rate in England where, statistically, there could be two homicides a day, but . . . this was not Brennan's field of expertise. He would tell Molly what he had found, and he would hope and pray that his cousin Conn had an alibi that would show he had not been in Elverton Street at the time of the Heath murder, and that the alibi did not place him anywhere near Essex County.

†

Brennan took the tube back to Kilburn and walked to Molly's flat. He was about to have a shower after his day in the hot, damp city, when the telephone rang.

"Hello?"

"Who's this?" The gruff Dublin voice sounded familiar. And none too happy.

"It's Brennan."

"Ah. Brennan. I heard you were in London. Well, I won't be seeing you there. The Tan fuckers detained me at the airport. Wouldn't let me into the country!"

"Finn!" His uncle in Dublin. "When was this?"

"This morning. I flew over there to see what the hell is going on with my son. Landed at Luton Airport, and yer man beckons me aside with a crook of his finger."

"Who?"

"Who do you think? Special Branch. Kept me on ice for three hours, then shipped me back to Dublin."

"And the reason for that would be . . ."

"That the Saxons haven't changed their attitude towards our people in eight hundred years. That's reason enough to keep a man in a tiny, overheated room for three hours without any explanation.

Three hours of interrogation and intimidation. Well, I'll have you know and I let them know I was not about to be intimidated."

No, Brennan was sure of that. His uncle was a tough old skin. "What did they interrogate you about?"

"They were very interested in my life story. I told them they could read all about it when I publish my memoirs." Brennan formed a picture in his mind of a book with his uncle's face on the cover, partly obscured by his customary dark glasses, and blank white spaces on every second page, where episodes of Finn Burke's life had to be withheld from the reading public. "But they seemed to know all about it anyway, or thought they did, the arrogant bastards. Then they started in on Conn. Well, they got nowhere with me about him. Except that he's an innocent man that they lifted on false charges for political reasons, while whoever really killed that peeler is still walking the streets of London, laughing at the whole crowd of them."

"Have you been in touch with Conn at all then?"

"Of course not. They'd be listening in on the call and recording it. Telling it to the judge." Finn launched into an impression of a highfalutin Englishman. "'And another thing, your Lordship. The accused man has been receiving calls from those Fenian bastards across the water. You know who I mean, my Lord.' 'I do indeed, Percival. We're all too familiar with that lot. Guilty as charged. Next Paddy on the docket, please!' I can just hear it now."

"So can I, Finn, thanks to you." Brennan did not try to hide his laughter. "But we'll take a run out and see Conn again, tell him what happened to you."

"Good. Who has he got handling his case? Fellow going to do the job?"

"Her name is Lorna MacIntyre. She seems to be on top of things."

"Glad to hear it. Let her know I'll be covering the lad's legal fees."

"I will. I'll be sticking around here for a while, Finn. I'm not going to leave with all this going on. Just have to call the home parish and square it with the boss."

"Good man. I'll rest a little easier with you there. See if you can find out what the fuck is going on, and how they managed to fit my boy up for this killing."

"I'll do my best. The blessings of God on you, Finn."

"Thank you, Brennan. Goodbye to you for now. You, too, officer." Click.

Brennan headed into the shower then and basked in the cool water sluicing down all over him. When he emerged wearing a pair of shorts and a T-shirt, he saw that his sister was home and she was not alone.

Two men were standing in the living room. One was tall and had on a pricey-looking suit; the other was shorter and pugnacious looking in a pair of baggy pants and a zip-up black nylon jacket.

Molly stood several feet away from them. It took a few seconds but Brennan recognized them: the two police officers who had been in the car outside Hannigan's bar. Special Branch. They turned their eyes on Brennan and scanned him for their files. Molly made no move to introduce him. But he had committed their names to memory at the time Molly described their previous visit. Chambers and Peck.

She said to the taller man, "Conn didn't do it, Detective Chambers. He's being fitted up for this because of who he is."

"And who is that, Miss Burke?"

"An Irish patriot."

Detective Constable Peck responded with a derisive snort, but DS Chambers tried for a bit more sophistication. "It's not a bad thing to love one's country, but there have been a lot of terrible things done in the name of Irish patriotism. Wouldn't you agree?"

"A terrible beauty is born," Molly replied, quoting Yeats. "Born out of the executions of the patriots of 1916."

"Right," said Peck, his Cockney accent coming through from the first word, "so you think something that happened seventy years ago excuses murder and bombings today."

"The history goes back considerably farther than that. The Anglo-Norman invasion of Ireland took place in 1169. And the most recent invasion, British troops in the North of Ireland, exactly eight hundred years later in 1969."

"So the IRA is going to be shooting people and blowing them up for another eight hundred years, is that it? Well, it's our job to make sure that doesn't happen."

"Clive, if I've learned one thing in this job, it's that you cannot reason with the . . ."

Chambers hesitated, and Brennan almost had to feel some sympathy. The man didn't want to say "the Irish," let alone "the Paddies" or even "these people."

The sergeant settled for "people who believe they have a long-standing grievance, with some justification, no question, but, well it's the old 'the end does not justify the means,' isn't it? And the means here was the cold-blooded murder of a police officer who, in very difficult circumstances, was trying to carry out his duties."

"Why are you here, Detective?" Molly asked then.

And, in a flash of insight, Brennan had the answer. Or part of the answer. Yes, the Special Branch coppers were doing their jobs, investigating a murder. But there was something else, at least for Detective Sergeant Chambers: he had taken a shine to his hostile witness. In an unguarded moment, Chambers looked at Molly while she was speaking. And although he didn't for one second buy what she was saying, Brennan could see that he liked her in spite of himself. He hadn't known her long. As far as Brennan knew, this was only his second visit to her home. Second interrogation. But how long had he had her under surveillance?

"If you truly think your cousin didn't do it, who do you think did?" Chambers said now.

"How would I know that?"

"It stands to reason, given the timing and location so close to the targets of the bomb plot, that it would be someone in, shall we say, Republican circles."

"Patriot circles, don't you mean, sir?" Peck interjected.

"So," Chambers continued, "if you can think of anyone else who might own up to this and get your cousin sprung from Brixton, do let us know, won't you?"

In the sergeant's mind, surely, "someone else" having committed the police murder would be as likely as Detective Constable Clive Peck being appointed to the House of Lords.

"I don't know anyone who would commit such a crime, Sergeant," said Molly, "and that includes Conn."

"You told us on an earlier occasion that you didn't see Conn Burke the day of the murder."

Brennan recalled how Molly had agonized over that spontaneous admission to the police. If Conn needed an alibi, she had scotched her chance of giving him one.

"That's right," she said now in a subdued voice. Then the fire was back in her. "But I know he wasn't out killing policemen!"

"If you think he was somewhere else that day, tell us."

She was wise enough to keep silent at this point. Wherever she suggested Conn might have been, his workplace, for instance, it was a dead certainty he hadn't been there. The police had checked on day one.

"Maybe 'e was ou' of town, was Conn," the Cockney police constable said, in a parody of a helpful tone.

Nothing from Molly.

"Took a little motoring 'oliday ou' in the countryside perhaps?"

What were they getting at now? Their position was that Conn was in London on April 25, killing the cop and calling in the bomb warnings. Brennan thought of the other murder, the one in Essex, an hour away from London. Had it ever been determined what time that man had been killed? Brennan would like to know more about that incident. Or would he?

"It looks as if there is nothing I can do for you gentlemen, so don't let us hold you up," said Molly.

"We're not finished here," said Chambers.

"She's made it plain that she has no information that can help you," Brennan said.

"We hear that frequently, Mr. . . . ." Chambers looked from sister to brother. "Burke. If we were deterred by that disclaimer every time we heard it, we'd never get a thing done." To Molly, he said, "What made you call off your plan to vandalize the statue of Cromwell?"

Molly's lips parted but no sound came out. Brennan willed her not to answer the *When did you stop beating your wife?* question. But of course she required no mental telepathy from her brother to sidestep this one. Brennan remembered all too clearly that she had received a coded warning to call off the Cromwell paint job.

Chambers was undeterred. He let the silence drag out for nearly a full minute before asking, "Have you ever been to a property at 33 Anson Road in Cricklewood?"

It was obvious that, on this one at least, she was utterly at sea. "I don't even know where that is."

"Very good then. That's all we need for now. Thank you for your time."

As they took their leave, Brennan knew he had not just imagined it. The senior man's eyes lingered on Molly as he said goodbye. It was not the sort of look a cop gives to a suspect.

"Good thing Terry wasn't on hand for that," he said.

"Yes, I have to say I was glad it was you and not him witnessing the interview. God only knows what he would have said to them."

"Well, he wasn't here, so you won't have to be slagged about that fellow having his eye on you."

"What are you on about, or do I even want to hear it?"

"The sergeant there, he has a *grá* for you."

"Are you daft?"

But her heart wasn't in the denial; she hadn't missed it herself. The detective fancied her. He had his eye on her, and his sights set on her cousin as the killer of his fellow officer in the Special Branch.

Chapter VIII

Let's be sacrificers, but not butchers, Caius . . .
Let's kill him boldly, but not wrathfully.

William Shakespeare, *Julius Caesar*

If Brennan had been in any doubt about staying on in London, the visit from Special Branch put all doubts to rest. He made a call to his home parish of St. Kieran's in New York and spoke to his pastor, Monsignor Brian O'Sullivan. Not a man of strong Republican sympathies, but a man strong on family ties, Monsignor O'Sullivan approved an extended period of leave for Father Burke. He would have Father Pietro Schiavone fill in. Brennan then brought up the idea of doing some parish work in London; he wanted to be usefully occupied during the hours not spent dealing with his family troubles. O'Sullivan shared Brennan's love of the traditional Latin Mass and suggested he talk to the priests at St. Andrew the Scot church in London.

"Sounds more Presbyterian than Romanish, doesn't it?" said Brennan.

"Aye, it does, laddie. But you and I know what's what."

They both knew that, back in Andrew's time in the ninth century, the word "Scot" meant "Irishman." As if there wasn't enough confusion about who's who in the world.

Brennan thanked O'Sullivan and made his next call to St. Andrew the Scot. The pastor there was neither Scottish nor Irish, but an Englishman who was fluent in Latin. He was grateful for Brennan's offer of assistance, and they agreed to meet soon and set something up.

Brennan then took the opportunity to fill Molly in on another old saint, Botolph, and the other results of his research at the British Library. He told her about the ruins of the abbeys in Colchester, Essex, where the second, or possibly the first, murder had occurred late in April.

"What have they said about the victim in that case?" Molly asked.

"Very little, at least the last time I heard any news about it. They had identified the body but not released the name because the family had not yet been notified. All I remember is that the woman who found him said he seemed like a nice fellow and he had been taking pictures of the old buildings. The question is whether the two killings are linked by more than timing and abbeys and Cromwell."

"Make that Cromwells, plural," said Molly. "There are two of them mixed up in this."

"Right. There was a Cromwell associated with Henry the Eighth."

"Thomas Cromwell, the first Earl of Essex. Henry's hatchet man, a one-man Gestapo. Absolutely ruthless, and not just in relation to the monasteries. But it is only the monasteries that concern us here. They were Thomas's 'file.' Eight hundred of them were dissolved in England, Wales, and Ireland in the century before Oliver Cromwell hacked his way through stone and flesh in this country and ours. Oliver was not descended from Thomas but from his sister, who married a man named Williams. But the Williamses took the Cromwell name to get in on all the glory. Never mind that Henry eventually had Thomas beheaded."

"And to think I found history dull when I was a schoolboy. That's because I didn't have a teacher like you."

"That's because it was presented as just another subject to get through in school; it wasn't presented as life. And as you and I know, life is anything but dull. Not in our family, at any rate."

"Painfully true. So, what would you say as an historian, Professor Burke? Is there a connection between the two killings, or are we merely looking at a coincidence?"

"What did I read a while ago? A quotation from a well-known person about coincidence? I used to have it taped up on my office wall, so I should . . . Einstein! He is reported to have said, 'Coincidence is God's way of remaining anonymous.'"

"I love that. I'll pin it up in my office when I get back. Unless all this is just a coincidence."

"And we mustn't forget DC Peck's question. Did Conn take a little trip out of town that day? If we could possibly find something to suggest the killings are linked, and that our young cousin was here in London . . ."

"Busying himself with the other matters that are being investigated. If he was not in Colchester killing the man there, it does not follow that he is innocent of the police killing. If the two crimes are related, it could just mean two different people were sent out to commit them."

"I know, Brennan, obviously. I'm trying desperately to hold on to Conn's denial to us. I cannot bear to think he would target innocent people or kill a police officer. It could hardly hurt us to find out more about this Colchester incident if there is a connection. The more we know about what's going on the better equipped we'll be to understand what Conn might or might not have been up to. We may regret whatever it is we learn, but remaining in ignorance is not going to help anyone either. So, fancy a road trip to Essex?"

"And what will we accomplish there, aside from seeing more examples of the destruction of great religious houses by king and parliament?"

"We shall interview our witness, one Babs Mundle, to see if we can ferret out more information than is contained in the news stories."

†

So that is what they did on Sunday after Mass. They boarded a train to Essex and admired the early May countryside as best they could, as it flew by outside the windows of the train.

"Let's hope we can get in and out of Essex without Special Branch tracking our movements," said Brennan.

It wasn't long before they arrived in Colchester, with nobody tailing them as far as they could see, and they soon found themselves standing before what remained of St. John's Abbey. The gatehouse was large and imposing, with a typical mediaeval arch and vaulted ceiling, and turrets at all four corners with pinnacles on top. Dark rain clouds now loomed over the remains of the building. Brennan tried to avoid imagining the abbot in a noose outside the gates, for resisting the depredations of the state. Brennan and Molly then went to see St. Botolph's. The elaborately carved west front was mostly intact, as was one wall of upper and lower Norman arches. Brennan bowed his head and said a prayer for the people who had died in the siege of Colchester, and for those who had built these once-majestic structures nearly a thousand years ago.

Then they asked questions around town until they found their witness. Babs Mundle invited Molly and Brennan into the living room of her small bungalow. Every chair had at least two colourful cushions, every armrest a knitted or crocheted doily on it, every shelf a china poodle, dachshund, frog, or hedgehog. A large television set dominated the room. Mrs. Mundle's hair was a faded blond, and she had it in short ringlets framing her plump face. She was the soul of friendliness, and she immediately went about making tea for them. The teapot and cups commemorated the royal wedding of 1981.

"It's not often I have visitors from London. My Clifford used to take me there a couple of times a year for an outing when we didn't go to Butlins Minehead."

"Where's that, Mrs. Mundle?" Molly asked.

"It's one of those holiday camps, you know, where they put you up in sort of a compound and they feed you and they provide all your entertainment between meals. They changed the name of it a couple of years ago but it'll always be Butlins Minehead to us. Once in a while, though, we'd go to London. It's too big, though, isn't it? I only go if I have to. So, how can I help you today? Milk? Sugar?"

They stated their preferences and were served their tea and crumpets. Were they crumpets, Brennan asked himself, or was he just thinking so because he was in England?

He thanked her, and Molly said, "This is lovely, Mrs. Mundle."

"Oh, you're welcome. And my name is Babs. I don't hold with all that formality."

"Very well, Babs. I'm Molly and this is Brennan. We were interested in what you told the papers about finding that man who was killed."

"Oh, that gave me a fright! But never mind me. That poor, poor man! And they haven't even said who he was, let alone who did it. But—" she bent towards them as if to impart a confidence "—word's got round that he was a fellow called Doyle. The victim of the murder, I mean. Coppers can't find the next of kin. Well, whoever they are, they're in for a horrible shock. Any murder is awful, I know, but to beat someone to a bloody pulp . . . why would someone have to do that? What is happening to this country?"

"Terrible, yes, and very upsetting for you coming upon him," Molly said. "The reason we are here—and I can understand why you may not welcome this explanation, Babs, but we want to be truthful—is that our young cousin is the man charged with the murder of the Special Branch detective in London."

"Bloody hell!"

"I know, and we can both assure you that our cousin had nothing to do with the killing. Honestly."

"How do you know that?"

"For one thing, we have known Conn Burke since the day he was born, and he would not do this. Secondly, we have information that we can't reveal, which shows he is innocent."

Brennan could not help but admire the patina of credibility with which his sister managed to coat the shaky edifice of her creation.

"Naturally, given the timing, and a few other factors, we are wondering whether the two killings are connected and whether there might be something about the Colchester murder that could help in some way to clear our cousin. So, is there anything you can tell me about the victim here, the fellow you met?"

"He seemed like a lovely man, really. I never had a conversation with him or anything like that but I saw him a few times over a period of a couple of months when I'd be out walking Frankie, and the bloke would be out there taking his pictures. He would smile at me. A sweet smile he had. Kind, like. Or that's what I thought."

"Can you describe him to us, Babs?"

"Well, now, he looked to be in his mid-thirties. Not all that tall. Around the same height as you, Molly. And not heavy. Fair hair, or light brown I'd call it. Not too long but not cut close to his head."

"And he was taking pictures of the local sights?"

"Down at St. John's Abbey Gatehouse, and I saw him at St. Botolph's as well. Shame about his camera being stolen. Or at least I think the murderer took it, because the man always had it with him."

"How many times would you have seen him?" Brennan asked.

"Two or three, I think, before that final time when I found the body outside the gatehouse."

"Was he with anyone?"

"No, always out walking by himself. Well, except for that one time."

"Oh?"

"Chap went up to him there. Must have been the second time I saw him. Chap in an anorak, with walking shoes on. Goes up to him and says, 'Hello! Are you a member of the Save the Buildings Society?' Or the Heritage Preservation Society. Something like that. And the dead man, or him that ended up dead, just gives a smile and kind of a jaunty salute to the fellow in the anorak. And they just kept on with their business."

"They went off together?"

"No, not together really. The dead man, Doyle if that's who he was, kept walking the way he was going, and the other man kept going in the same direction, but I don't know whether he caught up with him, or they went their separate ways or what, because I stopped in at the butcher shop, and I didn't see them after that."

"You told the police this."

"Oh, yes, I did. But that never came out in the paper. The police told me to keep that to myself. Well, I'm telling you but you're not with the papers."

"That's right. I suppose the police want to keep certain details to themselves."

"That's what they do."

"After this encounter with the second man, when did you see the murder victim again? Was it when you found the body?"

"No, no, I saw him alive again after that. So, yes, I saw him three times in all before he died, and it was the second time, when that other bloke came along."

"Are you able to describe that other man?"

"I just saw him from the back, dressed as I told you. He had a cap on, one of those tweed caps with the bill, you know. I didn't see his face and all and didn't see much of his hair. Can't remember anything about it."

"What did he sound like, this second man?"

"Nothing out of the ordinary."

"So, his voice," Molly began. Brennan suspected she was trying to avoid the C-word, class being a perpetual bugbear in England. And one of the surest ways to signal your station in life was to open your mouth and speak. "Did he sound like a regular sort of fellow, or a toff, or you know . . ."

"Just ordinary. Not London Cockney, not a Geordie, but not an Oxford don or anything like that."

That was the best they were going to get.

"Did you ever hear of the Heritage Preservation Society, or whatever it was, before this, Babs?"

"I know I've heard of groups with names like that but I wouldn't know one from the other, not off the top of my head. There's a whole lot of old buildings and houses, aren't there? People would want to preserve them."

"Yes, I'm sure they would."

Chapter IX

*I suppose that the chief cause of bringing in the Irish language amongst them
was specially their fostering and marrying with the Irish, the which are two
most dangerous infections.*

Edmund Spenser, *A View of the Present State of Ireland*

When they were back in Kilburn, Brennan offered to go out for some
take-away fish and chips for the two of them. When he came back
with the food, Brennan found Molly sitting in her armchair staring
into space.

"Is something wrong?"

She gave him a "not now" signal with her hands. Just then, Finbarr
emerged from his bedroom.

"Hi yeh, Brennan."

"How's it going, Finbarr?"

"Grand. Something smells good."

"Help yourself."

"Well, maybe I will. But before that, I have something for you,
Ma. In honour of your work on the intersection of English and Irish
history."

"Oh? What is it, darling?"

He headed for his room and called back, "I designed it myself and had it made up for you. One of a kind. Well, I got one for myself and Shelmalier, too. Not sure if she'll ever wear it."

"You've got me on the edge of my seat, Finbarr. Bring it out here!"

"Good thing you didn't have it earlier. You might have done even more time in prison if they'd caught you wearing this." He came into the room and held something out before him. "Drum roll, please!"

"Jesus, Mary, and Joseph!" his mother exclaimed. "Finbarr, that is brilliant!"

The joy on his face was like that of an eight-year-old boy who had finally got it right.

The gift was a black T-shirt, with tan lettering. On the front it said, "CROMWELL IRISH TOUR, 1649–1650!" There was an image of Oliver Cromwell's face superimposed on a guitar-playing rock musician. In place of the guitar he wielded a musket. At his feet were images of corpses. The back of the shirt advertised the tour again and bore an excerpt from a review: "*Rock Fortress Mag* predicts: He'll slay them in Drogheda and Wexford!" Below that was a list of towns on the tour, towns that had suffered the presence of Cromwell's army, including Drogheda, Wexford, New Ross, Clonmel, and Kilkenny, among others.

Molly's eyes were enormous as she took in the shirt her son had designed for her. "I love it! And I'll wear it even if it means risking arrest all over again."

"I should get one made up for Conn to wear in Brixton."

"Finbarr," Brennan said, "that is sheer genius. Where did you come up with the images for the shirt?"

"I did them myself."

"My son the artist," said Molly. "He's forever being asked to make posters for school events and adverts for a group of his mates who are in a rock band."

"Good on you, Finbarr. Could we get more of the shirts?"

"Sure! The bloke at the shop can print up as many as we want."

"I'll want one, and so will Terry. And we'll get some to bring to New York with us. You can let us know the prices."

"Super. Just write down the sizes, and I'll put the order in."

Finbarr looked as if he had improvised a blistering guitar riff at Wembley Stadium and the fans were on their feet. Then his eyes fell on the fish and chips. "I'm off to see one of the lads in my mechanics course. We're going to work on his old Mini Cooper, but I'm a bit peckish."

"Go right ahead."

The young fellow opened the paper, scooped up a serving of fish and chips, and dumped it on a plate. He wolfed it down and took a bottle of beer from the fridge as a chaser. He had that gone in a few short seconds.

"Finbarr, darling!" his mother said. "There's no need to hoover the food and drink into yourself at such a speed. Take your time."

"Got to get going. Takes me a while to get to his place. Since I don't have an *auto*. To practice on for my *auto* mechanics course."

"To everything there is a season, my lad."

"Speaking of seasons, this one seems bloody long, seeing how I'm spending it with the old man. Feels like I've been there since Christmas."

"It's only been since Easter, darling. We thought that, since you'd been staying here so much, it might be good if you stayed with your dad between Easter and the end of the school term. But it's always up to you, you know that."

"Yeah, yeah, I'll stick it out and stay the course. I'll pop in here as usual when I can."

"Good, Finbarr. I always love seeing you. Nobody pretends this is an ideal situation."

"Right, right. I know, Mum. I shouldn't be whinging about it. Anyway, I'm off."

"Thank you again for the shirt, *a chroí*."

"Glad you like it. See yez." And with that he was out the door.

"He's in good form this evening."

"He does have an amiable gene in his makeup even if he doesn't always show it. Much of the time he puts up a brittle shield, to protect himself, I suppose. From what, I'm not always sure."

"How is he getting along? Generally, I mean."

Molly sighed. "When Neville and I were married, and when we had the children, I never dreamed I'd be one of those parents having to jolly the kids into staying with the other parent. That would never happen to *us*. Now look what's become of us."

Brennan searched his mind for a silver, or at least a pewter, lining. "One good thing is that it didn't happen during their early years. Shelmalier was already in university, Finbarr in his mid-teens."

"I know, but still . . ."

"Now," Brennan said to his sister, "what accounted for the long face when I came in?"

"I had a phone call." She hesitated, and Brennan waited. "I could hardly hear what the person said. There was a lot of background noise, the sounds of traffic. All I could make out was a man saying 'Tell him his prints were on the driver's door.'"

"Tell who? Whose prints?"

She looked even more disturbed than she had when he arrived. "Well, he must have meant Conn."

"Why wouldn't he say so?"

"How do I know, Brennan? He may have done. There was so much noise. I had the impression he had said something before I was able to hear him properly. He may have said Conn's name. I just don't know. Then he rang off."

"So this was an anonymous caller, using a call box somewhere outside."

"Yes."

"What did he sound like? Young? Old?"

"His voice was raspy. It was obvious he was trying to disguise it."

"Was there anything at all that sounded familiar?"

"No, nothing. And it was BBC English. Could have been real, could have been fake. It was very hard to make out. And it was over in a second."

"Why would someone make this call to you?"

"The obvious answer is that someone wants me to believe Conn is guilty. Which is the last thing in the world I want to believe, Brennan."

"But why you? You're not his wife. You're not his mother. Why not call Tess, or Finn?"

"I don't know. Maybe the man knows I've been to see Conn's lawyer, been out to Brixton."

"Maybe. Now, who would know about the prints? *If* this person can be believed. It's the police who would have this information, obviously. Could it have been yer man from Special Branch?"

"If you mean Detective Sergeant Chambers, he would not be shy about letting me know directly, if he wanted to get that message across." She imitated the Special Branch man's superior tone of voice. "'Sorry to trouble you, my dear lady, but it looks as if your boy is guilty as charged. Pity. We lifted his prints right off the victim's car door. Perhaps he'll see the advantage of cooperating with the Crown, favouring us with the names of some of his fellow terrorists. This could do him a world of good at sentencing time on the murder charge.' Chambers would not disguise his voice and hide behind the noise of a busy street corner in order to deliver his verdict."

"No, I suppose not."

"What's the lawyer's number? We'd better make an appointment with Lorna and give her the bad news, if she hasn't received it already."

✝

Lorna MacIntyre had in fact not heard the news. Brennan and Molly were sitting in her office the morning after the disturbing phone call.

"I was just speaking to the Crown Prosecution Service today. Not a word about fingerprints. The official story is that the police are still investigating. I'm entitled to the Crown's evidence, but it's early days yet. For the process. Not for Conn. Every day must be an eternity to him, sitting out there in Brixton."

"And for Tess," Brennan said. "You know his girlfriend is pregnant?"

"I know," Lorna replied. "It's a very tough situation for all concerned. How is she doing with all this?"

"I rang her the other day," said Molly, "but I just caught her on her way out of the flat. She was going over to Belfast to see her family. She said she was holding up all right, but I can't imagine . . ."

"Just like Conn. My client and his girlfriend have been in England long enough to have developed a stiff upper lip!"

"We should all be so fortunate," Brennan remarked.

"About that call, Lorna," Molly began. "If it's true, what the caller said . . ."

"If it's true, it places Conn right there at the murder scene with his hand on the victim's car door. But we don't know that it's true. The police have not said, yet, that they have prints. And who else would have that information? And why the cloak and dagger call? The whole thing seems extremely dodgy to me. It may just be someone trying to wind Conn up. The killing of Heath has touched a chord, as we know. There are droves of people who would like to see Conn put away for life. Or worse. They can't call him in prison. Hence the call to you, as the next best thing. You wouldn't have to be a member of Special Branch to find the connection between you and your cousin. I know it's pointless to tell you to put it out of your mind. But really it may be nothing other than a crank call. I'll see what I can find out. But, as I say, the police tell me the investigation is in the early stages."

"Not so early that they haven't got our cousin banged up in Brixton on account of it," Brennan remarked.

"True. But leave it with me. I'd prefer not to show our hand to the police about the call just yet. I don't want to be the one to raise the matter of fingerprints. We'll find out soon enough what they have.

Best to play our cards close to our vest. We don't know who is out there or what is going on."

†

Brennan didn't know whether to stand outside the grand Victorian building in Maida Vale and admire the elegant white exterior, with its beautiful architectural detailing, or go inside the place and drink. And have lunch. He lingered for a minute or so, taking in the sight, then went in to find a sumptuous pub in warm gold and reddish colours with a marble fireplace, stained glass, and art nouveau friezes high on the walls. Little wonder his sister was a regular here at the Warrington.

They were sitting with drinks on the table and menus in their hands when Brennan said, "Don't look now, Molly, but there's a very proper-looking gentleman giving you the eye from across the room."

"Of course there's someone giving me the eye, Brennan. Just as there's a tall blond Swedish film star giving the eye to you. She'll be crushed when she learns of your commitment to the celibate state."

"No, really. Take a couple of moments, then look around to your left."

Molly spent a bit more time reading the menu, then took a casual look around, and said, "It galls me to give credence to your seemingly preposterous claim, but I think you're right. I saw him in here the other day. He looked at me as if he recognized me, but I'd never seen him before, so I paid no attention."

"Well, he's . . ."

Approaching the table. Brennan caught the man's eye and acknowledged him with a nod. The fellow appeared to be in his early fifties with well-cut fair hair going white. Even Brennan, no expert on fabric or fashion, could tell that his dark grey suit was costly; his bearing could only be described as aristocratic.

"I'm awfully sorry to disturb you," he said, in a voice that could

107

have come down from the House of Windsor, "but you are Molly Burke, if I'm not mistaken?"

"Yes, I am," she replied, looking up at him.

"I shan't keep you from your luncheon, but I wanted to say hello and pass along my compliments. I attended a symposium in which you made a presentation, and I was very taken by it."

"The Cromwell conference, you mean?"

"Cromwell? No, I missed that one."

Just as well, Brennan thought. But then again, this man was probably more of a royalist than a parliamentarian and so might have had his own beef against the king-killing Cromwell. But such a judgment would be hasty and perhaps completely wide of the mark.

The man was speaking again. "Cromwell's name did come up, though. I am referring to your paper on Spenser and Milton, and their political views. Milton's in favour of Cromwell and the revolution. Well, Milton was a civil servant under Cromwell, after all. And Spenser's less-than-salutary attitudes towards Ireland and its people."

"Spenser's advocacy of a scorched earth and famine policy for Ireland."

"Precisely."

"He was encouraged by the famine in Munster—Irish people crawling on their hands and knees, eating shamrocks and carcasses in the wild, and how that left very few of them alive. Spenser reasoned that if the Irish could be restrained from cultivating the land, and having their cattle, they would 'quickly consume themselves and devour one another.'"

'Yes, quite dreadful, all that. I thought you captured the poets' thinking brilliantly and made some of the Milton and Spenser scholars distinctly uncomfortable. Oh, where are my manners? Here I am accosting you and your companion, and I haven't even introduced myself. My name is Cedric Mawdsley, and it is my task in life to bore the students on the subject of Spenser and Milton at King's College,

Cambridge. My research brings me home to London frequently, and I come here to the Warrington as often as I can."

"It's a pleasure to meet you, Mr. Mawdsley, and thank you for the kind words about my presentation."

"Cedric, please. And you are most welcome."

"Cedric, this is Brennan Burke. My brother is visiting from New York, where we washed up some years ago from our native soil."

Brennan rose and shook hands with Mawdsley.

"Well, I shan't impose upon you any longer."

"It's not an imposition at all, Cedric. Would you like to join us?"

"Oh, no, I wouldn't think of it."

"Really, you are most welcome. We haven't ordered yet and would enjoy your company."

"Well, if you're sure . . ."

He pulled out a third chair at the table and sat down. Molly handed him her menu. "I don't know why I take the menu at all," she said, "given that I know every item off by heart and I order the same three things over and over."

"I'm like that myself. Used to drive my wife mad. Same restaurants, same meals, same wine, same clothing. Minor flaws, I thought, but apparently not. But enough of that. Except to say that I have branched out a bit, coming to this place and a couple of other spots. I saw you here the other day but didn't approach you. I've never seen myself as a bashful person, but I must be, a bit."

"I'm glad you came over and said hello, Cedric."

Mawdsley then returned to the subject of the English poets of the 1500s and 1600s, and he and Molly gabbed about that. They traded stories about some of the students they had encountered in their years of teaching, Molly at the University of London, Cedric Mawdsley at Cambridge. Mawdsley put on a convincing show of interest in Brennan's work in Renaissance music with his church choir. When the gathering broke up, after they had all cleaned their plates of everything from salmon to lamb to—Brennan preferred not to dwell on Mawdsley's choice—devilled kidneys, Brennan was under the distinct impression that the Cambridge scholar would like to see Professor Molly Burke again. Brennan's only hope was that she would not invite him to dinner and devil a pair of kidneys in her kitchen.

"Molly, haven't you had enough of these snooty English toffs? Why not get on the boat back to Dublin and find yourself a nice Irish lad?"

"I am not looking for a nice lad of any description, Brennan. I thought I'd made that clear. But," she said, reverting to the tones of the city where she had been born, "you're so t'ick you can't cop on to dat, you feckin' little gobshite. So why don't you *póg mo thóin*."

Brennan concluded that this might be a subject best left to another day.

Chapter X

Many in the past have joined the Army out of romantic notions, or sheer adventure, but when captured and jailed they had after-thoughts about their allegiance to the Army. . . . [A potential volunteer] should examine fully his own motives, knowing the dangers involved and knowing that he will find no romance within the Movement.

Irish Republican Army, *Green Book*

Later that afternoon, Brennan took the Victoria line train and had himself admitted once again to Brixton Prison, where he sat across from his cousin and prepared for another session of enigmatic signals, covering noise, and ineffective lip-reading.

"Any point in asking how you're doing in here, Conn?"

"Resting comfortably."

"Do they give you anything to do?"

Conn shrugged, then said, "Bit of exercise. Reading. Dodging psychopaths and bigots. Watching television."

"Are you optimistic that someone else will be picked up for this, and you'll be able to join us at Hannigan's again soon?"

"I have no interest in seeing anyone else arrested for this."

"What? Why on earth not?" No reply from the prisoner. "You don't want someone else arrested and yourself released from here? Is that what you're telling me? Because somebody killed the cop, so there's going to be somebody sitting here in prison for it. Either you or the other fellow. 'Nobody charged' is not an option." The silence was still unbroken. "This suggests to me that you know exactly who committed this murder. Otherwise you would be ranting and railing about why the police have not picked up the real killer, whoever he is, while you, an innocent man, sit here wasting your life in prison."

Conn put up his hand as if to say *Cease and desist, Brennan, you're wasting your time.*

But Brennan was not easily put off. "You're protecting someone. I don't know whether it's someone to whom you are loyal and devoted, or someone who has you terrorized."

Conn continued to be deaf to Brennan's inquiries, dumb to his desire for communication.

"Tell me this, then, since we're having a freewheeling exchange of ideas, Conn. What do you make of the other killing, the one in Essex County?"

The younger Burke remained inscrutable.

"Word has it the victim had an Irish name. Doyle. Of course he may have been long removed from Ireland."

"Perhaps so."

"Oh? Are we making casual conversation here now? Strangers speculating on a news story about a person nobody knows?"

"I'm sorry I can't make your visits here a bit more pleasant, Brennan. I'm not much of a host, I'm afraid."

"I've known better times, it's true. But then again, so have you. And one would think you would move heaven and earth to try to return to that life you lived so fully and riotously up to now. How do you expect to beat the murder charge, Conn?"

"Reasonable doubt. Have Lorna drive a stake into the heart of the British Crown's case against me."

"You didn't kill the copper, so why in the fuck will you not make it a whole lot easier on yourself, and tell what you know and get yourself sprung from here?"

Conn gave him a look that said *Have you gone off your head?* All Brennan could do was nod in weary resignation. They were Burkes, not informers; they did not grass to the peelers or any other agents of the state. Even if it meant wasting away in prison for someone else's crime.

But the murder was only part of the story. "Conn. Westminster Abbey was packed with enough explosives to blow it to the heavens. And the police say it was your voice on the phone giving the warning. What if they hadn't been able to get everyone away, and the place blew up? Innocent people killed and a magnificent piece of history destroyed? What do you have to say to me about that?"

"I don't blow things up, Brennan."

"I'm not asking whether you're the fellow who planted the bombs in there. I'm saying that if you had any role at all —"

"I don't blow things up, and I don't put civilian lives at risk." It was the first time Brennan had ever heard Conn raise his voice. The accusations had touched a nerve. Brennan did not want to think about the kind of person for whom such charges would not touch a nerve. He waited a few seconds and then changed course, if only slightly.

"When do you expect the charges to be tested in a court of law?"

"Whenever it is, I shall expect Molly to kit me out in a suit of clothes befitting an English gentleman; see if I can bamboozle the jury."

"Conn, for the love of Christ, help us to help you. And if you are, for some unfathomable reason, unconcerned about your own future, think about Tess. And your child."

Once again, Brennan had hit a tender spot. "What kind of man do you think I am, Brennan? Don't you think I spend hours on end here in this cell, day after day after fucking day, agonizing over Tess and our baby and our future?"

"I'm sure you do, Conn. Without question. So let's get to work here. Is there anything at all you can tell me that I can pass on to Lorna MacIntyre? Is there anybody who can vouch for your presence away from the murder scene?"

"I didn't do it, Brennan."

"Your word obviously is not good enough."

"That's right. My innocence will have no effect whatsoever on the course of justice as it rolls on and over me. I'm not the first to be held for something I didn't do. Won't be the first to be convicted, if in fact I get convicted. Lorna is doing her best to see that it doesn't go that far. Next question."

The words were those of a man who had resigned himself to an unfortunate fate, but the truth could be read in Conn's demeanour. He had the look of someone who had become accustomed to lying awake at three in the morning seeing his future as a long, slow descent into hell.

Brennan could think of nothing to say. The prisoner took up the slack.

"Are you a man for television at all, Brennan?"

"No."

"Neither am I unless it's football or hurling. Or the news." Conn caught Brennan's gaze and held it. "Of course the news is always bad."

Brennan would switch on the set when he returned to Molly's and catch a newscast.

"How's the family?" Conn asked then.

"Worried about you, young Conchobar. Your father called. I hope you haven't been sitting here wondering why you haven't heard from him."

"He wouldn't ring a place like this unless someone had him at the point of a bayonet."

"That's more or less what he told me. He suspected that your telephone conversations would not be private."

"He knows how the world works."

"Yes. Well, he made an attempt to breach these walls."

"No! There's a switch. One of our lads trying to get into a Brit prison instead of trying to break out."

"He didn't get anywhere near the place. They wouldn't even let him out of the airport. Detained him for a few hours at Luton, then shipped him back to Dublin."

"Fuckers. If you're talking to Da, let him know I appreciate his efforts. I know he'll be going mental thinking about me in here." Conn took a look around, locked eyes with one of the warders, and held his gaze till the other man blinked. Then Conn returned his attention to Brennan. "So how about the rest of the family? Terry enjoying the craic?"

"Oh, yeah. Loves the bars, and he's applied for permanent resident status at the RAF Museum."

"I can see that. How about Molly? Doing all right aside from this bit of aggravation?"

"Sure."

"Shelley? Getting on with her studies, I suppose?"

"Yes, she's up at Oxford again."

Where was this going?

The next name was mouthed in silence. "Finbarr?"

"I saw some of his artwork recently. He should do more of it. A talented young lad." This was not the place to describe the Cromwell rock tour T-shirts, so Brennan did not elaborate.

But art was not what Conn had in mind. "Keeping his nose clean, I hope." Again, a significant look across the divider.

His nose? Was the young fellow snorting coke, or was Brennan being a bit too literal in his interpretation? Was Conn's refusal to speak the young lad's name aloud just natural caution, or was Molly's son up to no good?

"Tell the lad from one who knows," Conn said, "that the life he wants to sign up for is not a Boys' Own Adventure, not a swashbuckling romance. Tell him from me to stay out of trouble. And to stay away from . . ." He stopped speaking but did something strange. He bent forward till he was hunched over and made his right hand jiggle around. What was he doing? He repeated the gesture, this time with his eyes focused on the moving hand. He looked like an old man with a . . . cane. *Stay away from Kane.*

Nobody was home when Brennan got back to Molly's, so he

opened a window and lit up a smoke. Ahhh! Then he reminded himself that he had intended to turn on the television, pursuant to what seemed to have been a hint from Conn. It took some channel-hopping, a practice heretofore foreign to Brennan, but he eventually found a newscast and, among the events reported, was a disturbing story about a man who had been admitted to hospital in London three days earlier with wounds consistent with a vicious and prolonged beating. Was this the story Conn had been hinting at? Was this why he had issued a warning to stay away from Kane?

"The man, whose name has not been released, told staff at the hospital he could not identify his attackers and therefore was not in a position to press charges. A police source told me he had seen these kinds of wounds on another man in north London last year. Like the victim in this week's attack, that victim was unable, or unwilling, to identify his assailants. 'We believe drugs are involved,' the source said. 'We also believe drugs are not the whole story. We will continue to investigate this violent attack, with or without the cooperation of the victim.' Perhaps not surprisingly, the victim declined to be interviewed for this story."

No identity for that poor soul, but the next story confirmed that the man murdered in Colchester, Essex County, was named Doyle. The police had identified the dead man as Patrick Michael Doyle, thirty-six, a gardener and landscaper who lived on the outskirts of Chelmsford in Essex County. The fact that the victim was of Irish descent was interesting, but was that enough to link him to the murder of an English detective in London during a bomb plot hatched in County Wexford?

Chapter XI

"And of this place," thought she, "I might have been mistress! With these rooms I might now have been familiarly acquainted! Instead of viewing them as a stranger, I might have rejoiced in them as my own . . ."

Jane Austen, *Pride and Prejudice*

"Get out your tweeds, lads, you've been invited to an outing in the country."

It was the day after Brennan's frustrating visit to Brixton, and he felt blessed to have done several hours of work with members of St. Andrew the Scot's parish in the east end of London. He had said an early Mass, served at a soup kitchen, and counselled some of the parishioners about their various troubles. Terry had flown in from New York, and he had made arrangements to step into the cockpit when his airline needed a substitute pilot for flights between London and continental Europe. Now they were all back in the Kilburn flat, and Molly presented them with an invitation.

"We're going up to a place called Blythewich."

"What is it?" Terry asked.

"One of the great houses of southern England, I believe."

"Is it close to Biggleswade?"

"I suspect not."

"Whose house is it? Someone from the university?"

"No, I'm not sure who owns it. But the invitation comes from a Cambridge don."

"That fellow in the grand pub where we had lunch," Brennan said. "What was his name? Mawdsley?"

"That's right. He was in the Warrington again today, and came over and mentioned this drinks party out at Blythewich, and invited me to come."

"Another suitor, my dear," said Brennan. "You won't have to worry about a future as a wallflower whenever you finally give Neville the heave-ho."

"Another?" Terry asked.

Brennan decided not to tip his hand to Terry about Detective Sergeant Chambers's extracurricular interest in their sister. He would spare her that. So he said, "How did Terry and I get invited to tag along?"

"Well, I told Cedric I have two brothers in tow now, and I'm sure he is wise to the fact that you two aren't the local gentry. Blow-ins from away who could benefit from seeing a bit of the countryside. So he included you. Oh, and he said, 'Tell your brothers the place has a well-stocked bar.' Don't quite know what to make of that."

"I do," said Brennan.

"He did have the grace to look a bit embarrassed after he said it. But anyway, we'll all go and see what is no doubt a lovely spot, no doubt a great building, Bren, from what he told me."

"Ah but sure, we'll go," said Terry in a thick Oirish brogue. "We'll all go on the batter till dey picks us up and boots us in the hole and t'rows us out the door of the big house."

"We might have to lose him on the way, Father," Molly said to Brennan. "Otherwise it could be dreadfully embarrassing."

"One shudders to contemplate it," Brennan agreed. "So, shall we wear our best hunting attire? I'm afraid my pink jacket never recovered from the last time I was thrown from my mount."

"Do your best, darling. You could set them reeling by turning up in your papist collar."

"No, I'll go in under cover. Plain clothes all the way. How are we getting there?"

"By rail. Cedric said someone will meet our train."

"Sending his man. I like that," said Terry.

"All right. Wash your faces and let's get started. We have to get the tube to the station at St. Pancras."

✝

They were met at the train by someone who must have been bred from a long line of butlers; either that, or an actor was chosen for the role after a successful audition as a courteous, self-effacing, and helpful servant. He helped them into a long, old-fashioned car that Brennan would have described as a saloon, and they drove out through the countryside until they came to the great house on a low hill. Blythewich was a neo-Classical house of the eighteenth century done in Portland stone with ionic columns and a pediment. Like many of the great houses, it stood on a lawn without a lot of trees or plantings up against it, presumably so it could be seen in all its glory from the road leading to it. But farther away from the building were walking paths through stands of trees and lush flower gardens and fountains.

"Welcome to Pemberley, Miss Bennett," Brennan whispered in Molly's ear. She affected not to hear.

Cedric Mawdsley may not have owned the house but one could be forgiven for thinking he did. He effortlessly gave the impression of a man accustomed to luxury. He mixed easily with the other toffs gathered in the marble hall. He came forward and welcomed the Burkes, introduced himself to Terry, and then introduced the three of them to some of the other guests. It seemed to be a gathering of rich property owners, architecture buffs, and some film people as well. Mawdsley then excused himself, with a promise to be right back with someone who would show them around the rooms.

When he was out of earshot, Terry said to his sister, "Well, this is a bit of a break from your usual, Mol." Imitating a London Cockney, he went on, "Not your regular night of guzzling and groping at the No-Tell 'otel."

She responded in an upper crust voice that echoed that of Mawdsley. "Be gone, you grubby little man. I have ambitions tonight, and I don't want you spoiling them."

"Righty-ho. I won't stand in the way of you and his lordship, Mol. Someday all this will be yours."

"Mr. Mawdsley is not a peer of the realm, you poor benighted colonial. At least not yet. And he does not own this pile."

"Ah. I knew he was frightfully common when all was said and done. Still, if you put out for him and do a bloody good job of it, that could be your ticket out of Kilburn and all those bog Irish who live around you."

"Terry, has anyone ever threatened to kneecap you for all your guff?"

"Yeah, everyone in the family has, at one time or another. And many an outsider as well. I'm gaining in unpopularity all the time."

"I can believe it. I should make it clear to you, just in case there is any need to, that I am here for the same reason you are. The evening is a pleasant diversion from our recent worries. As far as I know, Cedric Mawdsley is a married man and is only looking for another chat about the English poets. In a pleasant setting."

"He *was* married, the way I remember the conversation," said Brennan.

"Well, even if he is no longer married, I am. And until that changes, I shall be the very soul of respectability."

"Give Neville his walking papers. Even Brennan agrees. Right, Bren?"

"Hard to disagree. He's not doing you any good, so why waste any more time on him? I'll see if I can get you a foot in the door for a Church annulment, on the grounds that you didn't know he was a cad and a bounder when you gave your consent to the marriage."

A young woman came over and asked if they would like a little tour. Yes, they would, so she accompanied them from room to room, giving them a short history of the illustrious family that had built the place in the eighteenth century, and the changes that had been made to the house over the years. The décor varied from room to room, from clean lines and simple cornices that were pleasing to Brennan's eye to richly carved woodwork and gilt mirrors in the Rococo style.

When they were back in the great hall, Mawdsley rejoined them and asked what they would like to drink. Brennan asked for a whiskey, Terry a beer, and Molly a glass of red wine. Mawdsley caught the eye of a man in a dinner jacket, and the man came over. Mawdsley sent him to fetch the drinks, and then engaged Molly and her brothers in a bit of friendly conversation. Mawdsley said he had been teaching at Cambridge for over twenty years. He had two children, one boy who was studying theatre and another who was "doing absolutely nothing, but is pleasant to have round the house." Cedric's ex-wife was an amiable sort, all things considered. "And there you have it. Now, Molly, do you live near the Warrington? Maida Vale area?"

"Not far from there. Kilburn."

"Ah."

"Though I'm thinking of getting a flat in Bloomsbury again. I used to be able to walk to work and now I can't. But I shouldn't complain; it's only a few minutes on the tube."

"Quite so, yes."

"Kilburn is an interesting area to live in," she said, loyally, "Lots of places to go."

"Yes, yes, I'm sure there are. I'm not all that familiar with Kilburn, but that just shows my ignorance. You live in a city all your life and there are entire districts you've never taken the opportunity to know. You feel quite safe there? I don't mean, oh, I'm sorry, it's just that one hears things."

Brennan did his best to keep a straight face as the man stumbled through his apology. He probably lived in Belgravia or Mayfair, and never ventured anywhere near a place where there were bars like Janey Mack's or blocks of flats or, God knows, council housing estates.

"Quite safe," said Molly equably. "In fact—" she leaned forward a bit "—I have a pair of guardian angels looking out for me."

"Your brothers, I presume?" Mawdsley said, smiling at Brennan and Terry.

"No, not my brothers. I have found myself under surveillance."

"What on earth do you mean?" He looked more concerned than shocked and appalled.

She leaned in again, and whispered, "Special Branch."

"No!"

"Yes."

"Why on earth would they be interested in you? Not that you're not interesting, I don't mean that! But to have the police . . ." His face registered his distaste at the very idea.

"I shouldn't make light of it, Cedric. It's no laughing matter, actually. My cousin has been charged with a very serious offence."

"Good heavens!"

"Wrongly charged."

"Has he a good solicitor? I could recommend someone."

"Oh, yes, he has. It will all be straightened out, surely. Someone else committed the crime, but so far the police have not looked beyond Conn—that's my cousin—for a suspect. And why would they? Once they have someone in the frame . . ."

"I'm terribly sorry to hear it. Forgive me, but would this be the Burke who was arrested for the . . . the police officer who . . ."

"Yes, exactly. But he's innocent. Honestly."

Brennan could see Mawdsley making an effort to look as if he was giving this notion a fair hearing. "It must be very difficult for you people, I mean, you know, Irish people living in England, when one of their number gets into trouble and everyone gets tarred with the same brush. When of course it is completely unjustified to judge the many by the very few."

"It is," Molly agreed. "It can be very trying at times."

"So tell me about these plods who have insinuated themselves into your life."

This was presumably an occurrence completely outside the experience of Cedric Mawdsley, so why would he not want to hear about it? Get a little thrill from the brush with notoriety.

"They are both detectives. As I say, Special Branch. The constable is Clive Peck, kind of a rough and tumble fellow. The sergeant is John Chambers. Sounds like a well-educated man."

"Really!"

"That surprises you?"

"No, no, of course not. I just . . . sometimes the police . . ."

The poor old plods haven't had our advantages, Brennan translated.

"This Chambers does seem to be a very intelligent man," Molly said in the copper's defence.

"I don't question that at all, Molly. The police are very clever fellows. Very astute. And women officers, too, of course. The police have a hard job to do. They are indeed clever, our coppers, ingenious in fact in the way they are able to solve crimes. Sometimes they get it wrong, though, as presumably they have done with your cousin."

"Yes, they're wrong this time."

"What got them onto, um, Conn in the first place? Has he had troubles with the law in the past, or was he just in the wrong place at the wrong time?"

Looking at his sister, Brennan could see the mischief in her eyes as she made her decision. "He's acquainted with some people in the IRA."

That was understating things considerably but it had the effect she was looking for.

"Good Lord!" Mawdsley exclaimed, and he peered at Molly as if seeing her in a new and somewhat garish light.

"So you see why I'm a target, by association, in the eyes of Special Branch."

"Yes, I do see. It's a shame that you have to bear the . . ."

"Stigma?"

"No, well, yes, you do in a way, don't you? Having the same name as a young man with ties to the IRA. But, as you say, it seems they have arrested the wrong man. Perhaps for that very reason, his association with that group. In times like this, with people on edge, and bombs going off and so on, the general public seems to forget the 'innocent until proven guilty' principle."

Brennan translated this as *The old "innocent until guilty" bromide that nobody takes seriously.*

"Would you excuse me for a moment, Molly?"

"Certainly, Cedric."

He made off for the far corner of the room, with haste, Brennan thought.

"You've blown it there, Mol," Terry said, "owning up to an association with the bold IRA. It doesn't get any worse than that for the people in this room. And, fair play to them, you can see where they're coming from."

"Imagine what he'd think if he knew our family history," she said. "Christy, Da, Finn . . . This crowd would have us in shackles."

"Almost as bad, they haven't come by to offer us anything more from the bar. One drink and that's it for us. Time to take the train back to civilization and stop in for a pint at Hannigan's?"

"Let's not be overly hasty, but yes, that's what we'll do."

Before long, Mawdsley came towards them again, his face the very picture of forced bonhomie. "Well! I hope you've enjoyed seeing the house. It's been splendid having you here. I hope to see you at the Warrington again one of these days!"

✝

"That was that," said Terry as they seated themselves in the train bound for London. "I guess the likes of us won't be admitted to the big house again anytime soon. Though why would we ever want to go again and stand there gasping for a pint, and not a drop coming our way?"

"I'm glad we got to see the place," said Molly.

"But won't it just eat away at you, Mol, knowing what you can never have, a future as Lady Mawdsley in a house like that and no aggro from the police ever again? Yer man certainly had a condescending attitude towards the police, didn't he?"

"He did. Imagine if John Chambers could have heard that."

"It's John now, is it?"

"The police aren't just nameless servants of the state, Ter. But as for Mawdsley and his attitudes, he was formed by his upbringing just as we were. Not a bad fellow, I don't think. He's just inherited his outlook; he's a product of his class."

Not an hour later they were planted in Hannigan's with pints in front of them, feeling right at home, listening to a motley group of musicians doing a spirited rendition of "The Boys of the Old Brigade."

Chapter XII

For sleeping England long time have I watched;
Watching breeds leanness, leanness is gaunt.

William Shakespeare, *Richard II*

The next evening Terry was off on a flight to Zurich. Brennan and Molly had tickets to see *Metropolis* at the Piccadilly Theatre. They were about to leave the flat when the telephone rang. Molly said, "Oh, I shouldn't bother. We're running late."

"Answer it. We've got time."

"Hello. Who is this? What? I can't hear you. No, please, say it again. I don't understand. Tell me who you are. How do you know this?" A couple of seconds went by, then, "What did you say?"

Brennan moved towards her. He was about to grab the receiver, but he heard a click and the dial tone. Molly was so agitated she could not get the receiver back onto the hook. Brennan took it from her and replaced it.

"It was the same man. Same traffic noise in the background."

"What did he say?"

"He said, 'The Yard have the fingerprints from Heath's door. See what the prisoner has to say about that!'"

"What else did he say?"

"Nothing. Gobbledegook."

"Well, what was it, nothing or gobbledegook?"

"I think he was making a sick joke. You know, how the 'RA have codes. He seemed to be slagging me about that."

"Molly, what did he say?"

"He thinks I'm Conn's sister, which I guess explains why he's calling me. When I answered, he said, 'Tell your brother I haven't forgotten that we shared the loopy lady.' As if things weren't bad enough, he takes the opportunity to make a smutty remark about some woman. And if this is someone who really shared a girlfriend with Conn . . . or shared a tart . . . who the hell is he and why is he doing this to Conn? Would someone set him up for a murder charge because of an old sexual rivalry?" She looked closely at Brennan. "What?"

She must have caught something in his expression. Might as well own up. "It's possible."

"Men!"

"But he did call her 'loopy,' meaning crazy, so this may not have been a lasting love that he's been in mourning for."

"Well, it's beside the point anyway. The prints are the point."

"And we're back to the same question: who other than the police would know about them?"

"Put it out of your head for now, Brennan. The stage beckons."

Metropolis, disturbing in its depiction of a dystopian future with the working class toiling away at machines underground and the rich frolicking in skyscrapers above, prompted Brennan and his sister to imagine a cast composed of people they had met in England, including Cedric Mawdsley as one of the idle rich and Detective Constable Clive Peck fuming underground, while Babs Mundle made the tea.

"Where would we cast John Chambers?" Molly asked.

"We'd have him, in place of me, sitting beside you as you watched the show."

The excursion took their minds off their family troubles, at least for a while.

The BBC Radio news the next morning was of great interest in the Molly Burke residence in Kilburn.

"There has been a surprising development in connection with a murder in Essex earlier this spring. Our correspondent Emma Langford reports from Colchester."

"Essex police have announced that the man killed in Colchester at the end of April of this year, the man originally identified as Patrick Michael Doyle, was in actual fact Liam Michael O'Brien, a thirty-six-year-old immigrant from the Republic of Ireland. The police say Mr. O'Brien lived in a rural area outside Chelmsford in Essex County. It is now known as well that he was married and was the father of four children living in Ireland. Mr. O'Brien was originally from Kilmacthomas in County Waterford and had been living in England for the past seven years. He was a gardener by trade and operated his own landscaping business under the name Patrick Doyle. Earlier reports were that the man had been beaten to death, and that his injuries were such that it was difficult for anyone to recognize his face. Police say they have been provided with no information that would alter their conclusion as to the cause of death. Asked why Mr. O'Brien had been living under a false name, and how he was able to conceal his true identity, the police were tight-lipped except to say that this aspect of the story would obviously form an important part of the investigation."

Brennan looked at Molly. "An Irishman living here under a false name. This gets more and more shady by the day."

"And why do I suspect that the more we learn, the darker it's going to get?"

Two days later, Brennan left work at St. Andrew the Scot and met Molly in Kew Gardens, one of her favourite attractions in London. She offered a running commentary on the rhododendrons, water lilies, bluebells, and other spring flowers that dazzled the eye as she and Brennan walked some of the three hundred acres of parkland. Brennan particularly liked the glasshouses.

"Leave it to you, Brennan. Five million flowers and you like the buildings. But I'll grant you, the glasshouses are spectacular."

"As are the flowers," he was quick to say.

"If only life could be this beautiful all the time."

"You mean without people being murdered, and cousins being charged, and women and children facing an uncertain future, and you being spied upon and imprisoned without charge, all of that?"

"Yes, those are aspects of life I could do without. Though I have to say I had an interesting experience with the police today."

"What? I leave you alone for a day, to go off and serve the poor and the devout, and the police immediately move in on you?"

"No, it was more benign than that."

"Let's hear it."

"I looked out and saw Chambers. Saw his car. What they get out of sitting in front of someone's flat, I don't know."

"Whatever it is, I don't think we would regard it as benign. They're watching you and taking note of whoever comes and goes. Your rebel contacts."

"But what if there aren't any comings and goings? Which is most of the time. The only 'person of interest' the police would ever see is Conn. And they know he's not coming or going anywhere these days."

"So what happened? Did they sit out there all day?"

"I took pity on them. Made them a cup of tea."

"Jaysus! Taking tea out to the peelers who are spying on you and, for all we know, just waiting for a reason to cart you off to the nick again."

"Now, Brennan, they're just doing their jobs like the rest of us."

"All right. Go on. You went out with the tea. What was their reaction to that?"

"Well, it turned out it was Chambers by himself, having a smoke. Peck wasn't there."

"Ah."

"And I had two cups of tea, so I gestured with my head to the passenger door. He opened it, and I got in and handed him his cup and I had mine."

"What did he say? Did he look a little sheepish to be caught out?"

"Not at all. If there was any sheepishness, he covered it well."

Earlier that day

"It's not often I get such friendly service." He crushed his cigarette in the ashtray, then rolled down his window and tried to wave some of the smoke out of the car.

"Perhaps the fact that you're spying on people puts you on the wrong foot with them."

"Never thought of that." He raised his cup and took a sip. "All these years, sitting in the car conducting surveillance and wondering, 'Where's the tea? Where's the hospitality?' And now you tell me it may be my own doing."

Looking at him, Molly wished she had brought out a couple of scones or biscuits as well; even in the two weeks since his first visit—first interrogation—he seemed to have lost weight. His face was thinner and he looked as if he could use a few long nights of uninterrupted sleep.

"Lovely cup of tea. Delivered by—" he cleared his throat and went on "—a lovely subject of inquiry, if I may say so."

She was taken aback by the unexpected compliment but quickly recovered. "Nobody has ever said that to me before, Detective . . . or, may I call you John?"

"Please do. And if I might call you Molly . . ."

"Of course."

They took a moment to savour their tea.

"All this is new to me," said Molly.

"That's what they *want* you to think."

"What do you mean?"

"I'm only joking you. Isn't that what they say in your country of origin? Joking you?"

"It is. You should visit the place. Spend some time in Ireland. You'll find there's more to us than 'subjects of inquiry.'"

"I have been there. I've been to Belfast."

"Leave it to you, John, and God love you and save you, but leave it to a Special Branch man to think he's seen Ireland if he's seen Belfast in the midst of the latest Troubles."

"But Belfast is Ireland, according to your politics. Correct?"

"Aye aye, sir, correct. The entire island is Ireland and should be united without the border between the Republic and the Six Counties your lot kept to themselves. But there are great differences between the various parts of Ireland. A great deal of variety among the Twenty-Six Counties of the South as well. Just ask a Cork man about a Kerry man, or either of them about a jackeen from Dublin!"

"I'm sure that's true. I would like to see the country. Not in my official capacity."

"What do you do for holidays, John? Do you get away from it all? Take the family to the seaside? Skiing in Austria?"

"No family holidays for me. Not anymore."

Molly wasn't sure if she should follow up on that, but to ignore what he said might seem unsympathetic. "Why not?"

"My wife got good and fed up with me sitting out in my car all hours having tea with lovely female subversives."

"I'd like to own up to two of those three words."

"If the shoe fits . . ."

"But you say this sort of tea party is a rare experience in your line of duty, so it must have been something else that went wrong in your marriage."

He didn't respond but gazed out the window of the police car.

"I'm sorry, John, I shouldn't have asked. I'm not the prying type, usually. Really, I'm not."

He turned to her and smiled. "I don't consider it prying. And even if I did, who am I to complain? I spend all my working life prying into the lives of others. To answer your question, it was the long hours, the calls in the middle of the night, interrupted or cancelled holidays, concern about what would happen to me when I left for my shift, all of that. Plus the tension this sort of work inevitably brings to a person, to a relationship. I would be short-tempered with her for no rational reason, nothing she did. It was the buried tension coming out."

Everything he said about his work and the effect it had on his marriage sounded painfully real to Molly; wasn't that exactly what would happen? But, at the same time, it also had the sound of a pat answer. She could easily imagine any police officer or soldier giving the same response. She couldn't have said why, but she wondered if something else had happened, something else that accounted for the collapse of his marriage.

"But what am I doing?" he said. "I shouldn't be unloading all of this on you. You say you're not the prying sort, and I can tell you I'm not usually like this, banging on and on about deeply personal matters."

"I believe you, John. From the little I've seen of you, I think you are a very self-contained person, not one given to personal disclosures. I would suggest that you do more of this, not less. It's a cliché but I'll say it anyway: it is not good to keep things bottled up. Little wonder it comes out when little irritations crop up."

Chambers said, in the manner of a toffee-nosed aristocrat, "When one is British, one doesn't speak of such matters. One keeps calm and carries on."

"And you do that admirably, Detective Sergeant Chambers. Did I read that the father of John Mortimer, the barrister and author, was a lawyer too? The father, that is. And he was blind, and wouldn't admit it? And that nobody was to acknowledge it? Do I have that right?"

"Of course. He never let on. One doesn't let on."

"It's a good thing you have a sense of humour, John. That must make life a little easier for you. The things you must see in your line of work. I'm not the hardest of hardened criminals you've ever dealt with, surely."

"You're a tough nut to crack, Burke, but you are correct. I have seen worse in my day."

She looked at him and waited until she caught his gaze. "How much worse?"

All merriment gone, he replied. "You have no idea. No idea what one human being will do to another, and what we have to do sometimes in our work to try and stop it." He drained the rest of his tea as if it were whiskey. Or, well, gin.

"But you feel strongly about what you do. That you're doing the right thing?"

"I am doing the right thing, Molly. Of that I am certain."

✝

"Then his car radio crackled," Molly told her brother, "and he had to take a call, so I took my tea things and went back inside. I looked out a few minutes later and he had gone."

Chapter XIII

Rooster of a fighting stock
would you let a Saxon cock
crow out upon an Irish rock?
Fly up and teach him manners.

Patrick Joseph McCall, "Follow Me Up to Carlow"

On Sunday evening, Terry was back in London, and the three of them were sitting at Molly's table, having a dinner of beef and Guinness pie with extra spuds, roasted, on the side. Molly was accepting compliments, and they were all enjoying a drink of whiskey.

The telephone rang, and Molly regarded it as one might regard a large brown rat making its remorseless way towards the baby cradle. But she got up and made her way towards the instrument. Brennan got there ahead of her and grabbed the receiver. "Yes?" No reply. "Who is this?" There was a soft click at the other end of the line, as the person hung up.

"What was that?" Terry asked. "Another anonymous call about fingerprints?"

"Yes, but it was just empty air this time."

"Maybe the guy was spooked because you answered, Bren. Thought he'd get Molly."

"Or maybe it was nothing, someone who realized he or she had the wrong number."

"Sure. Tell me this. How long will it be before Conn goes to trial?"

"Lorna told us it could be months."

"And he's going to be sitting in a cell until that time."

"They're hardly going to let him out," Molly said, "someone they consider a terrorist and cop killer."

"But we don't consider him either of those things, right?" Brennan asked.

There was no answer from his brother or sister.

"Right?" he repeated.

Still no response from Terry. But Molly finally spoke up for the defendant. "I can't imagine Conn taking an innocent life."

"You should have been a lawyer, Mol," Brennan told her. "What constitutes an 'innocent life' to a member of the IRA? Is an English Special Branch police officer an innocent or a legitimate target?"

"Let's not get into that again."

"It's the perennial question," Brennan said. "It will never go away as long as human beings have to share the planet with others of their kind. I'm sure we all agree that Conn knows more about the murder than he's letting on. We all came away with that impression. We just don't know who he's trying to protect, someone he loves or someone he fears. Of course if we had that figured out, we'd have solved the case. And we're not likely to accomplish that."

"We may never want the case solved," Molly said in a quiet voice.

"You think he did it, don't you, Molly?"

"I don't want to think it, Terry, but Lorna told us the police recognized his voice in those warning calls, and the phone box was only minutes from the murder scene. The nine-millimetre bullets or whatever they were match some kind of gun used by the IRA."

"Browning Hi-Power semi-automatic," Terry said.

"Thank you, Air Marshal Burke. Then there's the fact that I got those two calls. From public phones, in a noisy, high-traffic area. So I'd be hard put ever to identify the voice. But the message was clear."

"Right," said Terry. "Conn's prints on the police car door."

"That and a coarse message about sharing the 'loopy lady.' As if this is an appropriate time for tawdry reminiscences."

"What did you say?"

Terry's tone of voice was uncharacteristically sharp, and Brennan looked closely at him. Molly replied, "I said how inappropriate it is to—"

"No, I mean, what did the man say on the phone?"

"He said, 'Tell your brother I haven't forgotten the time we shared the loopy lady.'"

"Jesus!"

"What is it, Terry?" Brennan asked.

"You're sure, Molly. Well, you couldn't have made it up!"

"This person who made the calls, he thinks I'm Conn's sister, apparently. Because he said 'Tell your brother' that nonsense about the woman."

"It's not nonsense. That message was for me."

"What?" Molly and Brennan demanded.

"I shared the loopy lady with him."

"With whom? What on earth are you on about?" Molly demanded. "Are you saying you shared a woman with some man, someone who would make an anonymous call . . . You're not making any sense, Terry. At least I hope to God you're not."

"It's Casey."

"Casey?" Molly asked. "Who is Casey?"

"Well . . ." Terry began. He shifted in his seat and looked at his brother and sister. "It's a long story, and I'm not sure how you're going to take it." It was a rare experience for Brennan to see his brother so reticent about a telling a story.

Terry got up and went to the drinks cabinet, brought the bottle of Jameson to the table, and refilled the three glasses.

"It all goes back to a trip I took to Belfast a few years ago, in 1983. I had a chance to substitute for another pilot on a flight from New York to Dublin, with a week of R and R afterwards. So I visited some of our clan in the oul hometown, one of whom was our uncle Finn behind the bar at Christy's. Had a few scoops there, heard some music. Great gas. But in conversation with Finn, it came out that he was a little concerned about his youngest, Conn, who had moved to Belfast a couple of years before. Finn felt unable to travel to Belfast himself at that time, for reasons he made no effort to explain. Anyway, he gave me Conn's address and number, the phone number for the building site where he was employed, and all that. I said that was grand; I had never been to Belfast and looked forward to seeing the city. Finn let out a snort at that and said, 'Going, yes, I appreciate it. But looking forward to it? Terry, are you cracked?'"

Belfast
July 8, 1983

Signs of the Troubles were immediate as soon as Terry boarded the train for Belfast. Warnings were posted in the train cars, urging passengers to be vigilant and telling them what to do if they spotted an unattended parcel. He heard two women across from him discussing someone they knew who had been killed on the train. The women made the sign of the cross when the train arrived at Drogheda. Terry looked out at the town on the River Boyne, the grey buildings and church spires, and recalled what he had heard about Drogheda, and Cromwell, while growing up. As the train chugged along, Terry took in the beautiful scenery around him, green fields and rolling hills, swans in the shining waters. It was not so pretty when they got to the Northern Irish border. Oh, the countryside was still lush and green. But he could see the motorway where cars were being stopped and searched by British soldiers dressed in camouflage fatigues and armed with rifles.

Things looked even worse when he got to Belfast, as might be expected. Coming in on the train, he saw buildings with the windows blown out and yards full of rubble. There was graffiti on gable walls, typically white paint on grey stone: JOIN THE IRA and SMASH H BLOCK, and the other side's efforts as well, NO SURRENDER and NO POPE HERE. Terry's hotel was a short walk from the train station, so he headed there.

July eighth was a Friday, a work day. Terry called the number for Conn's building company, and the woman who answered said Conn was busy but she would take a message, so Terry left his name and number.

Now, what to do, sit in my hotel room in the hope that the phone will ring, like a teenage wallflower? No, get out and see the sights.

Like everybody else, he had seen the latest Troubles on the television news, but nothing had prepared him for being on the ground in the embattled city. There were the murals, lurid and explicit, calling death down on the IRA on the one side or on the UVF/ UDA/UFF—the Protestant Loyalist paramilitaries—on the other. There were police barracks with enormous blast walls around them to protect against car bombs. Nationalist and Loyalist neighbourhoods, Catholic and Protestant, were separated from each other by jerry-built walls and barbed wire. But what struck him most was the overwhelming military presence, the soldiers walking or running past with rifles at the ready. This was the British Army; this part of the island was, rightly or wrongly, still part of the United Kingdom. Armoured vehicles lumbered along the streets and sirens screamed in the distance. Terry lined up with the locals to be groped—body-searched—at control points in the city centre. How could people live like this?

He walked for two hours in weather that spanned the spectrum from warm and sunny, to cool and cloudy, to mist and rain, to sun showers. When he looped back to his hotel, there were no messages for him. He headed out again, in search of a pint or a glass of whiskey and a bite to eat. He had spotted some bars in the area behind his hotel, so he walked in that direction. He noticed on the way a couple of piles of wooden pallets stacked up, and Union Jack and Ulster Red Hand flags flying.

He found a bar called the Rangers Pitch and walked in. The place was half-full, and every one of the drinkers looked up and inspected him when he came in the door. Not wanting to be identified instantly as a Yank, a rich kid, a blow-in from the USA, he discarded the New York inflections of his speech and took on the voice he was born to, born in Dublin the year before his father bundled them onto a ship that slipped out of Cobh harbour in the dark of night and carried them to the new world. Now, in Belfast, he spoke to the barman in the tones of a man just hours out of Dublin. That was his first mistake. In the Rangers Pitch bar, the worst thing you could be, far worse than a Yankee tourist, maybe even worse—he realized now—than a Celtics football club supporter, was a blow-in from Dublin. He knew that instantly from the hostile looks he got from the punters and the barman himself. So, on his first outing, he had banjaxed things as only a dumb tourist could do. Well, he was going to stick it out. But, in a concession to his surroundings, he ordered a Bushmills instead of a Jameson. Bushmills, good Protestant whiskey, along with his pint of Guinness. He took his glasses to a table and sat down.

"Got all your pallets in place for Monday, Billy?"

The raised voice, the harsh northern accent, came from a man at the table next to Terry's and was directed to the man's drinking companion. Both were muscular types with their hair buzzed close to their skulls.

"Aye, Georgie, piled high as the Pope's evil eye and as dry as a nun's heart. One match and it will catch like the fires of hell itself."

Right, Terry thought. Monday would be Bonfire Night, the eleventh, when the Orange Order lit fires to lead off the Twelfth of July celebrations. Celebrations marking the victory of King William of Orange over the Catholics of Ireland. Over Terry's people. The Orangemen were still crowing over the victory and parading through Catholic neighbourhoods nearly three hundred years later. And legally permitted to do it. Fuckers. Terry sank his glass of Bushmills and started on his pint.

"You'll see the flames all the way from the Falls Road," Billy said, "not that anybody in this bar would be going to the Falls Road."

"Right you are, Billy. Nobody from the Falls in this place. All local fellows here. Loyal to the Crown."

We don't want your kind in here was the message being lobbed at Terry Burke in the Rangers Pitch.

Terry had never been one to sit silent in a bar. Bars were for drinking and socializing and telling tall tales. He launched into one now, inventing as he went along.

"Just be careful around your fires this year, lads," he said.

"Oh, aye? And why should we do that?"

"If you see something flying over you, take cover."

"Our people don't take cover. Our people don't run away. Maybe you haven't seen our motto out there on the gable walls. No Surrender. No surrender to a bunch of Fenian terrorists!"

"Up to you. I'm just giving you fair warning."

"Warning of what?"

"Ever hear of something called the Green Slopper?" No answer. Terry took a long drink of Guinness and launched into his tale. "I've got a brother in the U.S. Air Force and he told me about it. It flies about five hundred feet up, operated by remote control. It's triggered by smoke. You know, like those smoke detectors that make an ungodly racket and wake you up so you don't burn to death in your home. But don't let me get distracted about people being burned out of their homes. Like what happened here, at the hands of some."

Terry figured he'd gone too far, and he'd better split. The anger on the faces of his drinking companions could erupt into violence any second. But he hadn't finished his story.

"I'm talking about an unmanned airship, looks like a small zeppelin. Developed in America. It's used to fight fires. Drops water on them mixed with a chemical. I don't know what the stuff is, but it has a side effect. When it reacts with human skin it turns it green. Big blotches of green. The effect lasts for about two weeks, and it's painful. Especially in the eyes. The Yanks won't say whether it does permanent damage. You wouldn't want to be standing around a bonfire looking up at this thing flying over. Wouldn't want your wife and kids looking up at it."

"Yeah, well, we've never seen one of those over here. So we won't be losing any sleep, will we, Georgie?"

"You're going to see one Monday night. You're going to see thousands of Orangemen and their families turning green. Green as an Irish Republican on Saint Patrick's day."

"Fuck you! If the IRA think they can get away with this, they'll wish they had never been born!"

"Lemme give you the heads-up, boys. It's not the IRA that got hold of this." He stood up and drained the last of his pint. "It's the Brits. They're fed up with the lot of you. They're wishing they'd given the whole country back to us in 1921 and washed their hands of the place. Come July twelfth, they'll be blaming the IRA for it. And the IRA may be happy to take the credit. But you'll know the real story of who snuffed out your fires and painted you green."

He raised his empty glass to them and sang them a line from an old rebel song, "Now FitzWilliam, have a care. Fallen is your star low," and made a hasty exit from the Rangers Pitch.

Seconds later he heard the sound of angry voices erupting from the bar, and he ducked into the shadows between two nearby buildings. He recognized the strident tones of Billy and Georgie calling death down on his head. He surveyed the area around him, as best he could, in case he needed to bolt to another hiding place or a public space with people around. Though how much sympathy he could expect from the public in this part of town was an open question. After a few minutes he heard no more, and he cautiously emerged from the shadows.

Not one to push his luck — well, not one to press it again after he'd already pushed it in somebody's fierce red face—he decided to forgo any further bar excursions for now. He made a beeline for his hotel and had his supper in the dining room, garnished with a couple more pints of Guinness. He was just finishing up his last satisfying sip when the hotel clerk came in to tell him there was a call for him.

Conn welcomed his cousin to Belfast and said he could not get away to see Terry that night, but they could get together the next day. How had he spent his first day in the city?

"Battled my way through all the tourists in the streets, walked along with my arms held out singing 'Sunshine, Lollipops, and Rainbows,' and everybody in the street burst into song and joined in. That sort of thing."

"Where did you say you spent the day? Sure as fuck wasn't Belfast."

"Oh, it was Belfast all right. Nearly got my ticket punched at the Rangers Pitch."

"What are you telling me? Are yeh daft, going into a bar in Sandy Row?"

"Well . . ."

"Stay away from there. You'll get yourself killed. You want a drink, I'll take you for a drink. I have to work again tomorrow but I'll collect you from your hotel tomorrow, half-six. Keep yourself tucked in your room till I get to you!"

✝

Terry had not seen his cousin since their grandfather's funeral thirteen years before, even though Terry had made the odd trip to Dublin in the intervening years. Conn picked Terry up in his Ford Escort and greeted him like the long-lost relation he was. Conn was now twenty-six years old, slim but muscular, with thick auburn hair and brown eyes; he hadn't had a shave for a couple of days. He drove Terry through the gritty streets to his home, an upper flat in a terrace of red-brick houses near the Falls Road in West Belfast. There was no doubt whose side the Falls Road was on, with its IRA and BRITS OUT graffiti and the green, white, and orange tricolour flying everywhere.

"See that?" Conn pointed to a high-rise building nearby, a tower block around twenty storeys high, done in red and white panels. Terry imagined the rant his brother Brennan would unleash in the presence of yet another ugly experiment in 1960s urban planning and architecture. Brennan may have abandoned architecture for the priesthood but he still carried a torch for magnificent buildings. He'd be carrying a flamethrower for this one.

"Who has the misfortune to live in there?" he asked Conn.

"That's Divis tower. It was built for poor Catholic folk to cram into," Conn replied, "but that's not why I'm showing it to you. There's something much more interesting about that building. Top two floors of it are occupied by the British security forces. It bristles with listening devices and cameras, so we're all under surveillance twenty-four hours a day. The army knows every house, every back alley, in some houses every room and the colour of the furniture. From up there, they can watch us Taigs here in the Falls, and the Prods in the Shankill if they've a mind to. But we haven't exactly welcomed them to the neighbourhood. It got so dangerous for the Brits here they have to fly in and out of the building by helicopter. They land it on the roof. Too perilous for them to be on the ground anywhere near the building. But pay them no mind. Come on inside."

They went up into the modest flat, with its second-hand furniture and posters displaying favoured bands and exhortations to true Irishmen to claim their country from the British Empire. A framed picture of the Sacred Heart of Jesus had pride of place above the other emblems of Conn Burke's life. There was a guitar leaning against the wall and an assortment of tin whistles on a table by the window. "You're a musician, are you? Or somebody is."

"I am. There's a session most nights at my local. I join in when I can. We'll head over there now."

Terry looked at him closely and only then noticed that his cousin was exhausted. His eyes were bloodshot and underscored by dark circles. "Is everything all right, Conn?" No answer. "Late nights?"

"I've had some long nights, but I'm able for it. Come on, we'll have a pint at Nolan's."

They walked down the Falls Road and turned into a side street. Nolan's was a small, dingy bar that looked as if it had been there for a couple of hundred years. Two of its window panes were boarded up with plywood, and there were pockmarks on the exterior walls. Bullet holes. Conn and Terry walked in and were greeted by the barman and assorted drinkers in the room. Conn returned their greetings and announced that this was his cousin Terry, from New York. That brought about what-about-ye's and raised glasses.

Terry noticed an old fellow in a tweed cap, standing in the corner with a pint in his hand. "And my tale ends thus," the man declared. "'Was that night on the marge of Lake Lebarge I cremated Sam McGee!'" There was a round of applause and the rhymer sat, looking pleased, and took a long draft from his glass.

Attention then turned to Conn as he stood at the bar waiting for two pints of Guinness to be properly poured. When they were ready, he handed one to Terry and led him to a table.

"Give us a story, Conn," someone urged him from the back of the room.

"I don't have one today."

"Never stopped you before. Make one up."

"I don't know now . . ."

"Get on with it."

So Conn took a leisurely sip of his pint, then stood and held his left arm out like a ham actor his first time onstage.

There was a young fella named Terry
Who didn't know Belfast from Derry.
The man's been around.

I thought he was sound.
But the truth was quite the contrary.

The poet took another drink, got his second wind, and continued.

Now we all want the same thing wherever we are.
To sit and relax, sure, and have us a jar.
So where does he head,
This fine Catholic lad?
He went into the Rangers Pitch bar.

This was greeted by an incredulous chorus of "No!" around the pub. Terry offered a sheepish acknowledgement of his gaffe.

Now the boys who inhabit the Rangers
Aren't kind to the Pope-loving strangers.
But our Terry stayed cool
On his barstool.
Had his pint and ignored all the dangers.

Conn's recital was met with appreciative applause, which he acknowledged with a theatrical bow. "Thank you for your kind attention." And more than one of the punters offered to buy a pint for Conn and his reckless relation.

When the regulars had returned to their drinking, Terry and Conn had the opportunity to catch up on each other's lives. Conn was working for a builder now but hoped to start his own company eventually. He would see how things went in Belfast. He wouldn't want to be here forever. He thought Terry's job had a little more to commend it.

"So you fly 747s, Terry. Doesn't get any better than flying six and a half miles above the fray. How did you work your way into a career like that?"

"Like a lot of fellas, I started with the Air Force, then moved over to civil aviation."

"I take it we're talking about the American forces? Did you see any action?"

"No wartime service, if that's what you mean. I signed up for the U.S. Air Force and had just completed my training when the Vietnam War ended."

"When your people had to be evacuated off the roof of your embassy in Saigon, you mean."

"Yeah."

"You'd think the U.S. would have stayed home after that lesson in humiliation, instead of getting involved in more foreign adventures around the world."

"Doesn't work that way, does it?"

"How did you feel about that war? Keen to be up in the skies blitzing the rice paddies?"

Terry replied,

> Nor law, nor duty bade me fight,
> Nor public men, nor cheering crowds.
> A lonely impulse of delight
> Drove to this tumult in the clouds.

"I know that one. Who was it, Yeats?"

"Yeah. 'An Irish Airman Foresees His Death.' Only poem I can recite by heart, except for the ones I make up myself. 'I know that I shall meet my fate somewhere among the clouds above.' But so far, so good."

"More dangerous on the ground, at least in this part of the world."

"I hear yeh. But back to your question, I would have been sent to fight in Nam, but I didn't support the war. The U.S. should never have gone in there. The anti-war movement was right. But that doesn't mean I supported the protesters who treated our returning soldiers like shit when they hobbled home, injured and demoralized. That was unforgivable. Protest government policy, yes. But don't take it out on the poor fuckers who were sent over there to do the job. Kind of like the Irish airmen Yeats was writing about. Airmen and soldiers who fought in the British Army in the First World War. Ostracized by many of their fellow Irishmen when they came home."

"You said a mouthful there."

Something about the expression on his cousin's face led Terry to believe he was not just tossing off a commonplace remark.

"What do you mean?"

But Conn waved him off and got up to order two more pints. When he returned he said, "It's a wonder you didn't foresee your death in the Rangers bar. That could have been the end of you."

"Yeah, I know. Had a bit of fun with them, though. If I was going down, I was going down in character!" He gave his cousin a summary of the nonsense he had made up about the Green Slopper raining on the Orangemen's parade.

"Jaysus! As if there weren't enough characters in the Burke family, now I've discovered another one. But wouldn't that be brilliant, that green thing? If it doesn't exist, somebody should invent it and sell it to us over here."

"Where's your initiative? Build it yourself and add it to the arsenal."

"I may do that. Listen," he said, checking his wristwatch, "I have to go soon. Make a call, maybe meet somebody. I could be late, but I won't see you stuck for a lift back to your hotel."

"I'll come with you."

Conn seemed to be thinking it over. "All right."

"Do we have time to drink up?"

"Sure, then we'll be off."

Conn was clearly distracted but they finished their drinks, saluted the other drinkers, and made their departure. They walked back to Conn's terrace. "Have to make a call from my flat."

When they were back inside, Conn picked up the phone and

punched in a number. Terry could hear the rings at the other end, and it rang for a long time. When there was an answering click, Conn listened to the faint voice coming over the line. Terry could not make it out. Conn finally said, "What should I bring? Neither do I! I can't bring anyone, you know that. I know, I know. I've been working on it. Right. I will." Click.

"What's the trouble, Conn?"

He didn't answer, but whatever he'd just heard had him disturbed. He got up and walked to the window. Stared out into the street. Then he turned and looked at Terry. "Do you know anything about, em, first aid?"

"Is someone injured?"

"Yeah."

"Is he in need of a doctor?"

"Can't do that."

"What do you mean?"

Conn shook his head and put his hand up. *Don't ask.*

"Is this an emergency?"

"It's serious enough," Conn replied.

"Well, I had military training when I joined the Air Force. So I have some knowledge of medical matters. I'm pretty well limited to battlefield injuries." He caught his cousin's gaze and held it. "Bullet wounds, that sort of thing."

Conn nodded. "Let's go."

They got into the car and drove in a zigzag pattern through the dark, narrow streets of the city. Terry wasn't half-bad as a navigator; even in an unfamiliar city, he noted that his driver was backtracking and retracing his route. And Conn spent a lot of time checking in his rear-view mirror. Making sure he wasn't followed. Something told Terry it wasn't the breathalyser he was worried about.

"Fuck!"

Conn brought the car to a screeching halt, reversed, and pulled away in the opposite direction. Terry, pinned to his seat, managed to twist around and look behind them. He saw two armoured trucks, with long bonnets and massive grilles, turning into the street. Conn careened away from the advancing army vehicles.

"Pigs," he said.

Terry made a noncommittal sound in response.

"Humber pigs, I mean. Kind of a pig-snout look about the front of the vehicles. Last thing we need is an encounter with two pigs full of Brits."

Conn drove until he arrived at a decrepit-looking block of flats. He surveyed the area and then made a turn into a crumbling asphalt parking area behind the building. "In here" was all he said. He used a key to gain entry from the back and headed up an iron staircase. They climbed in darkness to the third floor. Again, Conn's head turned left and right before he emerged into a shabby corridor and made his way to a steel door. He let himself in, pulled Terry in behind him, and locked and bolted the door. The place was lit by one low-watt bulb, and the windows were shaded with black-out curtains. There was a galley kitchen to the left. On the right was the living room with nothing in it but a chair with clothing draped over it, and a mattress on the floor, covered with a white sheet. On it lay a man with bandages on his left shoulder and left lower leg. His face was dripping with water or sweat, and his dark hair was matted to his skull. His eyes followed Conn's progress across the room. Then he caught sight of Terry and stared at him with alarm.

"My cousin. No worries," Conn said. "Terry, could you have a look at his wounds?"

"What?" the man croaked.

"Terry's had military training in America. He'll look you over, and we'll decide what to do."

"I can't fucking stay here, Conn. I'm going to die in this place." His voice broke and he turned away.

"We're going to suss things out, get you away from here."

Terry smiled at the man and gently pulled the bandages away from his shoulder. Blood had seeped through. There was no sign of infection but that could change at any time, he knew, depending upon what debris, such as cloth fibres, had gone into the flesh with the bullet. He refolded the bandage and looked at the leg wound; infection had definitely set in there. And there was no telling how close the bullets were to bone or connective tissue.

"This fellow needs to be in a hospital. I'm not telling you anything you don't know. Why is he in this place and not under a doctor's care?"

"He can't be seen anywhere" was the terse reply from Conn.

"I have to get out!"

"Yes, you do, and Conn and I will see that you're cared for. What have you had to drink and eat?"

"I've got supplies for him in the fridge," said Conn.

They left the wounded man with assurances that could not have sounded anything but hollow.

✝

When they were back in Conn's flat, after taking a circuitous route home, Conn went to a cupboard and withdrew a bottle of Paddy whiskey. He poured them both a glass, and they sat at the kitchen table.

"Why is the man hiding there?"

"I can't take the chance of having him walk out alone, and I can't take the chance of being seen with him. I can't get him out of the city on a train or a bus or a plane because somebody will spot him. Can't get him across the border. Out of the question."

"So I ask you again: why?"

Terry could see Conn battling with himself about whether to open up to his cousin or keep it all inside. Finally, Conn made his decision. "He's RUC."

"And that means . . ."

"Royal Ulster Constabulary. He's a cop."

"What? You've got a cop lying alone in a flat with bullet wounds, and you say he can't go to hospital?!"

"That's right."

"And he was shot by . . . ?"

"IRA."

"How did he come to be in the flat? With you as his caretaker?"

Conn looked away, then back at Terry. "I was there."

"You were there when he was shot."

"Right."

"And?"

"It wasn't me who fired the shots."

"So which side of the firing line were you on?"

"I only learned about the hit that night."

"So this was planned?"

"Not by me. By others. I got there too late to prevent it."

"Why was he targeted? Are all cops automatically targets?"

"Not necessarily. But he . . . he's a Catholic."

"So you shot one of your own."

"I didn't shoot him! I wanted to prevent it, but by the time I found out it was too late."

"Why did you want to stop it, you being a member—I assume—of the Provisional IRA? This man would have been considered a traitor to his people? Was that the thinking?"

"That was the thinking, but I didn't agree with it." The young man's face was haggard in the dim light of his kitchen. He looked old beyond his years. He took a long sip of his whiskey, put his glass down, and sighed.

"You remember when we spoke at Grandda's funeral. We sat beside each other."

"I remember it well. You were just a young fellow at the time."

"Thirteen."

"But you had studied your history. Must have made top grades in that subject."

"Learned at my father's knee and my grandfather's. I'd been close to Christy. Loved the man."

"And during the funeral procession, if my memory can be relied upon, you fell in with the . . ."

"The volunteers, yes, those who are fighting for a united Ireland. And the battle goes on, to get the Brits out of the Six Counties here in the North."

"You're taking on the British and also those long-time residents who are loyal to them. You're fighting on two fronts here."

"Our war is against the Brits. And there is no front. It's all around, everywhere. Guerrilla warfare."

"And bombings."

"I'm not a bomber."

"Didn't say you were."

"I'm not in favour of them here, and I'm not in favour of the bombing campaign that's been waged by our boys in England over the last ten years. We are an army; we should not be putting civilians at risk. Civilians are never targeted, but they are inevitably at risk in some of those actions. I'm against it, and the boys know I'm against it. Though they are right when they say that one bomb in London is worth a dozen in Belfast, if you want to capture the Brits' attention. Dead bodies in the North of Ireland just don't make the headlines like dead bodies in England."

"I don't doubt it, but that doesn't excuse it."

"No. Now back to our grandfather, and the day of his funeral. I told you about Kilmainham Gaol and Mick Collins?"

"Yes, an unforgettable scene. You told me about Christy being in there, and about his fellow prisoners when they learned that Michael Collins had been assassinated."

"Right. Mick's former comrades, who were now his enemies, jailed by his government. Hundreds of them on their knees, saying the beads at the news of his death."

"Speaks volumes about the man, about Collins, doesn't it?"

Conn nodded in agreement. "As much as the anti-treaty IRA disagreed, and still does, with the signing of the treaty, I have never doubted for a minute that Collins believed he had done the best he could for this country."

"Not to mention the fact that Britain had threatened Ireland with 'immediate and terrible war' if the delegation didn't sign!"

"Right, yeah. So he did the best he could. Now we have Jacky Casey, a Catholic from the Murph — the Ballymurphy housing estate here in Belfast — joining the Royal Ulster Constabulary, which has always been a bastion of Protestant power. Power deployed disproportionately against Catholics here in the North. Casey didn't join the RUC to prop up Protestant rule in Belfast; he joined to promote the interests of Catholics within the force and within the community. He urged other Catholic lads to do the same. 'Let's outbreed them and outman them in the police force.' That was his goal, and it was not to be sneered at. He should not have been targeted; he should have been supported."

Conn looked down at his glass, his hands tapping the table beside it. "He received a bullet and a Mass card in the post one day. So he knew what was coming. When I heard about the planned hit, I left my position that night and rushed to the scene. I was minutes out of time. Casey was lying there in the street in agony. I told the lads I heard there was a patrol coming by. Said I'd take him in my car and get him out of sight before the army rolled in. They didn't want that. They wanted his body on display as a lesson to others. But I told them it wasn't worth it for them all to be arrested and put out of commission. I said I'd bundle Casey into the car, take him out to the sea, finish him off with a bullet to the head, and dump the body. So while they were watching, I lifted him up, handled him roughly — just for show, praying that I wasn't doing further damage to him and drove him all over the city till I could be sure I wasn't being followed. Then I dragged him up into that flat, which is an old safe house I use from time to time. He was barely conscious but

I got the message across that I was going to get help for him and get him out of the city.

"That's where we are now. There's a great hue and cry over the fact that a young RUC officer is missing. I have to get him away from here and into a hospital where nobody will know him. But that's the problem. Any bus or train station, the airport, the border crossings, are all too dangerous. He'd be recognized, and both of us would be in danger. He'd be killed, and I'd be killed for not killing him! I even thought of getting a boat and trying to get him across to Scotland. A daft idea, but that's how desperate the situation is." He looked up at Terry. "What the fuck am I going to do?"

Terry sat there without speaking. He was running a few daft ideas of his own through his mind. Never one to turn away from the unlikely, the improbable, or the unworkable—after all, he could keep an aircraft weighing a million pounds afloat on nothing but air—he said, "Does Belfast have a flying club?"

Conn stared at him. Then Terry could see the animation returning to his face. "There are a few, here and in other parts of the North. Yeah, there are."

"Jacky Casey is a citizen of the United Kingdom."

Conn made a face. "Yeah, which is the reason for all this trouble in the first place."

"So he doesn't need a passport anywhere in the U.K. He'd have his police card or some identification on him."

"He would. He does, yeah."

"Leave it with me."

"You're serious?"

"Have you ever known me to be less than serious?"

"Em, well . . ."

"Leave it with me, cuz."

First thing the next morning, Terry was in a rented car and was on a mission. It took all the nerve he could muster, and he'd never been short of nerve, to walk in to the Antrim Aviators Club and find the right man to work on. The fellow was impressed with Terry's credentials and was amenable to his request for an aircraft. He offered to look at the ferry roster to see whether there was a plane that needed returning to England. No such luck, but Terry was able to arrange the rental of a Cessna 172 Skyhawk with a huge downpayment on his credit card, after a transatlantic call to the credit card company and a promise to help the club member's son embark on a flying career in New York, a promise Terry knew he would keep. That arranged, he went to a pharmacy and a grocery store for supplies for his patient, his refugee, and then went up to the flat where Casey was hiding, got him cleaned up and fed, stuffed him with painkillers, and then asked him casually if he knew anybody in England. He did. Some of his family had gone over there years before to find work. There were some Caseys in Luton, and his father's brother lived in Manchester. Terry told him what he had in mind, and Casey began to tremble. It took all of Terry's skills as a flight captain, father, and teller of tall tales, to get the poor, wounded, lonely, missing-and-presumed-dead policeman reassured.

The most difficult part of this breathtaking scheme was coming up with a distraction to allow Terry to get into the hangar in his rental car so he could sneak Casey onto the Cessna without being seen. But setting up the ambitious father in the flying club with a transatlantic call to an executive of Terry's airline in New York gave Terry time to hustle Casey on board.

For an experienced pilot the flight itself was routine, at least in the technical sense. But in all his years of flying, in blizzards and turbulence, in lightning and fog, with drunken, aggressive passengers, Terry had never had a case of the nerves like this. Well, except for the time a mild-looking fellow in a three-piece suit managed to get onboard with a concealed gun and tried to hijack the plane and had to be taken down by the flight crew. Now here was Terry, flying out over the Irish Sea with a passenger who gripped his armrests with shaking hands and never turned his head from the window. What was he expecting to see out there? An interceptor aircraft coming up on their starboard side? The situation brought to mind a story Terry had heard some years before. The British had arranged for secret talks about Northern Ireland in the early 1970s and flew a delegation of top-level IRA men to England for meetings. Before the flight to England, the IRA group was flown to Belfast in a British Army helicopter. Circling over the war-torn city in the chopper, every one of the lads had the same terrifying thought, which none of them could admit: they were afraid their fellow IRA men on the ground, unaware of the talks and of the presence of their leaders in the helicopter, would fire a rocket at the chopper and blow it out of the sky.

Terry had to break the tension somehow, for his sake and that of his passenger. Looking away from his instruments, Terry scanned the aircraft for a distraction. It wasn't hard to find. The interior of the plane looked like the interior of a brothel; never mind how Terry knew that.

"Jacky," he called above the roar of the engines, "when Misty comes up for air over there, send her to me, would you?"

Jacky Casey stared back, uncomprehending.

"Come on now. We're men of the world. We know what this place is: the scarlet fuzzy seat covers, the crimson curtains. It looks like a bordello on Valentine's Day."

Casey gazed around and seemed to notice his surroundings for the first time. It took a few minutes but Terry was able to engage him in a bit of banter about the gaudy interior of the plane. Someone had tried to make over the unremarkable cabin to look like a parlour, but whoever had done it had been looking in the wrong magazines. Pilot and passenger shared a laugh about that, which lightened the mood a bit. But the passenger was a young man with serious wounds, a man who was leaving his family, his colleagues, his country, to go into exile in order to save his life. Terry's heart went out to the lad when he had to leave him with his uncle at the airfield in Manchester.

The following night, when Terry was back in Belfast in his cousin's flat, Conn goggled at him across the kitchen table. "You really did this. You really got him there. You didn't just . . ."

"I didn't just fly him in circles over County Down and push him out of the plane, no. He is safe in England. His father's brother lives there, only about an hour from Manchester. Casey called him, and the man dropped everything to head out to the airport. He arrived and took charge of his nephew, and I refuelled and pulled out. Casey is going to get the medical attention he needs and take it from there. I have to tell you, Conn, I still get the heebie-jeebies when I think of all the things that could have gone wrong before we cleared Northern Irish airspace."

"This is unbelievable."

"Read some of the stories of the flyers in the First and Second World Wars, the scrapes they got into, the artillery they dodged, the stalls they pulled out of, the landings and crashes they survived, the subsequent missions with the same things happening all over again. You talk about unbelievable; some of those stories, true stories, will make your head spin."

"Jaysus, man, I owe you. What can I ever . . ."

Terry brushed it off. "I've already been rewarded. Took a flight I'd never taken before on a beautiful clear day and brought a man to safety. Maybe to start a new life in a country not wracked by war."

"That's because their war is over here."

Chapter XIV

He had no veteran soldiers but volunteers raw
Playing sweet Mauser music for Erin Go Bragh.

Peadar Kearney, "Erin Go Bragh"

Belfast
July 11–12, 1983

"All right, all right. Now, what's on tonight? I should get out and enjoy the night life on my last evening in town."

"I have to stay off the drink. I'm, well . . . I have some obligations tonight. After all you've done, I hate to leave you on your own, Terry, but . . ."

"I'll come along."

"No, no, you don't understand. I have to be out and . . ."

"You're on duty."

"I am."

Visions of the Belfast war zone flashed through Terry's mind. The armoured personnel carriers, the soldiers with guns, the bullet-pocked walls and bombed-out buildings, the menacing graffiti, the tense visit to Casey's flat. Sitting across from him was his young cousin, who would be heading out into the night to perform his "obligations."

What was Terry going to do, sit in a bar all night, skulling pints and chatting up the locals? Sit in his hotel and watch a game or a comedy on television, while a member of his family was out there risking his life?

"I'm coming with you."

"Terry, the last thing you need is to put yourself in harm's way again. This is the eleventh, bonfire night. The place will go up in flames at midnight to celebrate King Billy's victory over our people in 1690."

"Yeah, I know. We held a little symposium on the subject in the Rangers Pitch."

"You're having me on. Please tell me you're not thick enough, not stupid enough, to raise that subject in a Loyalist bar."

"It was just a few little remarks, Conn. Nothing wrong with that."

"And you want me to bring you along tonight? Maybe we can make a picnic lunch tomorrow and enjoy the parades while we're at it. The fecking Orangemen will be marching all day tomorrow, to rub our noses in it further, with their kick-the-Pope bands going by our churches and all over. And that will ratchet things up to an even more hysterical pitch. But we haven't got there yet. We still have tonight to get through. The police will be out in force. Army patrols will be stepped up. Worst night of the year for you to be out on the streets of Belfast."

"My wife would fucking kill me if she knew. What time do we head out?"

"Have you got a death wish, Terry?"

"Have you?"

"Far from it. I wish to Christ this could be resolved, and we could all get back to enjoying life, full time. But when I say resolved, I mean resolved on our terms. And history has shown us this is the only way to bring the Brits to terms. I don't expect you to—"

"I'm hardly going to sit in my hotel room, or in a guzzling den, while my little cousin is out there risking life and limb for the cause."

"Time to go, then. Hold on." Conn went into his bedroom and emerged with a black shirt, which he tossed to Terry. "Put that on. Light blue is out of fashion for night work." Terry did as he was told.

When they got outside, Terry headed to the Ford Escort but Conn went to another car. This was a Toyota Carina, a few years old. Conn caught Terry's eye and motioned him over.

"A single man is a two-car family now?"

"No, this has been put at my disposal for the night."

"Ah."

Conn unlocked the doors and got into the back seat.

"What are you doing back there? So impressed with my driving to England and back that you've promoted me to chauffeur?"

"No," Conn grunted, as he yanked at the interior door panel.

Terry got in on the other side, just as Conn pulled out a long package wrapped in dark rags. It wasn't a tire wrench.

"Got another one of those?"

"No."

Terry moved over and yanked at the panel. "Looks to me as if there's more than one item in that stash."

"Three."

"So give me one."

"Are you off your head?"

"If it's so dangerous you need an AR-15 to protect yourself, I don't intend to go unarmed."

"It's not for protection."

"It's for offensive action, not defence. That doesn't give me any comfort. Hand one over."

Conn let out a sharp sigh and reached in for a second rifle. He handed it to Terry without a word.

It was well oiled and cared for. Terry pushed the button and dropped the clip. Loaded.

"Yeah, it's loaded, Ter; not much use otherwise. Come up front and keep it under the seat."

Terry racked the charging handle back and checked the breech: no round in the chamber. Not yet. He replaced the magazine, and held the rifle down by his side.

"These came over on the *Queen Elizabeth II*—now that's a bit of irony for you—sailing out of New York. Irish crew members bought them and smuggled them on board for the voyage to Southampton. Then they were brought here to Belfast. Where they fell into the right hands."

They both got in the front, stashed their Armalites out of sight, and Conn started the engine. Before he shifted gears, Terry saw him make a furtive sign of the cross. Then, "Let's roll." He pulled out into the dark Belfast street. Terry heard the beating rotors of a helicopter and looked up in time to see an army chopper approaching the top of the Divis tower.

"*Sasanach* incoming," Conn announced.

They passed through a residential area but, despite the mild summer night, saw very few people out. Except . . . "What on earth?" Terry twisted around in his seat and stared. "There's a woman out there painting a wall. At this time of night?"

"Whitewashing it," Conn replied without turning to look.

"Yeah. What's with that? I've heard of being house-proud but that's a bit much."

"Not at all. Good Republican woman. The army would have come by and painted it black; she's restoring it to white."

"You've lost me, Conn."

"You're not thinking like a Belfast man, Terry. A white wall makes it easier for us to see the silhouette of a Brit soldier lurking in the neighbourhood. Brits don't like that so they paint the walls black. We paint them white again." Terry just shook his head. "You've a lot to learn, Burke. But the night is young."

"If there's anything I have to know, Burke, make sure I know it."

"I'll do my best."

"The bonfires have started, I see." There were flames shooting high all over the city and plumes of smoke. "These are all Loyalist fires?"

"These ones, yeah. Some in our crowd have a bonfire in August to commemorate the imposition of internment without trial back in 1971. Not on the scale of these ones. And before you ask, no, I don't attend. Why should we be imitating that shower of savages?" He jerked his head in the general direction of the fires, and those stoking them.

"So the reason for this is what?"

Conn turned to look at him. "A reason? Reason doesn't enter into it. They do it as a lead-in to the big celebrations tomorrow. The Glorious Twelfth, commemorating their victory over their Catholic neighbours nearly three hundred years ago. It's just as sweet for them today. You'll see them all marching tomorrow wearing their bowler hats and orange sashes, looking like a bunch of gobshites. You want to go over there, don't you, Terry? See one of those fires."

"Nah."

"Sure you do." Conn looked at his watch. "We've got a bit of time. Not much. Don't roll your window down. Don't make faces at them. And get your gun ready, just in case. Anything can happen on the Shankill Road. To two nice Catholic lads out for a tour of the city."

He stopped and reversed, and headed in the direction of the nearest pall of smoke. As they got closer, Terry could see the flames shooting high into the night sky. Smoke and fire roiled around in a hot gaseous cloud. There were UVF and UDA insignia on the gable walls, and Union Jacks and Ulster Red Hand flags on all the lamp posts. When they got close enough to see the activity, Conn pulled to the left and stopped with the engine running. He checked ahead and behind and all around them. Terry saw revellers dancing in the firelight, arms pumping in the air. One man had his paramilitary insignia branded on his bare back; he wore a red, white, and blue top hat, and he leapt about in a drunken frenzy. Small children ran around excitedly and threw rocks into the flames. There was something undeniably primitive about the scene.

Terry tried not to think how ugly things could get if the firesetters caught on that there were papists in their midst. Tried not to think, but his mind had a mind of its own. He could see all too clearly the group's feelings running high, a mob mentality taking over, Conn's car being surrounded, the windows smashed, himself and his cousin being pulled from the car. He glanced at Conn and saw the tension in his face.

But tension was quickly replaced by fury, as Conn's eyes fastened on something happening ahead of them.

"There's our man, successor to Saint Peter himself," he said, pointing to the top of a towering wood pile. Terry saw a figure in white collapse with the supporting beams, and it all came crashing to the earth. The crowd roared in triumph, their grins demonic in the orange light. The Pope had been burned in effigy by his sectarian opponents.

It was the kind of thing Terry would have expected to laugh off with a smart remark or a hastily composed limerick; it was merely the act of ignorant bigots, not worthy of attention. So his emotions took him completely by surprise; what he felt was a growing rage. It displaced the fear he'd been feeling only seconds before. "Why in the fuck are they allowed to get away with that? The government here allows it. That would be like, I don't know, whites in America having permission to go onto the so-called Indian reservations and get in the faces of the Native Americans. Here it's one guy's victory over the guy next door, and his wife . . . It's . . ."

"Don't tax your brain trying to put it in context, Terry. Had enough?"

"Fuck it."

Conn pulled out, made a turn, and left the scene. "Doesn't take long to get the feel of this place. Am I right, Terry?"

Terry grunted his reply and stared out at the passing show. He snapped back to attention when Conn slowed and turned into a narrow street.

"Where are we?"

"Welcome to the Murph. This is the Ballymurphy housing estate."

"Casey's from here."

"Yeah, it's a Nationalist area."

The graffiti bore that out, dedicated as it was to the Republican cause and the memory of the 1981 hunger strikers.

"We're heading over that way, to the Springhill area. Massacre there a few years back. Well, 1972. Brit snipers opened fire and killed five people, one of them a thirteen-year-old girl. One of the victims was the priest who went to assist her. They shot him too."

"Jesus Christ. A little girl."

"And two boys not much older."

"And the priest. They could hardly claim he was armed and dangerous, out there giving the last rites to the dying."

"Father Noel Fitzpatrick. He wasn't the first."

"What?"

"Same thing happened in the Murph the year before. Eleven murdered by the soldiers that time. Father Hugh Mullan went to assist one of the victims. He waved a white cloth, but they shot him dead."

"My God."

"See, Terry, me and the other lads, we're not out here for the sport. There's a reason we do what we do. Now, let's see who comes calling tonight."

A few minutes later, Conn pulled into a laneway and opened the door panels again. He drew out two black balaclavas and told Terry to put one on.

"I can't believe I'm doing this," he muttered as he brought the sinister-looking face mask down over his head.

Before long he found himself lying on a rooftop overlooking an intersection of two streets. The house was at the end of a row of identical attached houses with steep roofs and chimney pots on each one. Although he could not see them, he had been told that there was one man on the roof of each of the other three corner houses, covering the intersection. His balaclava was already saturated with the wood smoke from the fires around the city. He could see flames across the horizon.

Terry thought smuggling Jacky Casey out of Ireland in a Skyhawk had been a hair-raising escapade; now he might be on the verge of a gun battle, facing some of the best-trained soldiers in the world. What the hell was he doing here? Yes, he supported the Republican ideal; he had learned Irish nationalism at his father's knee. But he had never considered leaving New York to take up the cause in Belfast. Now, through a set of circumstances he could not have foreseen, he found himself in the midst of the Troubles, with a rifle in his hand. The sensible thing, the rational thing, would be to stand down. But what was he going to do, climb down from the rooftop, leaving his younger cousin to face danger while he, Terry, the former Air Force officer, slunk off to safety? If word got out, he'd be a coward in his family's eyes forever after. Terry knew he would not be able to look at himself in the mirror again, let alone look Conn Burke in the eye. He could hear his wife, Sheila, now. As she signed the divorce papers. Or the death certificate. *Men!* But that's what he was, and this was something he had to do. He turned his mind to some relaxation techniques he had picked up early in his training, in order to keep his nerves under control. And he comforted himself with the thought — the hope, the belief — that he was being melodramatic, and that the evening would turn out to be an anticlimax. He and the younger Burke would climb down from the roof, having seen no action at all, and would soon be belting out "Come Out, Ye Black and Tans" in the safety of the residents' bar at Terry's hotel.

"No matter which way they come in," Conn said to him in a low voice, "if an army patrol enters this intersection, we have them covered. If this is the night they're going to kick in the doors of people living on this estate, and drag them out of their homes for interrogation, we'll send the Brits packing."

"And if they just roll through, and don't get out to bother anybody?"

"We'll take it as it comes. See what happens."

They heard a rattling in the street then, and Terry tensed up at the sound; his cousin did the same.

"Stay down," Conn whispered.

Dim headlights appeared, and Terry peered over the edge of the roof.

"Only a lorry," Conn said, relief audible in his voice.

"And if it hadn't been?"

Conn gave him a look. "You seem a little squeamish here, Terry. Didn't you train in the U.S. military to do exactly this? Kill for your country?"

"But this is . . ."

"No, it isn't. It isn't different. British soldiers have killed our people, beaten and tortured our lads in detention. Shot a woman in the face, mother of eleven children. Shot her with one of those huge rubber bullets and blinded her, right in front of her family. I told you about the Ballymurphy and Springhill massacres. This is war, Terry."

"Those actions are unforgiveable, Christ knows," Terry whispered in reply, "but the IRA has done some unforgiveable things, too."

"That's true. I can't deny it. But this is war and we didn't start it. Back in 1969 when the civil rights marchers were attacked in Derry, and Catholics burnt out of their homes in Belfast, the IRA was unprepared. A bunch of Marxist blatherers, more interested in theory than practice. That's when the Provisionals split off, armed themselves, and took up the defence of our communities. And the people appreciated—"

That's when they heard it. Terry knew right away it was not just a lorry.

"Piglet," Conn whispered. "Get down."

Theory turned to practice in an instant on the Belfast rooftop.

The vehicle rumbled into the intersection from their right. It was a three-quarter-ton Land Rover. Terry had seen this kind of rig somewhere. A documentary? He knew it had an armour kit added to it, specifically designed for service in the North of Ireland. And it wasn't the only army vehicle with that distinction. It came to a stop, and Conn rose enough to get a line of sight; he trained his rifle on it and waited. The first thing that emerged from the left-hand door of the armoured car was the long barrel of a gun. A soldier came into view then, stepped into the street and pivoted around, pointing his rifle ahead of him. Another soldier got out and did the same. Then both ran to the front door of the corner house across from Terry and Conn. One soldier knocked while the other faced the street, again turning from side to side with his rifle raised. Lights were on in the house, but no one came to the door. The soldiers waited. No response. They returned to the vehicle. All the while, Conn watched them like a hawk from above.

The soldiers emerged from the piglet again. This time they had a battering ram. They started for the house. Two more men came out of the vehicle with rifles, and looked around and upwards. One apparently spied someone on one of the rooftops, and he raised his rifle to firing position. Conn fired, and the soldier went down.

Two seconds later, a bullet came whizzing past Terry from behind. He whipped around and saw a second piglet in the street behind them. It had crept into the area with no lights; they had missed it, while concentrating on the patrol in the intersection. Terry saw a soldier beside the second vehicle take aim at Conn. Terry fired. He hit the side panel of the Land Rover, and the soldier flew to the rear of the truck. Had he made a dive for safety, or had the bullet ricocheted and struck him? Terry didn't know. No time to think. Conn got two shots off at the first patrol, and a rain of bullets fell on it from the other three rooftops. The soldier Conn had hit rose from the ground and was pulled into the carrier. The two with the battering ram jumped back in, and the patrol barrelled off down the street to the left.

Conn turned and aimed at the second Land Rover behind them. A soldier was crouched beside it, his rifle pointed at a gunman on the roof across the street. Conn fired at the soldier and made a direct hit on the barrel of his gun. Defenceless, the soldier hoisted himself into the vehicle, and it moved forward into and through the intersec-tion. Several shots rang out again from the rooftops, and there was answering fire from the back of the Land Rover. As Terry watched, a man tottered at the edge of the roof of the house opposite. The man dropped his rifle, clutched at his neck, and then fell from the roof into the street. The vehicle roared away.

Conn yelled at Terry to follow him. They descended from the roof, jumped to the ground, and Conn rapped at the back door of the house. A man came to the door, fully dressed. "Ambulance, Donal" was all Conn said. The man nodded and withdrew.

For the second time since coming to Belfast, Terry found himself tending a wounded man. Conn and two others stood facing out-wards, rifles at their shoulders, providing what cover they could. Terry eased the balaclava up off the face of the fellow on the ground. He looked to be about twenty-one, with golden curls and light blue eyes that stared sightless at the heavens.

"What shape is he in?" Conn asked. Terry raised his head to see his cousin. Conn was continuously scanning the area, ready to fire.

"He's not going to make it."

Terry looked up at the riflemen in time to see each of them take his right hand off his weapon and make a quick sign of the cross. Standing in the street with rifles poised, they then began to pray. "Hail Mary, full of grace . . ." Terry joined in the prayer. An ambu-lance siren was approaching, and smoke wafted over them from the hellish fires across the city. "Pray for us sinners, now and at the hour of our death."

It was a quiet trip back to Terry's hotel at the end of the night, the cousins both lost in their own thoughts about the firefight they had just survived.

When they arrived at their destination, Conn turned to Terry and made an effort at lightheartedness. "So, aside from that, Mr. Burke, how was your trip to Belfast?"

"Jesus."

"Well, you can take comfort in the fact that you saved two lives in your short time here."

"What?"

"You flew Jacky Casey to safety and you took out the soldier who had me in his sights."

"I didn't kill him!"

"Maybe, maybe not. We don't know whether your round hit him and they dragged him into the piglet, or he got up and climbed in under his own power. Either way, your shot took him out of action at the crucial time. I'd have been a dead warrior beside you. You would have had to break the news to the family back in Dublin. Good work."

It was one of those rare times when Terry was lost for a reply.

"Look at it this way, brother. You fired a shot for the cause." Conn leaned over and quickly embraced him. "God go with you, Terry," he said, and Terry got out of the car. He turned back to wave, and Conn raised his hand to his forehead and gave him a salute.

Terry did not stick around for the Glorious Twelfth parades.

†

Terry's eyes refocused on Molly and Brennan, sitting across from him in a London flat in 1989.

"Where to begin after hearing that?" Brennan asked.

Molly was perfectly still, utterly at a loss for words.

"One thing is clear," said Brennan. "I wondered a while ago about a little remark Finbarr made."

"What?" asked Molly, looking as if she might prefer not to hear it.

"He was slagging you about what you were wearing. 'Even a sniper wouldn't take you out looking like that.' Then he added, 'Eh, Conn?' Conn didn't seem to laugh it off the way one might have expected. Gave Finbarr a silent 'fuck off' or something. Did this mean Conn was a sniper? Terry here put me off when I mentioned it. But now we know."

"Now you know," said a subdued Terry Burke.

But Conn was not the only person who had played a dramatic role in the Belfast adventure. Brennan said, "You were handy with a rifle yourself, Terrence."

"When the occasion demanded it."

"Jesus, Mary, and all the saints! I can't believe the tale you just told me."

"I still get the janglers thinking about it, Brennan, six years after the fact. But imagine how I'd feel if I'd gone out and partied, or I'd gone back to the hotel to sleep, and something had happened to Conn . . ." Terry picked up the Jameson and poured everyone a refill. "Of course Conn was out there all those other nights, I know. But, when I was in town, I just felt I had to back him up."

"What I really find hard to believe," Brennan said, "is that I never heard this from you before."

"Never told anybody."

"That's not like you."

"Neither was lying on a rooftop in Belfast in sniper position with an AR-15, facing two contingents of British troops." He took a drink of his whiskey and savoured it for a long moment. "I've never known what to make of the whole thing, what attitude to take towards it. Whether I should be . . ."

"Bragging or complaining."

"Yeah, whether I should be proud of it or ashamed."

"So you fought with the IRA in the Six Counties, and our oul man doesn't know about it?"

Terry laughed then. "He'd enjoy the story."

"He would. What did you say to Uncle Finn, after him sending you up there in the first place to check on the young fellow?"

"I told him Conn might be putting himself in the way of harm. But Finn already knew that. That's why Conn moved up there, I'm sure."

"Whatever happened to the young cop you dropped off here in England? Did he ever get back to Ireland?"

"Well now, that's what got me started on the tale in the first place. I had no idea what happened to Jacky Casey. I never saw Conn again till this trip with you and Molly, and didn't have the opportunity to get into it with Conn. But now you tell me a man made a mysterious phone call and said, 'Tell your brother we shared the loopy lady.' I'm the brother. It was a message to me, from Casey."

"Just when we thought this trip to London couldn't get any more bizarre," Brennan muttered.

Molly nodded. "The only thing missing is a love interest, Brennan. Maybe Terry will fill that in for us. You seem convinced that it was Jacky Casey who made the call, Ter, but we didn't hear anything about sharing a 'lady' in the story you just recounted. And I'm not sure we want to."

"I told you about the Cessna Skyhawk Casey and I flew in. Not known for their elegant interiors, the Skyhawks. Since this one was tarted up like a whorehouse, we got this joke going about the owner's wife and her decorating efforts. The Tacky Tart, the Dotty Dowager, the Loopy Lady. That's where that line came from."

"Thank God it was bad design and not some poor love-struck woman left behind by the pair of you," Molly said. "So this man may still be in England, if there was a price on his head in Belfast. Exiled because he was a target of the Irish Republican Army."

"That would not dispose him to think too kindly of the IRA," Brennan put in. "And if they killed a police officer here in London . . ."

"But," Terry interrupted, "he would presumably think kindly of Conn."

"And you," Brennan said, "for the mercy flight out of Belfast. So why would he send a message through Molly to you, to make sure you heard about Conn's fingerprints on the car?"

"Maybe," Molly suggested, "he is telling you, 'Terry, you lifted me out of Belfast. You saved my life. And so did Conn. But look what he's done now. I'm a policeman. I can't let this go.'"

They considered this in silence for a few minutes, till Brennan spoke up again. "But why tell you? This is the kind of information only the police would have. So they already have it. What is to be gained by telling any of us?"

Chapter XV

In the street stood Ireland's hero, brave Republican was he.
All the Staters with their rifles, no surrender would they see.
Then he raised his gun and fired one more round for Ireland true,
And a hail of bullets felled him, our great martyr Cathal Brugha.

Áine Ni Mhurchadha, "Cathal Brugha"

Brennan returned from his parish work early the next day and, after spending a couple of hours loafing in the flat, listening to music and sampling some of Molly's history books, he answered a phone call.

"Hello, is Molly in?"

"No, she isn't. I'm not sure where she is, probably at work. Is this Tess?"

"It is, yeah. Are you one of her brothers?"

"Yes, it's Brennan."

"'Bout ye, Brennan?"

"How are you doing, Tess?"

"Oh, I'm all right. I'm just back from Belfast, seeing my mam and da and the rest of them. It was good to be home."

"I'm sure it was."

"I'm going to Brixton today. Was wondering if Molly might want to come with me. I hate going into that place on my own. But maybe we can go together another time."

"Why don't I go with you?"

"Would you?"

"Of course."

✝

Brennan and Tess stood together, waiting to be shown, one after the other, into the visiting area. A warder came towards them and said, "You here for Burke?"

"We're here for Conn Burke, yes," Brennan replied.

"Down those stairs, then first door on your right."

"Both of us?" Tess asked.

"Yes, both." He gestured for them to go ahead. This was the opposite direction from the visiting area. What was happening?

"Where are we going?" Brennan demanded to know.

"Move along. Down the stairs."

Brennan took Tess's arm and moved towards the stairs. He was glad the young woman wasn't here by herself. If something had gone wrong with Conn in this place, he wanted to be here to help her deal with it.

They went down the stairs and stood by the first room on the right. The warder came up behind them with a ring of keys, opened the door, and ushered them inside. And there was Conn in blue jeans and a T-shirt, sitting with one leg crossed over the other, looking as if he didn't have a care in the world. He got up and put his arms around Tess, gave her a prolonged kiss, and then spoke softly into her ear. Nobody barked an order at them about "no contact." When they pulled apart from one another, Conn gave Brennan a quick embrace and they all sat down, including the warder.

"You've met Albert Smithson," said Conn. "Albert, this is my bride-to-be, Tess, and my cousin Brennan."

Albert leaned towards them and shook hands with both of the visitors. Tess beamed at the benevolent official who had engineered this little reprieve for her and her man.

"Welcome to our guest suite," Albert said, laughing.

He sounded as if he might be from Liverpool, but Brennan wondered if that conclusion had been influenced by the fact that the man looked like a younger brother to Ringo Starr. The same face and, now that they were out of public view, the same friendly demeanour. Brennan refrained from making a crack about sticks and skins. He was sure the fellow had heard it all before.

"Albert stands out in this place," Conn told them, "for his kindness and his wisdom. He is wise enough, for instance, to know that I am not going to *kill* him, or you, Tess, or you, Brennan, if the four of us are in here having a little hooley — if a gathering without a drop of drink to be had can be called a hooley, and I don't fault you for that at all, Albert — a little party with me unshackled and Albert unarmed, and all of us together. No danger to anyone whatsoever."

"I'd be sacked if the powers-that-be found out about this gathering even without me setting up a bar in the corner, so . . ."

"So you're saying you might as well bring in a slab of beer for us? Might as well be hanged for a sheep as a lamb."

"It's the death penalty for supplying liquor to dangerous foreign agitators in the prison."

"When did they get so humourless?"

"Must have been last week. Did you see Hobson standing there, po-faced, while you insisted on teaching me some of your rebel songs? Good songs, I have to admit. I loved the line 'He died of lead pyeson o'er Erin Go Bragh.' Sounds like an old fellow we had in here a couple of years back. Bobby somebody. One of your lot. He talked like that. Poison sounded like pyeson, and he was always singing those songs. Not everybody here appreciates that music, though, I'm sure you'd agree."

"That must have been what soured them on us foreign agitators. Now, Albert, you're the best man in this entire godforsaken, soul-destroying complex of buildings, so I think it only right that you be the best man at our wedding. Amn't I right, Tess?"

"Aye, Conn, you took the words right out of my mouth. I'm so grateful for him arranging this get-together, I'd almost fancy him as the groom!"

"Now, I wouldn't want to step on any toes," said Albert.

"Listen, you two, you've got me concerned here. If he takes too much of a liking to you, he might just keep me in here for years."

"I assure you that I shall be a gentleman, Conn."

"Thank you, Albert. Now if you come as best man to the ceremony in Belfast, you might make a few of our guests nervous, particularly my family from Dublin, you being an Englishman and all. So come prepared to be searched. Patted down. You know the drill."

"Searched by a bunch of IRA blokes? That might get a bit rough."

"IRA? What are they saying about me in this place? Don't be listening to a load of bollocks. No, in Irish tradition, security at a wedding is the responsibility of the bridesmaids."

"I didn't know that!" Albert played along.

"Oh yes. And, as best man, it will be your privilege to be searched by the maid of honour. So, something to look forward to."

"I'm getting keener by the minute."

"But you can't show up in your uniform, Albert."

"What's wrong with my ensemble? I've been wearing the same thing every day, thinking I looked quite dapper."

"No, mate, it's all wrong. Everyone in Belfast city will clock you as a screw right away. You wouldn't want that. And it would reflect badly on myself as well. When someone thinks *screw*, they think *prison*, *prisoner*, *criminal*. And that's not the image I'll be striving for at our wedding. Now Tessie, what have you got there? Is that a bride I see on the cover of that publication? Why has she got such a big enormous head on her?"

"It's a wedding magazine someone left out there. The latest fashions for brides and grooms. And yer one looks like that because big hair is in style now."

"And big shoulders by the look of that dress. She looks like an

American football player. But let's see what else is in there. We don't want to be standing at the altar like a pair of unfashionable gobshites."

"Here it is about men, Conn. Your hair just won't do. It was all right yesterday but not anymore. Listen to this: 'Perms for men will create a wilder, fuller head. And your hair will no longer be controlled by gels and sprays.'"

"I am due for a new perm," Conn conceded, patting his shaggy auburn hair. "I do look a fright. But I am not, simply not, going to give up my hairspray! A man without hairspray, a man without gel . . ."

"Is a man on the slippery slope down to hell," responded Tess.

"But a man with a perm is a man with respect."

"Not in this place," the warder declared, "he's a bloody insect!"

"Well done, Albert. Not only will you be our best man, you'll be the court poet when we start our noble house. Poets were very important members of the aristocratic households, you know. Well, that would be obvious from the immortal lines we recited here today."

Tess snickered as she read more diktats from the führers of fashion. "Shoulders are going to get narrow, but hemlines wide. Guess that means I'll have to toss out everything I own today and buy all new clobber."

"I suppose that's the idea," said Albert.

"But I won't go along with that. I'll be a rebel with a narrow hemline and a wide belly. And if they don't like it, they can get stuffed. Oh. Here it tells you to decide on a theme for your wedding."

"What will we have for our theme, Tess, a smart young couple like us?"

"The theme will likely be *Hurry it up can't you, Father? Give us your blessing, my contractions are starting!*"

"Think you can handle that for us, Father Burke?"

"Conn, my lad, I am nothing if not flexible. If you'd like to have the baptismal font wheeled in for the wedding, you can have two sacraments for the price of one."

They were startled then by a loud bang at the door. Two uniformed men burst into the room.

"Smithson!" one of them shouted. "What's going on here?"

Albert Smithson jumped up from his seat and faced the newcomers.

"What is this man doing on this floor?"

The older of the two pointed at Conn, who looked at him with a kind of lazy insolence.

"This is Mr. Burke's wife-to-be, sir. And this is his priest. Because they are getting married, I thought—"

"You're not paid to think, Smithson. Your responsibility is to keep order, and to keep the inmates in their proper quarters, not allow them to consort with females whenever they get the itch."

"They're hardly consorting, sir. As I said, this is their priest. They—"

"Get these people out of here. Now. Smithson, upstairs and wait for me. Roberts," he said to his fellow warder, "search him."

Roberts commanded Conn to get up against the wall with his legs spread and arms up.

Brennan turned to see his cousin being manhandled, not at all gently, by the screw. "There's no need of that. We didn't pass anything to him."

"We'll decide what's needed here," the older warder said to him. "Up the stairs."

Tess went ahead and Brennan followed her. Just as they reached the top of the staircase, Brennan heard a clatter from the room, as if a chair had been knocked over, followed by "My name's not Paddy, you fuckin' Tan." Then there were more sounds of a struggle before the door at the top of the staircase was slammed shut, and Brennan heard no more.

Conn, for the love of Christ, Brennan pleaded silently, don't make it any worse for yourself in here.

After their unceremonious ejection from the Brixton Prison, Brennan did his best to offer comfort to Tess as they sat together in the tube. She was in tears. "What's happening to him in there, Brennan? He didn't do anything wrong. We were just having a visit. Now he's being punished."

"He'll be all right, Tess," Brennan said, in an effort to convince them both. "Things will settle down. He did nothing wrong, as you say."

"And what will happen to Albert? He was so kind. He didn't do anything wrong either. It's not as if we were all in there using drugs, or plotting an escape. I hope he doesn't lose his job, though how he can stand working in a place like that, I don't know."

"He'll probably be disciplined in some way. A note in his file," Brennan improvised, "and it will all be forgotten."

Tess was silent for a while. She sat staring at the dark window across from them as the train hurtled along beneath the streets of London. Then she said, "What's going to happen to us, Brennan? I keep telling myself it will all be cleared up, and Conn will get out, and we'll have our . . . our baby and get on with our life together. But what if he never gets out? I'll be raising our child alone. A child without a father. Or, I mean, a father in prison. What kind of a life would that be for a little girl or boy? Conn will be the most wonderful, most loving father in the world, but what if he loses his chance? What if our child spends his or her whole life never receiving that love, only on weekend visits to that horrid prison? And imagine how the other children will treat our little one, here in England, where I'll have to stay if Conn is here."

Brennan reached over and gently wiped the tears from Tess's cheeks, then put his hand over hers. "Molly and Terry and I are going to do everything we possibly can to get information that will clear him of the charges. But tell me this, Tess." She looked up and met his eyes. "If there is anything you know about this, anything at all, tell me now."

"He didn't do it, Brennan. I'm not one of those girls who thinks her man never did anything wrong in his life. He's a volunteer. I know that." In other words, a member of the IRA. "And I know he's done things he can't tell me about. That's exactly what he says. 'I can't tell you, love. Don't ask me.' But he swore to me on my cross—" she fingered the small gold Celtic cross she wore on a chain around her neck "—he pointed to it and swore he did not kill that policeman. I know he was telling me the truth."

Brennan experienced relief all over again, at Conn's insistence that he had not murdered the Special Branch officer. He asked Tess, "Is there anything at all you know about it that could help us? Any name, any fact . . ."

She was shaking her head. "If I knew, I'd tell you."

He believed her. Whatever Conn knew about the killing, he was keeping to himself. But how long could this go on? Here was a woman who would be giving birth to Conn's son or daughter in a few months' time. Were mother and child destined to remain in a foreign country, away from family and friends, making periodic visits to the child's father under the eyes of the warders of Brixton Prison? This should have been the most joyful time of Tess Rooney's life, looking forward to her marriage and the birth of the baby, and their life together, the three of them, with maybe more children to come. Instead, she looked young and helpless and miserable. What effect might her emotional condition have on the child she was carrying? Brennan could hardly bear to think about it.

Molly was home when Brennan returned, and he filled her in on the events of the afternoon. The first thing she did was call Tess, and commiserate with her over the situation with Conn and the prison and the months ahead. After the call, Brennan asked Molly about her day, and she confessed to once again taking tea to her Special Branch pursuer in his car outside her flat.

Earlier that day

"People are going to talk."

"Wouldn't want that in your line of work, John, unless they're spilling their subversive secrets into a hidden microphone. Or onto a tape spinning in an interrogation room."

"How cynical you've become, my dear. I hope I'm not to blame."

"You are. I never had even a moment of paranoia till I came to the attention of the Special Branch."

"If that's the case, I shall depart immediately, with apologies for having targeted the wrong person. Case of mistaken identity. We tend to pick people at random and follow them if the traffic lights cooperate. There's one; let's follow her. No wait. We have a red light. Turn left and follow that other one instead."

"Long years of training required for that."

"No, they use the same random process to select and promote us."

"So who else have you got on your radar these days, besides us Paddies?"

"Haven't really looked around for anyone else, you lot keep us so busy." Then he said, "Molly, I am not an anti-Irish bigot. Honestly. There is so much I admire about the Irish people."

She stopped herself from making a tart reply. It was obvious that Detective Sergeant John Chambers was absolutely sincere in what he was saying, as awkward as it was in the telling.

He spoke again. "Ireland is renowned for its literature, poetry, music, its rich culture . . . nobody would deny that. And the Irish people I've met—at least those I've met unofficially!—splendid people, really."

"But?"

"No buts. Our work is against individuals who, in their understandable but misguided quest to right the wrongs of the past, kill or maim innocent people. What kind of government, what kind of police force, would sit back and let that happen to its citizens? But, having said that, Molly, let me tell you I have found much to admire even in some of those who waged the war for your country's freedom from the British yoke. I've read a bit of history in my day. Well, we have to know what it's all about, don't we? Special Branch, I mean, if we're going to deal effectively with . . ."

"Know thine enemy," Molly put in.

"Yes, yes, I know. But it's not just that. Really. Britain did some terrible things in Ireland. You'll never hear me deny it. And some bone-headed things too. How stupid, as well as brutal, how stupid was our government to execute the leaders of the Rising in 1916? I've seen documentaries where Irish people have said modern Ireland was born, not in the Rising itself, but in the aftermath when the leaders — teachers and poets, as I understand it — were shot by firing squad. People were so outraged that the tide of public opinion turned against England and in favour of rebellion."

"That's right. The grounds of Kilmainham Gaol, birthplace of modern Ireland. They even took one injured man, James Connolly, and strapped him to a chair so they could shoot him."

"Yes, I had heard that. So I completely understand why there was a rebel movement. And I have to say I was quite taken by the story I read about Cathal Brugha. Forgive me if I've mispronounced it — some of those Irish names are impossible for the rest of us. He was wounded multiple times in the Rising. And he lived to fight again. Imagine the man walking about, all those bullets rattling around inside him. Then he fights on the anti-treaty side in the Civil War, holed up with other Irregulars in a hotel in Dublin. When he knew it was all over for him, what did he do? Told his men to surrender. But there was no surrender for him. He walked out of the hotel to face the rifles of the Free State army arrayed against him. He walked out with his gun blazing — in some versions I read, it was a gun in each hand — and went down in a hail of rifle fire. Now there was a man with the courage to die for his country. Hard not to admire a man like that."

Chambers seemed to have forgotten Molly's presence. He stared out the windscreen of the police car, imagining perhaps the scene in front of the Hammam Hotel in O'Connell Street, still called Sackville Street back then, when the old IRA warrior went down in a blaze of glory.

Molly lifted her cup to her lips. The movement brought Chambers back to the present. He turned and gave her a searching look. Not knowing what to do under his intense gaze, she mumbled about going back up to her flat, getting things done. A man accustomed to hearing lies, he regarded her with amusement, handed back his teacup, and thanked her for her hospitality. She turned when she got to her door and saw him lighting a cigarette. He watched her through the haze of smoke.

†

"He has the loveliest blue eyes," Molly said, as if to herself.

"Oh?" said Brennan. "Gazing into his eyes, were you?"

"Just an observation, Brennan, dear. I was about to say that it's a waste, such lovely eyes being used to peer into the dark corners of people's lives."

"Somebody has to do it. Somebody has to keep at bay whatever might slither out of those dark corners. The state needs its policemen."

"Yes, it certainly does. Only I wish . . ."

Brennan raised an eyebrow and waited for his sister to elaborate. She did not. What was it she wished, that a certain Special Branch Detective Sergeant could set his sights on other targets, leaving him to meet her as something other than a suspect or a witness or a close associate of the foreign shit-disturbers he was sworn to shut down?

†

On Tuesday, Brennan, Molly, and Terry were being ushered into the office of Lorna MacIntyre. She had called and asked them to come in. Lorna faced them across her desk and filled them in on information disclosed to her by the Crown Prosecution Service.

"The information confirms what you heard from your anonymous caller. Conn's fingerprints were on the driver's door of the police car."

Molly slumped in her seat as if she had been buoyed until now by the hope that the allegation about the prints would be refuted.

"But we all knew he was there, didn't we?" Lorna said. "He was seen by a witness nearby, and the calls warning of the bombs came from the same area, and the police believe it was Conn's voice on the phone. The bullets came from a Browning Hi-Power pistol, which many of the IRA have and, according to the disclosure, Conn himself was known to possess."

"Knowing all that is one thing," Molly said in a small voice. "But prints on the car are, well . . ."

"Direct as opposed to circumstantial evidence when it comes to the murder."

"So Casey's info was correct after all," Terry said.

"Casey?" the lawyer asked. Silence from the Burkes across from her desk. "Who is Casey?"

Brennan and Molly looked to Terry, as if to say, *You popped your head up out of the trench. Now it's up to you to rise and walk across the field.*

There was nothing to be gained from withholding the information from Conn's lawyer, and they all knew it. Terry fessed up. "The calls Molly received. We figured out they came from a fellow by the name of Casey."

"And you're going to tell me how you know this. And who this man is. Aren't you, Terry?" Lorna MacIntyre looked perturbed, and little wonder.

"Several years ago, Conn and I arranged to spirit this Casey out of Belfast. He had been wounded. His life was in danger. If he stayed in Belfast, the gunmen would have finished the job." The solicitor sat stony-faced through the recital. "I wasn't there when the two calls came in to Molly. Only later did she mention what appeared to be a throwaway line. The man gave Molly a message to pass along to her brother, that is, me, a line about the 'loopy lady,' which was a joke about the plane we flew over in. The message was a code of sorts. So these calls . . ."

MacIntyre held up her hand for silence. "Flew where?"

"Belfast to Manchester."

"When?"

"In 1983."

"Who is Casey? An IRA man?"

"No, he was a cop in Belfast."

This time, surprise was evident on the lawyer's face. "Casey is a police officer!"

"Was. He was a member of the Royal Ulster Constabulary."

"And he was targeted by whom? Provisional IRA? Loyalist paramilitaries?"

"He was a Catholic, and he was targeted by the IRA for joining the Protestant police force."

"He had joined up," Brennan put in, "to try to boost the Catholic presence on the force, to improve things for Catholics in terms of law enforcement."

"The IRA didn't see it that way," MacIntyre said.

"They should have. Conn did," Terry replied. "He saved Jacky Casey's life and put his own life in danger as a result."

"Where is Casey now?"

"Never heard from him or about him again. Till now."

"Till he called with confidential information that only the police had at the time."

"I guess you're right. We couldn't figure out why he called."

"He knows what's going on, and he knows you're in London," Lorna said to Terry.

"Right."

She turned to Molly. "You told me the caller sounded English?"

"Yes, but it was very noisy, and I had the impression he was trying to disguise his voice."

"Casey's voice when I met him was pure Belfast," Terry said.

"Which might explain why he didn't stay on the phone long with Molly. Hard to cover all those Belfast vowels, no matter how hard you work at it. He would be very concerned about being discovered, presumably, if he is working as a police officer again now. A police officer passing along information to help clear an IRA murder suspect."

"Help clear?!" Molly and Terry both spoke at once. "But he said . . ."

Lorna raised her eyebrows. "Yes?"

"Well, he made a point of telling us Conn's prints were on the car."

"Conn saved his life."

"But the IRA shot him and left him for dead, so he must have been telling us that, as much as he appreciated what Conn did, the murder of a policeman by an IRA man, Conn or anyone else, was something he could not let go, and he had the smoking gun, so to speak, the prints, and . . ." Molly wound down, and nobody spoke for a long few seconds.

"The information from the Crown is that Richard Heath was shot from the left-hand side, the passenger side, of his car."

"Not through the driver's window," Brennan remarked.

"That's right."

"But they know Conn touched the driver's door."

"The driver's door, yes. The police did not pick up any prints from Conn on the passenger side of the vehicle, inside or out."

"So that tells us . . ." Brennan began.

"It provides us with the opportunity to argue that, whatever Conn was doing on one side of the car, there is nothing to put him in the passenger seat whence came the shots that killed Richard Heath."

"Well, this is good!" If there were straws floating about in the room, Molly was grasping at them.

"And Casey knew it?" asked Terry. "Is that what you're saying, Lorna? He called to give us evidence of Conn's innocence, not his guilt?"

"Could be. But it's not that clear, unfortunately. The indications are that prints were wiped from the passenger side, interior and exterior."

"Oh, God!" Molly had come crashing down to earth once again.

"This may mean that someone else was in the car," the lawyer said.

"Yes!"

"Or that Conn went round to the passenger side and got in without leaving any prints."

"So," Brennan said, "he, em . . . whoever it was . . . wiped his prints off one side of the car but left them on the other. Would anyone do that?"

"Someone might, Brennan, being in a panic to get away."

Chapter XVI

Here in this graveyard that's still No Man's Land
The countless white crosses in mute witness stand
To man's blind indifference to his fellow man,
And a whole generation who were butchered and damned.

Eric Bogle, "No Man's Land"

"You're mitching off classes today, are you, Shelley?" Terry asked when he, Molly, and Brennan returned to the flat in Kilburn and found Shelmalier lying on the sofa listening to an old Beatles tune on the radio. Not that there were any new Beatles tunes.

"I had one lecture this morning. I don't have any this afternoon or tomorrow. And neither do you lot, so you'll all be free to come to dinner tomorrow evening at Edward's. May seventeenth is his birthday."

"Count us in for dinner anywhere. But I suppose it's not good form to wash up at Edward's for dinner and not ask who Edward is. Splendid fellow, I'm sure, whoever he might be."

"Edward is my beloved, Terry. An *older man*. He's turning thirty, and his mum and dad are having a birthday dinner for him at their place in Twickenham. They've extended the invitation to my entire family. My own dad is in Wales at the moment and won't be able to attend, but I hope all of you will join us."

"Lovely, darling," said Molly. "I'll ring Finbarr."

Molly went to the phone and picked up the receiver. Her daughter walked over and took it out of her hand, gently replacing it on the hook.

"That won't be necessary, Mum."

"But why . . ."

"He won't come. No point in asking."

"How do you know if you don't ask?"

"I know," she said, in a tone that brooked no argument.

This brought back a vague memory for Brennan, some little altercation or exchange of words between Shelmalier and her brother. Something about the British military? He couldn't remember the details.

"Now," Shelley said, "I'll go out and pick up a couple of nice bottles of wine to bring along."

"We'll take care of that," Brennan said. "What do you think they'd like?"

"Easy. A Shiraz and a Pinot Grigio."

"I know just the thing. I'll pick them up when I'm out."

"All right. You do that and I'll shop for cards. I already have his gift."

✝

The next evening the Burkes found themselves on the doorstep of a large brick house on a tree-lined street in Twickenham, southwest of London. It looked as if there was a sizeable garden in the back. They were welcomed by a casually dressed, handsome man who looked somewhat older than the thirty years he was celebrating tonight. He was tall and angular with light brown hair and grey eyes that seemed, to Brennan, to have a wary look about them. But the wariness vanished when, having searched the arriving party, he located Shelmalier. At her greeting, the man's face creased into a smile and he opened his arms to her. She embraced him and then introduced Brennan and Terry to Edward Hathaway. Molly greeted him warmly, and he invited them inside.

Brennan handed Edward a brown paper bag containing four bottles of wine, and Edward thanked him and placed them on a side table. An older couple came into the room then. The woman had silver hair and was stylishly kitted out in a pale blue wool suit; the man was tall and fit and wore a brown cardigan, white shirt, and tie. Edward's parents, Brennan assumed.

"How lovely to see you, Molly," the woman said. "And these must be your brothers. Shelley told us about your visit."

"That's right, Amelia. Meet Terry and Brennan. Amelia and Boy Hathaway."

"How do you do?" said Amelia.

Boy gave them both a hearty shake of the hand and said, "Boswell. I've been known as Boy since my school days. Do come in and make yourselves comfortable. What can I get you? A G and T?"

"That would be just the thing," Terry said.

Everyone sat down and made small talk about the drizzly weather, the upcoming tennis schedule at Wimbledon, and, closer to Brennan's heart, the opera *Don Carlo* at Covent Garden.

"Magnificent, wasn't it, Boy?"

"Long, my dear, but magnificent indeed. Spectacular music but then it's Verdi. What else would one expect?"

"I saw the French version," Brennan said. "I wish I had seen the Italian. Some day."

"It's probably still on, Brennan. If you set out walking at a good clip, you'll probably catch the last half."

"Tempting, Boy. I'll enjoy my gin and tonic, and give it some thought."

"Lots of time, no rush."

Brennan looked at his brother, whose eyes were focused on the far wall of the room. It was covered with framed black and white pictures, including photos of two massive four-engine airplanes, and several flight crews. The planes looked familiar; well, to Brennan, they looked much the same. Had these been on display at the RAF Museum?

"Go ahead, Terry," Brennan said. "You know you want to, and I'm sure our hosts won't mind. Airplane buff," he said to Amelia and Boy.

"Oh, my dear fellow, go and have a look," said Boy.

They all did.

"Are these your crews, Boy?"

"Yes, that's me and a passel of young rogues."

"You flew a Halifax, did you?"

"In '42. Just after they sank the *Tirpitz*. Missed out on that. Then they put me in the Lancaster."

"Were you the pilot, Boy?"

"Good heavens, no. Amelia says I shouldn't even be licensed to drive on the ground."

"Nonsense, Boy, I said no such thing."

"I was the navigator. Had a good few missions in the old Lanc in '43, before I retired and sat out the rest of the war. Sat on my bum and reminisced with a bunch of other airmen. You're keen on aircraft, are you, Terry?"

"I am. I'm a commercial pilot flying out of New York."

"Well, then! You must find our old bombers a bit on the antique side."

"No, I love the old planes. Love the old airscrews."

"Don't listen to my father," Edward said. Brennan and family were a bit taken aback until Edward continued. "Dad didn't retire midway through the war. He was shot down over Bremen, was the only one of his crew who survived, and was rounded up and sent to Stalag Luft Three."

Terry's eyes widened. "No! Did you take part in the Great Escape?"

"Looked on from the sidelines, more like."

"He was sidelined with a broken leg," his son said. "And the reason for that is that one of the men flipped out and tried to go over the wall. Dad went up after him just as the German guards appeared with their guns. Dad got everybody calmed, saved his fellow officer from being shot, but landed on his leg when he jumped down and fractured it."

"Broken leg? Nothing but a flesh wound," Boy exclaimed, in apparent homage to the black knight in *Monty Python and the Holy Grail*.

"And he did not sit on his bum in the years following that," said Edward. "He was decorated by the king for his bravery, and he carried on serving our country. He went on to become a very highly regarded member of the Intelligence Corps. He won't tell us what he got up to there, but we know they thought the world of him. Various people who served with him over the years gave me and Mum the nod and the wink. Not giving anything away, mind you, but letting us know our Boy was top drawer."

"One of the officers set out to write a book," Amelia said, "about intelligence work during the war. Wanted Boy to contribute a few anecdotes but Boy didn't think that was right, even after all this time."

"Personally," said Edward, "I think Dad is still involved in intelligence work. But, no way of knowing, short of following him about. And he's trained to spot that sort of thing!"

"We'd better stay on safe ground then," Terry said. "Something uncontroversial, like the German P.O.W. camp."

"I have to say, Terry, I handled my time in Stalag Three better than my time in school. You wouldn't be familiar with the institution known as the English 'public' school. Which, as you may know, actually means 'private' school. Mine was a boarding school, quite the usual practice in those days. I was a shy sort of fellow, didn't put myself forward, not particularly good at sport. And so I found myself being bullied unmercifully by the older boys, caned by the masters, and, if one wasn't on one's guard, being sized up for future buggery by the headmaster."

"Boy!" Amelia admonished him. Turning to her guests, she said,

"Let's look at the other pictures and try to forget my husband's ribaldry."

She pointed to a news photo of the royal family during the war, with a quotation from the wartime queen below it: "The Princesses will not leave us. I cannot leave the King. And the King will never leave."

Amelia said, "One used to see them, Their Majesties, visiting the bombed-out ruins of the east end during the Blitz. Hard for people to appreciate now how terrified we all were, with bombs raining down on us every night. Europe was occupied by the Nazis, and we were next. We really thought the Germans would invade and occupy our country. Here we were on this island, so close to the European mainland, and on our own. Of course we had the Canadians fighting with us, the Commonwealth, but the Americans weren't in it yet and we despaired of ever having them join in. Britons were greatly encouraged by the royals staying in London at such great risk to themselves. And, well . . . enough of all that. Shall we have our dinner?"

They moved to the dining table and were served heaps of — Brennan had to be told or he would not have known — braised oxtail ragout.

"Oh, this is lovely. We've only had it once at home, and even then it had to be catered!" said Molly. "My son, Finbarr, would eat three plates of this, and still be looking for more. Have you met Finbarr, Edward?"

"Yes." Edward gave a thin smile, looking as if he would like to smile more broadly but just couldn't manage it. "Wine?" he said, rising from his place and heading for the side table. He topped up everyone's glass and poured a good measure into his own.

"Are you going in to the office tomorrow, darling?" his mother inquired.

"Yes, going in first thing. And I assure you, Mother, a glass of wine or two will not put the nation's business at risk."

"You work for the government, do you, Edward?" asked Terry.

"Yes, Ministry of Defence. All very hush-hush." Edward had the appearance of enjoying a private little joke. "If they're doing random urine tests tomorrow, Mother, I shall pass with flying colours."

"I deserve that," Amelia said to her guests. "When your son turns thirty, it's long past time for motherly fretting about a glass of wine or two the night before a work day. Happy birthday, darling." She raised her glass to her son and regarded him with love and good humour.

That was the cue for people to rise and get the cards they had brought and hand them to Edward with the best of wishes. His eyes shone with delight when he opened his present from Shelmalier: a poster and two vinyl albums featuring Gerry and the Pacemakers. "I don't have these!"

"I know! And there's more where those came from. I found them in a little out-of-the-way shop in Soho. I'll take you there and we can pick up some more things." Shelley turned to her uncles. "Edward's dream is to open a café. More fun than his job with the government. And the theme will be the British Invasion."

Brennan saw Edward waiting for a reaction from his guests. Brennan's was favourable. "The rock invasion, I presume?"

"Exactly," said Edward. "Not any of our other invasions. I have posters and adverts from the Beatles' gigs in Hamburg, from *The Ed Sullivan Show* in the United States. I have shelves filled with albums. All sorts of great stuff. Oh, and I can make coffee. Can't cook, so I'll hire a pastry chef. Shelley is going to help design the shop." He smiled and said, "Guess what I'm going to call the place. Wait, I'll show you." He got up from the table and left the room. They could hear footsteps on stairs.

"Wait till you see this!" said Shelley.

Edward returned with a poster rolled up. He unfurled it, and said, "Ta *da*!"

The poster showed a shop front done in grey bricks with white graffiti. It had the look of a wall in Belfast, but with a twist. The white lettering said, "BRITS IN!" Brennan and the others had to laugh.

"I know I couldn't possibly get away with it," Edward said.

"No," his father agreed. "The place would be bombed, either by our own side or . . ."

His voice lurched to a sudden halt but everybody heard "or your lot," even though the words had not been uttered aloud. Boy Hathaway actually blushed a bit, but nobody let on.

"That was my first idea for the design and the name," said Edward, "and I only wish I could use it. Impossible, though. I'll have to change it from Brits In to something bland and inoffensive, like The Good Music Shop or Eddie's English Sounds and Scones. But still, fun thinking about it."

Molly said, "I hope you get to do it, Edward, whatever you end up calling it. It sounds wonderful. I'll become a regular. You'll have to enlist Shelley's assistance to dislodge me. 'Time to go, Mother. You have to get home to take your pills and go beddy-bye.'"

"Of course," said Edward, "I'd probably be the Basil Fawlty of the café society. Running the Fawlty Towers hotel would have been so easy and so much more pleasant if it weren't for the damn guests. For me it will be 'Shut up, won't you? I'll get to your coffee when the "Satisfaction" guitar riff is over, and not a second before. Bloody hell!'"

"What you need is a Sybil," Terry suggested. "Train Shelley here to bark at you the way Sybil did at Basil. You need to become terrified of her, and you'll be so afraid to incur her wrath that you'll carry out your duties to the letter. *Edward!*" Terry screeched, in the manner of Sybil Fawlty.

Edward's reaction was gratifying. He lurched back in his chair and put his hands up in a defensive posture. The look in his eyes was one of genuine terror.

Terry laughed. "Yep, that will work. You've got it down pat already, Ed."

He started to say more but the words died on his lips as Shelley got up and went to Edward, putting her arms around him and whispering, "It's all right, Edward. There's nothing happening. Just my uncle joking about the television show, about our café. How about us taking a little walk in the garden before we have our pudding?"

"War service," Boy said in explanation, after the two had left. "You know how it is. Shall we wait for the young people to return, my dear, or should we bring out the sweets now?"

"Oh, we'll have them now," said Amelia. "Everybody likes a sweet. And I'll put the coffee on."

Edward and Shelmalier returned a few minutes later. Nothing was said. And the evening passed pleasantly after that. They said their goodbyes, but Molly stayed on at the front door chatting with Amelia about her recipe for the ragout. Brennan lit up a smoke while he, Terry, and Shelmalier stood in the front garden and waited.

"Thanks for bringing us along, Shel," said Terry. "I've been running on pub and airline food. It's great to have a home-cooked meal like the one I just scoffed down."

"Amelia is a wonderful cook. She makes all kinds of concoctions for church fairs and charities. Auctions off her cakes, things like that." She looked up at the two women still gabbing by the door. "I just hope Mum doesn't mention Finbarr again."

Brennan recalled Edward's short response to the mention of Finbarr's name.

"Why?" Terry asked.

"Well, she probably won't."

"Why don't you want her to?"

"Oh, where do I begin when it comes to my brother? You've heard the saying: you can dress him up but you can't take him anywhere."

"Does he not get along with Edward?"

Nobody had asked about the incident with Edward at the table, and Brennan was not about to. If Shelley wanted to explain, she would.

Now she gave a sigh, and it was in regard to her brother. "I made the mistake of bringing him here to the Hathaways for tea one day.

They had graciously included him in the invitation. That won't be happening again anytime soon."

Two months ago

"Edward, this is Finbarr."

The two shook hands, and then Edward's parents came in for another round of introductions.

"Do sit down, both of you," Amelia said. "I shall bring the tea in shortly."

Finbarr sat on the sofa with Shelmalier beside him on his right, and the others settled themselves in armchairs.

Boy sought to engage his guest in conversation. "You're still in school, I suppose, Finbarr."

"Yeah, unfortunately. Can't wait till it's over."

"It will pass quicker than you think. What would you like to do when you've done with all that?"

Finbarr answered, "Be a soldier, I'm thinking. And I mean . . ."

Oh God, here it comes. Shelmalier did what she had to do: she folded her arms across her chest so her left arm partly covered her right, and darted her right hand out to her brother's side. She grabbed a hunk of his flesh and twisted it painfully, as a warning to keep his mouth in check. He jerked away from her, and the Hathaways regarded him with curious eyes. *Well, so be it.* A brother with some sort of ungainly twitch was preferable to a brother who would say whatever Finbarr had been about to say.

"How splendid!" Boy Hathaway exclaimed. "Military service runs in our family, as you might be able to tell from the memorabilia on display." Boy gestured with his hand to the wall of framed photos from World War Two. "Did a stint in the Air Force myself, while the wife served as an ARP warden during the Blitz. Air raid precautions, you know. Our Amelia out there every night with her 'W' helmet on, checking for lights that could give the game away. I'm telling you that if she commanded me to put my black-out curtains up, I'd bloody well hop to it. Well, I do now. If she commands, I obey."

"The Emergency, right," said Finbarr. "Ireland was neutral in all of that."

Shelmalier tried to elbow her brother into silence, but he evaded her attack. The last thing anyone in this room needed to hear was a spiel about Ireland's neutrality during World War Two, known as the "Emergency" over there. I'll neutral him, she thought. Ireland had its reasons, yes, but this little wanker is not going to sit here in the Hathaways' home and dismiss the entire Second World War, with tens of millions dead, and the country we're sitting in subject to the Blitzkrieg, and Boy here flying bombing runs over Nazi Germany and being taken prisoner, and Amelia out there in the dark, and my oik of a brother . . .

Shelmalier tuned back into the conversation. And wished she hadn't.

"And Edward is army all the way. But I, as an old flyboy, don't hold that against him."

"You're in the army?" Finbarr asked Edward. *Now?*

Edward responded with a little laugh. "Now as opposed to when? I could hardly have served before I was born. When I became of age to serve my country, I answered the call, as all soldiers do. We go whenever, and wherever, we are deployed."

Shelmalier braced herself. The only thing worse than whatever her brother might say would be . . .

"Edward served with our troops in Northern Ireland, early part of this decade," said Boy.

Finbarr, who had slumped away from his sister's incursions into his territory on the sofa, now sat bolt upright.

"It takes a lot of bottle to serve in that posting," Boy went on, "as you can well imagine. Every time our men leave the barracks, they don't know if they're going to be shot by a sniper or blown up by a terrorist. Lose their lives or their limbs. A dreadful business."

There would be no stopping her brother now.

"But those are the risks," Finbarr replied, "when an army occupies someone else's country."

"It's not someone else's country, though, is it?" Boy said. "Northern Ireland is part of the U.K."

Boy Hathaway was a man who knew what was what. Shelmalier had no illusions about that. He was well informed, and he kept company with other military men, so she had always proceeded on the assumption that he knew bloody well what the Burkes of Ireland were about. Gentleman that he was, he had always been too polite to mention it, and that suited Shelmalier to a T. Such tact was so far beyond her brother's capabilities that she lost all hope of rescuing the evening, all hope of saving her relationship with Edward and his family.

Finbarr responded right on cue. "Yeah, well, the North of Ireland is part of the U.K. only because you've taken it by force. And you're keeping it by force. What you call Northern Ireland is an illegitimate state, with boundaries rigged so the toadies who are loyal to Britain have all the power. The British Army is there to prop it up by force. And a brutal force it is."

"My dear fellow!" Boy protested.

"And he's a part of it." Finbarr pointed at Edward. "How many Irish did you kill when you were over there?"

"Really! I don't . . ." Edward began, but Finbarr rode right over him.

"How many lads did you and your unit drag out of their houses in front of the wife and kids to be thrown into . . ."

This time Shelmalier used her heel. It had always worked at the dining table at home. She dug into her brother's foot, and he suppressed a little yelp and yanked his foot away.

Before he could speak again she—well, she had already put her foot down—she spoke up in a tone she hoped would do what the physical force tradition had failed to accomplish. "Finbarr, this is not the time or the place for this discussion."

He whirled on her. "Is there a better time and place for it? Would you rather wait till me and him are looking at each other through the sights of a rifle?"

"Finbarr, for the love of God!"

"Who would you side with then, Shel? Your brother and your mother? Your uncles and cousins? Or your boyfriend?"

There was no point in reminding him that he and she were both half English. And perhaps there was no point in sitting in the Hathaways' home any longer and abusing their hospitality. She stood and said, "I suspect Edward will never speak to me again after this episode, Finbarr, and I wouldn't blame him. So the question is moot. We should be on our way."

What she feared most of all, even more than Edward seeing her off at the door for the last time ever, was that Finbarr's outburst might aggravate Edward's symptoms. She could not bear for her brother to see Edward upset if that should happen.

But Boy rose to the occasion. "Bit of healthy debate, that's what democracy is all about. But perhaps we'll put the question aside for now."

Amelia Hathaway's expression throughout all this had been unreadable. She rose from her seat and said, "You'll stay. Now, shall we have tea?"

Fortunately, Boy Hathaway was the sort of fellow who could talk the birds out of the trees, or the Kommandant of a German camp out of shooting a prisoner, so the awkwardness was held at bay for the duration of the evening.

†

"If Edward and I ever marry," Shelmalier said to Brennan and Terry now, "we'll have to elope in order to avoid another excruciating scene."

"You were right," Terry said. "There's a time and a place for every-thing and that wasn't it."

"The Hathaways are such lovely people, gracious and kind and courageous. And tolerant! And Boy is such a card. Of course it was beyond Finbarr's limited social abilities to appreciate and enjoy them. I couldn't help but contrast him with our cousin Conn. Imagine how it would have been if Conn were sitting in the Hathaways' house with a cup of tea. Who is more of a diehard Irish Republican than Conn? If Anglo-Irish history came up, he would have given them his spiel and listened to theirs. He would have engaged in pleasant conversation, would have given them a song, would have had them in stitches laughing. And in the end he'd have charmed them into making monthly donations to Sinn Féin!"

She wasn't far off. Brennan remembered the amicable warden at Brixton saying Conn had taught him some rebel songs.

"Finbarr should take a page from Conn's book for sure," Terry agreed. "Not a whole chapter, mind you, but a page at least. When did Edward serve in the North?"

"His first tour of duty was in Derry, in 1982. He was home for a bit, then sent back over to County Armagh in, I believe, 1983. He went directly from there to Belfast until he was pulled out in 1984."

Brennan asked, "Is Edward still in the army? He said he works for the Ministry of Defence."

"Very hush-hush, he says," added Terry.

"The only thing about it that's hush-hush is that nobody speaks of what he really does. We're not talking official secrets here. Edward works as a parking attendant at one of the defence buildings outside London."

"Oh."

"Here is a man thirty years old, with eight years in the army and, before that, a bachelor's degree in engineering, working in a booth in a parking lot."

"What's the story behind that?" asked Brennan.

"Shell shock. They call it post-traumatic stress disorder now. PTSD. Edward's experiences in the North of Ireland were so horrific — the things he saw, the things he experienced — that he had a breakdown and had to be brought home. After a while he tried various jobs, but anything too demanding was beyond him. I don't mean he couldn't handle it intellectually; no worries there. But anything stressful, with aggravating co-workers or superiors, or anything involving noise or conflict, he was just a wreck. Well, you saw him tonight."

"I'm sorry for my part in that," Terry said. "I didn't know and then, when it happened, wasn't sure what to make of it."

"No need to apologize, Terry. You couldn't have known, and Edward understands that."

"What a shame," Brennan said. "He's a fine fellow, and I'm sure he was a good soldier under very difficult circumstances."

"Yes, he is, and he was. And of course he grew up idolizing his father, dashing airman in the war, shot down in Germany, survived and served time in the P.O.W. camp, and risked his life to save another P.O.W. And Old Hathaway — that's the grandfather — just managed to survive the pointless slaughter of World War One. And now Edward feels as if he's not up to snuff. He —" Shelley's voice faltered, and she looked down at her hands. "His parents are absolutely wonderful. They understand completely but, at the same time, they don't treat him as an object of pity. They don't dwell on it. His dad's take on it, from his own war experience, is 'Saw a lot of that. Perfectly understandable.' They know Edward goes off every day to work in the booth. Everyone just refers to it as the office."

Chapter XVII

The Irish Republic is entitled to, and hereby claims, the allegiance of every Irish man and Irish woman.

The Proclamation of the Irish Republic, 1916

The gospel according to Matthew exhorts us to visit the imprisoned. Father Brennan Burke, true to his calling, made the journey to Brixton Prison once again, this time in response to a brief call from his cousin. He was alarmed at the changes in Conn since his last visit. The young man seemed to be shrinking under the brown and yellow prison uniform, and the skin beneath his eyes look bruised.

"There's nothing left of you, Conn."

"Sure, me stomach thinks me throat's been cut."

"I should have a word with the authorities about the conditions here."

"D'yeh think they'd listen to yeh? The food is shite. I might as well be on hunger strike."

"Did they rough you up after they caught you offside with me and Tess last time? I heard a bit of a row going on when we left."

"They belted me a couple of times. Par for the course. But they decided against going any further."

"Oh? Why was that?"

"There was a crowd of other Irish fellas nearby at the time. The Hun might have got the idea we'd become hard to manage if one of us was given a bollocking with everyone knowing about it. You know how touchy we are."

"How's Albert Smithson these days? Did he take some flak for granting us extra visiting privileges?"

"Never saw him again."

"Christ. Did you hear anything?"

"Screws aren't going to tell me anything. But some of the lads say he got the sack. Just for having a heart."

"That's a shame."

"Shameful yes, surprising no. Now, to the reason I rang you, Father."

"Yes?"

"If you can —" and here he mouthed "read my lips" "— we can dispense with the rattle and hum we performed on previous occasions."

Brennan mouthed "I'll try," and Conn nodded in affirmation.

After surveying the room to see whom the warders were watching, he commenced his silent communication. "O'Brien. Essex." So far so good: O'Brien, the man who had been killed in Essex. "His wife." Again, that much was clear. Whatever Conn mimed next, though, Brennan could not make out. Conn looked at the screws again, then exaggerated his lip movements till Brennan caught "Chelmsford. Go see her." Brennan signalled his assent. Conn pantomimed checking over his left shoulder, and "Make sure you're not followed." He wound up with a strange request. "Ask her about the body. Was there anything in his mouth?"

Brennan, who had been told his face rarely betrayed his emotions, must have looked nonplussed, because his cousin returned to the spoken word. "Anything?" he said aloud and put his hands out as if to receive a gift. "A toy?"

A toy?

Conn caught Brennan's confusion and offered an explanation. "A clown. Someone who fucked up."

"Ah."

"Or grass? Or drugs?"

Brennan looked over and saw a warder with his eyes on him and Conn. Playing along, Brennan said, "I'm sorry, my lad. I came empty-handed today."

Conn then managed to convey the words "in O'Brien's mouth" and raised his eyebrows to indicate he was wondering, asking a question.

The remainder of the conversation, despite the surroundings, seemed utterly commonplace compared to the bizarre request that constituted the reason for the visit.

†

First thing the next morning, a gleaming blue 1980 MGB roadster was on its way from London to the County of Essex, with an enthusiastic Terry Burke at the controls. If you're going to hire a car for a trip into the English countryside, why not travel in fine English style? They decided that Brennan should wear his collar, which might serve to reassure the widow that the two men appearing at her door were on a legitimate errand. They also decided they would stop before reaching the house to put the top up on the car, not wanting to portray a serious errand as a joyride.

"God is my co-pilot," Terry said in homage to Father Burke in the passenger seat.

"I am humbled," Brennan replied.

"Well, there's a first."

"Surely not."

"All right, there was that time I saw you lying face down on the floor of the church."

"You're referring to my ordination, I take it."

"Why? Was there another time you were flat on the floor of a church?"

"No, that was it. Prostrating myself before the Archbishop of New York."

"I have to tell you, Brennan, you were the last guy on earth I could imagine subjugating your will to another. Signing up for a life of celibacy and obedience."

"There you go then. I am perceived to be unworthy of my calling. Another humbling experience for me today. Now let me do my navigating."

"Saint Brennan the Navigator."

"That was Saint Brendan, but you're close. Now pay attention. We're looking for the exit to Chelmsford."

"Roger."

Once they had left the city traffic behind, the drive to Chelmsford went quickly, all the more so in a sports car. Brennan estimated the distance from the city at forty miles or less. He had done some research before picking up the car, that is, he had consulted the news article Molly had clipped from one of the papers, about Liam Michael O'Brien, formerly known as Patrick Michael Doyle. When Terry and Brennan took the turnoff to Chelmsford, they pulled into the first petrol station they found and asked for directions to Doyle's former place of business. Given the recent notoriety surrounding the place, it was not surprising that directions were easy to come by. Prompted by Brennan, Terry put the top up on the MG and then drove to a nearby secondary road, which quickly brought them to their destination.

The house was an immaculate small white bungalow with a clay tile roof. It was surrounded by gardens that looked almost tropical, with enormous pink blooms and small trees with gigantic leaves soaking up the sun.

Brennan and Terry decided that only one of them should go to the door, at least in the beginning, and that would be Father Burke in his clerical attire. A woman whose husband had been murdered would be understandably nervous in the house, particularly with the crime unsolved and the killer still on the loose.

"What are you going to say to her? That you're the cousin of one Conn Burke, currently on remand for a murder that took place around the same time as that of her husband? And that the murders may well be related?"

"I'll have to wing it. Nothing else I can do."

Brennan got out of the car and rang the bell, then stepped back so that he could be seen by someone from any of the front rooms of the house. Out of the corner of his eye, he saw a curtain move in the picture window. He affected not to notice. A few seconds later, the door opened, and a woman emerged. She was in her mid-thirties with a strawberry blond ponytail, a freckled face, and green eyes. She looked as if she had just woken up.

"Mrs. O'Brien?"

"Yes?"

"I am Father Brennan Burke. I was very sorry to hear about your husband's death."

"Thank you, Father. I'm still, well, I haven't been able to . . ."

She stood staring at him, mute. He wished he knew what to say to comfort her.

She made an effort to compose herself and spoke again. "Father, this has all been so terrible. Liam gone just like that." Mrs. O'Brien had the speech patterns distinctive to County Waterford in Ireland. "You never know when you tie your boots on in the morning who's going to be taking them off of you."

"True enough, Mrs. O'Brien. I was wondering whether I could have a word with you. I should tell you straight up that I did not know Liam, and I have nothing to offer you in the way of information. I'm here to ask you a couple of questions, and I'll explain why."

"Oh, that would be fine. Would you like to come in, or . . ."

"We can speak out here, if you would prefer."

She looked beyond him, to the car. "You didn't drive yourself here, Father. There's somebody else with you."

"Yes, my brother, Terry. But, em, we didn't want to alarm you by having two strangers turn up on your doorstep. He can stay in the car. Or we both can, for that matter, if you'd rather not have company."

"No, no, you're grand. Come in and I'll wet the tea."

God love and protect her, Brennan thought. Her husband has been murdered, two unknown men show up, and she invites them into her home. He would do his best to put her at ease and then warn her to be careful in the future.

Terry emerged from the car, expressed his condolences, and introduced himself. Mrs. O'Brien asked them to call her Mairéad. They followed her into the house, which was simply furnished and sparkling clean, and she invited them to sit at the kitchen table. She got to work with the kettle and the tea bags.

"Beautiful gardens, Mairéad," said Terry, "especially on a day like this."

"Sure it's a day you'd write away for, isn't it? Liam was a gardener and had his own landscaping company, as you may know. To see his work like this, well, I'm gutted thinking about it."

Brennan could see her making a determined effort not to break down. "Liam's father is here, helping with things. He's gone into the town, to take Liam's old car into the garage for repairs. I'm expecting him back any time now."

"Good," Brennan said. "You'll not be alone. Am I right in thinking you haven't been living here? You live in Ireland?"

"That's right, Father. Liam and I, well, we weren't divorced or anything like that, you understand. But, em, I moved back home with the children two years ago. I tried it here in England, but Liam's life here . . ."

She wound down, and Brennan was not surprised. Whatever it was about Liam's life that got him murdered would not be something she would readily discuss with strangers. Liam O'Brien was an Irishman living in England under an assumed name, so it might not stretch the imagination too far to see a political shadow over this death. Add to that Conn's question about "grass," which was another word for "informer."

Questions along these lines might rattle the poor man's widow, but perhaps a little confession from the inquisitor would ease the way.

"Mairéad, you may have heard or read in the news about a young fellow who's been arrested in London. Conn Burke."

The recognition was immediate. "Oh, yes," she said, with a touch of wariness.

"Well, Conn is our cousin. His father is Finn Burke. Our father is Declan, Finn's brother." Brennan had the impression that Finn's name, like Conn's, was known to Mairéad O'Brien. "I'm sure you're familiar with the term 'well-known Republican family.' Well, that's us."

"I understand," she said.

"We know that Conn did not kill the Special Branch man," Brennan asserted, with all the conviction he regularly devoted to the Apostles' Creed. "The police know Conn was in London, but they are way off the mark in thinking he committed murder." He hoped this would reassure Mairéad that his cousin was not in, say, County Essex around the time of the killings.

"Liam and his family are strong Republicans," Mairéad said.

"Do you think that was the reason for Liam's death?"

She looked him in the eye and nodded.

"We think so, too," said Brennan. He in fact had no idea what might have accounted for Liam O'Brien's death, but the circumstantial evidence was piling up against a random act or robbery as the motive. "The timing of the two murders leads us to wonder whether there is a connection. And there is a selfish impulse on our part as well as genuine concern over the death of your husband. We are wondering if there is anything we can learn about Liam's death that might help Conn fight the charges against him in London."

"I believe he knew Conn. Liam did."

"Ah."

"But I never met Conn myself."

She produced a plate of biscuits and poured tea for all of them. *"Bainne?"*

"Please," they both said to the offer of milk, and they helped themselves to the sugar, thanking the widow.

Brennan took the lead in the interrogation. "Now, Mairéad, there are a couple of things I have to ask you. And I'm sorry, it won't be easy for you."

"That's all right. You can ask me."

"About the condition of Liam's body . . ."

"They beat him so bad you wouldn't recognize him!" Brennan almost had to look away from the anguish in the woman's face. "How could anyone do that to a person?"

"I can't imagine how terrible it must have been."

"I had to identify him. Well, that's only right. I'm his wife. Liam's father rang me at home. Word had got round that it might be Liam who was dead. Rory Óg—that's Liam's father—was away doing some business in Dublin, but said he'd come over and meet me here, and we'd go together to see . . . the remains. I left that very day, caught the ferry at Rosslare and made my way to Chelmsford. I waited here at the house for Rory Óg, but then I got a call from him, from Dublin, that he was in the hospital there. He has lung trouble. All that smoking, God save him. And they wouldn't let him out. He was wicked distressed not to be able to be at my side when I'd be seeing the body, because both of us just knew it was going to be Liam. I understood entirely. So I went to the police and they took me to see what was left of my husband."

"I know it must have been excruciating to see him like that." Brennan hesitated, then asked, "But can you say if there was anything . . . unusual . . . about the body, Mairéad? Any sign or article placed with it, perhaps?"

She looked at him in horror. "What do you mean?"

"I'm sorry. It's just that if there was something like a message left with the body, or some item meant to convey a message, it might offer a clue at least to the motive behind the killing. To someone in the know, it might offer a clue to the killer's identity."

"He had all his clothes on and I only saw his face and his hands. But that was enough! His poor face was all cut and bruised and swollen up. Same with his hands. The police didn't say anything about a message or an object being left on Liam, and I certainly never saw anything myself. And they would have told me, don't you think? In case it was familiar to me?"

She sat staring into her teacup. Brennan realized she had drained it, so he got up and refilled it for her. He laid a comforting hand on her shoulder, then returned to his seat. He did not want to cause Mairéad O'Brien any more distress, even though there were other questions to be asked.

As if they were operating as a tag team, Terry took up where his brother left off. "Did Liam ever mention anyone he was afraid of? Anyone he knew to have a grudge?"

"He never told me he was afraid. Of course he'd never admit to me that he was ever afraid of anything! As for a grudge, well, he was living in a country that he considered himself to be at war with. But only . . . he didn't regard every English person as an enemy! And I don't think the English people he knew regarded him that way either. He lived in peace here for seven years before this happened."

"Did he mention someone new coming into his life, or someone new with an interest in the Republican struggle?"

Mairéad did not answer right away. She took a sip of her tea and looked out the kitchen window at a tiny bird flitting from branch to branch of an ornamental tree that was abloom with deep pink flowers. Then she turned back to her guests and seemed to come to a decision.

"There was a fellow who came here to Essex, him and two other lads. Liam didn't want me to meet them. I had left the children with my sister back home in Kilmacthomas, and I was over to visit Liam. I was supposed to be heading back on the train to Wales, to catch the ferry back to Rosslare, but I stayed here instead. I didn't like the feeling I was getting off of Liam. He would barely look me in the eye and he didn't want me coming out that night with him. So I said to myself, 'Stop the lights!' I was going to find out what my husband was up to."

"Who could blame you?" said Terry.

"That's right. So I went along with Liam that night to the bar." The *a* in *bar* was like the *a* in *cat*. "And there were three fellows sitting at a table at the back. There was one extra chair pulled up to the table. They were eyeing Liam and me when we arrived, and one of them signalled for Liam to come over. Then he jerked his thumb at one of the other lads to find another chair, for me. Liam brought me over and introduced me to them, but not them to me. I didn't get their names at all. Anyway, Liam and I went to the bar, ordered our pints, and then sat down.

"You could tell right away which of them was in charge, because the other two were forever looking at him as if waiting for orders. This fellow had his hair cut really short, and you should have seen the skinny, evil eyes he had. You only had to look at him to know he was the type who'd hang Jesus from the cross."

Brennan was forming a picture in his mind, and it had a familiar look about it.

"There was a session. Rebel songs, a bit of harmless craic, you know? Good thing for me, because yer man with the slitty eyes took my husband away to some other part of the building, and I was left there with the other two. Thick as pig shite, the pair of them, if you'll excuse my language, Father."

"No, you're grand, Mairéad. How long were Liam and the other fellow gone?"

"Seemed like forever and ever, amen, but maybe an hour and they were back. Liam had a worried look about him. And the other fellow wasn't pleased either, but I thought it was the other two, his own two gurriers, that had him annoyed. They had lashings of drink, and he didn't like that. He had two pints and, when he finished the second one, he put it down on the table and looked around at everybody else as if to say, 'This is how much drink a man should have and that should be the end of it.' Of course there does be a valuable lesson in that, but not from him!"

"What else went on that night?"

"Well, the secret meeting was over, so we listened to more of the rebel songs and talked about them, which rebellion they were about, and all that. You know, just general conversation about the things we all—" she directed a quick, uncertain glance at Brennan and Terry "—we all believe in. I mean, we're right and we know that. Fight for a united Ireland, with the Brits out, is the right thing to do. And they won't go on their own, so physical force is the only language they'll understand. It's what's called, I guess, a 'just war.' But some of the things being done for the cause . . . some things are just wrong. Even if the cause itself, the war . . ."

"The war itself has to be just, *jus ad bellum*," Brennan said, "and it also has to be waged in a way that is just, *jus in bello*. The first criterion, why you fight, is difficult enough to meet. The second, how you fight, to fight justly, is rarely met. Certainly not with any consistency."

"Right. Should have had you with us, Father."

"Wouldn't have helped much, I suspect."

"I suspect you're right about that. Anyway, we listened to a bit more of the music, and then Liam rang for a taxi to take me home. That wasn't like Liam, to treat me with so little consideration. But by that time, I was happy enough to be getting out of there. Still, I was concerned about Liam being with the likes of them. So I waited up for him."

"What was he like when he got home?" Brennan asked.

"He was distracted. He had something on his mind, but he wouldn't answer me when I pestered him about it. Then I got myself all in a lather about the things he might be doing over here, you know, for the cause, and how worried I was about him. And he said, 'Don't be concerning yourself about me, pet. There are some things I will never do, even for my country.'"

"Was he referring to something specific, do you think? Or was he making a comment on things other people might do?"

"I had no idea then and I have no idea now what he meant."

"How long ago did this happen?"

"Would have been about two weeks before he died."

They heard a car engine outside, then the slamming of a car door, and a few seconds later someone came into the house and called out, "Mairéad, I've got that old banger of a car working, but it was fierce money to get it moving again. I really should feck it out and get a horse for you; a good horse would get a person around faster, and it's less dear to fuel up." The word *car* sounded halfway between *car* and *care*, *horse* was *harse*, *person* was *pairsson*. The man who came into the room, presumably Liam O'Brien's father, had white hair and a handsome rugged face reddened and lined by the sun. A countryman with the thickest County Waterford accent Brennan had ever heard.

"Who are these fellows?"

"Rory Óg, this is Father Brennan Burke and his brother, Terry. This is Rory Óg O'Brien, Liam's father."

The Burkes got up and shook Rory Óg's hand and offered their condolences.

"You were friends of Liam?"

"No, unfortunately, we didn't know him," Brennan said.

"Then you were spared the pain of losing him."

All Brennan could do was nod in agreement.

"They're just over from New York, Rory Óg. They're originally from Dublin."

"Ah but sure, New York is a long way to be exiled. But what am I saying? My own son was working here in the Saxons' country, wasn't he? Lived and died on foreign soil. And when I find the Saxon fucker who did it to him, I'll tear the fucker's head off." O'Brien looked down then, and said, "Ah, my manners. Sorry, Mairéad. These boots. I'll go take them off."

"Don't mind them, Rory Óg. You'll be in and out. Sit down and have a cup of tea."

He sat, and she poured his tea. He picked up his cup and raised it to his daughter-in-law. "Thank you, pet."

"Father Burke here and Terry are nephews of Finn Burke, Rory."

The man had his cup halfway to his lip, and it stayed there. He stared over the rim at the two visitors.

Brennan explained to him why they were there, expressing sympathy again, and suggesting that if the two murders were related, they might be able help each other out.

"Nephews of Finn. So Conn is your cousin."

"That's right."

"How . . . yez are from New York now. How often would you be in touch with Finn?"

What was it he wanted to know? Brennan hazarded a guess. "Not as much as we'd like to be, of course. It's really only on social occasions we get to see him. Have a few jars at the pub when we're in Dublin." In other words, Brennan and Terry were not privy to whatever machinations Finn might be involved in, not privy to his secrets.

O'Brien seemed to understand this, because his body relaxed, and he had a sip of his tea.

Mairéad said, "They were asking me if there was anything strange about Liam's body."

"I know you didn't see the body yourself, Rory Óg, but maybe you heard something?" Brennan asked.

The man sent his daughter-in-law a glance, Brennan noticed, then almost immediately looked abashed and returned his gaze to the table in front of him. It was as if Mairéad had been caught telling tales out of school. Well, perhaps the father was embarrassed about the fact that he had missed the viewing of his son's body, leaving the widow to deal with the horrific event all by herself.

"But," Brennan continued, "Conn raised the question whether

you heard anything, from the police or whomever, about messages or signs or something left with the body."

Mrs. O'Brien was getting upset again, and little wonder.

Her father-in-law said, "Mairéad, *a chroí*, why don't you go out and have a little walk around the garden so you don't have to listen to this, and live it all over again?"

"I'll do that. I'm sorry, I'm just not able for it."

"Understandable, Mairéad," Brennan said. He got up from his seat and the other men did as well, when the widow rose and left the room.

"My boy was tortured! Not only was he bet up, but they smashed the bones of his fingers! And they also went at him with the claw part of the hammer! There were marks all over his body, which, by the mercy of God, Mairéad wasn't shown. The information I got was that there was loads of alcohol in his blood. Whoever had him must have lulled him with drink and then tied him up in order to commit such savagery on him. Someone was punishing him, or trying to get information out of him. Barbarians!"

"I am so sorry, Rory Óg," Brennan said, and waited for a minute before speaking again. "There was nothing like that released to the public, was there?"

"They keep a lot to themselves, the peelers. There's information they don't make public. And I'm thinking they patched over things a bit for herself when she saw him, because she doesn't know that part of it."

"So how do you know this, Rory Óg?"

"I know," he answered with an air of finality.

"Was there . . . was there anything in his mouth?"

"What do you mean?" The dead man's father looked as if he wanted to ram his fist into someone's mouth and leave it there till the person ceased to breathe.

"Yes, it's sick. I know that. But Conn says if there was anything like that, it would be vitally important evidence."

"What kind of thing are you talking about, that would be stuck in someone's mouth? If some dirty old pervert killed my son and then desecrated his body . . ."

"The sort of thing I'm talking about could be drugs . . ."

"My son was not a drug user, or a drug dealer, let alone a drug dealer invading someone else's turf."

"I know. Or a toy."

"A fuckin' toy!"

"A little clown figure maybe. Or blades of grass."

O'Brien shot up out of his chair, nearly knocking it over. "My son wasn't some little *amadán* who banjaxed his assignments, and he wasn't an informer!"

"No, sir, I'm sure he wasn't," said Terry in a voice he might have used to humour a hijacker and ease him out of the cockpit.

"I'm sorry, lads," O'Brien said then, and dropped into his seat.

He looked from Terry to Brennan and said in a voice barely above a whisper, "It's Kane you're talking about, isn't it?" Apparently, it was. "I heard that about him. He leaves messages. Telecom Éireann, he's known as, in some circles."

O'Brien got up again, calmly this time, and left the room. He returned almost instantly with a bottle of Tullamore Dew and got three glasses from the press. Without asking, he poured a generous shot of whiskey into each of the glasses and passed them around. The three men drank silently for a few seconds.

"Are you thinking that evil bastard killed my boy?"

"That must be what Conn was thinking. But if it turned out that there were no messages, no objects or whatever, left in Liam's . . . found with Liam, that would suggest it was not Kane. Not Kane's modus operandi, if you will."

"Well, you can be sure I'll be looking into this." O'Brien gave the appearance of a man who would be looking into it through the sight of an automatic rifle. "And if he cannot provide a good account of himself for the twenty-fifth of April . . ." He polished off his whiskey and poured himself another. "I should have moved heaven and earth to get there and see Liam's body before they sent him off to be cut up. Lot of good it would do me to see it now."

"Because of the autopsy, you mean?"

"Right. They had to wait for family to identify him. And Mairéad did that, God be good to her. I was stuck in Dublin."

"Well, let's hope the autopsy gives the police more to go on," said Terry.

"They don't give a flying fuck about a dead Paddy. And that's particularly true if it turns out that Kane had nothing to do with it. And when you think about it, what would he have against Liam? Liam was not a tout; he wouldn't grass to the peelers or to the Black and Tans or to anyone else. It's just not in him. More likely, it was some Tan fucker who beat my son to a pulp and left him for dead. And the peelers won't be putting in any overtime claims for that."

There were many questions Brennan wanted to ask Rory Óg O'Brien, including why his son was living under a false name in England. But that would sound too much like an investigation of the victim for O'Brien's liking.

Mairéad returned then and took her seat at the table. "Were you able to help them any, Rory Óg?"

"No. As much as I'd like to, I've nothing to give them."

"Do you think they know who did it? The police, I mean?" She addressed the question to her father-in-law.

"Wouldn't put it past them. And they're keeping their gobs shut for reasons of their own."

"I told you about that fellow Liam met at the bar."

"Yes, his name is Kane, and he's a skinful of evil. If you ever catch sight of him anywhere, here or back home, you let me know."

"I will. But the police may be able to find him through the telephone records. I mean, if he rang Liam to arrange meeting him in the bar. They came here with Liam's phone records, the police did, and they asked me about them. Especially some calls Liam got from London."

The dead man's father was silent across the table. Brennan decided not to break the silence, and Terry obviously caught on as well. When information is flowing, don't interrupt it.

"There was nothing I could tell them about calls from London. I don't know anyone there. But maybe this Kane lives in London now. Do you know, Rory Óg? He had a fierce strong Dublin accent, but maybe he works over here."

"That would make sense. From the talk I've heard, he spends time here in England, so maybe the London number is Kane's."

"Well, they should be able to track that down. And they'll want to, because one of those calls that had them curious came two days before Liam was killed!"

"You can be sure they're looking into that," Terry said.

"And if it was Kane, he had the nerve to call here before I went up to identify Liam's body."

"What?" Brennan asked. "You spoke to Kane on the phone?"

"No, no, I didn't. But the same London phone number came up that day as on the twenty-third of April, before the murder. So he must have rung here that day, before I went to make the identification, and I wasn't here to take the call. Liam had bought one of those answerphones, to take messages for the business. Whoever called the day of the viewing didn't leave a message, but the calls came through, two of them from that number on the records. Thank God and his Blessed Mother I didn't hear that man's voice if it was Kane!"

"Thank God you didn't is right," Brennan said, "but we don't know for sure it was Kane."

"That's true. But the police will find out one way or the other. The things they can do nowadays. We're lucky to be living in 1989, and not back in the day when they couldn't trace a phone number. Or, well, maybe they always could. What do I know?"

"The wonders of twentieth-century technology," Terry agreed.

"But they can't do long distance," she said.

"Sure they can."

"No, I don't think so, Terry, because Rory Óg's call from Dublin, from the hospital, didn't show up on the records. And I talked to him myself, did I not, Rory?"

Rory Óg took a long swallow of his whiskey and agreed that she did indeed talk to him that day.

†

Back in Kilburn, Brennan and Terry reported their findings to Molly. She told them she had turned on the television earlier in the day and heard it announced that the news team had prepared a short documentary on the life of murdered Special Branch officer Richard Heath. So she recorded it on her VCR and had it ready to go.

The program opened with a black and white photo of Heath as a schoolboy, out on the playing field in his rugby gear, and then there were clips from interviews with former schoolmates. Richard was a force to be reckoned with, by the sound of things, on and off the playing field. One man said Richard had styled himself the "Duke of Do It Or Else." Something of a daredevil, was Richard. "It was like what your mother would say to you, trying to reason with you about the company you were keeping. 'If so and so told you to jump in the lake, would you do it?' And if it was Richard telling you, by God, you would! You did things with Richard you wouldn't otherwise even have considered. Or else! He challenged you, you know?"

"I wonder what the 'or else' amounted to," Terry commented.

The program then showed Heath with a wife and two boys, posing at the seaside. One boy grinned while the other stared intently at the camera. The wife was thin and shivering with cold. She, too, stared at the camera, like someone who did not much enjoy being photographed. Heath was doing a comic turn as a muscleman, striking an exaggerated pose with his biceps flexed. This was followed by interviews with some of Heath's fellow officers of the Met. A couple of them appeared on camera. Others were voices only, as various pictures were presented of Heath as a uniformed officer and then, later, in plain clothes when he joined the Special Branch. To a man, the officers praised Heath as a colleague and as a policeman; they lauded his drive and his courage.

Next up was a man just coming off a tennis court. His forehead glistened, and he gave it a wipe with his arm. "Dickie Heath was a great sportsman. If it was a shooting party in Wiltshire, it wasn't only the pheasants who had to keep their beaks up. Dickie would let you know if your shooting wasn't up to par. He inspired you to be at your best. Because you'd hear about it afterwards if you were not! Very competitive, was Dickie. And that's what raises the quality of any endeavour, isn't it? He enjoyed a game of rugger, or cricket or tennis, and same thing there: you had to be on your toes to keep up, or you'd get the jibes from Dickie. He raised the level of any sport he played."

"Sounds like a bit of bully to me," said Molly.

The show closed with the Commissioner of Police vowing that justice would be done, and that the callous murder of a committed, loyal, and courageous officer would not deter the Metropolitan Police and other police forces from carrying out their vital and dangerous work for the people of Great Britain.

†

It was back to lip-reading and talking over table tapping and humming at Brixton Prison, when Brennan reported to Conn on his trip to Essex.

"There is no indication that any object or message was found on the body," said Brennan. He watched as Conn processed this information.

A few seconds passed, then Brennan asked, "Does this rule something out now? Does it rule out a certain suspect you have in mind?"

"It doesn't rule anything out. It may just mean that people have changed their methods. Or that there was more than one operating mind behind this. Or that he, or they, got interrupted before the job could be finished. Or that no message was necessary, that the deed speaks for itself."

"Given the condition of the poor man's body, after what was done to him, I'd opt for your last suggestion."

Conn swallowed, said nothing.

"Well?"

"Brennan, the absence of a message may mean nothing at all."

"You're not helping matters here, Conn."

"I know. I dragooned you fellas into travelling to Essex, and now there's nothing I can tell you."

"You can't tell me, because you really don't know? Or you just won't tell me?"

"A place like this is a hotbed of rumour. There are as many theories about Liam O'Brien's death as there are Micks in the cells. But no reliable information at all. So I don't know what to tell you from here."

"Are there rumours swirling about the death of Detective Sergeant Heath as well? I imagine that would be a subject of some interest."

"Nobody's mentioned it."

"Right."

"Leave it, Brennan."

"Are you making any effort to fight the charges, Conn? Planning a home and a future with Tess and your child? Or just sitting here like a stoic, awaiting your fate without a word of complaint? Lorna MacIntyre strikes me as a very capable lawyer. Are you helping her at all?"

"She wants to use the 'wild geese' defence."

"What on earth is that?"

"You know who the wild geese were."

"Irish soldiers who left the country to fight in Europe in centuries past, often as mercenaries. The 'flight of the wild geese.' What is Lorna going to do, claim that an Irish regiment operating out of Spain sailed up the Thames in a full-rigged galleon and executed Richard Heath, and then sailed home again without anyone being the wiser?"

"It needs work, I admit."

"Conn, for fuck's sake!"

"She succeeded with that defence in the past."

"She did, in your hole. Smarten up here."

"Go talk to her, Brennan. For obvious reasons, I cannot elaborate on my legal strategy whilst sitting in here."

"I get it now. An insanity defence. Go ahead and elaborate. The more of this talk that comes out of you, the more convincing your defence will be. If the warders here can make out what you're saying, you can call them as witnesses on your behalf. 'Oh, yes, Your Lordship, he's quite daft. Positively barmy, if you ask me.'"

"I would have expected more sympathy for my condition, Father Burke. Just think of it as visiting the sick and visiting the imprisoned all rolled up in one."

Brennan shook his head and made ready to leave. "I hope you'll be talking sense next time I see you."

"Go see Lorna."

Chapter XVIII

If it were possible to make an accurate calculation
of the evils which police regulations occasion,
and of those which they prevent,
the number of the former would, in all cases, exceed that of the latter.

Wilhelm von Humboldt, *The Sphere and Duties of Government*

On Saturday, Terry announced that he had to spend some time at the office, that being the cockpit of a Boeing 747 flying from London to Rome. Molly joked that they would wave goodbye to him as he headed out over the Channel. With one thing and another, that led to Brennan and Molly deciding to do exactly that, hire a car and drive out to the Channel for a little day trip. They didn't see Terry's plane go over, or at least they didn't recognize it, but they saw the white cliffs of Dover and the sparkling waters of the English Channel and had a fine, relaxing day of sightseeing.

When they were back in London, Brennan turned in to his sister's street and began the hunt for a parking space. A car was a great thing for touring the country, but not so great for parking in the city. As far as he could tell, the spaces were all taken. Wait, there was one car with a man sitting at the wheel. Had he just arrived or was he leaving? Brennan pulled in near the corner to wait and see. No movement yet. Molly said, "If we leave it here, we'll get a ticket. We might be better off returning it to the car hire place now, rather than—"

They both whipped around in their seats at the sound of the rear door being wrenched open behind Molly.

Brennan found himself looking into the cold blue eyes of Special Branch Detective John Chambers.

"Pull out, Brennan, and drive straight ahead."

"You're on parking patrol now, Detective?"

"A parking fine will be the least of your problems. Keep driving and follow my directions."

"I don't think so."

"Do as I say."

This time when Brennan turned, it wasn't the detective's eyes he was looking into, but the barrel of a gun.

"What on earth are you doing? If you want to talk to us, why . . ."

"Don't question it. Just do it. Take the next left and follow it to the lights."

"Where are we going?" Molly asked. "There's no need of this, John. We haven't provided you with information for the simple reason that we—"

"Molly, save it. Don't make me point this at you. All right, Brennan, when you get to the lights, turn right. And don't even think of trying to call any attention to your predicament here. I've got the gun on you, and I'll have it on you till we get to our destination."

"Are we under arrest, John?" Molly asked.

He didn't answer. He issued a few more commands and Brennan followed them, not wanting to provoke an armed man while Molly was in the car. His mind was racing. Was this a legitimate police tactic in England, or was something very sinister happening here? He feared the latter; he knew it. This was a residential neighbourhood, and an unsavoury one. There was no police station anywhere in sight. He tried to figure out how he could take Chambers by surprise and wrest the gun from him. The best place for that to happen, surely, would be on a public street. If Chambers succeeded in getting them inside somewhere, with no witnesses . . . Or were there other people waiting at their destination, wherever it was?

"Pull up there and park," Chambers said.

They were next to a terrace of rundown brick houses. There wasn't another person in sight.

"Get out of the car. You first, Molly."

"Listen, Sergeant," Brennan said, "whatever this is, why don't we take care of it, just the two of us? Let my sister go. You know her well enough to know she's not a talker. She's not going to call anyone and report this. Maybe that's the problem, that you are frustrated by a lack of information coming from us. Well, anything Molly knows about recent events, I know, too. So let her go and . . ."

"Can't do that, Brennan. Both of you, out of the car, and don't linger on the pavement. Go through that door and into the house. It's open. Don't try anything clever, either of you."

Brennan turned off the ignition, pocketed the keys, and got out. He wanted to go to Molly and protect her but the better tactic was to stay apart from her, forcing Chambers to point his gun at Brennan, not Molly. Brennan held back while Molly went to the house and opened the door. She stepped inside and stood in the doorway facing the street.

Brennan turned to Chambers. "John, there is no need of this. Molly—"

"Burke, get the fuck inside the door or I'll blow your head off."

There was an edge of desperation in the voice of the normally cool detective. Of all the things that had happened in these last harrowing minutes, Brennan found that the most unnerving. The most frightening. The cop was not in control of himself. Brennan couldn't let this go on.

It was the last moment for action. Brennan whirled on the detective, grabbed him by the throat with his left hand, and tried with his right to get the gun. He failed to grasp it, but it fell from the cop's hand and went skittering across the pavement. Brennan didn't dare turn his back on Chambers to go after the gun. Instead he got Chambers in a headlock and was about to call out to Molly to make her escape down the road, when Chambers delivered a kick to Brennan's right leg, causing them both to crash to the ground. They wrestled on the concrete, and Brennan managed to gain the upper hand. He rose to stand above Chambers and lifted his left foot, ready to drive it down onto the cop's throat. He couldn't bring himself to do it.

Molly spoke from the doorway. Brennan registered the icy calm in her voice. "Brennan. John. Stop this. For the love of God, will you both calm down and back away before someone gets killed?"

Brennan disregarded her plea and took sideways steps towards the weapon, keeping Chambers in his sight. Just as Brennan bent down to retrieve the gun, Chambers made a move and said, "Don't touch it." He had pulled out a second pistol. "Get into that house or I'll fucking kill you right here and now."

Brennan and his sister had run out of options. They entered the house. There was no light. Dark curtains covered all the windows.

"Back room," the detective commanded, and they kept walking. Chambers entered the room behind them and locked the door. He had picked up the first gun from the pavement.

"Sit."

Molly sat on the sofa and Brennan made for an armchair on the other side of the room, again with the hope of forcing his opponent to fight on two fronts.

"Together." Chambers gestured with the right-hand gun, and Brennan went to the sofa and sat down. They were both in his sights. Chambers checked the safety catch on the left-hand pistol and shoved it into his jacket pocket.

Brennan felt himself growing weak in the aftermath of the adrenaline rush. But he was determined to brazen it out. He kept his eyes on Chambers, who, Brennan suspected, was suffering the same after-shock and was equally determined not to show it.

"One hears about the Irish temper," the Special Branch man finally said. "Not just folklore after all, it seems."

Brennan's sister knew him well enough to give him a hard nudge with her knee to make sure he didn't inflame things further with a sharp remark or a string of curses. It took all the willpower he could manage because, now that the cop's breathing had returned to normal and he was in control once again, he gave the appearance of one who was vastly amused by the events of the day. Brennan couldn't let it pass unremarked; it just wasn't in him.

"This is a bit of craic for you on a dull day, is it, Chambers? Enjoying this, are you, having an innocent woman at gunpoint?"

"I don't expect there will be any need to point this at your sister; she's too intelligent to provoke a tense situation and make it infinitely more dangerous. You, on the other hand . . . Where did you learn those moves, Burke? Hand-to-hand combat training with your fellow, um, what's the word I'm looking for? Let's just say your well-known Republican family. The Burkes of Dublin. Long history, from what I hear. Lots of fighting men round your table of an evening."

Brennan could have confirmed this, that he had in fact learned those moves from his well-known Republican father, Declan, after they were jumped by a couple of punks in the streets of New York following their forced emigration from Ireland. Declan had flattened the pair of them and left them terrified, and young Brennan had insisted that his da teach him how to do that. Now, facing a gun in the hand of a British peeler, Brennan refused to admit that the man had it right.

"Why are you doing this to us, John?" Molly asked.

The detective smiled at her then. "Because we can't talk at your place."

"What do you mean?"

"The flat is bugged. As is the telephone."

"You have been listening to my conversations?!"

"You're surprised at this, Molly?" Brennan said. "The man is Special Branch, and they are obviously out to—"

"Not us," said Chambers.

"What do you mean, it's not you?" Brennan demanded. "You've got us here at gunpoint and you're denying the lesser sin of eavesdropping on our conversations?"

"It's not us. It's the Security Service."

"We are targets of MI5 now?!" Molly again.

"Not you, specifically."

"Who then? Conn? But, as everyone knows, he's far out of hearing range, at Brixton Prison. Though he's bloody careful what he says out there, too."

"There must be a traffic jam outside my sister's building," Brennan said. "You watching us from your car, the other spooks watching from theirs."

Chambers gave a "that's the way of the world" shrug. Then he said, "Five intercepted the call you received about Conn's fingerprints on the door of the car of the officer who was killed."

"Jesus the Christ and son of God. When did they start all this eavesdropping?" Brennan asked.

"Don't know. Recently, I expect."

"What's involved in planting these listening devices?"

"They go in."

"What goes in? Who?"

"MI5."

"So these spooks broke into the flat."

"Right."

"But," Brennan persisted, "it's not just Molly in the place now. My brother and I are there. They see us go out, but that doesn't mean they can predict when one of us will come back."

"This work can be done fairly quickly; the security services in this country are very adept at what they do. As are we in Special Branch."

"I don't doubt it."

"But they may have employed a ruse to get all of you out of the place for a good stretch of time to make sure they wouldn't be caught in the act."

"I can't recall anything offhand. Building on fire? No. Come collect your winnings from the football pool, all three of you? No."

"It will come to you. Anyway, what's done is done. And I cannot stress this enough: you must not let on you know. Carry on as usual. Don't stop talking, or change your habits, or they'll know you've been tipped off. Do you listen to the radio while you're home? Television?"

"She has BBC Radio on morning, noon, and night."

"Good. Keep it on. That will cover a lot of your conversation in the flat. Won't help with the phone tap."

Brennan took a quick glance at Molly, whose left hand had begun to tremble; that had always been a tell for his sister, a sign that she was nervous.

"About the fingerprints," Chambers said, "we already knew about those, of course. The Met did, I mean. And Five no doubt had the information as well. That wasn't the point."

"So the point is . . ." Brennan began.

"MI5 quite naturally wants to keep tabs on what the IRA is doing in this country. And if Molly Burke makes or receives calls from people involved or associated with that organization, well, those calls might well be worth recording."

"I can't believe this," Brennan muttered. "Special Branch. The Security Service. Molly and I under the gun in a . . . a . . ."

"A safe house in northwest London. I brought you here because I needed a place where we could speak without being seen or overheard." He looked at the gun in his hand and put it in a holster behind his back. "I'm sorry. Truly. Please understand that I had no intention of harming either of you, regardless of how things turned out. Though I guess you wouldn't be able to say the same with respect to me, Brennan."

"After you taking us out of public view and threatening us with a gun. I'd do the same again."

"I have no doubt you would. But I had to speak with you, had to get you out of sight as quickly as possible, and, if anyone was watching, it had to look as if I was taking you in, not consorting with you."

"Consorting with us! Somebody might think we're pals?"

"And I wanted to make sure you did not cause a scene. So much for that plan. Good thing you caused it here and not at Molly's place, where, for all we know, the eyes of MI5 were on us all."

"What difference would it make to you if MI5's eyes were on you?"

"MI5 are on the hunt for a mole."

"What the fuck are you saying now? A traitor, you mean? You've been watching too many spy movies, Chambers."

"Yes, a traitor. Either within Five itself or within Special Branch. Someone whose loyalties lie elsewhere."

"So they're watching each other and watching the police."

"I assume so."

"Today's episode wouldn't look too good for you, Detective Chambers. Your rival agency witnessing a nearly fatal encounter between you and a blameless visitor to this country."

"Well, at least they'd know I'm not the mole," Chambers grumbled. "And to think I was worried that talking to you might have raised suspicions about me!"

"What did you want to speak to us about, John?" Molly asked. "Before . . . before all this happened?"

He glanced at Brennan, then focused an intense gaze on Molly. "I cannot in good conscience go on any longer without telling you something you have to know. About your cousin."

"Oh, God!" Molly blurted out.

"Conn Burke did not kill Detective Sergeant Heath."

"Oh, God!" Molly exclaimed again.

"Are you serious?" Brennan asked him.

"Conn was not the killer, but he was present when it happened. I expect he'd be reluctant to tell you that, even though you probably know enough about the evidence to know he was on the scene. The fingerprints, the calls from the phone box nearby, all of that."

Brennan was haunted almost as much by Conn's being on the scene of a bomb attack as he was by the murder charge, but he was not about to raise that with Special Branch. At least, *Deo gratias*, Conn was not guilty of the police killing.

"I should tell you also," Chambers said, "that the charges are not a set-up. My colleagues, my fellow officers, genuinely believe he did it."

"But, John, if the police believe he is guilty, how will we ever convince them otherwise?"

"I can assure you that I will put every effort into finding the other individual who was on the street that day, the man who pulled the trigger on Richard Heath."

"You're going to help behind the scenes?" Molly asked. "I don't know what to say, John . . . that you would do this for us . . ."

"So now I have to put myself in your hands. I urge you not to tell Conn Burke what I have said here today. Not yet. There is a risk that everything will fall apart if it gets out that I have revealed this. I'll be taken off the case and disciplined, and that won't help anybody. Reassure your cousin that you know he is innocent, that he wouldn't have committed the crime, however you want to put it to him. But keep our conversation between the three of us for now."

"Getting back to Conn's innocence, how do you know this, Detective?" Brennan asked.

"I have very reliable evidence from a witness," Chambers replied, "and I am working the case on my own. But, as I say, I find myself hobbled by the suspicions circulating within the Branch and within MI5 about a mole. I daren't come out with this information until I have certain things wrapped up."

"This mole," Brennan said, "whose side is he on? Who is he passing information to, or whatever he is doing?"

"The Irish."

"The *Irish*? You're covering a lot of ground with that term, aren't you? Who are we talking about? The government of the Irish Republic?

Garda Special Branch in Dublin? Some crowd in the North? The merry drinkers in the Kilburn High Road?"

"No," he said drawing the word out with the vowel sound peculiar to the English when saying that word, "that is not what I mean."

"Thought not."

"The story—and I must say I find it less than credible myself—is that this individual is a double agent, working in the interests of the Provisional IRA. As I say, hard to believe."

"Wouldn't want to be that fella when they nab him," Brennan remarked.

"No. He'll need a whole parcel of priests saying prayers for him, that man will."

"So, would this be an Englishman sympathetic to Irish nationalism? Or an Irishman who infiltrated the police or Security Service? Hard to imagine either one, in my book."

"Exactly. There are of course people in England who are sympathetic to the Irish people and their various troubles over the years. How could there not be? But those people, well . . ."

"Don't tend to sign up for law enforcement. Is that what you're saying? Because the obverse of that is: people in law enforcement in England would not be sympathetic to the poor oul Oirish at all, at all."

"Of course that's not what I'm saying. What I can say is that we have many, many people of Irish origin in the ranks of the police. And the Security Service. And damned good officers, too."

Brennan had to laugh at the policeman's efforts to sound accommodating on the subject.

"But the IRA, well, that's beyond the pale," Chambers said.

"Pardoning the expression, of course."

"What's that?"

"Beyond the pale, the Pale being the part of Ireland ruled by the English in the late Middle Ages, with the rest of the country being inhabited by the wild Irish natives."

"Yes, yes, quite. Point taken. To be more precise, the IRA have declared Britain their sworn enemy. Difficult to believe an IRA operative could sit in London and pass information to his comrades in London or Dublin or Belfast without anyone noticing."

"But someone has noticed."

"Someone has raised suspicions at least. Wouldn't want to be that bloke if he really exists. Nor would I want to be mistaken for him by meeting you two where I could be spotted. Though I think my loyalty is well known."

"I think so too, Detective," Brennan could not help saying.

"But," said Chambers, "the Provisional IRA as an organization is one thing; a man wrongly charged with murder, even if he is misguided in his politics, is quite another. And now, you are free to go. I have taken a great risk in engaging in this cloak and dagger behaviour, and giving you this information. But it would be a grievous miscarriage of justice if your cousin were convicted of the murder when in fact he is innocent. I assume it will be obvious to you that you must be very, very careful what you say, where you say it, and to whom you say it. I urge you not to alter your behaviour in any way when you are at home, so Five does not catch on that you are aware of the listening devices. If they realize you have been warned off, that will start a whole new nightmare. For everyone. So," he said, rising from his seat, "give me five minutes, then carry on. Oh, if you get a parking fine, I'm afraid I am not in a position to help you!"

†

"What are we to make of that?" Brennan asked his sister when they were in the car on their way back to the rental office, with no parking ticket for their trouble.

"I'll be having nightmares about the initial part of the encounter for I don't know how long. Did he really need a gun to get us away from my flat?"

"It galls me to defend his actions, but would we have gone with him willingly to a shabby flat in an unknown neighbourhood? No, we would not have."

"You didn't make things any better, I have to say, Brennan. You could have got yourself killed. Or, you could have killed him. And we'd have two Burkes in prison for murder, only one of them innocent."

"I know, I know, sweetheart. But he was taking us into a secluded place at gunpoint and we didn't know why. I had to do something. You were remarkably calm, Mol."

"He wasn't going to shoot us, Brennan."

"Oh, you know that, do you? Knew it at the time?"

"He wouldn't shoot me."

"What makes you so sure?"

"Well, you said it yourself a while ago. And I think you were right, that, in spite of everything, John . . . doesn't dislike me."

Brennan turned to look at her. "Is that Britspeak for 'he's head over heels in love'?"

"Of course not!"

"Of course not," Brennan repeated in a facsimile of John Chambers's voice. "One doesn't fall in love, at least not with the targets of one's investigation. One maintains propriety at all times. Except for those times when weapons have to be pulled, however distasteful that may be."

"Don't try my patience, Brenny."

"Don't fucking call me Brenny if you want me off your case."

"We're back in our childhood, by the sound of things. Men are just grown-up little boys. Ever hear that saying?"

"No and I'm not hearing it now. I'm hearing one thing and one thing only: my name being called over and over by Mr. John Jameson somewhere in a dark and smoky bar. When we get this vehicle dropped off, we're going for a drink."

"Can't argue with that."

When they were back in familiar territory, that being Hannigan's bar, with drinks in front of them and a cigarette hanging out of Brennan's mouth, Molly said, "Was John making all that up, about the traitor in the ranks? Why would he, though? Not the sort of thing Special Branch would want bandied about."

"I wondered briefly whether that's exactly what he wants. Wants word to get out, if he thinks the traitor is in MI5. You always hear about the rivalry between these various organizations. But you know as well as I do he wasn't making it up. There must be a conscience in him, to tell us Conn is innocent of the charges. If he was being straight with us, he really did want to avoid discussing all this in our flat where, to hear him tell it, the walls have ears."

"That makes my flesh crawl. They are listening to everything we say. Wait till Terry hears this. I hope he won't start telling wild stories into the light fixtures. You used to hear about politicians visiting the Soviet Union, staying in hotels and speaking loudly into the lamps: 'I'd love a bowl of oranges about now.' And lo and behold, room service would arrive with the oranges."

"I don't think we have to worry, Mol. Terry keeps his cool flying jumbo jets in turbulence and lightning storms. He's not going to lose it over this."

"And when were they in there? When did they know we'd all be out of the flat long enough to get these things planted?"

"Hardly matters now, does it?"

Molly took a good, long swallow of her Guinness. Then she made a sign of the cross and said, "Thank God in heaven, Conn didn't kill that copper."

Brennan blew out a mouthful of smoke and put his cigarette in the ashtray. "Thank God and Mary and Saint Patrick and all the angels and saints. But how long is he going to be the good soldier, wasting away in a cell for someone else's crime? Someone else's crime committed in connection with a terrorist attack. I think we're agreed on the fact that he knows who the killer is." His sister didn't respond. "Unless he was there on the scene and a complete stranger arrived and shot the cop. Or someone appeared wearing a balaclava. Be a fool not to, whoever it was. But the more likely scenario is that Conn does know who did it. So who would he cover up for, at the cost of a possible conviction for murder and a life in prison? Whoever it is, it must be someone pretty damned important to him."

After a long silence, she replied, "The people most important to him are Tess and his family. Including us. I've met a few of his drinking pals. Well, you would have seen them at Hannigan's. And you saw Dáithí, who plays the uilleann pipes. There are a couple of other musicians he teams up with. And fellows he works with at the building site of course, but I don't know any of them. And I certainly don't know his brothers-in-arms, the lads operating in Republican circles over here. I'm sure he's loyal to them, whoever they might be. Them and his family, I guess, would top the list." She fell into an uneasy silence.

"What is it, Molly?" Brennan asked. She merely shook her head. "What about other people you've met? How about somebody from the lesser of the Cromwell plots, the red paint scheme? Do you see any of them, whoever they are, as people who would go a lot farther than vandalism to promote the cause?"

"No."

"Well, you can be sure it's someone very important to him. Or someone who has him terrified."

Chapter XIX

Was it for this the wild geese spread
The grey wing upon every tide;
For this that all that blood was shed?

William Butler Yeats, "September 1913"

Brennan needed a refuge from the world of crime and suspicion he had been living in for the past three weeks. So he looked forward more than ever to his morning Mass. *Immaculata Mater Dei, Regina caelorum, Mater misericordiae, Advocata et Refugium peccatorum, ora pro nobis*, he prayed silently on the tube ride to St. Andrew's church. Immaculate Mother of God, Queen of the Heavens, Mother of Mercy, Advocate and Refuge of sinners, pray for us. It was Sunday, and the ten thirty Mass was the traditional Latin rite.

As Father Burke walked up the aisle wearing his vestments and a black biretta on his head, with a procession of altar boys bearing candles ahead of him, he noticed several familiar faces in the congregation, namely Molly, Shelmalier, and her boyfriend, Edward. Brennan sang his Mass in the ancient tongue and was joined by a passably good choir in the loft. The magnificent ritual lifted him above the cares of his worldly existence. The processional hymn was the *Salve Regina*, sung by priest, choir, and congregation. *Ad te clamamus exsules filii Hevae*. To thee do we cry, poor banished children of Eve.

As he greeted the parishioners after Mass, it occurred to him just how far from the mainstream of English life he was at this moment. Catholics were a small minority in this country, and the incense and the kneeling, the papal encyclicals cited in the sermon, the Latin, and the prayers beseeching the Blessed Virgin Mary were as Catholic, as popish, as you could get. This struck him even more forcefully when Shelmalier and Edward came forward to say hello after the parishioners had left. Edward had a dazed look about him.

"Not your usual cup of tea, perhaps, Edward?" Brennan said to him, shaking his hand.

"Quite foreign to my experience, Brennan, as you say. But I'm chuffed to be here. It was lovely."

"Gratias tibi ago."

Molly came up to him then. "When I see you like that," she said, "performing the sacraments, looking and singing like an angel in heaven, I cannot believe it's my little brother up there. It was absolutely divine, in every sense of the word, darling."

He drew her towards him and kissed her. "Thank you, *acushla*."

"There's some shopping I have to do, so I thought I'd go to Oxford Street and have a bit of lunch while I'm at it. If anyone would like to join me, you're more than welcome."

Brennan turned to Shelmalier. She was looking him in the eye, but he couldn't quite read the situation so he improvised. "You have been studying Dante, mediaeval Italian dialects, if I'm not mistaken, Shelley?"

"For my paper, yes."

"Well, if you'd like to stick around for a minute, I'll show you something in the old Latin scriptures that might be of interest to a Dante scholar."

"I'm hardly that, but I'd love to see it. And Mum prefers to shop alone anyway. Gets it over faster that way. Am I right, Mum?"

"Well, there's some truth in that. I'm not much fun as a shopping companion. In, out, done, home. That's my modus operandi."

"Grand, then," said Brennan. "Why don't you go ahead, and we'll pore over old books."

When Molly departed, Brennan confessed, "I just committed the sin of lying. *Mea culpa, mea culpa, mea maxima culpa.* I have nothing to show you that relates to Dante, though I do have Latin scriptures by the yard. But I thought maybe you wanted to have a word?"

"Thanks for catching on, Brennan. Yes, I do. We do, Edward and I."

Edward looked distinctly uncomfortable. "Er, perhaps I should absent myself whilst you and Shelley have a chat."

"No, Edward. I want you with me. We're in this together."

"Very well, darling."

"Have a seat," Brennan said. "There's nobody else here now."

The three of them sat in a pew near the back of the church, as the morning light streamed in on them, coloured red, blue, gold, and green from the gorgeous stained glass windows.

Brennan waited for his niece to begin. She took Edward's hand in hers. "Edward and I hope to be married."

"Wonderful!" Brennan replied. "That's great news."

"It won't happen right away. I'll want to finish my studies, and Edward would like to open his café and get a start with that. So the wedding will be a ways off yet. But there are difficulties, as you might imagine."

"Religious differences, you mean? Those are finessed fairly easily these days. You won't be shunted off to the rectory for the ceremony."

"No, that's not it. I'll want to be married in the church, and Edward is more than agreeable to that."

"Full Latin Mass, you'll be wanting, Edward? Smells and bells and Latin and a blessing from His Holiness the Pope?"

Edward laughed. "If that's what she wants, that's what she'll have. Might need a medical team on standby for some of the older members of my family, but they'll just have to maintain flexible knees and stiff upper lips, won't they?"

"No, Brennan," Shelmalier said, "it's not our churches. It's our families."

"Ah."

"The Hathaways know what . . . who we are. The background of Mum's and your side of the family."

"Right."

"And they are very, well, tolerant."

"Steady on, darling!" said Edward. "Let's not damn them with faint praise. They're more than 'tolerant.' They are very welcoming of your mother and her family; they always have been."

"You're right, Eddie. Bad choice of words on my part." She let a moment go by and then said, "When I speak of my family, Brennan, I have one particular individual in mind. One person who causes me concern. One brother."

It certainly spoke volumes about her brother that he was the sticking point, and not the member of the family who was sitting in prison awaiting trial for the murder of an English policeman.

"Even though this is not a question of religion, I thought maybe we could talk to you. I know it would be too painful for Mum to hear me rattling on and on about Finbarr. I love my brother. But, really, he is impossible. And it's a serious obstacle for me and Edward."

"He's not the most tactful individual," Brennan agreed.

"He needs to grow up."

"He's only seventeen, though. We have to remember that."

"True, but he should be mature enough to recognize that other people have positions that differ from his, and it is their right to do so. And they should not be subjected to his, well, his acting out."

"What do you have to say about this, Edward?"

"Discretion is the better part of valour," he said, then blushed painfully, presumably at the word "valour." Brennan affected not to notice. His heart went out to the young man who had fought, no doubt valiantly, in the dirty war in the North of Ireland and returned home damaged as a result of the horrors he had seen and endured. After a moment, Edward returned to the conversation. "When you marry someone, you often have a person in your new family that you, well, don't see eye to eye with. That's part of life."

"The oafish brother-in-law," Shelmalier said, "right off the casting couch. Perhaps I could write a farce about it and have it staged in the west end."

"Oh, that would go a long way to ease the tension, Shelley."

"Not likely to happen, Ed. But seriously, Brennan, Finbarr refuses to consider any position more sophisticated and nuanced than 'Irish good, English bad.' Anything England ever did with respect to Ireland, whether it was eight days ago or eight centuries, has to be avenged with a whole lot of noise and violence. And I told you about the scene at Edward's home, when Finbarr refused to take my hints and get off the subject."

"Your hints, darling?" Edward said. "Or the physical violence you perpetrated on him to shut him up?"

"Well, there was a little of that. Brothers and sisters . . . I'm sure you know how it is, Brennan."

"Sure, I received a few jabs from my siblings back in the day, and I probably should confess to delivering a few myself," Brennan agreed.

"Right. I tried to prevent a full frontal assault from my militant little brother in the home of my future in-laws. Boy and Amelia didn't deserve that, in return for their hospitality. Any more than you deserved it yourself, Edward."

"Well, it wasn't anything we hadn't heard before. Disagreements over our policy in Northern Ireland are not exactly new."

"I could picture it getting all too personal, Eddie." She turned to Brennan. "Finbarr doesn't know, thank God, what Edward is going through as a result of his service in Ireland."

"Now, Shelley . . ." Edward began.

"You have a very real disorder, medically certified, as a result of what you suffered over there, Edward."

"Be that as it may, I should be able to handle your seventeen-year-old brother and his jibes about British foreign policy without having to take up your uncle's time here today. Not my idea, by the way. Whatever must you think of me, Brennan?"

"Edward, soldiers have been bringing wounds home from battle as long as man has been walking upright on this planet, and oftentimes those wounds are not physical, not visible to anyone else. We should all be thankful that the situation is finally being acknowledged and treated." Brennan could not imagine how agonizing this all was for Edward, son of Boy and Amelia Hathaway who had both, Brennan recalled, played heroic roles in the Second World War.

"Boy has been doing some work with soldiers suffering from post-traumatic stress," Shelmalier said.

"That's great to hear," said Brennan. "A person who has seen battle, been under fire himself, is the person best placed to understand what another soldier has gone through."

"That's right. Edward's dad knows what it's like. And he's been volunteering his time to the cause ever since he retired."

"Sometimes I wonder just how 'retired' Dad is," said Edward. "There are times when I suspect he's still at it."

"What makes you say that, darling?"

"Well, you remember the time we dropped in a couple of weeks ago, and he wasn't there and Mother was positively sphinx-like concerning his whereabouts. And that's not the first time it's happened."

"Well, it's quite a leap from that to Boy skulking around spying on people. He may have been at his local pub, and your mother didn't want to reveal that he was out in the gin mills playing the lad."

"Oh, I think she'd have owned up to that. She takes a glass of gin herself. Not to mention the occasional sherry."

"Boy belongs to a group of war veterans who get together and discuss old campaigns, so he may have been out with those fellows."

"There, again, she would have no reason to be coy about it. And before you say so, she would not tiptoe round the subject of the old gents' exploits in the war on my account."

"No, of course she wouldn't."

"But I don't think they've met since Heath died."

"Heath?" Brennan asked. "The detective who was killed?"

"No, well, yes. Since DS Heath died, but the man my father chums around with is his brother."

"Speaking of brothers," Shelley said, her voice loaded with meaning.

"What's this about Sergeant Heath's brother? Pain in the arse, is he? Or what?"

"No, no, it's not Clarence Heath who's the pain. It was Richard, the copper who was killed. They hadn't spoken in years. There wasn't much said about the murder of Richard at your family's table, Edward. Your parents were the soul of discretion when they had Molly, Brennan, and Terry over for dinner. Nobody mentioned the Heath murder at all. Typical British restraint about the sordid? Or was it something else? Were Boy and Amelia afraid they might blurt out 'Served the bastard right!'"

"Good Lord! Shelley!"

"Of course the fact that my mother's cousin is charged in the murder might have had something to do with their reticence. Good manners and all that."

"What accounted for the brothers falling out?" Brennan asked.

"Oh, just a family squabble."

"Edward, love, Richard Heath was a heartless prick who defamed his own brother over . . ."

"I don't want to hear any more about the Heaths, Shelley, if you don't mind."

"All right, Eddie. I'm sorry."

"Now, shouldn't we be on our way? I'm giving you a lift back to Oxford unless you wanted to stay on in the city."

"No, we'll head up to Oxford."

They were quiet for a few seconds, then Brennan said, "Would you like me to have a word with young Finbarr?"

"That will earn you some time off purgatory, Father," his niece said, "sitting down with Finbarr and trying to get him to see reason."

"I'm more than willing to try."

"Thank you, Brennan."

Edward looked at Brennan and raised his eyes heavenward. There was little doubt that Edward found Finbarr a pain, but it was equally clear that he had only agreed to this meeting to please his intended.

"Let's be on our way, then. Thank you, Brennan," said Shelmalier. "And that was a lovely Mass. If I ever hear guitars and 'Kumbaya' in a church again, I shall run screaming for St. Andrew's and all those Latin chants and scriptures!"

✝

On Monday morning, Brennan made an appointment to see Lorna MacIntyre, to give her the good news—and he had little doubt that it would come as news—that her client was innocent.

"Och, it's not every day I hear that one of my clients didn't commit the crime. Now, may I ask how you know this?"

"I heard it from someone in the know."

"Someone willing to put himself up there in a court of law and testify to Conn's innocence?"

"Out of the question. At least for now."

"I rather thought so."

"So you're going to need something beyond 'Mr. Burke is innocent. Somebody told me that. Can't say anymore. Can we all go home now?'"

"Aye, I've tried that one in the past, to no avail. They're a stony-hearted lot, the English courts."

"To my mind, Lorna, Conn doesn't seem to be taking this seriously."

"Being a bit of an eedle-doddle, is he?"

"A what?"

"Tha's wha' we in Scotland call a fellow who's being a wee bit too easygoing."

"That's him. He told me your strategy is going to be a 'wild geese defence.' Now that's him and not me. I'm sure you'll do an excellent job for him, but whatever he meant . . ."

"He's right. That's one of the defences I'm considering for him." She peered at Brennan and gave a hoot of laughter. "I only wish witnesses in court could master the art of receiving outlandish news with a complete lack of expression the way you're doing now. Well done, Brennan!"

He joined in the laughter. "You may well have me in court as a character witness for your easygoing young client, so it's as well that I've mastered the art of not having my gob hanging open and my eyes out on sticks."

"You'll be the first on my list. But let me explain. I used the wild geese defence successfully in the past. I was representing an IRA man, and he was acquitted at trial."

"Well! This is a day for surprises."

"There aren't many days in this business without surprises, I can tell you. Anyway, you know who the wild geese were: soldiers who left Ireland in the sixteenth, seventeenth, and eighteenth centuries, sometimes voluntarily, sometimes at the toe of the boot of their English overlords. They fought in various armies in continental Europe, normally the armies of Catholic states. Sometimes the Irishmen fought out of conviction, and sometimes as soldiers of fortune. Mercenaries, in other words. Hold still a moment whilst I look for something to read to you."

She walked over to her ceiling-high bookshelf and pulled out several volumes until she found what she was seeking. "You'll appreciate this, I think, Brennan. This was written to King Philip the Third of Spain by one of his military advisers: 'Every year Your Highness should order to recruit in Ireland some Irish soldiers, who are people tough and strong, and nor the cold weather or bad food could kill them easily as they would with the Spanish, as in their island, which is much colder than this one, they are almost naked, they sleep on the floor and eat oats, bread, meat, and water, without drinking any wine.'" Lorna MacIntyre looked at Brennan. "What do you think of that as a description of your countrymen?"

"Hard to fault it. We're tough, we're strong, and we spend a lot of our time naked. And bad food sure as fuck hasn't killed us. But what year was this?"

"End of the sixteenth century."

"We'd been importing wine into Ireland for centuries by then."

"Really?"

"Really. We were quite the trading nation in the Middle Ages, and I read somewhere that wine was our main import for much of that time."

"Well, according to the king's advisor here, you were not over-indulging."

"Of course not."

"I shall leave that statement uncontradicted, and return to the subject of my former client, the IRA man who was acquitted. This was a few years back. He was charged with murder, and it looked like an open-and-shut case, typical IRA hit. We put forward a case that the murder had in fact been committed by a IRA-trained mercenary, a hired killer, who had been retained by an enemy of the victim to commit the murder and make it look like a political killing. And we did this without producing the hit man or the man who hired him."

"How on earth did you manage to do that?"

The solicitor smiled at him. "I'm good at what I do. And I had a very fine barrister conducting the trial."

"I believe you! Was there ever a hit man, or was this purely a fantasy spun by a very good courtroom storyteller?"

"Oh, there was indeed a hit man. He may still be out there, for all

I know. And we were able to call expert evidence of his methods and all that, which fit with the facts of our case. And it didn't hurt us any that the victim had a long list of people in his life who had reason to want him dead."

"Well done, Lorna."

"Thank you."

"So in order for this to work for Conn, you would need to present evidence that, one, your IRA-trained hit man really existed and still exists, and, two, that Detective Sergeant Richard Heath had a list of enemies who wished him dead."

"I only need one. And anyone who knew Richard Heath knew he was an insufferable prick."

"Are you serious?" But he was not as surprised as he made himself out to be, not after Shelmalier's comments about the man, commentary that had been squelched by Edward's intervention.

"Absolutely. He was a callous, abrasive man who showed no mercy to the people he arrested, to those he interrogated, even to people in his personal life. His colleagues in the Metropolitan Police may have thought he was a capital fellow; after all, his attitude and methods brought results and made them all look good. But never mind his pals in Special Branch. I imagine he left a lot of hurt feelings and wounded egos behind him in personal and sporting circles. Did you happen to see that little documentary about him recently on the telly?"

"Yes, I did."

"All that talk about how 'competitive' he was? What a daredevil he was, and how he 'challenged' his schoolmates to do things they would never otherwise do? 'Do it or else,' wasn't that it? Not hard to read between the lines there. We'll be able to shanghai a few of his former acquaintances in to testify as to his character, if we play our cards right. We won't get any fellow coppers. As I say, they praised him to the skies. But we won't need them."

"And the hit man?"

"I'll dust off my notes from last time."

"So you're telling me there is a man out there, with IRA training or affiliation, who is moonlighting as a killer for hire. Doesn't sound to me like a true believer."

"Money makes many a man a true believer, at least in his assignment of the day."

"I wonder what the members of the IRA think of someone like that."

"Why don't you ask them?"

"Touché."

Chapter XX

Away from the light steals home my heavy son,
And private in his chamber pens himself . . .
Black and portentous must this humour prove
Unless good counsel may the cause remove.

William Shakespeare, *Romeo and Juliet*

"My dinner is *ruined*!" Terry grabbed a dishtowel, bunched it up in his hand, and threw it down on the floor, in a parody of the disgruntled housewife. "I slave over a hot stove all day and what thanks do I get? You waltz in at seven o'clock in the evening, Mol, and expect your dinner hot on the table, and me in a pretty frock smiling although my heart is breaking, and—"

"What did you make for me, sunshine?"

"Take-away from the local chipper."

"Perfect."

She went into her room and emerged a few minutes later, and headed for the take-out containers. "So where did you fly in from today? Rome, was it?"

"I took off from Fiumicino in the clear blue sky and flew into severe turbulence over France and then came in for landing at Heathrow in fog that was nearly black. As soon as my wheels touched the tarmac, the passengers broke into applause."

"That was nice of them."

"No, it wasn't. I hate that. What did they think was going to happen? Did they think doing my job and getting the plane down onto terra firma was optional?"

"Good point. How about you, Brennan?"

"I worked at St. Andrew's, then came back here and had a restful time until Terry blasted in, with his heart-stopping tales from the air."

Or at least that was Brennan's story for now. He could not recount his conversation with Lorna MacIntyre earlier that day, let alone tell Terry about the two-gun hijacking by the Special Branch detective, the revelation of Conn's innocence, or the news that MI5 had the place bugged. Could not get into any of this, not with the place bugged and the spooks listening in.

"How about you, Molly?" Brennan asked, while making a signal that he hoped she would catch: *Don't say anything you don't want recorded by the state's security apparatus.*

"I just . . . good chips." She bent her head over the grub and put fork to mouth.

"You just what?" Terry asked.

"Hmm?"

"Today, you . . ."

"I don't have to tell you two everything I do. And I certainly don't want to know everything you get up to." She gave Brennan the eye. She had not forgotten for a moment that, even over the plummy voice of the BBC presenter, their conversation might be overheard by unseen persons in unmarked quarters. They had to avoid controversial matters and act to the best of their ability as if nothing had changed. But what was controversial about Molly's afternoon?

"After I scoff this down, I'll join you for a pint if you two haven't drained the pub dry over the last few weeks."

"No, we left some for all those pissheads and alcos who seem to gravitate to the place."

"Always thinking of others, Ter."

When she had finished her fish and chips, they all left the flat.

"I'm not really going to the bar. I'd just like a bit of a walk in the fresh air. Fewer bugs out here."

"Fewer than where?" Terry asked.

"My place."

"Your place! If there was so much as a single ant in your flat, a poor little ant limping across the floor with two of his legs in little ant-sized casts, asking only for a wee grain of sugar and then he'd be gone, do you think Brennan would be staying there?"

So they filled him in on all the news.

"That sounds like a story I'd come up with after enjoying a few bottles at Janey Mack's!"

"We know, we know," said Brennan, and that was without a word about the dust-up between him and Chambers outside the safe house.

"But back to you, Molly," he said. "How did your day go?"

"I took a little train trip out of town. Nice to get away from the city once in a while."

"Where did you go?"

"Em, I went to Bath. It's gorgeous. You should go there while you're here, Brennan. It is architectural heaven, with magnificent neo-Classical buildings, everything beautifully laid out. And of course the Roman artifacts and the baths, and statues of the Roman emperors. You'd love it. Some place names for you from that area, too. Limpley Stoke, Dodleaze Wood, Slittems Wood, to name a few. And for you, Terry, the hanging loos."

"The what?"

"You'd find them most entertaining, I'm sure. When the houses were first built of course nobody had indoor toilets. So, in later times, some of the owners erected little buildings or compartments attached to the outside walls of the houses. Suspended off the façade several storeys up. Hanging loos."

"I never could have invented that, no matter how much drink I'd taken to fuel my imagination."

"Well, I took a picture for you. Drove by it the first time without realizing what it was, but went back for the photo. When I get my film developed, I'll send it to you. Amaze your friends! Anyway, that was my day. And since I'm not going drinking tonight, but you fellows probably are, I'll head back home and leave you to it."

"You could have told us that in the comfort of your home," said Terry, "even with the spies taking notes. Unless a lady doesn't engage in toilet talk in front of unseen strangers."

Brennan looked at her. "You drove back to take the picture? I thought you took the train."

"I did take the train. To get there, but then . . ."

Her eyes went from Brennan to Terry, and back to Brennan. Then she made a decision. To come clean. "I met John there."

"John?" Brennan asked. "You don't mean John Chambers."

She nodded.

"You agreed to meet the man who not so long ago abducted us at gunpoint? Pulled a gun on us even after you and he had seemingly become friends?"

"Abducted us to make sure we went with him to a place of safety so he could tell us, without being overheard, that our cousin is innocent of murder. John explained why he felt he had to do it that way. So, as I was saying, we made this plan to go to Bath. He rang me at work, on a phone line he knew to be secure. I travelled to Bath on the train, and he arrived by car. We couldn't be seen travelling together, him a detective and me a person of interest in his investigation!"

Earlier that day

John was waiting for her in his car when she got off the train in Bath. If he hadn't waved to her, she might have passed by without recognizing him. Gone was the severe-looking business suit and the cold, professional demeanour. He was dressed in a grey and blue striped rugby shirt, and his hair was tousled, as if he had run his fingers through it after showering, and not bothered to comb it down for a day on the beat. The smile he gave her was nearly a grin, and he looked ten years younger than he did when carrying out the grim duties of his profession.

They leaned towards each other when she got into the car, then both backed away when they realized what they had been about to do.

"Well, then," he said, looking a little embarrassed, "let's get on with things. A little motor tour about the city to see what's what, and then perhaps a stroll through the streets?"

"Sounds just right, John."

"It's, um, well, it's good to see you, Molly, if I may say so."

"You may."

"Good to see you off-duty."

"You look like a new man, just by being a hundred miles from your headquarters."

"That must be it."

He pulled away from the station and into Dorchester Street.

"This may be the most beautiful city in all of England," Molly said as they passed along an elegant colonnaded street. "There's a Jane Austen connection too, which adds even more lustre to the place."

"Yes, she lived here for a spell and set two of her books here."

"An Austen fan, are you?"

"Well, actually, I thought perhaps you were, so I looked it up before I came. Knew there was something, but I'd no idea what."

"There you are, a wiser and better man already."

"You're a good influence on me, no matter what they might say about you back at HQ."

"I can only hope that back at headquarters they have satisfied themselves I am a dead end as far as any investigation goes."

"I hope so too."

"You could put in a word for me."

"But then I'd have no excuse to sit outside your flat and take tea with you."

"Very well then. Keep me under suspicion."

"But I'm not working your case right now. We're on holiday. And I've brought some music, especially for this occasion."

He reached down between the seats and brought out a cassette tape in a bright green cover. A band of four men and one woman, all dressed in various shades of green, raised pints of green-tinted beer in a toast to one another. They all had demented grins on their faces, and one man winked rakishly at the camera. The title of the album was *Ireland O'Rama!* John must have caught something in the expression on his passenger's face, because he glanced at the cover, and said, "Well, all right, they look like a bunch of prats, but the music's great. I've listened to it. All the good old Irish songs."

She opened the abominable thing and inserted it into the player. As expected, the opening number was "When Irish Eyes Are Smiling." John sang along with it, and his voice wasn't half-bad, though she had to grit her teeth through the faux-Irish doggerel. "When Irish eyes are smiling, sure they'll steal your heart away!"

It was the equivalent of asking for English music, meaning the William Byrd *Mass for Four Voices*, or "Wild Horses" by the Rolling Stones, and getting "I've Got a Lovely Bunch of Coconuts." She looked at her companion and only then saw the mischief in his eyes.

"Look in the glove box; the good one is in there. The chap in the music shop was an Irishman," John told her. "He was appalled when I insisted on buying the *O'Rama* thing, until he caught on it was being done in jest. Then I asked him for authentic Irish music, and he showed me a tape by Planxty. I've never heard them, but I'm about to."

She opened the box and found *The Woman I Loved So Well*. That was more like it. She put it in the slot and cranked up the brilliant modern-day traditional music of Planxty.

Soon after that they were out walking the streets, chatting easily while admiring the crescents and avenues, the Palladian-revival splendour, the buildings of golden Bath stone, luminous in the sun. They saw the sixteenth-century abbey, the fifteenth-century church of

Saint Thomas à Becket, and the steamy first-century Roman baths. A tour guide explained that two hundred forty thousand gallons of hot water had been rising here from the Sacred Spring every day for thousands of years.

"I don't know if it's all that water, or just the time of day, but I've a bit of a thirst."

"You're not a man for the drink, I hope, John."

"Perish the thought. A cup of tea, the occasional glass of sherry whilst wearing the old school tie, the very rare splash of gin at my club."

"Splendid. Only what I would expect of an English gent. I must say I'm a little peckish, so let's look for a place that serves food and drink."

Ten minutes later they were facing each other across a table in the main lounge of the Star Inn, each of them with a pint of Draught Bass ale, a specialty of the house. The pub had been in business since 1760. Molly overheard one man call out to another upon arrival, "See you in a minute, Hopkins. I'll be on death row."

"John? Is there something I should know about this place?"

John shrugged. Molly was sufficiently curious to make inquiries of a young fellow who was clearing tables. He pointed to one of the other rooms. "Death row, that's the bench in there. In the small bar."

"I guess I should be grateful that you didn't sit me down in there, Detective Sergeant."

"Wouldn't think of it. I intend to take you alive."

She thought it wise not to respond, or to dwell on the images his words gave rise to in her imagination.

He raised his glass to her. "Cheers!"

"Sláinte!" she replied, and they both took a long, cool draught of their ale.

"I'd like to visit Ireland again," he said. "The South, I mean. Not just Belfast this time."

"Good idea, John."

"Of course I'd want a trusty guide with me, so I wouldn't go astray, say the wrong thing, and get myself in trouble!"

"Sure, you'd want to watch your words if you had a few bottles in one of the bars. That's where you could take a page from the IRA handbook, the *Green Book*. It warns its members to avoid 'drink-induced loose talk.'"

"Never thought I'd take the advice of *that* lot, but can't argue with them there. So that's what I'll do. Visit Ireland, drink only moderately, and watch what I say."

"You may as well stay home in that case!"

"True. I'd miss all the fun and they'd know I wasn't a local boy anyway."

"Safe to say you'd be spotted as a blow-in."

"As long as they didn't take me for a modern-day Cromwell, I'd be all right."

"You'll not want to utter that name anywhere in the Twenty-Six Counties."

John took a swig of his beer and looked at her. "Don't you think, Molly, that three and a half centuries is a long time to hold a grudge? I'm talking about Cromwell, and—" he held up his hand to ward off whatever she would almost certainly say "—I know what he did and I assure you that I don't make light of the way he treated the Irish people. But don't you think the passage of that much time makes revenge a bit, well, beside the point? Look at the situation in Belfast and Londonderry. Look at the marches the Orangemen hold every year in July. What are they marching for? To commemorate the Protestant victory over the Catholics at the Battle of the Boyne in 1690. Don't you regard them as, well . . ."

"Bigoted cranks."

"Yes, quite. And doesn't it go through your mind that they should get over the victory of William of Orange, get over it and move on, and stop marching through Catholic neighbourhoods crowing about it? And, if so, shouldn't the same logic apply to the Republican side? Time to forget Cromwell and get on with other things?"

"The reason, John, that the idea of revenge for Cromwell hasn't gone away is that the problem hasn't gone away. They're back again, Cromwell's men. The British Army is once again on Irish soil. And many of them, I have to say, are not behaving like gentlemen." She took a sip from her pint and went on. "And you raise the subject of the Orangemen. Let's look at them and the rest of the Loyalists. Loyal to Britain, they'd be the first to tell you, not to Ireland. The campaign they have waged against Catholics and Nationalists cries out for revenge. Particularly when you consider that the Loyalists can often count on the collusion of the police and security forces. And, by the way, it's an open secret that many of their killings have been planned, supported, and covered up by the intelligence services—" she paused and waited for a reaction but the police, as they say, remained tight-lipped "—all of that bolsters the argument in favour of continued action by Republicans."

John gazed at her intently for a few seconds, then said, "I have to tell you, in all honesty, Molly, the Loyalists in Ulster make me cringe. Speaking as an Englishman, I'm telling you that, if I had my way, we'd be rid of those so-called Loyalists who are causing so much trouble. I'm not alone in thinking Britain would be better off if we had washed our hands of the whole lot of them in 1924, or whatever year it was. Signed the whole thing over and said *Tally-ho, Ireland, good luck to you and goodbye.* And sailed home. End of story. If only!"

"The Government of Ireland Act was in 1920, the treaty in 1921. I'm an historian, can't help myself. But otherwise I'm in agreement with you: when the English pulled out of the South, they should have left the island of Ireland as one nation, instead of partitioning it. And should have gone home and forgotten all about us. Think of all the trouble, the money, the aggravation, you would have been spared. But you had an intransigent, irascible population in the North who were determined to stay British and wouldn't let you go."

"Am I hearing you correctly? You're absolving us of responsibility?"

"No, sorry, you don't get off that lightly. Because England is still propping up an illegitimate state, a state in which borders and voting districts were gerrymandered in order to keep the Loyalist-Unionists in power."

"And that justifies all the terrorism that has been committed by the IRA?"

"Some acts can never be justified. You'll not be hearing me apologize for terrorism, no matter who the perpetrator is." She could not read the expression on the face of the man across from her. She drained her glass, and put it down. "Isn't this where the matriarch of the family rises and says, 'Now perhaps the gentlemen would like to retire to the library for brandy and cigars?'"

"This gentleman would like another pint. Would the lady care to join me?"

"I thought you'd never ask."

John got up and ordered two again. "I'll have to stop after this one. It wouldn't do to have me stopped by the *police* for driving whilst under the influence. You know what they're like."

"Impossible to reason with." She shook her head. "Absolutely impossible."

"You're bearing up well, then, under the circumstances. Being in my company and all that."

"I've been living in this country long enough, John, to have taken on some English characteristics. One of them, obviously, is *keep calm and carry on*."

"Very sporting of you, Molly. Well done!"

"Thank you, Sergeant. You know, I have to admit I did not see the humorous side of your personality when we first met."

"No? I can't imagine what you mean."

"But I suppose if you were seen to be friendly at all, you would be an object of suspicion in Special Branch."

"Well, I'd like to think I can be civil to the people I question without being put under suspicion as a double agent."

"Does your force really believe there is a traitor in its midst?"

"Not necessarily in our midst. Possibly in MI5, if there are any grounds for believing the rumour at all. Another possibility that has been raised is that there is someone in the Intelligence Corps, military intelligence, who is playing with the wrong stick. I don't have to tell you that all this is strictly confidential. I should never have opened my mouth about it, but, well, I did. Whatever the case, I seriously doubt it could be anyone in Special Branch."

"What, in our house?"

"Right."

"Shakespeare."

"Ah. I really must do more swotting if I have the good fortune to spend time with you again. I did the Austen research but never thought to consult the bard in preparation for our day together. Should have done. One can hardly spend a day in this country, in educated company, without a Shakespearean moment or two."

"Don't worry. If you do spend more time with me, you'll soon see how ignorant and uninformed I am about anything other than history and literature."

"Oh, I can't quite see you as ignorant and uninformed. But—" his expression turned serious "—you may be a bit naive. No, that's not the word I'm looking for. It's insulting, and I don't mean it that way. But you may not appreciate the pitfalls of the activities undertaken by some of the people near and dear to you. I've already told you that your cousin Conn is innocent of the murder of Detective Sergeant Heath. But he may not be innocent of other activities. He should watch his back, in prison and out of it. It's a dangerous game he's playing. And Conn Burke is not the only one. We, that is, Special Branch, are aware of numerous Republicans who are almost certainly plotting more mayhem here in England. It won't go well for them if they are caught. That is, if they don't piss off their own people first and get punished. Or worse."

"Why are you telling me this?"

"I suppose because I wouldn't want to see you suffer as a result of the actions of people you care about. And of course there is a benefit to me as well. A benefit to the police and to this country, if Conn Burke and other Republicans were to see the light and cease their activities against British targets."

"Surely, you don't think a word from me would cause any of the local Republicans to give up the struggle to which they are committed."

He drank deeply of his pint, then put it down and said, "What I think is that we should take advantage of the fact that we are away from our workaday cares, and find more pleasant subjects to discuss."

✝

"So that's what we did, lads," she said to her brothers that evening as they walked along the street in Kilburn. "John told some entertaining stories, and some harrowing ones as well, about his early days as a copper. I told him about some of my students and colleagues, some of the oddballs around the university, no doubt reinforcing every stereotype he likely had about the eggheads who populate the halls of academe. And I recounted some tales from our childhood in Dublin, without giving up anything that might be of official interest to Special Branch.

"But here's the thing. He insisted on buying our drinks and snacks, even though I offered, and he switched from pints to glasses of orange juice. But I'd swear there was more in the juice than vitamin C. Vodka or something. I didn't lean over and stick my nose in his glass to find out, but things got a little heated later in the afternoon, and I think there was drink involved. Almost inevitably, John's work came up again. There had been a bomb planted at one of the train stations just outside London the day before. Thank God and Mary and all the holy men and women, it was dismantled and rendered harmless.

✝

"It's likely that lot in Cricklewood again."

"The 'usual suspects' by the sound of things, John?"

"We wouldn't be doing our duty if we didn't concentrate on the most likely suspects. Though I suppose we could engage in a public relations exercise, and question a broad section of the community, so nobody could accuse us of having preconceived notions. Or prejudices against any particular group or nationality. We could bring in a bunch of pensioners, round them up after chapel, and beat them about the head for appearances' sake. And there's a Swiss group in the country at the moment, doing some bird-watching. Might want to have them in and intern them without trial. Or a gaggle of school-girls. 'Excuse me, Miss Smithers, but we believe some of these young ladies might have been involved in setting a bomb. Or they might not have. Hard to know, really.' That would make us the most incompetent police force on the planet, but at least it wouldn't show us as fixated on one ethnic group."

The tone was jocular, but Molly sensed more than a trace of bitterness behind the humour.

"I don't support bombings, John," she felt compelled to say.

"I don't for a minute think you do. But it's not just bombs, is it? It's arms smuggling and shootings and intimidation, and all the rest of it. This entire campaign, be it here in England or over in Ulster—no good can come of it, Molly. It's been going on for twenty years now, and what has it accomplished?"

"You're asking the wrong person, John."

He leaned towards her then and spoke intently. "Molly, you don't want your children mixed up in any of this stuff."

Her children. Molly felt a chill go down her spine and out to the tips of her fingers. She had begun to think of John Chambers as a friend—even, she had to admit to herself, something more. Was she being naive after all? John was an agent of the state, the same state that had taken Molly herself out of her home in the middle of the night and locked her up in prison. On the flimsiest of excuses. Now, here was Special Branch Detective John Chambers talking about her children.

"You have a daughter who is dating the son of a war hero and brilliant intelligence officer, Boy Hathaway. And you have a son who is registered in a night course in auto mechanics but, as far as anyone can determine, he hasn't attended a class in seven weeks."

"You've been spying on my children!"

He gazed at her, unperturbed. "Of course we've been watching your children. We had you in the nick for suspected IRA activity. Your cousin is charged with the murder of one of our own. Your family in Ireland has a long history of . . . let's be polite and call it Republican activism, stretching back to Fenian days. Are you really surprised that we checked out the rest of the clan?"

She felt a tremor in her left hand, something that frequently happened when she was upset. She had no idea why emotional turmoil was channelled into this kind of symptom, but there it was. She slid her hand back and gripped the edge of the table with it, hoping to steady it before Chambers could detect her weakness. But, as he said, she should not have been surprised at his words. Special Branch—the political police, as she thought of them—would not have been living up to their job description if they had not looked into all her relations and associates. What disturbed her every bit as much as the confirmation of what she should have known was the information he had imparted about Finbarr. Any time she had asked her son about the night course, he had rattled off a plausible answer. Often it was a snide remark about the idiocy of one of his fellow students, which, Finbarr no doubt knew, would sound more like him than a précis of the evening's lesson. And the fact that he was spending this term at his father's house made any irregularities in his habits that much harder to track. What was she to make of the situation now?

"Is this why you invited me on this outing, John? To interrogate me about my own children?"

"Am I interrogating you? Or am I once again giving you a warning, at considerable risk to my career? Like when I tipped my hand to you about your cousin's innocence." There was a steely edge to his voice, and Molly was convinced then that he had been ordering something else to fortify his orange juice.

"You know I am very, very grateful that you told me Conn is innocent of the murder. The police have the wrong idea entirely if—"

"Conn Burke has made a name for himself in the Provisional IRA—he has established his credentials, shall we say—to the point where he has some choice in his assignments. He can say no and hand off operations to someone else, at least when the orders are coming from someone over here. I don't think he could blow off a command coming down from the top, but generally he is nobody's errand boy. The same cannot be said of more junior personnel making their way up the ranks. Someone tells a young recruit to jump, the young recruit says, 'How high and shall I kiss your arse on my way up, *sir*?'"

"Who do you mean by young recruits?" Molly could barely recognize her own voice, so timorous did she sound.

"Keep your eyes open, Molly. Ask questions."

"Are you suggesting I have been lax as a parent? You know, that goes right to the heart of me, John."

"I imagine it does. Children are a gift. I hope that doesn't sound too mawkish. So if I had a son who was—"

"My God, you really do think I'm a bad mother!"

"Hear me out, won't you?"

"Do you have children, John?"

The answer was a terse no.

The "no" was so loaded that Molly could not return to her own grievances without first asking him about his own. "Was that a . . . matter of choice, John, you and your wife having no children? Or . . ."

His left arm came up and made a slashing motion, cutting off her questions. If John's answers about a cop's life had seemed rehearsed that day when they first spoke in his car, this reaction was unpremeditated, instinctive. This was a no-go area.

She was about to apologize for being out of line with her questions, all of them well meant, though obviously unwelcome. But before she could begin, he was back to the matter of Finbarr.

"The last thing I want, Molly, is to turn up at your door some night and tell you your boy has been arrested. Or has suffered an even worse fate. So if you think he has been—"

"I can tell you, John, that I would know if he was up to something more than hero-worshipping a few hard men or striking a pose as a young rebel—"

"You know shite! You wouldn't *know* if he was engaging in criminal or dangerous activities. Sure he's not going to tell you that." The detective's voice was raised, and he was mimicking the Irish while he was at it. "It sounds to me as if the little bollocks is telling you he is one place, and he's really someplace else. Do you even know what city he's in from one day to the next? You might want to be looking a little closer."

"John! What . . ."

Chambers got to his feet, drained the last of his drink, and walked out of the bar.

Molly stared after him. It was the first time she had seen any sign of a temper in Detective Sergeant Chambers. She didn't know what was worse, the hints that Finbarr was implicated in something, or the implied criticism of her as a parent. But of course she knew what was worse: Finbarr's well-being took precedence over her own sensitivities, without question. The Special Branch man's mockery of her native speech was far down the line in importance.

She sat for a few minutes trying to calm down, planning a confrontation with Finbarr, trying again to calm herself. Then she rose, went to the loo, and freshened up. When she emerged from the Star Inn, she saw Chambers in a phone box. He was smoking a cigarette and blowing smoke out the open door of the box as he listened to whatever was being said at the other end of the line. It almost made her laugh, despite the tension she still felt after the conversation in the bar: here was a member of the Metropolitan Police, Special Branch, forced to use a public phone like any other member of the public. His private car was not equipped with a police radio or any of the other gear he would use in his daily work.

He was facing away from her, so she walked softly up to the call box and tried to catch what he was saying. It was not likely anything about her or her family — or so she hoped — but she could not fight down the temptation. She wished she had.

"Well, I don't give a fuck. I don't care what understanding you think you had with the family, DC Thompson. Your understanding — *my* understanding — was that we expected something in return. And we got zero, not a whispered word from any of them. Detain the lot of them. What? That's their problem. We don't run a child-minding service. And if they start crying about it, tell them, 'Lassies, yew should never hae left Glasgow!' Get it done."

He slammed down the receiver and took a long drag of his cigarette, then threw it onto the pavement outside and crushed it with his foot. He looked up and saw her then. At least he had the grace to look embarrassed.

"Tough day at the office?" she asked him.

He merely shook his head. They walked in silence to his car, parked near the railway station. He unlocked it and opened the passenger door.

"I'll go wait for my train," she said.

"Get in, Molly." When she made no reply, he said, "I'm sorry. Really, I am. I hope you'll let me make it up to you sometime. The work has been taking a lot out of me, all of us on the force. I'm a little tense these days, but I shouldn't make you bear the brunt of it. Especially after such a, well, such a pleasant day otherwise. A pleasant day in your company. Come inside for a minute."

She got in, and he went around to the driver's side.

She knew this would not go over well; still, she could not help but ask. "Are you all right to be driving, John?"

"I'm fine to drive, Molly."

"Typical man!"

"I suppose. But I'm fine. And if some young traffic copper stops me, I'll pull rank on the bastard. Jesus, Molly, I'm joking. I see I have a lot of fence-mending to do with you."

He reached across and covered her right hand with his left. She started to pull away, but his grasp was firm. She kept her hand in John's and waited for whatever he might say next. "There are some very dangerous individuals operating here in the U.K., Molly. If your son starts travelling that same road, he will find himself in a very dark and terrifying place."

†

"So, boys," Molly said now as she and her brothers turned back into her street in Kilburn, "I don't know what to think anymore. John was his calm, controlled, kind-seeming self at the end. The John Chambers I think I've come to know. And he wouldn't be warning me about these things unless he . . . well, unless he was concerned about me in some way."

Terry said, "I'm wondering why he got so worked up when you asked him about kids. Most guys would say 'It just never happened,' or 'We sure had a good time trying.' Something like that. You sure touched a nerve there."

"His reaction made me wonder," Molly said, "whether he might have had a child and something happened. The child died or had an accident, or maybe was a victim of a crime, or . . . well, there's no point in trying to speculate."

"You'll want to know him a bit better," Terry said, "before you set up house together in Barkingside."

"Barkingside?"

"Another interesting place name I saw today."

"I don't imagine we'll be house-hunting any time soon. But . . ."

"But what?"

"I am fond of him. I just wish I could figure him out. He's usually been kind, courteous, funny—and he did give us top secret information about our cousin. We mustn't forget that. But on today's outing I caught a glimpse of another side of him, and I wouldn't want to cross it."

"I wouldn't want to be those poor Scots he ordered detained either!" Terry commented. "He didn't show much mercy to them."

Brennan asked himself, Will that be us at some point down the road?

Chapter XXI

Did you really believe them when they told you "The Cause"?
Did you really believe that this war would end wars?
Well, the suffering, the sorrow, the glory, the shame,
The killing, the dying, it was all done in vain,
For, Willie McBride, it all happened again,
And again and again and again and again.

Eric Bogle, "No Man's Land"

Molly was sitting at the table the following day, consulting a stack of thick books and scribbling notes on a pad of paper.

Brennan said, "You look as if you have something more lofty to do than accompany your brothers to Hannigan's and get gilled."

"I do. A tutorial. But I can't keep my mind on it. I rang Neville hoping to speak to Finbarr and ask him . . . a few pointed questions. But Finbarr wasn't there. Neville said he had gone off to stay with a pal from school for a few days. Davey and his family. Neville himself is going away, so he thought it was a good idea. Better than leaving Finbarr with the run of the house in Neville's absence. I can see his point! But I can hardly concentrate on the material for my tutorial here."

He started to ask about her work but they both heard the BBC news reader mention Colchester, and they tuned in to the radio.

". . . new information in the case of the death of Liam Michael O'Brien. O'Brien is the Irish man who was found beaten to death in Colchester in April of this year. Our correspondent Emma Langford reports from Colchester."

"Police had originally identified the dead man as Patrick Michael Doyle, only to discover later that his real name was Liam Michael O'Brien. They would not speculate at the time as to why Mr. O'Brien had been living in this country under a false name. Now, though, we may have the answer to that question. The *Essex County Standard* reported today that Mr. O'Brien had been working with law enforcement for many years. Quoting unnamed sources close to the investigation, the paper said Mr. O'Brien had been a confidential informant in relation to criminal matters and also matters of national security. We spoke to the police in Colchester, but they would not confirm that Mr. O'Brien had been an informant. They said it is not their practice to comment on police procedures or tactics, whether they involve informants or not. Nor would they comment on whether the Provisional IRA is a factor in this case. A police spokesman did say the investigation is making progress.

"Liam O'Brien was a native of Kilmacthomas in County Waterford, Ireland. He left a wife and four children. The family lived in England for some years and then returned to Ireland. Mr. O'Brien worked as a landscaper in the Chelmsford area under the name Patrick Doyle. Neighbours described him as friendly and helpful, with a ready smile and a good sense of humour. They were of course shocked at his death, and also say they are surprised by reports that he had anything to do with police or political matters."

"Well, I suppose *we* shouldn't be all that surprised," Brennan said, "at the suggestion that O'Brien was an informer, given the way he was killed."

Molly gave him the warning sign. The walls, literally, have ears.

He had to say something now, so the listeners, or recorders, would not catch on that he had caught on.

"A beating like that is a punishment, and we all know that informers are severely punished."

"Dreadful," she agreed.

Molly headed into her bedroom, and Brennan followed. They

had reasoned that anyone wanting to hear the conversations Molly had with the members of her family, and Republican outlaws, would likely have concentrated on the dining or living area of the flat.

Still, Brennan spoke in hushed tones. "Liam O'Brien's father said Liam was tortured, God rest him."

"I thought you told me his father never made it over to see the body."

"He didn't, but he got the information somewhere."

"God help anybody who's suspected of being a tout."

"Suspected, is right. He may have been one, or he may just have been suspected. Either way, he was destined for a grisly end. Anyway, where were we before that unwelcome bit of reportage came our way? Hannigan's, wasn't it? Coming for a few scoops at your local?"

"An evening of drink and song would do me the world of good right now. I'm trying to come up with some new insights for a tutorial on Spenser and Milton, but I'd much rather go to Hannigan's and recite blood-curdling tales from our native land."

"When is the tutorial?" Brennan asked.

"Not till next week."

"Well, then."

"Oh, I should stick with it, even if I'm not getting anywhere. Earlier today I tried to find something by Cedric Mawdsley to spice up my presentation."

"Mawdsley? Did you ever see him again, after we got the bum's rush out at that country house?"

"No, I never saw him again."

"Spooked by your IRA connections."

"Put him off his food, apparently. I haven't seen him in the Warrington since that evening at Blythewich. Poor man. The expression on his face when I told him about Conn!"

"No wonder we never got another dhrop to dhrink at the big house."

"True, but I was thinking today that it would be interesting to get his perspective on Spenser and Milton. I wonder if someone of Mawdsley's class and background would have written anything about the poets' less-than-benevolent attitude towards Ireland and its inhabitants."

"Why didn't you look it up? Surely he has published a paper or two on the poets."

"I looked. Couldn't find anything. Neither could our librarian."

"So it wasn't his main field of research. Did you find anything else he's done?"

"Didn't think to ask."

"No worries. One thing I've been wanting to do when I'm in England is go and hear Evensong with the King's College Choir. Now I have two reasons to travel to Cambridge. I'll go early and drop in to see Mawdsley in his office. 'Hello, Cedric, old chap. You may remember me, a member of one of the old families. We knew each other at Blythewich.'"

"One of the old Fenian families, you mean," said Terry, coming in through the bedroom door with a slab of beer under his right arm. He dropped it on the bed. "Thought you'd be in here." He, too, spoke *sotto voce*. "What we should do is stage a performance for the spooks who are listening in. Someone mentions Conn, and how we can't communicate properly with him in the prison because we're afraid the screws are listening in. One of us says then, 'They probably have his flat bugged too, the peelers, since they think he's a fucking terrorist.' That leads one of us to get paranoid about this place, and we clam up. We go out and hire a security firm to come in and do a sweep."

"That's not a bad idea, Terry, if we can pull it off," Brennan said. "You write the script, and we'll take it from there."

"So what were you saying before I interrupted in my soft little voice? Something about our friendship with Cedric Mawdsley, was it?"

"Yes. Brennan is going to see Cedric at Cambridge. I'm looking for any research he might have done on Milton and Spenser."

"Yer man Cedric will turn pale at the sight of you, Bren, and call security." Terry said to Molly, "You know what they used to call this fellow when he taught at St. Kieran's High School? And the name followed him when he became a professor at the seminary."

"What did they call him?"

"The Assassin."

"You do have that look about you, Brennan," his sister agreed. "The hawk nose, those black eyes . . . You're even more sinister gliding round in a black soutane, I have no doubt. If they ever make a movie about a Vatican hit squad, you'll have the leading role."

True to form, Terry embellished it a bit. "A Vatican hit squad recruited from disaffected snipers in the IRA."

"Well, that's it then," said Brennan. "I'll go to Cambridge as a former IRA sniper, now working as a Vatican enforcer—what could be more natural?—and I'll intimidate Mawdsley into producing something scandalous on Milton and Spenser, something Molly can reveal and rail against in her tutorial."

Molly waved a dismissive hand at her brothers. "All right, children, I've heard enough from you today. I have work to do. Why don't you go out and play blind man's bluff in the traffic round Trafalgar Square?"

†

When Brennan and Terry got to Hannigan's, there was no place to stand at the bar, and not a barstool to be had, so they each ordered a pint and a glass of Jameson and took a table near the back of the pub. Along with the rest of the crowd, they kept an eye on the hurling match being broadcast from Ireland, Cork vs. Clare. This kept their minds off the family troubles for the first hour or so, until the news came on, and Ireland led the coverage there, too. Two Protestant paramilitary members and two passersby were killed by an IRA bomb at a chip shop in Belfast. Across town, three Catholics were killed, and two seriously injured, when a pub was firebombed. One of the injured was the barman's twelve-year-old daughter, who was on the premises to arrange pots of flowers for a wake that was to be held there that evening. Also coming out of Belfast were accusations of collusion by the state security forces in the shooting death three months earlier of Pat Finucane, a prominent civil rights lawyer. Nearly every eye in the bar was on the television, and the chat was muted.

Molly walked in during the litany of woe and peered through a pall of cigarette smoke looking for her brothers. Brennan stood and waved, and she signalled that she would join them once she had her pint in hand.

"I had enough of Spenser and Milton, so I decided to join you lads, the poets of the twentieth century. You, at least, Ter. We can expect some doggerel out of you, surely."

> I think that I shall never see a poem lovely as a tree,
> A tree from which a branch doth spring, a Special Branch
>   for you and me.
> But more for you, my dear, than me, that branch doth
>   stretch and stiffen there.
> And if thy gentle hand doth —

"I don't like where this is going, you foul-mouthed little brat, so mind your feckin' manners and shut your cake hole, or I'll shut it for you."

"Yes, Miss Manners."

"That's more like it."

"As low a person as he is, Molly," said Brennan, "his adolescent humour almost comes as a welcome relief after what we've been hearing on the news. Several dead in the North, including civilians. Which is foreseeable any time the weapon is a bomb."

He lit a cigarette and savoured the hit of nicotine. He tried to turn his mind from the atrocities in the Six Counties to the relative strengths of Cork and Clare in hurling, but his mind would not cooperate. Instead of "Who is going to win the cup?" he said, "Who is a legitimate target in a war? We say non-combatants, civilians, should never be targeted. And they should not become 'collateral damage,' to use a contemporary military euphemism. So that leaves those whose task it is to make war or defend their countries. The military. The command structure, military installations, and the soldiers, sailors, airmen, and others who do the fighting. They are paid to fight, and part of the risk they sign up for is to take a bullet for their country. Guerrilla forces fit in there, too. Anybody who takes up arms to fight. But what about involuntary service? What about those who serve as soldiers not by choice or to earn a wage, but because they have been drafted against their will?"

"Seems to me a soldier is a soldier," Terry responded. "Certainly from the point of view of their enemies."

"But wouldn't a drafted soldier be in the same position as a civilian? Neither of them chose to fight. And even those who are there willingly: can we take it for granted that they are legitimate fodder? Look at the slaughter of millions of soldiers in the First World War. Line after line of them sent out across the fields, mowed down by opposing fire. And for what? It all started up again twenty-one years later. Are we morally justified in sending those poor devils out onto the field for our country's ambitions? That has certainly been the accepted practice throughout history."

"Nobody guarantees the life of a soldier. Or, as I remember from my own days in uniform, the life of an Air Force pilot." Terry looked at Brennan's two empty glasses. "Ready for more?"

"Yeah."

"You, Mol?"

"No, I'll be a while with this one."

When Terry returned, Brennan took a sip of his whiskey, then of his pint, and returned to the philosophy of war. "Say, for the sake of argument right now, that the poor grunt in uniform should not have to pay for the policies forged by his political masters, the wars started for empire or greed or revenge, or for whatever reason."

"Back to World War One," Molly said. "This makes me think of the German and the English soldiers in the trenches, singing 'Silent Night' together at Christmastime. That story always moves me to tears."

"Me, too," said Terry.

Molly looked at her brother, obviously expecting a punchline. But he was as serious as she was. She said, "That incident tells me that those soldiers out in the field had more in common with one another than they had with their commanding officers or, God knows, with the leaders of their countries. Makes you think of mass mutiny, but then I guess you might wind up with a military coup, and the horrors that always arise from that."

"So," asked Brennan, "who should be held responsible for the actions a country takes? Surely it should be the people in power, the ones who make the decisions. By this logic, political assassination may be the most legitimate kind of attack. During the War of Independence, Cathal Brugha wanted the IRA to wipe out the entire British cabinet. Richard Mulcahy and Michael Collins were aghast at the idea, and it's not as if those two were afraid to get their hands dirty, Mulcahy being chief of staff of the IRA at the time, and Collins director of intelligence. Collins had his own squad of assassins at work in Ireland, getting rid of the Brits' spies and informers."

"Five years ago, they actually did try to do it," said Molly. "The IRA set out to assassinate the cabinet and the prime minister. I've heard Margaret Thatcher described as the most hated person in Ireland since Cromwell. The Conservative Party Conference was on at the Grand Hotel in Brighton, and the IRA planted a bomb. But, as we know, they didn't get the PM or her cabinet. Several other people weren't so fortunate."

"Always seems to be the case, doesn't it?" Terry remarked.

Brennan turned from practice to theory once again. "Talking

about governments, if a regime is a dictatorship, imposed on its people by force, can the people be held morally accountable for what the government does at home or abroad? What if the government is a democracy? If the people making the decisions have been voted in by the populace, the civilians, are attacks on those civilians then cloaked in a mantel of legitimacy?"

The hurling match reappeared on the television, and the mood of the room changed accordingly. But not for Brennan.

"Just for the record here," he said, "I would not condone the killing of civilians, ever, no matter where the arguments lead us. And it's not only people, is it? There is also the legacy human societies have left to future generations, whether the builders ever looked that far ahead or not. The great buildings that have endured through history. Mankind's heritage. The Parthenon, the Taj Mahal, Westminster Abbey. They belong to the ages. Destruction of anything like that, anywhere by anyone, would be unconscionable. But, then, who decides at what point, or under what criteria, a building or a work of art attains the status that would protect it from destruction?"

"Brennan," his brother demanded to know, "can't you just come into a bar and down a few pints and talk about games and goals and girls?"

"I can, but the situation we're in, our family is in, calls for a bit more gravitas. You took up arms yourself, Terry, in the guerrilla war being fought in the North of Ireland. Yet you hoped that your shot did not kill that British soldier beside the armoured vehicle. That soldier would have killed Conn, or you, or any of the other IRA men in Ballymurphy that night, if he could have. One of your lads was killed. Your killing the soldier would have been no worse than his killing any of you, no worse than the deaths he caused before that night or after, while carrying out his duties on behalf of British rule. Yet you did not want to have the man's death on your conscience."

"That's right. I still don't know what to think about my role that night, and I've gone through military training. I was in the U.S. Air Force, for Christ's sake, and I don't have the answers."

"And what about the members of the Cromwell Association?" Brennan looked at his sister. "If that bomb had been allowed to go off, and some of them had been killed, would that have been justified? We come from a country where Cromwell directed the massacres of thousands of people and sent others into slavery. The English people alive now of course bear no responsibility for what he did. But the Cromwell Association is made up of people who honour him. Their respect may be based on Cromwell as a parliamentarian, of sorts, but the fact remains that they are honouring someone who today would be considered a war criminal. In any act of revenge for the deeds of Cromwell, aren't they exactly the people who should be targeted?"

Terry turned to Molly. "Would you have been willing to kill one of them, Mol, if your red paint campaign had somehow escalated around the statue?"

"No."

"Difficult to draw any lines here, isn't it?" Terry continued. "Our cousin Conn was a gunman with the IRA. A sniper. Maybe still is. But he draws a firm line between that and taking part in a bombing campaign."

"I think we all would." Her brothers were in agreement there.

"And yet," Brennan said, after finishing off his latest pint, "if you take no action at all, you've accepted the occupation of your country by a force you believe has no right to be there. And you accede to the violence perpetrated on your own people by the occupiers to maintain that occupation."

Terry jerked his thumb in the direction of his brother. "How buckled would this fellow have to be before he'd lose the ability to pronounce ac . . . ash . . . acsheed?"

"Well," Molly replied, "whatever stage he would have to reach to lose the power of coherent thought and speech, I'll have to miss it. I'm just having this one, and going home. Early night for me. Mind yourself, lads."

†

Brennan awoke the next morning feeling as if the wrath of God had been visited upon his head and his stomach. A night of skulling pints with whiskey as a chaser. Or was it the other way around? This wouldn't be the time to say his daily Mass; he simply wasn't able for it. *Domine, non sum dignus.* Lord, I am not worthy. He would see how he got through the day and would hope that, by evening, he would prove more worthy of the Eucharist. He debated rolling over from his back to his front but was afraid his stomach would react with violence. The idea of whatever was in there sloshing around . . . No, he would just stay like this for . . . well, for as far as he could see into the future. He gingerly raised his head to look at the clock. One o'clock. In the afternoon? Couldn't be. He couldn't keep his head up. He sank back down and said to himself, Never, ever again.

He heard a gentle knock at the door. Was this death come calling? If so, he almost welcomed it. But, no. "Brennan," Molly whispered through a crack in the door.

"I died. Without the sacraments. Leave me to my torment."

"I would, but there's a message here for you."

"For me? Unless it's from the Pope himself . . ."

"For you and Terry, maybe. But he went out this morning. You'd better come and have a look."

"All right. Steer clear of me." Last thing he wanted to do—what if it in fact was the last thing he ever did, his final act on earth?—was eject the contents of his stomach at his sister's feet.

She wisely removed herself from the path between his room and the bathroom, and he lurched towards the facilities. The less said the better about what went on in there, except to say that the episode culminated in him brushing his teeth, taking a shower, and emerging from the bathroom wrapped in a towel. The room was spinning around him. But he plunked himself down on a chair across from Molly. She eyed him across the table.

"Seek pleasure and avoid pain, Brennan, darling. A laboratory rat can learn that much. When certain behaviours repeatedly result in painful consequences, like, say, an electric shock, or a painful hangover, the rat avoids those behaviours in future. It's called learning."

"I didn't know you were a radical behaviourist."

"You're this hungover and yet you can remember the term for the school of thought that might well describe you as less intelligent than the humble white rat?"

"What?"

"Nothing, darling. But you really, really should ease off on the drink."

"Yes, yes, you're right. A bit of behaviour modification might be in order. Stick my hand in an electrical socket whenever I reach for my eleventh pint."

"Well before that, I'm thinking. Now, here's why I dragged you from your bed. This was under the door when I got up."

She reached behind her, grabbed an envelope, and handed it to Brennan. He opened the flap and pulled out a piece of paper. He read it silently. "Burke brothers, please meet me at Janey M's this afternoon. Rory Óg. Don't ask for me by name when you come in!"

†

The last place on earth Brennan wanted to be on the afternoon of Wednesday, May 24, 1989, was a bar. He knew from long experience that the "hair of the dog" would go a long way to easing the symptoms of his hangover. But that was a cycle he wanted to avoid, a cycle hard to break once you got going on it. Nevertheless, he was not about to ignore the request of the bereaved father of Liam O'Brien for a meeting. So there Brennan was, being transported through the pissing London rain in the back of a taxi with a driver who skidded and careened around corners as if he was driving the Tilt-A-Whirl, and who talked nonstop about nothing but the pissing London rain. Competing with the beat of the rain on the roof, and the driver's endless natter, was a singer on the radio whose voice kept breaking into a bad falsetto whenever she went above a B-flat in the middle of the staff. He had to tune that out or he would go off his head. But the only alternative that came to him was not the consolation of a Gregorian chant, as he had hoped, but lines he knew well from "Carrickfergus":

> I'll sing no more now till I get a drink.
> For I'm drunk today and I'm seldom sober,
> A handsome rover from town to town.
> Ah, but I'm sick now. My days are numbered.

As bad as the ride was for Brennan's stomach and his head, the idea of heaving himself up and out of the cab was almost too much to contemplate. But he got on with it and found himself walking in the door of Janey Mack's bar in Cricklewood, his stomach churning, his head spinning.

He looked around, recognized a few faces, and smiled at them. But he saw no sign of Rory Óg O'Brien. The barman caught his eye, though, and said, "Would you like to sit in the snug today, sir?"

"Em, yes, I would."

"What would you like?"

There was nothing for it but to order a pint. He waited for it to settle, then paid up, thanked the barman, and headed to the snug.

O'Brien was sitting inside, his back to the wall, a pint half gone and an empty glass beside it. A cigarette was burning in an ashtray. O'Brien got up and put out his hand. Brennan placed his glass on the table and shook O'Brien's hand. Then he sat down and lit up a smoke.

"Those Tan fuckers are defaming my son by claiming he was a tout. He was not."

Brennan of course had no idea whether young O'Brien had been a tout, but he would not even consider saying as much to his father. In the circles in which Rory Óg O'Brien and most of Brennan's own relations travelled, the worst accusation that could be made against you was that you were an informer. It could get you tortured and killed.

"But," O'Brien continued, "if somebody was saying that about him, it might have been enough to get the army wound up against him."

"But the British Army . . ."

"No, our army. The IRA, the lads operating over here. I know there were no messages on his body, but that could just mean Kane has changed the way he works. No longer wants to leave a calling card that might as well say in giant letters 'Kane the Officer Commanding of the Psycho Brigade of the IRA Was Here.'"

"That may well be."

"But I also heard Kane has been doing some recruiting, bringing some new young lads under his command. He's got those two brides-maids that are always by his side, but they're nothing more than ladies in waiting, there to carry out his whims from one moment to the next. He's in the process of forming his own band of men. Fellows who aren't afraid of the sight of blood."

"How does this Kane get to wield so much power?"

"The command structure back home may not be in love with him, but they find him useful. He gets results. So what I'm saying is that Kane may be responsible for my boy's death, but he had somebody else commit the atrocity for him."

"Have you names for any of these foot soldiers?"

O'Brien took a moment, thinking it over, or perhaps weighing the advantages and disadvantages of having this knowledge. In the end he said, simply, "No" and downed the remainder of his pint. The man was showing signs that the drink was getting to him, and his Waterford accent became more pronounced as the meeting went on. Brennan had the impression that Janey Mack's was not his first stop of the day. Or perhaps he had enjoyed a few cans at home before heading out.

"I'm ready for another. You'll have the same, Brennan?"

"No, I won't, but thank you, Rory Óg."

"Now, Brennan, no bird ever flew on one wing." He got up and went to the bar and returned shortly with a pint for each of them.

Brennan took a good, long swallow of his unwanted pint and realized the sickness in his stomach was gone. His head was feeling fine as well.

O'Brien drew a coin from his pocket and tapped it against the side of his glass. He made no move to drink but returned to his analysis. "I'm thinking that slander about Liam being a tout was a smoke-screen put up by the *Sasanachs*, maybe because they thought the IRA would step in and take him out. More likely to my mind, they killed him themselves. It would serve the Brits very nicely to have it about that Liam was an informer, so everyone would lay the blame on the 'RA. There go those Paddies, murdering their own on English soil."

"Why would they want him dead?"

"Because he was an Irish patriot, that's why!"

"He was . . . active in the cause here in England?"

"He did what he could."

"That doesn't tell me much of anything, Rory Óg." And it didn't shine any light on the real motive, if there was one, for the British to want Liam as a dead body rather than a successful and public arrest for the books.

O'Brien tapped the coin against his glass again and muttered, "It has a better ring to it now. Even for a London pint." He lifted it and took a long, leisurely drink. "This much I can tell you, Brennan: Liam was ferocious worried for his safety."

"When?"

"In the days before he died."

"So you were in touch with him shortly before he was murdered?"

"Sure, I was speaking to him on the phone."

"Did he say he'd been threatened?"

"He believed he was being followed."

"By someone on foot, in a car, what?"

"He didn't tell me that. Just said he got the feeling he was being watched."

"He probably was, if he was known to be active in Republican circles here. My sister got thrown into prison. Special Branch had been watching her for ages."

"The Brits threw your sister in prison. And they killed my son. I'd stake my life on it. When they're not shooting our people, or beating them to death in detention centres over in Ireland, they're killing them here."

There was a sudden crashing sound at the front of the bar, and a shout. O'Brien jumped and looked ready to spring. He was so tense that Brennan got up and walked out of the snug to see what had happened. By this time, the people in the bar were laughing. A man had come in, fluthered, and had knocked over another fellow who had been carrying two full glasses. Nothing for Brennan's jumpy companion to worry about. He reported as much to O'Brien when he rejoined him in the snug. But he still had a worried air about him.

"Rory Óg?"

The man put his hand up. "Quiet with the name, remember?"

Brennan had said the name so softly that nobody could have heard it outside the walls of the snug.

O'Brien visibly relaxed after a few seconds had passed. "Now, Brennan, you mentioned prison. After a long song and dance, that's why I asked you to come and meet me today. There are a few of our lads in the prisons here. From what I hear of your cousin Conn — and it's all good — he's well connected. Knows who's who in London and beyond. So whenever you pay him a visit, you might pass on what I've told you . . ."

"You haven't given me much to go on."

"That's because I'm in the dark. Liam was being followed. Then he was subjected to torture, either to punish him or extract information from him, and he was killed. There's nothing else I know. But if you could ask Conn to keep his ear to the ground . . . And if he's heard anything you could let me know. And if there ever comes a time when I can return the favour, to you or your cousin, I will. Here's my number in Kilmacthomas." He drew a slip of paper from his pocket, with a phone number scribbled on it, and handed it to Brennan.

O'Brien knew of Conn, and it was all good, even though Conn was in prison charged with murder. Did this suggest that O'Brien thought Conn was innocent, or that if Conn had really killed the English policeman, this too would be a mark in his favour?

All Brennan said was "I'll do my best. Now, Rory Óg, is there anything you've heard about the other man who was killed at the same time as Liam? The Special Branch man?"

O'Brien just shook his head.

†

Brennan boarded the train for Cambridge the following day and noticed that one of the places along the route was Biggleswade. He considered getting off and having a look at the place, if only to ask somebody what the name meant. But he decided to stick with his plan to arrive in Cambridge early and have a look around before taking his seat in the King's College Chapel to hear one of the greatest choirs in the world. It was a brilliant sunny day, and he walked all over the stunningly beautiful city with its glorious Gothic buildings and lovely bridges over the River Cam.

He could have walked all day, all year for that matter, in awe of the beauty around him, but he had an errand to run for his sister, a bit of research for her upcoming tutorial. He was not about to gate-crash the office of Professor Cedric Mawdsley and ask him to hand over whatever screeds he may have written on the poets of the sixteenth and seventeenth centuries. Molly would be mortified at the very thought.

Brennan did wonder fleetingly what notice, if any, Mawdsley might have taken of the poets' attitudes to the people of Ireland. Milton served under Cromwell, Brennan knew. What was it Molly had said about Spenser? He had advocated starving the Irish into submission to England's will? A man ahead of his time; how gratified Spenser would have been by the advent of the Irish famine in the mid-1800s, which resulted in a million deaths in a country next door to the richest nation on earth. Brennan wondered where Spenser's grave was. Someone should dump a lorry-load of spuds on it with a sign, "The famine is over, Edmund. Some of us are still alive." Just thinking about it got Brennan agitated. But there was no reason to think Mawdsley shared those abhorrent views. Brennan had no intention of appearing at the professor's door, but he would make a stop at the university library to see what was on the shelves in Mawdsley's name. If there was anything of interest, he would make a photocopy for Molly.

It took him a while to determine which of many libraries was the one he wanted, but he eventually found it and walked up to a reference desk with his inquiry. "Excuse me, I'm wondering if you could point me in the right direction. I'm looking for any publications by Professor Mawdsley, particularly on the subject of . . ."

"Who?"

"Cedric Mawdsley, in the English Department."

The librarian shook her head. "You don't mean Cecilia Mawdsley, do you? Of course, she's in the maths department. Or Simon Mawdsley? Economics?"

"No, I'm, em, doing some work on Spenser and Milton, and I was hoping to find something by Cedric Mawdsley. King's College."

"There's nobody by that name on the faculty here. We have a considerable amount of scholarship on Spenser and Milton of course, and I would be happy to assist you."

"No, but thank you all the same. I must have been mistaken about Mawdsley."

Brennan pushed the question to the back of his mind while he basked in the incomparable English sound of Evensong done to perfection by the King's College Choir. But as he boarded the train back to London, the question asserted itself again: Who in the hell was the Cedric Mawdsley we met in London and at the country house?

†

"Why introduce himself and make all that up?" Molly asked when Brennan returned to her Kilburn flat with the news. "Why invite us to the country and then drop us like — help me avoid a potato simile here, Brennan."

"There's no getting around it, sorry."

"I mean, I can see him dumping us after learning of our family history. But why come to us in the first place?"

"Who knows? Maybe his family history is even more controversial than ours, and that's why he misrepresents himself. Another fellow whose family history I wonder about —" Brennan caught himself just in time and substituted a name already known to the shadowy figures at the other end of the listening devices in the flat "— is that poor devil, Liam O'Brien." He gave Molly the eye, and she nodded in resignation.

"What could he have done to bring that upon himself?"

"I don't imagine we'll have the answer to that till the peelers or the tabloids do."

They made small talk for a few minutes until the conversation came to a natural end, and then Molly went into her bedroom Brennan poured himself a glass of orange juice, gulped it down, and went into the room to join her.

"Rory Óg is the fellow I'm wondering about. He doesn't want his name overheard, and he nearly jumped out of his skin when there was a noise in the bar yesterday. I can't help thinking he, like our young relation in Brixton, knows more than he's letting on. But I don't imagine the information will be flowing from him anytime soon. He had loads of drink on him yesterday, and he didn't let anything slip.

"I would like to talk to Mairéad again, though. Liam's widow. There was something she said about a call from London. She said she didn't know anyone in London but Liam may have. We wondered if Kane had made a call. The police have the phone records. Of course there may not be anything of interest at all. And I can't bring myself to ring and interrogate the poor woman."

Terry had no such hesitation. After he arrived and scoffed down a bit of supper, he led the way to a call box in the Kilburn High Road. Brennan went along, but Molly stayed behind. If there was anything of interest, they would let her know. Terry called directory assistance to get the phone number for the Patrick Doyle Landscaping Company and dialled the number. It took a few rings but he got Mairéad O'Brien on the line. He reintroduced himself, asked after her well-being, and then got to the point. He held up the receiver so Brennan could hear the conversation.

"Mairéad, we were wondering again about those telephone records the police showed you."

"Oh, yes?"

"What was it you told us? The police were interested in calls from a London number?"

"Right. Because a call had come in on the day I formally identified Liam's body. And there was a call from the same number a couple of days before he died. And I didn't recognize the number. I never spoke to anyone from London."

"And I remember you saying something about long distance. What was that?"

"Oh, just that the records apparently don't show long distance calls. Or at least that's what I figured out, because I had a call from Dublin, and it didn't appear on those records."

"The call from Dublin was from?"

"Rory Óg, Liam's father, saying he couldn't get out of the hospital that day to come over to England for the identification of Liam."

"Yes, I remember now. Sorry to bother you about this again."

"No, no, you're grand. Is this going to help find who did this, do you think?"

"Probably not, Mairéad, I'm sorry to say. But I didn't want to leave the loose end about the police checking phone calls. It might become clear later what they were looking for."

"I hope so."

"But now that I think of it, you and Liam must have made long distance calls to one another, between Chelmsford and where is it? Kilmacthomas back in Ireland?"

"Oh, yes, we did. And of course I rang England from home, trying to reach him, after, you know . . . when I didn't know he was dead, wondering where he was. I didn't leave any messages on his answerphone because I knew I'd just try again later."

"But you didn't see any record of those calls to or from Kilmacthomas."

"Oh, Terry, I can't remember now. I had lost the plot entirely by that time. I may have seen them and not copped on. Or they may not have shown me any records of calls in the weeks before he died. The earliest one I remember seeing was from London just those two days before the murder."

"Thank you, sweetheart. I apologize for bringing this all up with you again. If we ever hear anything that could conceivably help in the search for the killer, we'll let you know right away."

"Thanks, Terry. Bye. God bless."

Terry replaced the receiver and said, "Of course the telephone company can provide records of long distance calls. She's too flummoxed to remember whether she saw Kilmacthomas or not. But we don't care about that, Brennan. The point for us is that she didn't see anything from Dublin even though she got a call from her father-in-law on the day of the viewing."

"And the call she got that day came not from Dublin but from

London, from the same number that called two days before Liam was killed. So Rory Óg O'Brien was in England, in London, on the day of the viewing. And he was in London two days before all hell broke loose, including the murder of his son, and he didn't want anyone to know."

Chapter XXII

We're children of a fighting race
That never yet has known disgrace.

Peadar Kearney, "The Soldier's Song"
(*Amhrán na bhFiann*, the Irish National Anthem)

When they returned to the flat, Molly said she had had a brief chat over the phone—brief indeed, Brennan was sure—with Tess, and Tess had invited them over for a visit. Terry said he wanted to stay in to see a BBC television documentary on the training of British Commonwealth air crews in Canada during the Second World War. So Brennan and Molly headed out. They stopped at a bakery to pick up a few treats for Tess on their way to the tube station.

Tess lived in a tiny studio flat near the King's Cross station. She gave Molly a hug when they arrived and thanked them for the items from the bakery. She took them out of the box and arranged them in three rows of four on a plate. Brennan had never seen such an orderly living space; everything was in its place, and everything was immaculately clean. Tess's thick red hair was loose around her shoulders, damp and smelling of shampoo. She was nearly three months pregnant, Brennan knew, but if there was anything showing, it was covered by a loose Oxford shirt.

"Come in and sit *dyne* while I serve the drinks. I've made cocoa. Is that all right?"

"Perfect," Molly said, and Brennan nodded his agreement.

"Have yez seen Conn lately?" Tess asked them.

Brennan described his latest trip to Brixton, and Molly said she had had a quick visit the week before.

"I haven't been out there in a while. He doesn't want me there. Must think it's bad scran to the baby or something, to have all those bad fellows eyeing me. And after that scene with the warder Albert — Conn said he never ever saw that lovely man again."

They turned the conversation to inconsequential things while Tess set out mugs and saucers and poured the cocoa. The table was tiny, and they all crowded around it in their chairs. "Not much room in this wee place, but Conn doesn't want me moving into his flat; he worries about security there because he's so infamous! When he gets out, we'll find a nice place for the four of us."

"The four of you?" Molly asked. "Is someone else going to move in with you?"

Her mother? Brennan wondered. Or a member of Conn's active service unit of the IRA? What kind of a life would that be for a young married couple?

But Tess's hazel eyes were sparkling in a way that bespoke not mother, not IRA gunman, but . . . "You're the first to hear my news. I'm having twins!"

"Jesus, Mary, and Joseph, that's brilliant news, Tess!" Molly squeezed herself out of the chair to reach over and put her arms around the mother-to-be.

"Lovely, Tess!" said Brennan. "There haven't been twins in the family for two generations. We'll all be looking forward to their arrival."

"I haven't announced it till now. I'm superstitious about things like that. Name it and it disappears. That's why I haven't bought any nursery things yet. Complete nonsense, I know, but anyway . . ."

"What did Conn have to say to that?" Molly asked.

Tess looked embarrassed. "I haven't told him yet. I didn't want to give him the news over the phone because, well, I want to see his face when he hears it. I want to know whether he'll be happy or thrown into a panic. Though I've never seen him in a panic about anything. And whatever he would say to me on the phone in the prison with all that lot listening in would not be his true reaction. And I really can't see how it would be much better sitting across from him in that manky old visiting area."

"There will be lots of time for him to enjoy the news, Tess. Surely there will be a break in the case, and Lorna MacIntyre will be able to get him out of there."

"He didn't do it! And he's stuck out there, and his life has come to a stop, and we can't get on with our plans. He said we might have to have a jailhouse wedding like, what were their names?"

"Grace Gifford and Joseph Plunkett," Molly replied. "They were married in the chapel at Kilmainham Gaol, hours be—" She stopped speaking, mortified.

"I know, Molly, hours before he was taken out and shot for his part in the Rising."

Molly reached over and covered Tess's hand with her own. "Conn will walk out of there on his own two legs, Tess, and you'll have a splendid wedding. We'll all be in attendance."

"But how long does it take to get a trial over here? I really want us to be married before the children are born, and they're due in just over six months' time. If it takes months to get a trial, and even then we won't know if . . . But what am I saying? I sound like one of those bubble heads in that fashion magazine, fretting about the wedding ceremony. That's the least of our troubles. I should be thinking of Conn and our children and what is going to happen if the court decides to punish Conn for somebody else's crime, if they keep him in jail forever. How could I raise two children here in London, where everything is so dear, and me having to work and my family not here? But I couldn't leave Conn and take the kids away from him!"

Brennan could practically see the hope leaching out of her as she contemplated a dismal future.

"Somebody else killed the copper," Molly declared, sounding for all the world as if she were the judge and jury and had come to a verdict of not guilty after all the facts were in and the real killer unmasked. "Conn will be out, and he'll be your man and a father to his children. It will happen, Tess."

Tess pushed herself up from her chair. "But you didn't come over to see me throw a wobbler."

"If that's a wobbler, Conn can look forward to a long life of peace and calm and good humour with his beloved wife."

"Thank you, Brennan. What I'm looking forward to, beyond having Conn back in my life of course, is meeting more of his family. If they're all like you and Molly, and Shelmalier, I'll be blessed. What say we get into some of those chocolate things you brought me?"

They got into the chocolate things and drank more cocoa and kept the talk away from Brixton Prison and murder trials.

"What work do you do, Tess?" Brennan asked her.

"I do printing and engraving. I work in a shop near here. My father had a shop in Ardoyne in Belfast, and he trained me in the job, but then I had to take other work when he, em, lost the business. And I wanted to move over here to be with Conn anyway, so."

"What happened to the business in Belfast?" Molly asked.

"Got bombed."

"How dreadful. I'm sorry to hear that, Tess. Was anyone hurt?"

"No, they did it at night."

"They?"

"Well, at first I thought it was the Huns that did it, us being Catholics and all. But turned out it wasn't the Prods at all." She looked over at her guests. "I shouldn't be talking like this, calling the Prods Huns and all that. I don't label them all that way, I really don't. I'm not in Belfast now and I have to learn to watch my mouth. But you, well, you're almost family. If my man ever comes home, and the wedding ever happens!"

"Consider us family now," Brennan said. "I know we think that way about you."

"Really? Thank you!" Her eyes were glistening, and she blinked a couple of times. "I appreciate you saying that. It gets a little, well, lonely at times. All I do is work and come home here. Can hardly be out in the bars and on the piss in my condition! And I'm not one for the drink anyway. Conn will tell you that. But, what was I saying?" She looked at Molly.

"You were telling us about your father's shop."

"Aye, the printing business. It was bad enough before the bomb. It was a struggle for my da to keep the business going. Hard times in Belfast as well you know. And then some fellows threw a bomb in the front window of the shop, and half-destroyed the place."

"How awful, Tess."

"It was. Thanks be to God, nobody was hurt. It ended up all right because we got money from the insurance company, and that put us to rights again because my da did not have to replace everything. He just made the business smaller."

Brennan asked, "And you say it wasn't the Loyalists? So it was . . ."

She cast a look behind her shoulder as if, even this far from Ardoyne, her words might reach the wrong pair of ears. "The 'RA," she said.

"Why do you think the IRA targeted your father, Tess?" Molly asked gently.

"He wouldn't talk about it."

Brennan was not sure whether to ask, but he did. "What did Conn have to say?"

"He was here in London. He didn't have anything to do with it!"

"Oh, I know that, pet. I just wondered, you know, what his take was on it."

Tess now looked as if she was sorry she had brought the whole thing to light, but she responded, "He told me he'd go over to Belfast and talk to some people, and I guess he did, because when he came back he told me my da had nothing to worry about from then on. And he said not to talk about it. To anyone." She looked warily at her new family.

"You can be sure we won't say a word, Tess," Brennan reassured her. "Not even to Conn."

"Amen," said Molly. "Now, Tess, why don't we make a plan for the whole crowd of us — the Burkes of London — to get together for dinner somewhere nice? And, if you want to, you can make your announcement about the twins. But of course that's up to you. You may want to give the news to Conn before then, but again, up to you. So why don't we think of a place, and I'll call round this week and set it up?"

"Aye, that would be lovely, Molly."

The two women talked restaurants and menus, and Brennan's mind drifted to Belfast, to bombs exploding and glass flying, and silence in the smoking aftermath.

†

"That poor man," Molly said to Brennan as they rode back to Kilburn on the tube. "I wonder what he did to deserve that."

"We'll get him on the batter at the wedding and ask him how he wrong-footed himself with the Provos. Of course half the wedding guests may be IRA themselves, so it may be a subject to be avoided."

"Disturbing that Conn would know who to talk to about it over in Belfast."

"Disturbing but not surprising. I believe him, by the way, when he says he's not a man for lobbing bombs. He told me that himself, and he said the same thing to Terry the night they fought side by side in Belfast. Though that hardly jibes with him knowing enough about the Westminster Abbey bomb plot to have his hands on the car of the cop who was trying to stop it."

"I'm stating the obvious here, Brennan, when I say we are missing huge pieces of this picture. But I hope you're sending up heaps of prayers that Conn will be a free man by the time Tess gives birth to their twins. Can't you just see him, a great big grin on his face, showing off those babies to the world? Her having to lug the dear little things into the Brixton Prison visiting room just doesn't bear thinking about."

"I've called in all the angels and saints; I've got them on the case. I wonder how serious Lorna MacIntyre is about pursuing her wild geese defence, the theory that somebody paid a mercenary to do away with Richard Heath."

"Let's hope she comes up with a Plan B. The mercenary theory might be a bit hard to sell to a jury, given that the detective was shot at a time and place so closely connected to the planned IRA bombing of the Cromwell statue and Westminster Abbey."

"But if the killer was an IRA hit man, he may have been tracking Heath's movements. And a man with IRA connections may well have been aware of the bomb plot, and knew that would be a particularly good day to follow him and take him out. It would look, well, the way it looks, like a hit on a cop committed in the midst of a terrorist attack. Of course we go through all these mental acrobatics and we keep coming back to the one fact that is known: Conn was there. So he knows who did it."

"How much do we know about the timing, though, Brennan? How much time may have elapsed between the instant when Heath stopped his car, or was forced to stop, and the instant he was shot? Could Conn have been there long enough to put his prints on the car, grabbing the door handle, for example, and then leaving before the shooting? Or was the killer wearing a balaclava, and Conn truly has no idea who he was?"

"We've been through all this before, Mol."

"I know, I know."

"I've got an idea: let's ask him. Oh, right, our bold boyo isn't talking."

"Brennan, I, em, spoke to John."

"Detective Sergeant Chambers."

"Yes."

"What sort of cheer was he in this time?"

"He was fine. He apologized for what he called his 'outburst' in Bath. Said again that he's been under stress with all he has to deal with at work. Didn't allude to the fact that much of what he deals with at work is havoc caused by Paddies like us."

"Well, that's a good sign, I suppose."

"But, em, I told him about the hit man theory."

"You told Special Branch about our theory that one of the people Detective Sergeant Heath had arrested and sent to jail got out and hired an IRA hit man to pull off the murder and make it look like an IRA assassination. Or that someone in Heath's personal life did this to avenge an old hurt."

"Right."

"I imagine Special Branch needs a good hearty laugh once in a while to relieve the stress of the job. Yer man must love you even more now, Mol. The way to a man's heart is through his —"

"He didn't laugh it off."

"He didn't?"

"No. He stared at me. It was as if he was trying to decide how to react. And no doubt he was."

"No doubt."

"Bear with me here, Brennan. He virtually confirmed it."

"What?"

"Oh, not the bit about Heath having a list of enemies. To hear Chambers tell it, Heath was a hail fellow, well met. Splendid chap. But the hit man? There's something to it."

"With IRA connections."

"I didn't even say IRA when I brought up the subject. But he did."

"Well, when you think of it, he is Special Branch. And he probably thinks the worst of the 'RA, as a man in his position would do. Understandably. So the idea of an IRA man taking money to kill people would not be unthinkable."

"Not only thinkable, but something already on the police blotter, by the sound of things."

"Lorna MacIntyre and her team presented a whole case with this as the centrepiece. So it stands to reason Special Branch would have caught wind of it."

"I think John Chambers knows exactly who this man is, Brennan."

"Oh?"

"Yes. He couched it all in general terms. 'We are aware of an individual who goes in and out of the country, and there seems to be an association between his travels and certain activities.' Well, you get the idea. Copspeak. Trying to say something without actually saying it. I couldn't tell whether he was trying to protect his information, or trying to cover up the fact that he doesn't have enough information to act on."

"So, how did you reach John Chambers to ask him about this? Sitting outside the flat again, was he?"

"No. He rang me at my office, to make his apologies and all that. And we met in a park outside London."

"This is sounding serious. Should I be refreshing myself on the protocol for mixed marriages? Prods and Taigs, cops and robbers? I'm assuming you'll want me to preside at the wedding."

"Preside at *this*, you gobshite! And may ravens gnaw on your neck."

"All right, all right, I apologize, darlin'. What else did Chambers have to say?"

"He warned me to be careful."

"I'd like to think you would not be in immediate danger from some shadowy mercenary who no doubt commands big money for his services."

"No, I'd probably be low on his list of targets. And anyone I know would be too poor or too cheap to pay the fee to have me offed! But a warning might be in order if I have this information and I get buckled some night at Hannigan's and start blathering about it. Or if, God forbid, this is a person I actually know or have met."

Chapter XXIII

Molly wasted no time getting down to the planning of the dinner for Tess. As soon as she got home, she began working on the guest list. That necessitated a call to her estranged husband. She turned the volume down on the BBC and made the call.

"Neville, how was your trip? Wales, was it? Good. Is Finbarr there? We're having a little get-together for Tess, and I'm hoping he'll attend. Tess. Conn's girlfriend. They're getting married. I told you that. No, but if he isn't sprung, it won't be the first time one of our people had to have his wedding in the lockup. But I'm confident he'll be released in plenty of time for the . . . Neville, I don't want to hear it. Just tell Finbarr to come round and . . ." There was silence and then, "What are you saying? I do keep track of our son, as I'm hoping you do when he's with you. Now, where is he, so I can make the arrangements? I don't understand. He's at your place this term, and you told me he went to spend a few days with Davey and his family. Now—" Silence again, then Molly could no longer keep the alarm out of her voice. "Since when? What did they say?"

She turned to Brennan, her face ashen. "Neville says when he got back from Wales he rang Davey's mother, and it turns out Finbarr hadn't spent even one night there, ever. Now Neville tells me this wasn't the first time Finbarr claimed to be staying with Davey. So Neville was going to call me today to ask what was going on."

Distracted, she replaced the receiver without another word to her husband. In the heat of the moment, Brennan had forgotten that the phones were tapped. No point in reminding Molly right now that someone in the Security Service had just been put on notice that ex-prisoner Molly Burke's hothead of a son was among the missing. He didn't want to provide them with any more personal information, so he turned the radio back to its usual volume and said, "You're shaking. Why don't you go lie down, and we'll try to look at the situation calmly."

She understood why he was directing her to the bedroom so she went without another word. Brennan decided then and there in favour of Terry's plan to stage a scene for the benefit of the listeners, raising the fear that their phone might be tapped and hiring someone to check the place out. Terry was not at home, and Brennan thought he knew just where to find him.

In the meantime, he and Molly huddled in her room and spoke softly.

"All right. When did you last see him?"

"A week or so ago. He stopped by for a visit. You and Terry weren't here. But Terry had left the names of all the family in New York, and estimated sizes for the T-shirts, you know, the Cromwell band tour shirts. So Finbarr and I had a bit of fun about that. He is going to order the shirts. Or he was . . ."

"Oh, we'll all have the shirts, don't worry. What else did he have to say?"

"Nothing but his usual."

"Which is what?"

"School is a waste of time. He'd rather be working on the ships, seeing the world."

"How is he doing in school?"

"Working below his potential, his reports always say, and it's true. He is just as clever as Shelmalier, but I suspect he feels she has cornered the market on academic achievement in the family. There's room for more than one, Finbarr! We've tried to make that point, not in so many words, of course."

"Is this something that would make him . . ."

"Run away? I can't imagine why. The worst that would happen from his point of view is that Neville and I would make a strong case for finishing school. He only has one year left to go. But we wouldn't use physical force on him! If he left school, he would always have the option to return later."

"Is there anything else that might motivate him to bolt?"

"He and Neville don't get on, Brennan, haven't done for years. Finbarr tends to come here when the situation flares up. Neville resents that, understandably, but . . ."

"But he hasn't come here this time. Tell me, though, what it is that puts them at odds with one another."

"Well, education and achievement are part of it. Neville has high expectations. Of both the kids. Over the years, Neville has turned into quite a demanding father, which accounts partly for why we separated. And partly for the way Finbarr acts out sometimes. Shelmalier just lets it run off her back. 'Get stuffed, Dad,' is her response. But she is a high achiever anyway, in spite of him as much as because of him. Finbarr is a more fiery personality and can't let it go. And Neville is fully aware that Finbarr does not aspire to be just like his father when he grows up; he wants to be like Conn! This is all very painful for Neville, though he would rather be eaten alive by rat-tailed maggots, or even blackballed from his club, than admit it. Fathers and sons, Brennan. You and Declan had a few major rows in your day."

"There's no denying it."

"It wasn't because you were a slacker in school. You managed to earn top marks even though you were . . ."

"A hotheaded young arsehole with a fondness for drink."

"And for sex, drugs, and rock and roll. But look at you now, Father."

"I'm off the drugs at least."

"I won't follow up on that any further, darling."

Brennan could see the effort she was making to keep the conversation light. She couldn't keep it up.

"I am his mother, Brennan, and I have allowed this to happen! He hates staying with Neville, but I persuaded him to go there because I didn't think it was right for me to have him to myself all the time, leaving his father out of things. And now look what I've done. Let him out of my sight so long he's missing, and I didn't even know! I'll never forgive myself—"

"Molly. You are not responsible for whatever it is that Finbarr has decided to do."

"I don't think he would just run off without contacting me. I'm afraid . . ." Her voice gave out on her, and a few seconds passed before she could go on. "I'm terrified for him, Bren. He's long had a fascination for a certain crowd of, well, some of our people who go way beyond the bounds of what I'd call acceptable protest."

"He's involved with the IRA here in London, is that what you're telling me?"

"I don't know, Brennan. I always thought it was more of a 'wannabe' situation. I know Conn keeps an eye on him. But Finbarr seems to be a little too admiring of this fellow . . . this Kane. We saw him at Janey Mack's one night."

"I remember. It was like an old Western movie where the man in the black hat walks in and all the rest of the hombres fall silent. The honky-tonk piano stops playing. It was that kind of moment."

"Yes. You could feel the chill of fear throughout the room. From the little I've heard, it's well deserved. Yet in spite of this, or maybe because of it, even our Conn got up and followed his bidding to a secret meeting."

"I noticed Conn kept Finbarr from following the rest of the crowd."

"Oh, Finbarr was wild about that. And now Conn is not around to keep my son in line. Perhaps a trip out to Brixton is in order, to ask Conn what he thinks might . . ."

Brennan shook his head. "I doubt Conn would enlighten us. But I can tell you this much. He warned me to keep Finbarr away from Kane."

"Oh my God. I know, from things I've heard, that Kane is an enforcer. He metes out punishment to those suspected of being informers."

"I don't imagine Finbarr is in that category."

"No, but informers aren't the only ones to be disciplined. Anyone who runs afoul of Kane's group of hard men from Dublin and Belfast, anyone who cocks things up . . . This has me petrified, Brennan. I've even heard, on good authority, that a couple of people have disappeared. Vanished into thin air."

"This is getting us nowhere, Molly. Finbarr is out there someplace. Terry and I will track him down. I'm going out to fetch Terry right now." He said in an even softer tone, "Play along with whatever foolishness you hear from us when we come in." He mimed a person listening through a set of headphones.

Brennan hoofed it over to the Kilburn High Road and into Hannigan's. Sure enough, there was his brother, leaning over the bar, pint in hand, talking to a couple of old fellows who were giving him their undivided attention. Well, whatever the tale was, the old gents would have to wait for the punchline. Terry was needed at home.

They worked out their lines on the walk to the flat. When they came through the door, Terry staggering in a fit of sudden and convenient drunkenness, they continued an argument that had, supposedly, been raging all the way home.

"You're off your head," Brennan said.

"The fellow I was talking to swore on his mother's grave, Bren. His flat was bugged!"

"I thought you said it was his brother's place."

"It was, the brother. And he was just an errand boy. He wasn't even IR—"

"Shut the fuck up."

"See? You believe it too!"

"You've been watching too many movies. Ever hear the word 'paranoid'?"

"Oh yeah? Then how come you're talking in a whisper? Listen to me, Brennan. They're after Conn. They'll have his place bugged and maybe other places he goes. And there's only one way to find out."

"And what's that? Shout into the lampshade and wait to hear if there's a peeler squealing somewhere down the line?"

Molly emerged then. "What's the matter with the pair of you? Terry, you're mangled here. Maybe you should give Hannigan's a miss for a couple of nights."

"No, I'm not. I only had a few pints. I'm just saying—" he stretched up and yelled at the overhead light "— Mr. Bond, we'd like a word!"

By noon the following day, the problem was solved. They consulted the phone directory and found a home security outfit; a man came to Molly's, performed an electronic sweep of some kind, and removed two devices, one from the phone and another from a picture frame on the wall beside the dining table.

✝

Shelmalier came down from Oxford after her lectures on Friday, to comfort her mother and offer any assistance she could provide.

She spent the morning with Molly, then went out and did a bit of shopping for lunch. She made them a delicious meal of lamb burgers with sweet onion and feta cheese. She suggested a walk afterwards but Molly did not want to leave the flat, in other words, the phone. Terry said he would stay with her, so Shelmalier and Brennan headed out. They decided to take the tube in to the city centre and stroll there.

Their walk brought them to Trafalgar Square, where Brennan once again got his great-building fix, and they entertained themselves by watching the thousands of people passing through the square. A man wearing a pair of fins, goggles, and a snorkel—and nothing else—stood and saluted Admiralty Gate, then Nelson's Column, then leapt into one of the fountains.

"Welcome to London, Father Burke."

"Thank you, my dear. I see your admiral is still standing."

"Is there any reason why he shouldn't be?"

"He got toppled over in Dublin some years back."

"Destroyed as a long-delayed act of revenge by the French?"

"Destroyed, yes. But, em, not by the French."

"I know. I had it sussed."

"Shelley, where do you think your brother is?"

"If I were any more superstitious than I am, I would think he had come to a horrible end somewhere as a direct result of my uncharitable remarks about him during the course of your visit here. You must think me the worst sister in the world, and deservedly so."

"Not at all, pet. We're family. We have to talk things out from time to time and, if we're having trouble with one another, family is the best place to let it out. You said nothing out of line. In fact, I thought you showed considerable restraint!"

"Thank you, Brennan. I'm terrified for him. And for Mum. I always suspected she would be like a Spartan mother to Finbarr, her being a rebel and him heading down that same road. You know, seeing her son go off to war and saying, 'Come home with your shield, or on it.' But she's gutted about him being gone. She's putting on a brave front around me, but I'm not taken in." Shelmalier reached out and put her arms around Brennan, and he held her in a long embrace.

"I know," he said, "but Terry and I are on the case. We'll have that little bundle of joy back to you so soon you'll be saying, 'What was the hurry?'"

"I only wish we could skip ahead to that day, when I have him before me and can give him a swift kick up the arse for putting us all through this."

"First step in the search is to ask you what you know. As much as you and Finbarr differ in outlook . . ."

"Uncle Brennan, forgive me for saying so, but nothing I've ever heard about you would have led me to expect such delicacy, such tact from you!"

"I am so meek, my dear, that I shall turn down my inheritance of the earth when it comes in, and will just spend my time picking wildflowers to give away on the street corner. So, as I was saying, even though you and your brother regularly go at it tooth and nail, he probably tells you things he would not tell his mother. Something like me not telling my own mother that yours was in prison."

"You didn't tell Gran?"

"It would only worry her, as they say. But more importantly, it would have set my oul fella on the warpath. Perhaps literally."

"I am descended from a long, long line of Irish rebels, aren't I? Maybe I'm the odd one out. Well, obviously I am. It's my English side. Finbarr is the one who fits the mould. He's exactly the son the family would want."

"You are exactly the daughter we'd all want, Shelley. Make no mistake about it."

"Thank you, Brennan." It was the first time Brennan had ever seen her close to tears. "Finbarr doesn't tell me much. Probably because he knows how I'd react. I know he is involved with Irish Republican elements here in London, but I've never met or even seen any of them. Apart from our Conn, of course. And I should say here, Brennan, that I understand their point of view. I know about the injustices that were committed and are at times still being committed against the Irish people. I even understand why Ireland stayed neutral in the Second

World War—not surprising, since the Irish had fought a bloody war against England twenty years before. It's not that I don't sympathize. And I respect Mum for standing up for her beliefs on the subject. Conn too, though, with him, I'm not sure how far he goes beyond what I'd be able to accept. But still I admire him for fighting for a cause he so deeply believes in. And it helps that he is so full of personality. Any time I've spent an evening in his company, I'm ready to go out and smuggle guns into the country under my coat. I'm also, if I've had a few drinks with him, ready to get up on stage and belt out his repertoire of rebel songs. It's my heritage, after all, well, half of it. The other half, my father, don't even ask what he says about 'the bloody Irish.' How he and Mum ever got together, I can't imagine."

"I must have been too scuttered at their wedding to notice if there were any ethnic tensions that early in the game. With your father going on about the 'bloody Irish' and your brother railing against the 'feckin' English,' there must have been some unholy rows at the dinner table at your place."

"Oh, Dad was never that direct. His comments were always offstage, and I just happened to overhear them once in a while. Though Finbarr loved to needle him by getting up from dinner and saying he had to attend a 'council of war.' Or he'd start speaking like someone from the docklands in Dublin. And aside from the irritation he meant it to cause Dad, there's nothing wrong with that, necessarily; Finbarr is as much Irish as he is English. But, well, I'll leave it to you to decide what to make of it. And, related to that, he talked a lot about moving to Ireland when he finished school. Or, preferably from his point of view, before he finished. I don't know whether he meant to go to the South or to the North, where he could try to push the Brits off Irish soil."

"Maybe that's exactly what he's done, gone to Ireland."

"I don't care where he's gone, as long as he's all right. The idea of what might have happened to him, with these murders and beatings and what not . . ."

Brennan could see his niece struggling to maintain her composure.

"I imagine he's gone off on an adventure or a mission of some kind, Shelley. Your mum is calling everyone she can think of to see if there's been any word of him. If she doesn't hear anything, Terry and I will board a plane for Ireland and make some inquiries over there."

"You certainly got more than you bargained for when you left New York!"

Shelmalier gazed around her for a minute or so. A group of very young schoolchildren in uniform trooped into the square, escorted by a teacher. "It isn't polite to stare, children," the teacher admonished them when she caught them gawping at the naked man cavorting in the fountain. "Now raise your eyes to Admiral Nelson. He is the object of our lesson today. A man who, for us as Britons, embodies everything we should strive to be."

"Thank Christ it isn't Cromwell," Brennan muttered.

"He may be next. The day is young. Do you ever get the desire to return to Ireland, Brennan? I mean, you spent your early years there. Do you miss it?"

"I do. And I've often thought of returning. But with one thing and another cropping up, I've never made the move. I go there as often as I can, though. And if you think there's a chance Finbarr headed that way, I may be there again, sooner than anticipated."

"You know, in spite of Finbarr's attitude, when I spoke to Edward today he was the soul of kindness. Reassuring me that Finbarr is probably fine, asking what he can do to help. Of course the whole history of what Edward went through in Northern Ireland, fighting the IRA, is too fraught to place in front of someone like Finbarr. But if Finbarr could sit down with Boy and Amelia and hear their stories of how Britain fought in World War Two, standing up against the Nazis, it might give him some perspective. Boy has some sort of club or group of veterans he sees, people who fought in various wars and lived to tell about it. If Finbarr ever grows up . . . Oh, God, I shouldn't have said that. What if . . . I've made him out to be such a, well, such an arsehole. But it's just about his politics, his endorsement of the "physical force tradition," as he calls it. In other ways, he is a delightful brother. Honestly. He's loads of fun most of the time, and he was forever dropping whatever he was doing to help me do this or that, or get me out of a scrape. And I did the same for him. Though you'd never know it from the way I bang on and on about him. I'll never forgive myself . . ."

"He's fine, Shelley. He's up to no good maybe, but he's alive and kicking and effing and blinding somewhere. And we'll find him."

"I know. I'm sure you're right."

"You mentioned this group of veterans when we spoke before. What was the connection with the murdered cop? I remember that Heath's name came up. There was something about his brother?"

"Clarence Heath. I only heard about it recently. And only a few tantalizing bits at that. The Hathaways were not about to discuss the Heath murder with me, the accused man's first cousin once removed, sitting at the table eating their pudding. But eventually it came up. Clarence was Richard Heath's older brother. Their father was in the army during the war, so the father used to attend these get-togethers with Boy Hathaway and the others. They have a ceremonial sword dating back to the days of the mediaeval knights, and they set that up on a table wherever they're meeting. A little ritual of some sort. Anyway, occasionally, Clarence would accompany his father and, when the father died, Clarence still dropped in once in a while. Clarence wasn't military but was a police officer like Richard. Not Special Branch, just a copper on the beat.

"Anyway, something happened with Clarence on the job years ago. Boy said there were different versions of the story, but they all revolved around one central fact. It was a domestic dispute in one of the council estates, a husband beating his wife, same old thing. Clarence was on duty and responded to the situation. While he was there, the husband pulled a gun, and the wife ended up dead on the floor. Clarence had forged ahead without his partner so, by the time the other copper got there, it was all over, and it was Clarence's word against that of the husband. The husband's version of events was a jumble, changing from one day to the next. There was an internal inquiry and they found no evidence that Clarence acted improperly. But his own brother, Richard, put it about that Clarence panicked and dove behind the sofa, or under the bed, or used the woman as a shield, or something like that. The Heath family of course tried to keep the whole thing quiet, but Richard had no such qualms. Went about calling Clarence names such as Lord Clarence of Bedsheetshire, or Clarence-Behind-The-Skirts. It was dreadful. Amelia heard that Clarence had attempted suicide at one point. That's all I know."

"What the hell is wrong with people? Years of study and theological training, and hearing confessions, and I still don't have the answer to that."

"People are beastly. Or at least many of them are. This whole thing was very distressing to Boy Hathaway, particularly given the situation with Edward. Boy will not sit still and let anyone throw the word 'coward' around. 'Poor devil,' he'd say about Clarence, 'didn't have a chance with Richard Heath as his brother. He should have run the bastard through with our ceremonial sword. We wouldn't even have washed the blood off it.'"

"Offers a whole new perspective on Detective Sergeant Heath, doesn't it?" Brennan said. "If he treated his own brother like that, imagine what other enemies he might have made."

Chapter XXIV

'Twas down by the glenside, I met an old woman.
A-plucking young nettles, she ne'er saw me coming.
I listened awhile to the song she was humming,
Glory O, Glory O, to the bold Fenian men.

Peadar Kearney, "Down by the Glenside"

"Brennan, I'm going with you. Obviously. My son is missing. I've run out of leads here, so he must have followed through on his threats to shag off to Ireland. I don't know how I'll ever come to terms with the fact that he would run away, that I didn't take the threats seriously, that I failed him so utterly . . . But what if he didn't run? What if—"

"You're not coming with us. If Finbarr is in Ireland, Terry and I will find him. If we have to make the rounds all over the island, it will be too hard on you. Stay in London with Shelmalier; it will be better for both of you that way. And you have to be here if he calls."

Molly was not happy about it. How could she be? But whether she stayed in England or undertook the journey to Ireland, she would be going through hell until her son was found. A directionless and frustrating journey around Ireland would only add to the pain and distress.

"I'll give you a couple of pictures of him to show around." She went into her room and came back with an envelope of photos.

Brennan looked through them and had to stifle a laugh. There was Terry with his middle finger raised to the statue of Oliver Cromwell.

"Do you want to sort these out before I take them?"

She waved her hand at them. It was a pointless distraction so he took the whole collection. Once again he tried to reassure her, then he and Terry left the flat.

Terry had booked the flight to Dublin for that Friday evening, and they landed in Ireland's capital just over an hour after leaving British soil.

Their first stop—the first stop for any member of the Burke family visiting Dublin—was Christy Burke's pub on Mountjoy Street. Christy's name was stamped in gold letters on a band of black that ran around the cream-coloured building. Christy, Brennan's grandfather, had bought the place in 1919. It had served as a drinking hole and, at times, a hiding place for the Old IRA during the war against the British from 1919 to 1921.

Christy's son, Finn, had worked the bar alongside the old man until his death in 1970, and Finn took over then as owner. He usually worked the bar himself and today was no exception. If, as had often been said, Brennan was at times a stony-faced individual, his uncle Finn was made of granite. He gave no sign of recognition when his two nephews walked in. What made the man even harder to read was the dark glasses he always wore, day and night, in or out of doors.

"Finn, a couple of pints for a pair of weary travellers."

Finn nodded, said, "Lads," and began the two-part pour for each of the glasses.

When the Guinness had settled, Brennan took a sip and sighed with pleasure. Was there a pint anywhere in the world to equal this?

"The blessings of God on you, Finn."

"And on you, Father. Count yourself blessed as well, Terrence."

"*Go raibh maith agat*, Finn."

"Now what brings you boys my way?"

They told him about Molly's missing son, and their hope that he might be located in Ireland. But Finn, who was known to be in the know about Republican matters in the South and in the North of Ireland, had not heard a whisper about Finbarr.

Brennan and Terry told their uncle a bit about the young fellow and filled him in about their parents and other family members in New York. Finn gave them a rundown on the Dublin contingent. Everyone was doing nicely except their great aunt Rosaleen; she had not been well, and Finn thought that seeing Father Burke would do her a world of good.

"I'd love to see her."

"Grand. I'll ring and let her know." Finn picked up the phone and dialled. 'Hi yeh, Bronagh. How's she doing today? Oh, she'll be fit to be tied about that. She'll be hearing the roar of the crowd through her window, and her not able to go and watch it." Finn said to Terry and Brennan, "I've got Rosaleen's nurse here. The doctor told Rosa she's not able for walking over to Croke Park and up into the stands for tomorrow's match against Limerick. And, what's that? She had to miss a performance of *Shadow of a Gunman* last week at the Gate Theatre. Put her on for me, can you, Bronagh?" Next thing Brennan heard was his uncle reciting poetry. Mangan, was it? "'O my dark Rosaleen, do not sigh, do not weep! The priests are on the ocean green; they march along the deep.' They are indeed. Would I lie to you? One, at least. Father Brennan Burke is on his way to you. Good, my dear. See you Sunday, and Brennan will see you sooner."

So Brennan had a quick smoke, finished his pint, and set off on his errand of mercy. That was fine with him; he had always liked old Rosaleen. Terry elected to stay at the bar.

Brennan made a stop at the hotel to change into his clerical suit and collar and headed out on foot to see the youngest sister of his grandfather, the late Christy Burke. Rosaleen Burke McCarthy was in her early nineties. You could see the iconic Croke Park stadium from the pavement in front of her north side house, and he knew from past experience that one could indeed hear the crowds when a

Gaelic football or hurling match was on. When Brennan arrived, a nurse opened the door and greeted him. "You must be Bronagh," he said and introduced himself. She led him to the old lady's bedroom, announced his arrival, and withdrew.

A frail-looking Rosaleen was lying in her bed, thin grey hair fanned out on her pillow and a pair of out-sized eyeglasses skewed across her face. She was hooked up to some sort of apparatus that was delivering fluids into her arm. Neither of them mentioned it.

"Brennan, aren't you a fine man now, and very much a priestly man in your appearance. It does me good to see you."

He bent and took her free hand, and kissed her on the cheek. "Rosaleen, I'm happy to be here. What can I get for you, anything?"

She motioned him to come close again. "Send yer one out for something. A loaf of bread. No, a box of chocolates from Butler's across town. And when she clears the threshold, pour me a glass of Tullamore's, would you?"

"Em, are you allowed to mix your fluids in that way, Rosa?"

"I'm ninety-one years old, Brennan. I can sit out in the sun all day, or the rain or the snow. I can smoke twenty fags a day, sniff cocaine, or shoot heroin into my veins. I can tattoo an image of King Billy on my arse and sit on it till the moon turns blue. I can lounge around in Christy's bar, God rest him, and sink pints from morning to night, if I so choose. Doesn't make any difference now. You'll find the whiskey and the glasses on a side table in the sitting room. You'll find me here when you've poured me a generous helping, and one for yourself."

"Yes, dear."

Brennan handed the nurse some money for chocolate for herself and for her patient and waited until she, reluctantly, left the property. Then he did his great aunt's bidding and went into the sitting room. It could have been a set for a film on Irish life. There was a picture of the Pope, and another of John F. Kennedy speaking in New Ross, County Wexford, a few months before his assassination. There was a print of the famous painting of the Mass Rock, a winter scene with a priest in his vestments raising the sacred host over a rock used as an altar in penal times when the Mass was outlawed. The faithful knelt in the snow. A party of scouts was approaching from the right, warning of the Redcoats, the British, advancing on them with rifles in hand. On another wall was a photo of the Dublin All-Ireland Gaelic football team of 1983. Breaking with these themes was a large colour newspaper photo of a dashing man in sunglasses. He looked familiar. Brennan peered at the picture and saw that it was the Italian film star, Marcello Mastroianni. She had an eye for a handsome face, had Rosaleen. Brennan poured them both a glass of Tullamore Dew, returned to Rosaleen's bedside, and pulled up a chair. She was sitting up, and her glasses had been righted over her eyes.

"Sláinte mhaith!" She smiled as she clinked Brennan's glass and downed a mouthful of the golden whiskey. "Now you're here for a short visit, you say. You've seen Finn?"

"I have."

"Had a pint at Christy's, did you?"

"Only the one, before coming to see you, Rosaleen."

"Bless you, Father. There's more in the taps there for you to enjoy after you've done your duty here."

"I'm in no hurry at all."

"Now, what brings you to Dublin, Brennan, when all the action is in London?"

"You're aware then of young Conn's predicament."

"Oh yes. A terrible thing. He'll need a fierce good lawyer. But if they've decided to fit him up for the crime, he'll never see the light of day again. Is that what brings you over from America?"

"No, that happened after I arrived. My visit was prompted by a call from Molly."

"Molly is a dote. She comes to me any time she's home in Dublin. What did she ring you about?"

"My sister has made quite a name for herself in London, Aunt Rosa. She is now a person known to police."

"Conn and Molly. Well, they are treading in well-worn footsteps. Our entire family seems to be known to the peelers. Here in Ireland and now we're in the soup again over there. What's brought her into their sights in this day and age?"

"They said she was promoting the interests of a forbidden organization."

"Ah."

"The meeting was about causing a ruckus at a statue of Oliver Cromwell."

The old lady's eyes narrowed behind the thick lenses. "The Irish-hating, Catholic-hating oul fiend! And him claiming to be doing God's work while slaughtering our people. You can be sure he's far from the sight of God now, roasting and roaring in the everlasting fires of hell."

"I expect you're right."

"Exactly. And you a priest. You'd know. And you say they're after building a statue of him?"

"Yes, way back. They started rehabilitating him, so to speak, in Victorian times. Regarded him as a hero of democracy."

"Democracy, in your hole! Ask them in Drogheda how much democracy they got from Cromwell! Ask them in Wexford. Well, I suppose, he killed indiscriminately; there's his democracy for you. And the Brits themselves got no joy out of him. He banned drink in England! Can you imagine it? He closed the theatres and sent out Puritan soldiers to grab women in the streets and scrub the makeup off their faces!"

But, Brennan remembered from Molly's presentation, Cromwell had no hesitation in shipping young women to Barbados for the pleasure of the English planters. "Molly calls him a pimp."

"Jaysus! The Puritan pimp! Good on her. And they put up a statue to the likes of him. Wouldn't I give that the evil eye if I could see it."

"You can see it if you like. I have a picture here." Brennan drew out his wallet and flipped through Molly's photos of Finbarr. He knew he also had a picture of the Cromwell statue with Terry standing beside it, giving it the finger. He held it up for his great aunt to see. She snatched it from his hand and glared daggers at it. *"Loscadh is dó ort!"*

She looked at Brennan and saw him struggling to translate. "Scorching and burning on you!" she said. "On Cromwell." She made no comment on the man standing next to the statue making the rude gesture. Presumably, in her mind, any statue of the hated man would quite naturally have someone alongside it, flipping it the bird.

"There was a plan to deface it," Brennan informed her.

"Defacing it would be too good for him. They should have cut off its head and hanged and drawn and quartered it. For starters."

"Well, that's what the English did, back in 1661. They dug up Cromwell's body and held a post-mortem execution, for his role in killing the king."

"We should have got to him first."

"Well, there was a more extreme plan in the works than just a splash of red paint."

"Oh?"

"Some of the lads were going to blow the statue to bits. Along with Westminster Abbey."

The old woman raised her eyebrows but offered no comment.

"They called in a warning, and the police cleared people off. Found the bombs and disabled them."

"Mmm."

"The murder of the police officer occurred the same day."

"And they've decided on our Conn for that. Was the shooting connected to the bombing?"

"Not sure. But the police seem to think so."

"What's this got to do with Molly?"

"They thought she knew something about it."

"Did she?"

"No. Actually, I think they were just pretending to believe she knew something. Likely they were hoping to spook her into telling them about some of our people living in London."

"What did they do to spook our little Molly?"

"Banged her up in jail for two nights"

"Tan bastards!"

"And they've since been round to question her."

"Who, the peelers?"

"Not just the uniformed police, but Special Branch."

"Special *Irish* Branch, you mean."

Brennan laughed. "I suppose."

"No supposition necessary, *avic*. That was the name of the organization when they created it. The Special Irish Branch."

"Are you serious?"

"We're talking a hundred years ago," his great aunt explained. "The Special Irish Branch was formed in the 1880s to combat the Fenians and the dynamiters who were setting off bombs in London at the time."

"At the time."

"Yes, the distant past. What goes around comes around, I guess. That outfit was set up to deal with our Fenian ancestors and here they are trailing after us a hundred years later. They dropped *Irish* from their name, but we'll not be fooled by that."

"Did we have ancestors causing grief over there, Rosa?"

"Sure, your great-great grandfather Sean and his brother Tommy were not unknown to the Special Irish Branch in their day. The Fenian heart beats strong in the breast of the Burkes; you don't need me to tell you that."

"True enough. But our Molly has not been blowing anything up in London or elsewhere."

"No, I'm sure that's not what the lads had in mind when they had their council of war back in the day."

"Council of war?"

"Oh, you know, when they all got together back in the forties. My brother had to settle them down."

"Do you mean the time Christy and my father went down to Wexford?" The meeting Brennan had stumbled upon in 1949, after fleeing the ruins of the abbey.

"Sure, the boys from Wexford, Waterford, Carlow, that crowd. Whatever their plan was, Christy knew it would never work. But they cooked up something else. And whatever it was, I believe it was still on the agenda more than twenty years later, when they came here for Christy's wake. I remember lashings of drink, and a lot of intense talk, and eye meeting eye over the coffin. But, whatever it was, you can be sure it didn't involve little Molly Burke running around with explosives."

"I hope they leave her be, the Special Irish Branch, find someone else to annoy. Her, a university professor, and the mother of two lovely children, and they bang her up in jail." Rosaleen took refuge in her whiskey. "That *Sasanach* she married. Sutton. I never liked him."

"Not just because he's English, I hope, Rosaleen."

"Of course not! What do you think I am, a bigot? The fellow I liked in fact was his brother. Neville Sutton's brother. I can't recall his name now, but he was sound. He was kind, considerate, clever, and very funny. He had me nearly wetting myself laughing the times I met him. She should have married him, not that Neville."

"Do you know her children at all?"

"Oh, yes, she's brought them to me on several occasions. Clever as a Jesuit, that Shelmalier, and a bit of a wit she is, too. The boy, now he's a handful. Molly will want to keep a close eye on him. He has his funny side, too, though. And a fine mimic. He had us in stitches one time doing an imitation of Ian Paisley; he had that barbed-wire Belfast voice down pat. And he does a fine take-off on his own father, Neville, that nobby English voice. He can speak perfectly well with no accent at all, can Finbarr."

"No accent at all" must mean a strong north side Dublin accent,

Brennan concluded, which Auntie Rosaleen could not differentiate from her own, couldn't even hear.

"The lad could be an actor," she said. "We'll wait and see how things turn out for him."

"Things aren't going well for him right now, as a matter of fact. He's missing."

"What?"

"He hasn't been in touch with either of his parents. Molly is beside herself with worry."

"And well she might be."

"That's why I'm over here."

"Why here?"

"He's disaffected with his life in England, with life in England in general, and he has ambitions to assist in the struggle for a united Ireland. We think this is something he might have done, come over here. We'll do what we can. If we don't get anywhere here, we'll start again in England."

Rosaleen mulled this over. "You've spoken to Finn?"

"Yes, but he has no idea. Hasn't heard a word about the young fellow."

"That is worrisome, Brennan. If the lad is over here for patriotic reasons and Finn Burke hasn't heard about it, well . . ."

"What are you telling me, Rosaleen?"

"If someone here doesn't want Finn to know about it, it could mean someone has got the boy involved in underhanded activity, something dangerous. Or it could mean . . ."

"Yes?"

"That someone has taken action against him. Hurt him or . . . or worse. And poor Molly, God be with her. She's joined a long list, hasn't she?"

"List?"

"The long list of us women, waiting at home for our men to come back. How many times, over how many years, was I in my room praying the rosary for my husband, my brothers, my sons to return safely from their battles? Now it's Molly's turn. My heart goes out to her."

And, Brennan realized, it was Tess's turn as well, waiting for Conn. And if Conn somehow managed to win his case, he'd be off on further missions, Brennan knew. Tess was in for a long spell of waiting and worrying. And Mairéad O'Brien; she'd had years of living apart from her husband, only to lose him to a brutal killer in England.

"It's the same the world over," Rosaleen said, "always has been. I've always wished I'd joined up myself, Cumann na mBan, the women's auxiliary. Or, in later years, the 'RA itself. Better to be out there in the thick of things than sitting by the window fretting and rattling the beads. But, Brennan, *a chroí*, don't be wasting your time with an oul one like me. I'll send you on your way."

"We'll wait for Bronagh to return so you won't be on your own."

She waved that off. "They haven't got me under twenty-four-hour surveillance. Not yet, they haven't. You're fine to go." She tried to heave herself out of her bed and let loose with a string of curses when her body failed her. "Get me a piece of paper and a pen out of that drawer." She flapped her hand impatiently at the dresser in the corner. "Top drawer."

He opened it and found a scratch pad and a fountain pen, and handed them to his great aunt. She held the pad up before her eyes and scribbled some words, tore the page out, and gave it to Brennan. "Go see the fellow at this address. It's on the ground floor fronting the street. Go under cover of darkness and make sure nobody sees you going there. Which, I have to tell you, will be difficult because you'll have to rap on the window to get his attention."

Brennan took his leave of her then, giving her a blessing before he left the house.

He took a detour to his hotel to change into civilian clothes, grabbed a chicken and stuffing sandwich at a convenience store, then walked back to Christy Burke's. There he found his brother savouring a pint and enjoying a party with several men and women at two tables pushed together near the back of the pub. Terry kissed the hand of one of the women and offered to fly her to the moon. Or at least to Cork Airport. He would be honoured to have her as his guest in the cockpit. This gave rise to some ribald comments at the two tables about joysticks and lift-off and variations of the same.

Brennan's uncle looked out from the bar through his dark glasses. Noting Brennan's arrival, he announced, "Behold the Lamb of God."

"Who taketh away the sins of the world," Brennan replied, as he tooketh his brother by the arm and prepared to take him away.

†

As far as Brennan could tell, there were no eyes on him and Terry as they approached the block of flats on Sean MacDermott Street Upper. It was late, it was dark, and many of the apartments in the red-brick building had their lights off for the night. They had no luck trying to get buzzed in so they fell back on Rosaleen's advice to knock on the window. After several minutes, during which they wondered if they would be nicked for loitering, a hostile-looking face appeared behind the glass. Now what? Brennan had no choice but to engage in a pantomime indicating that they wanted to have a word with the fellow. So much for remaining inconspicuous. Brennan saw a Garda car slowly making its way along Gardiner Street. But, after stopping for a few seconds, it went on its way. Eventually he and Terry were, if not welcomed, at least admitted as far as the door of the flat.

A man peered at them through the crack in his door. His left hand and foot held the door firm. His right hand remained out of sight.

"What are you doing here?"

"We're looking for somebody," Terry replied.

"Nobody here but me and the missus in the cot. You have the wrong address. Fuck off." He started to shut the door.

Terry put his hand out to keep the door open, and in the next instant, Brennan saw a gun pointing at his brother's face.

"We have the right address," Brennan said calmly, "given to us by Rosaleen Burke McCarthy, and we do apologize for waking you."

"You're coming from Rosaleen?"

"We're grandsons of Christy."

"Ah." The man visibly relaxed. He ran his gun hand through his hair and looked around, as if wondering whether he'd be able to accommodate two guests. He jerked his head up as if to say *All right, come in.*

They entered a small sitting room notable for a complete absence of any personal touches. No framed photos on the side table. Nothing on the walls.

Their host was of medium height and narrow-bodied but muscular; his dark hair was sticking up as if he had been sleeping on it. Given the late hour, he undoubtedly had been. But he was fully awake, and his dark eyes seemed to catalogue every detail of his visitors. He had a black shirt and a pair of grey gym pants on. The gun was now in his right-hand pocket.

"Sit down then. What can I do for you? Drink?"

"No, no, but *go raibh maith agat*," said Brennan, perching himself on the edge of an armchair.

Terry sat forward on one of the other chairs and said nothing. Brennan had to admire the native wisdom of his brother. The normally gabby Terrence Burke had the insight to know when silence was the better part of a nocturnal visit with a gunman in the shadows.

"Rosaleen thought you might be able to help us," Brennan said. "Give us an idea where to look. We have a nephew called Finbarr. Finbarr Sutton, and he's gone walkabout. We have to find him."

"Finbarr Sutton? Never heard that name."

But Brennan thought he had detected a sign of recognition on the man's face when he gave the name Finbarr. He thought about it and said, "Or Finbarr Burke."

"That has a better ring to it," the man said.

"You know who I'm talking about then." Silence from the man. "He's young. He has responsibilities elsewhere."

"He may have decided, as young as he is, to rearrange his priorities."

"In what way?"

"Putting himself at the service of others, perhaps, in times of need."

"Where?" Brennan asked.

"Not here."

"Where?" Brennan repeated.

"Try the Occupied Territories."

"Could you be a little more specific?"

Brennan pulled out his pen and the paper with the Sean MacDermott Street address on it and waited.

"Give me that, for fuck's sake." The man snatched the paper from his hand and tore it to shreds.

Brennan reached into his jacket and the man tensed. Brennan put his hands up in a I-have-nothing-to-hide gesture. "Just getting my smokes. I'll write on the pack."

"You won't need to write it because I can't give you the location. I don't know it. All I have is the name of a publican in Belfast, Paddy Murphy."

"Paddy Murphy. How many of those might there be? And how many using that name when their name is really something else?"

"That's the name."

"Where would we find him?"

"I don't know. Try Ardoyne. Try the Falls. Give me a fag, would you? Herself smoked my last one."

"Here, take the pack." Brennan handed it over. "We appreciate your help. We'll let ourselves out."

The man lit his cigarette and waved it at them. "Mind how you go, lads."

When they left the building, Brennan spotted a Garda car again on Gardiner Street. This time it turned the corner and cruised past them at a crawl. They affected not to notice.

Chapter XXV

Martyrs' blood flows once again,
Stains our green and white and gold.
Hear the boots of Cromwell's men,
With us as in days of old.

Áine Ni Mhurchadha, "A Fighting Nation Once Again"

Then it was Belfast. Brennan and Terry rented a car Saturday afternoon and headed north out of Dublin. British soldiers at the border crossing gave them the evil eye, grilled them, and searched the car. Only the grace of God enabled them both to keep their tempers in check as they submitted to what the Burke family had, for centuries, regarded as an occupying force.

It wasn't long before Brennan was wishing the publican they were seeking in Belfast had a name like Botolph Murphy and not Paddy Murphy; surely Botolph the barman would be one of a kind. They had decided to start their search on the Falls Road and the streets running off it. This was one of the main Catholic/Nationalist areas of Belfast, separated in places from the Shankill, the Protestant/Loyalist area, by barriers and barbed wire. Under other circumstances, the assignment would be a pleasant one, sampling a succession of bars in a search for the right spot. Well, pleasant if you could ignore the bellicose graffiti, the sirens, and the armoured cars roaring by carrying rifle-wielding British soldiers.

"All this would be familiar to you, I guess, Terrence, from your days in an active service unit here."

"Yeah, it's all coming back to me. Not that it ever went away. Conn didn't live far from here."

"He may be wishing about now that he'd stayed."

"He should have stayed in Dublin and cheered the boys on from the safety and comfort of Christy Burke's bar."

"Oh, I'm thinking the boys get more than cheerleading out of Christy's. And that's as true under Finn's management of the place as it was under Christy himself."

"I suspect you're right, Bren. Well, Conn didn't stay home and that decision is long behind him now. Let's find his young admirer and bundle him off to London if we can."

They checked bar after bar, asking for Paddy Murphy. At each place they attended, they were met with the understandable suspicion with which two strangers were regarded upon entering the bars of Belfast. But their names, and their ability to say the right things, eased their way. Finally, after meeting or hearing about three Paddy Murphys, they landed in the right place. The Banned Flag was an unabashedly Republican bar replete with photos of the old and the new IRA, and the ten H Block prisoners who had died on hunger strike. There was a huge green, white, and orange Irish tricolour on one wall over the words "The Flag They BANNED!" A small plaque explained: "The Flag and Emblems Display Act of 1954 gave the Royal Ulster Constabulary the duty to take down any flag they considered likely to cause a breach of the peace. The British Union Jack was specifically exempted, leaving the green, white, and *gold* the only flag routinely pulled down."

"Darren, take over for me for a spell here." With that, the burly and bearded Paddy Murphy of the Banned Flag pub left his duties to a young subordinate and motioned Brennan and Terry to his quarters behind the bar.

Murphy sat on the corner of an old wooden desk and he welcomed his visitors to take two of the several barstools available in the office.

"How can I help you?"

Brennan introduced himself and Terry, and said, "Thanks for seeing us, Mr. Murphy."

"Paddy."

"Paddy, we're trying to find our nephew." Going on the assumption that the young fellow was using his mother's Irish surname, he said, "Finbarr Burke. We were given information in Dublin that you might be able to help us out."

"What Burkes would you be now—" *nye* "—the two of you?"

"Grandsons of Christy in Dublin. You may know . . ."

"Aye."

"So if there is anything at all you can tell us . . ."

Murphy sat quiet for a moment, thinking things over. "Why don't you go out there and have a pint, and I'll join you in a few minutes."

"Will do," Terry replied, and the brothers repaired to the bar, ordered their pints, and found a seat at a table beneath a poster displaying the lyrics of "The Men Behind the Wire," the song Paddy McGuigan had written about the men who were imprisoned after the British introduced internment without trial. The tanks and armoured cars and other paraphernalia of an occupied territory mentioned in the lyrics were everyday sights to the people in this neighbourhood. McGuigan himself was interned after he wrote the hit song.

"What do you suppose Murphy's doing back there?" Terry asked. "Calling around to find Finbarr, I hope."

"Checking our credentials, more like."

"Fair play to him. Can't blame him for that."

Brennan looked around him at the drinkers, male and female, young and old. A subdued lot. Every time the door opened, every head turned; every eye in the place examined the newcomers. At one point there was a loud rumbling sound in the street, following by a bang. Everybody froze, glasses in hand. An old fellow wearing a tweed jacket and a pair of overalls got up and poked his head out the door, then returned and reported to the crowd.

"One of the three wee pigs ran into a barricade around the corner."

Terry said, "Must be one of the armoured vehicles known as pigs. Army."

The old man went on to offer his analysis. "The obstacle must have been huffed and puffed into place by the big bad wolf, because there was no barricade there when I came in."

"There was no street when you came in, Shammy, no pavement, just a cow path, you've been here so long, you ancient fucker."

"Mock ye not but seek ye my wisdom, children! And in return I ask nothing but a wee drop to wet my lips."

"Bring the man a jar, Darren," someone called out. "He's the only one of us who had the brass to get up off his arse and see what happened out there."

Shammy's intelligence report must have reassured the crowd in the Banned Flag; they resumed drinking and talking in quiet voices. The sound of heavy objects clattering to the ground could be heard from outside, then a vehicle gearing up and moving off. A non-event, thanks be to God.

A few minutes after that, Paddy Murphy emerged from his office and signalled Brennan and Terry to come inside.

"You were asking after Finbarr Burke. He's not here."

"But we were told—" Terry began.

Brennan cut him off. "Is there anything at all you can tell us, Paddy?"

"You should be looking south of the border."

"We just came up from there!" said Terry.

"It's Dundalk I'm talking about. Lots of the boys from Belfast are OTR. On the run. And that's where they go to bide their time. So what I suggest you do is go in to Phelim's bar and ask for Owen. If my information is correct, Owen is acquainted with somebody who sounds like your young relation."

"Thank you, Paddy. We'll head there now."

"You're going tonight?"

"Sure, it's early and it's only an hour's drive. God's blessings upon you, Paddy."

They shook hands all round, and the Burkes left for the next leg of their journey.

This time there was no messing about. They were entering the Republic of Ireland and were detained for mere seconds by the Irish authorities at a border checkpoint. They drove into the town of Dundalk, where they had no trouble finding Phelim's in a red-brick building just off the market square. Their contact, Owen, knew exactly what they wanted and did not pretend otherwise. The Burke brothers' credentials must have been checked and found to be in order on both sides of the border.

"You're going to the Dougherty farm. Here, I'll draw you a map." He found a stubby pencil behind the bar and sketched a map on the back of a Powers whiskey coaster. "Pull in behind the house, between it and the barn, dim your lights and wait. Don't get out of the car till somebody comes to collect you."

They thanked the man and started out again. They took a couple of wrong turns on the mucky, rutted roads leading to their destination but they were there soon enough, idling behind the farmhouse in which only one light was burning. From what Brennan could see, the white exterior walls were stained with age, and some of the black slates on the roof were cracked or missing. The barn door was wide open and there wasn't a sound within, suggesting that no animals reposed there.

A few minutes after their arrival the back door of the house opened, and two young fellows emerged. They were about eighteen years old and slight of build, one dark and one red-haired. They came up to the car, and Brennan rolled down his window.

"You the Burkes?" the ginger asked.

"We are. I'm Brennan and this is Terry."

"Aye. Owen tells us you're sound. Come in."

They were led into a large kitchen with a stone floor, old rusty appliances, and a huge wooden table marred by blackened gouges in the wood. There were six heavy wooden chairs. Straddling one of them backwards was Finbarr Burke Sutton, sporting a patchy light brown beard and wearing an olive-green army jacket. He was fiddling with a radio that looked as if it had been ordered from the catalogue in 1951. Static and squawks were the only sounds it emitted as he turned the tuning dial.

"There's better reception where you're going, my lad. Pack your bag."

He jerked around at the sound of Terry's voice and stared at him, gobsmacked. Clearly, he had not been given advance notice of the visit.

"How did you find me?" he blurted out, sounding all of thirteen as his voice ascended the scale.

"We've been around the block a few times, Finbarr."

"Does anyone else know I'm here?"

The two other lads exchanged glances.

"Nobody outside of Counties Antrim and Louth apparently," Brennan said. "We're here to tell you that your ship has come in. So no need to stick around here any longer. Pack up your gear and come with us."

"But I can't leave here."

"Why not?"

Finbarr's eyes went to his two companions, then slid away.

"On yer bike, Finbarr. We'll be out in the car. You've got five minutes."

"Did you hear me, Brennan? I can't fucking leave!" With that, he untangled himself from the chair and made for the back stairs at the side of the kitchen and disappeared from sight.

Brennan looked at Terry. "I'll go up. See if I can reason with him." Unspoken was *and you see what you can find out from these two*.

When Brennan went up the stairs, he found Finbarr sitting on a bed with his head down, arms wrapped around his knees. When he looked up, his young face was a portrait of misery. "I can't cross the border back into the U.K., Brennan."

"What have you done?"

"I can't fucking tell you that."

"Your mother is afraid your body's lying somewhere, with a hood on your head and your kneecaps blown out."

"Well, you can report that I'm alive and, if you're up for telling stories, you can tell her I'm well."

"What are you going to do, hide out in Dundalk for the rest of your natural life?"

"That's pretty well what I've been told to do."

"Told by whom?"

"A fellow came to see me back in London."

"Who?"

"Don't know his name."

Brennan told himself to be patient, not an easy task under these circumstances. "All right. This unidentified person came to see you. Where did this happen?"

"Told me to meet him outside the Arsenal football stadium. North part of London."

"How did he contact you in the first place?"

"Passed me in the street, whispered his message, and kept on walking."

"So you went to meet him. Did he look familiar to you at all? Any guesses as to who he was?" Finbarr shook his head. "English? Irish?"

"Über Irish."

"Dublin? Belfast?"

"Neither, I don't think. Didn't sound like our family in Dublin. And not from the North. But from Ireland somewhere."

"Why did he want to meet you?"

"To warn me." He stopped speaking and put his head down again.

"Warn you of what?"

"That the peelers were investigating . . . some things that had happened, and that my name hadn't come up yet but they were closing in on . . ."

"On what, for Christ's sake, Finbarr?"

"Something, some things they think I did."

"And did you? Do something?"

"I tried to help the lads out. They needed a job done."

"What kind of a job?"

"Who do you think I am, the presenter on the nightly news?"

"Whatever it is, you're exiled now from England and the North of Ireland. You have to stay crouched beneath the border here clinging to the edge of the Republic. For how long?"

"How the fuck do I know, Brennan? Just go and leave me alone."

"What about your family? Doesn't it trouble you that they're worried to death about you?"

"My ma is the only one who'll give a shite. So give her my love and tell her I'm fine. Just lying low for a while. I'll be in touch with her when I can."

"Don't you think your father must be frantic, wondering what the hell has become of you?"

"My father does not get 'frantic,' Brennan. If you ever hear Neville Sutton say, 'Good Lord, it's hardly the most pleasant day to be walking about,' you can start running for the shelters, because the bomb's just been dropped."

"What about your sister? You don't think she—"

"Shelmalier despises me."

"Why would she despise you?"

"For my views, my support for the Irish Republican cause."

"Perhaps she doesn't like the way you express your views."

"She's going with a Brit soldier, for fuck's sake."

"Fair play to her. She loves him. And she loves you. She's capable of doing both."

Just when Brennan least expected it, the mask of defiance crumpled, and what Brennan saw on the bed was a young boy fighting back tears.

"I know. I've spoilt things forever with Shel, because I acted like an arsewipe in front of her boyfriend and his family. Don't get me wrong! I don't accept for a minute the British policy or actions in Ireland!"

Brennan couldn't help but smile. "Nobody would ever accuse you of that, Finbarr. I don't accept it either. But we can't shove that into the face of every English person we know."

"I don't! Some of my best mates . . . Guess you're not allowed to say that anymore. Not sure why. Harmless statement of the facts, as far as I can see."

"Now, what are we going to do about you?"

"Nothing we can do. I told you that, Brennan. Funny in a way, isn't it? I'm half English, but I've always felt more Irish, more like my mother than my father. And I've always dreamed of moving to Ireland. Now I'm in Ireland, and I'm not free to see any of the country beyond Dundalk. Dundalk's a lovely town, but I'm going to go absolutely mad being confined to this farmhouse!"

There was no need for Brennan to state the obvious: that Finbarr had made his bed and now had to lie in it.

"I've read the 'RA's *Green Book*," his nephew said then. "It warns us that this is the least of what we have to expect when we sign up."

"And have you signed up?"

Finbarr looked away. "Well, I'm not official."

"Do you mean you're not a member of the Official IRA, or you're not officially a member of the Provisional IRA?"

"Not officially Provisional, I guess is what I should say. That would make a brilliant T-shirt, what? Image of one of the lads all kitted out at a funeral or the Wolfe Tone commemoration, and over him it would say 'Officially Provisional.'"

"If you were just making T-shirts for the movement, we'd all breathe a little easier."

"I could make some great ones for—" He cut off whatever he was about to say, and Brennan could see a pink flush creeping up on his cheeks.

"For what?"

"I overheard Shelmalier and Edward talking one day about the café he wants to open. Brits In! With the graffiti look and all that. Even though I'd probably get struck by lightning for even saying the words 'Brits In,' it sounds like an ace idea. I was thinking of all these ways I could help them design and build the shop, and droll little remarks we could stick on the menus, like quotes from members of the bands from the sixties and puns on song titles. But . . ."

"But?"

"I burned my bridges with him before I even . . . before I even got to know him. What if they are married someday? I don't want to be on the outs with him. Personally, I'm talking about. That doesn't mean I agree with what British soldiers—"

"That goes without saying, my son, and doesn't need to be said again."

"Right. Well, Brennan, there's no need for me to hold you up. I can't go with you. Tell Ma you tried. I'll ring her when I can."

Brennan knew that nothing short of physical force was going to dislodge Finbarr Burke Sutton from his safe house in Ireland, nothing short of wrestling him to the ground and tying him up in chains. Imagine trying to explain that to the immigration officers, or Special Branch, at Heathrow airport. So Brennan returned to the kitchen below.

When they were on the road again, Terry filled him in on the conversation in the kitchen, such as it was.

"I asked the two young fellows why Finbarr was there, and all they did was look at each other. Didn't answer. I raised my voice a couple of notches and asked again. Told them we were not there to get these lads in the soup, but that we had to find out why our nephew was there and how long he would be in Dundalk. I assured them that whatever they told me would never come back to bite them. One of them finally spoke up. 'We were told he could help us with some, em, fundraising for the struggle.'

"What kind of fundraising, I wanted to know. Was Finbarr baking pies for the cause? Selling his own art? They laughed but made no comment. I persisted. Bank jobs, drug dealing, what?

"'Nothing like that.'

"'You got that right,' the second fellow agreed with a little smirk on his face.

"Then I did something I didn't want to do. I got up and stood over one of the two. Crowded him and looked down at him. 'Do you want word going up the line that you're not being cooperative here?'

"'We don't know what he's after doing! We were just told to keep him here. That's all.'

"And I believed him. Either that, or he was more terrified of the command structure finding out he talked than of the command structure finding him uncooperative. I wasn't about to terrify him further.

"'All right,' I said, and I put my hand on the boy's arm, and he flinched. If I had felt like a shit intimidating this child with words, I felt like a fucking monster when the touch of my hand set him quaking. Anyway, I thanked them for seeing us, and for taking care of Finbarr. They looked ready to pass out with relief.

"After a couple of minutes, I engaged them in some small talk. They relaxed, and we gabbed about GAA football and hurling till you came down."

†

It was two in the morning before Brennan and Terry got back to their hotel in Dublin, but Brennan rang Molly even so. There is no bad time to receive good news when your child is missing. He was considering how to word his report, so that Molly would hear what she needed to hear, and anyone else listening . . . Then he remembered that they had cleared the place of listening devices.

He could hear the trepidation in her voice when she answered. "Yes?"

"He's fine, he's not hurt, he's his regular self."

"Oh, thank God! Is he with you? Where—"

He told her what he knew, softening it a bit about his living accommodations and his comments concerning his father and sister.

†

Relief alternated with alarm when they were back in London, and Molly heard about their encounter with her son, hiding out in a safe house just south of the border. Hiding out for reasons none of them understood.

"What on earth is he up to, that he has to hide out in Ireland? What has he done?"

"Something in the North, maybe," said Terry, "which would explain why he's taken refuge on the Southern Irish side of the border."

Molly was silent for a few seconds, then said softly, "The same logic would apply if he had done something here in England." She looked to her brothers. "Will we ever get him back again?"

Chapter XXVI

They loved dear old Ireland and they never feared danger.
Glory O, Glory O, to the bold Fenian men.

Peadar Kearney, "Down by the Glenside"

Sunday was pretty well a write-off for Brennan, with the exception of his morning Mass. He returned to the flat directly afterwards and spent the day lazing about and recovering from the exertions of the trip to Dublin, Belfast, and Dundalk. Molly was, to state the obvious, enormously thankful that her son had been found, but she was distressed that he was—for how long?—beyond her reach. It was a relief when her friend Jane called, inviting her to lunch the following day at the Warrington.

But they all perked up Sunday evening when a call came for Terry. Brennan heard his brother asking after the other person's health, and then they were catching up on each other's lives. The conversation was brief. Terry wished the other person well, said "God bless," and then hung up.

"That was someone I once flew a mission with. Mercy flight a few years back."

"You don't mean Casey!" Molly said.

"That's right, Jacky Casey. I wanted to track him down earlier, but couldn't very well make the calls when our phone was bugged! Anyway, it took me a couple of days but I knew his father's brother lived near Manchester. I managed to find the right family and I left a message. A *coded* message, something like the ones he left for me. Jacky says he's living here in England, is married now, and has a little girl. Sounds as if he's doing quite all right. He told me he's doing police work but was cagey about what or where. Little wonder, after what he went through."

"Has he been back to Ireland?" Brennan asked. Terry shook his head. "Imagine what that must be like for him."

"Imagine what it must be like for our oul man. It's been nearly forty years since Declan sank a footprint into Irish turf."

"True enough. Did Casey say anything about the calls he made to the flat here?"

"Just that he'd heard some details of the investigation and knew about the prints. Knew there were prints from Conn on the driver's side of the cop's car and none on the passenger side where the shots came from. Said he wished he could have done more for Conn, but that was as far as he dared go. I said we were all very grateful, and he said it was the least he could do, after the airlift out of Belfast."

✝

On Monday Brennan put in a day's work at St. Andrew the Scot's church and returned to Molly's in the late afternoon.

"How was your day at the office, dear?" she asked him.

"Costs are up, revenues are down, the typist is off sick, and the boss called me on the carpet and told me I have to shape up or ship out; I'm not indispensable, you know."

"Really?"

"No, I just figured that's what goes on in an office."

"That's exactly how it is," Terry said, "which is why I appreciate being able to get thirty-five thousand feet above it all during my work days."

"There's something to be said for that. How was lunch at the Warrington, Molly? Everything up to its usual standard?"

"It was lovely."

"Any sign of your old friend Cedric Mawdsley? He was a bit of a regular there for a while."

"No, the Cambridge University don who wasn't, wasn't there."

"Why do you suppose he invented that persona? Just to impress you?"

"If so, he seems to have decided he is not impressed with *me*. Not the sort of girl he would take home to mother, obviously."

"No, Mrs. Mawdsley would smell a rat if you came to tea with a bouquet of lilies in one hand and an Armalite rifle in the other. Not our sort, darling. Of course maybe the Mawdsleys aren't grand at all. We don't know how much was put on."

"Maybe they're not even Mawdsleys. Maybe the name was fictional too. But why?"

"Who knows? There are so many odd characters orbiting around you lately, Mol, that nobody can make sense of it."

"But, really, Brennan, what does it matter? Whoever he is, he got us out for an evening at a lovely country house, which we never would have seen otherwise . . ."

Brother and sister looked at each other, and said in unison, "He got us out. Out of the flat."

✝

A few minutes later, the telephone rang.

"What fresh hell is this?" Molly muttered as she reached for it.

"Hello. Conn! Are you all right, darling? You don't sound . . . no, I know you can't. I'm sure they are—standing right beside you, I expect. Conn! Don't provoke them! Jesus!"

She looked over at Terry. "He just told me to get you to hijack a helicopter, land it in the exercise yard, and spring all the Irish lads from the prison! He's writing the lyrics already, he says."

"Could work. It's been done before," said Terry. "Mountjoy Prison, 1973."

"Well," Molly said into the receiver, "let me assure all the good folks who maintain order at Her Majesty's Prison at Brixton that it's not going to be done now. Seriously, Conn, it's so rare that you make a call, you've got me concerned. How you're holding on to your sanity in there is beyond me. Yes? She did? A stilted conversation, I'm sure. Certainly. Good idea. Wish you could be with us. And you will be soon, darling. I have complete confidence in Lorna MacIntyre. She'll get you out from under this. Good then. I'll ring Tess and we'll set it up. Take care of yourself, Connie."

Brennan and Terry waited for the news.

"He doesn't sound at all well, in spite of his little jest about the prison break. He's going to get himself in trouble someday needling the warders like that. The reason he called is that he rang Tess and they talked for a while on the phone. She is trying to put a good face on things but she's feeling lost and helpless. Well, we know that. Here they are in love and expecting their baby and he's . . . She obviously didn't tell him about the twins." Molly stopped to take a couple of deep breaths. "Anyway, he said Tess is home right now and he suggested we make plans to go out together. There is always a session at Hannigan's on Monday, and of course Conn knows the musicians there; he thinks Tess would benefit from the outing. Then — typical Conn — he said, 'See that my wife and child stay off the drink.'"

"All right," said Brennan, "get her on the phone. We'll pick her up early and treat her to a meal. It would be grand if we could get the whole family out for this, since Tess is family now too. What are the chances of Shelmalier coming down again from Oxford?"

"I'll ring her and ask. It's only an hour's trip, after all. If only . . ."

"Finbarr will be back annoying people at family gatherings someday soon, never fear." Brennan felt far less confident than he sounded about Finbarr's eventual reappearance, but he kept that to himself.

"We'll make sure everyone enjoys the evening," he said. "Tomorrow we'll pay Lorna MacIntyre a visit and ask her to level with us about Conn's chances, about what kind of defence she can realistically expect to put on for him. We have to be thinking of the babies, and how we can help Tess if Conn . . . Well, let's just make the best of the craic tonight."

✝

Hannigan's was jammed but Seamus managed to find a table for the Burkes. Tess was pale, and there were dark circles under her eyes, but she insisted that she was in the pink, and her doctor had given her a glowing report on her twins' health when she had a checkup three days ago. Her mum had been over from Belfast and urged her to come home while she waited for 'Conn's situation to get sorted.' But Tess had assured her mother that she was doing all right and would wait things out — *wayett things ite* — in London. Molly urged her to eat the chicken stew she had ordered. But nobody needed encouragement; the food was delectable.

Shelmalier had come down from Oxford, and there was clearly a bond between the two young women; Shelley was delighted to hear about the twins. And it wasn't long before she had Tess in fits of laughter about some of the brilliant eccentrics she encountered regularly at Oxford. "I'm thinking my first published work will be *Endearing Kooks I Have Known.*"

"You're studying with kooks up there in Oxford?" Terry asked. "Your mother may want to demand her money back."

"You really must broaden your outlook, Terry," Shelley retorted. "No less a figure than John Stuart Mill said, 'The amount of eccentricity in a society has generally been proportional to the amount of genius, mental vigour, and moral courage it contained.' England is blessed with all those virtues, no matter what we may think of some of its actions as an imperial power. Oxford University of course has bragging rights to William Archibald Spooner, who was on the faculty some decades ago. His name and his mixing up of words and letters gave rise to the term 'spoonerism.' Such as: 'Let us glaze our asses to the queer old dean,' for 'Let us raise our glasses to the dear old queen.'

"My current favourite among the eccentrics at Oxford is Reginald Spoole-Blevins in the maths department. He's the ninth earl of something or other but he renounced the title, if you can do that, and insists on being called simply Reggie. He may have shucked off his title but, oddly, he has bestowed titles on the family of badgers and weasels he has living in his house. He has a little Debrett's Peerage sort of chart pasted on the wall, naming them all in order of precedence. Squeaks might be the Marquess of Mobberley, Lord Stinkbottom, the Earl of Egg Buckland. He prints up an honours list on New Year's Day, and they all have a little celebration.

"The animals have their own china, and Reggie regularly has tea with them. Students contrive to get over there at tea time just to see it. I did, too, with a couple of friends. We used the excuse that we were swotting for our exam and were having trouble with the Frobenius endomorphism. Maths aren't even a part of my program but I'm taking his course just to bask in his genius. We knocked on his door and he invited us in, and there were the animals. A few of them were seated at the table, others grubbing about in the corners of the room. And get this: he had some of them kitted out in little frock coats and dresses. The ladies — if indeed they were the females; I didn't lift their tails — had elaborate hats tied on. In the style of the queen and the queen mother. Reggie greeted us with a rather sheepish expression on his face, and said, 'I must ask you to excuse the shambles. It's always like this here, at this time of day. You know how it is.'"

Shelley's recital was met with the reception one would expect from the assembly. Then Tess asked, "And what was the Oxford don himself wearing?"

"Oh, nothing outlandish at all. Blue jeans, a pair of trainers, and white shirt. Looked like a banker dressing down for the holidays. His wife had just gone home, wherever that is, so he was taking it easy. One of my friends asked him to refresh our memories of the Frobenius endomorphism. I'm sure nobody *here* needs a refresher course in commutative algebra, but we pretended we had lost the finer points after repeated bouts of heavy drinking over the course of the term. If he thought we were taking the piss, he was too polite to mention it. So he obliged us with a clear, cogent explanation of the theory, complete with equations recited out of his head and scribbled with a black marker on the wall beside the dining table."

"Must have to repaint every time a pack of students leaves," Molly said.

"I shouldn't think so. The wall was done up in William Morris wallpaper. When Reggie wrapped up his lecture, he said, 'Tea?' And of course we all said yes and sat down with the weasels and the badgers in their noble finery, and we all had a lovely time."

Terry Burke sat gazing with delight at his young relation; no doubt he saw Shelley Burke Sutton as a fitting heir to his role as barroom bon vivant and raconteur. Tess looked as if her troubles had, for the moment, been packed up in an old kit bag.

Musicians made their way to their regular tables at the front of the room, and the session started up with a set of jigs and reels. The crowd clapped their hands, slapped their legs, tapped their feet, and a couple of young girls got up and did a step dance. After that they heard the opening verse of "Boolavogue," a song about the rebellion of 1798.

> At Boolavogue as the sun was setting
> O'er the bright May meadows of Shelmalier,
> A rebel hand set the heather blazing
> And brought the neighbours from far and near.

It took two lines before realization set in, and all heads at the table turned at once. There, voice raised in song, pint in hand, tweed cap on head, stood Conn Burke as if he had never been away.

It was all they could do to sit and let him finish the song. He acknowledged the thunderous applause and gave his name as "the *seanchaí* formerly known as Conn, now performing under the inevitable trade name Ex-Conn." After that, they queued up behind the mother of his unborn children. She too had been left in the dark to enjoy the big surprise. Tess lavished him with kisses and then clung to him, laughing and crying all at once. She told him, "Never go away like that again!" When she finally let go, everyone else piled onto him with hugs, kisses, and tears from some, and quick manly embraces from others. Their table was awash in pints and jars of whiskey brought by well-wishers but, after a few minutes of celebration, the bar patrons left him alone with his family. Conn pulled Tess's chair up tight next to his and wrapped his left arm around her.

Conn savoured his pint of Guinness for a bit, then put it down and said, "I suppose you're wondering why I called this meeting."

"If you have anything to share with the group, we'd like to hear it," said Molly.

"They released me this morning. Came in and told me the charges had been withdrawn. No explanation given."

This brought on another round of hugs and thanks to the Man Above.

Terry gave voice to the question on everyone's mind. "I guess this means they've got somebody else for it?"

"Not that I've heard."

Brennan was not sure what to make of that, and neither was anyone else, if the silence at the table was any indication.

Shelmalier finally spoke up. "Well, it wasn't you, Conn, and thank Christ your innocence has been acknowledged at last. Whoever did this has murder on his conscience, and not only that. He also has to live with the fact that he sat back and let them arrest you and lock you up; you could have spent the rest of your life in there."

Brennan caught Conn's gaze and held it. Brennan knew that "whoever did this, whoever sat back" was almost certainly a person known to Conn, a person on the scene at the same time. Special Branch Detective John Chambers had confided that information to him and Molly the day he had hijacked them at gunpoint, at great risk to his future at Scotland Yard, to let them know their cousin was innocent. Brennan could not begin to fathom how Conn felt about all this; nor could he imagine what had really happened on Elverton Street that day. But one thing was clear if there had been no new arrest: Conn had not informed on the other man present at the scene.

"You should sue them, Conn," Shelley said. "Bleed them for damages. We'll all be your character witnesses."

"And if he needs more characters," said Terry, "we'll call in that weasel fellow, Spoole-Blevins."

"But let's not speak of courtroom drama now," Molly urged them. "Let's celebrate with our cousin, and get something into his stomach that is not prison food. What did you eat today, Conn?"

"I had the best and biggest plate of greasy chips and deep-fried fish I have ever tasted."

"When was that, love?"

"That was at lunch time and I went back and had it again for supper!"

"Understandable, under the circumstances. If you'd like anything from the menu here, just say the word."

"No, no, I'll have a pint or two, Molly, and that's all I need for tonight." He turned to Tess. "Nothing but a wee glass of *bainne* for you!"

"A wee glass?" She looked over at the barman. "If you do have milk in the place, I'll take a great, huge glass of it. After all," she said, turning back to Conn, "I'm drinking for three."

It took him a couple of seconds to catch on. Then he stared at her, his eyes enormous. "Are you codding me? No? You are the most brilliant girl in the world. And—" he spoke to the room at large "—am

I a man or what? Twins! Two childer on the way." To Tess, he said, "I love you to bits. Let's have our wedding waltz now, and we'll get you to the altar next week, if there's one still standing over in the North. Play us a slow one, would you, Seamus?"

Seamus reached for a CD behind the bar. "How about 'Carrickfergus'?"

"Good man." Conn gestured to the room at large. "Everybody on the floor, all of yez."

Terry bowed to Shelmalier and asked for the favour of her company on the dance floor. Brennan linked up with Molly. And everyone else who wasn't entirely legless with drink got up and found a partner. They all danced and sang along with the lovely old melody.

> The water is wide and I cannot swim over.
> Neither have I the wings to fly.
> I wish I could meet a handy boatman to ferry me over,
> My love and I.

The innocent man danced his bride around the room, both of them beaming. There was no Special Branch police car lurking outside the bar when they left for the night.

✝

They gathered outside Molly's building, and Tess ran inside to call a taxi for herself and Conn. Shelmalier and Terry were deep in conversation, perhaps about her upcoming book, *Endearing Kooks*.

Molly turned to Conn and said, "It's wonderful to see you amongst the living again, Conn."

"Sure, it's wonderful to be walking the earth again," he agreed.

"But, em . . ." Molly looked as if she didn't quite know what to say. "Is it really over for you, Conn? Or will they come after you about the . . . the plan to damage the statue and the abbey?"

"There was no plan to damage Westminster Abbey."

"But, Conn, there were explosives planted all through the building. The police say it could have been reduced to rubble."

"First of all, Molly, the amount of explosive material in the building was wildly exaggerated by the police. And, two, the explosives were never primed. They were never going to go off."

"What?"

"The aim of that operation was propaganda, not ruination. It was to say 'Look what we could have done to *your* great abbey, in revenge for what was done to ours. We could have done it, and we could do it again. Maybe for real, next time.'"

Molly stared at her cousin, dumbfounded.

Brennan spoke up then. "I don't recall hearing that message any time after the incident. There was a phone call from a person — ahem! — claiming to speak for the Boys of Wexford. But nothing subsequently about 'no detonators' or 'not primed.' All we've heard is that the police cleared the abbey and dismantled the bombs."

"That should tell you that the peelers have their own reasons for not wanting to admit the thing was a hoax, that there was no danger to life or property. Better to have everyone believe that the Irish were once again putting innocent people at risk. And the individuals behind the plot have not yet announced that it was a hoax. They will, when they feel the time is right."

"So," said Brennan, "nobody was going to get hurt in that incident. But a lot of people have been hurt, or killed, as the result of IRA bombs here and in the North of Ireland. How do you justify that?"

"I don't. I don't go along with it, Brennan. I told you that. I don't support the bombing campaign even though indiscriminate attacks are not part of the strategy, and civilians are not the targets. The fact that civilians get killed 'incidentally' is enough for me to condemn it. I didn't even like the hoax at Westminster Abbey but I agreed to help out, since I knew it was just for show."

"But on the larger question, if you don't agree with what the IRA is doing, why do you stay in the organization?"

"We consider the Irish Republican Army the legitimate army of the Republic that was set up following the election of 1918. I stay in the hope that I can eventually gain some influence, and have a voice in persuading those in command that the IRA should return to its beginnings, to the ideals of the Old IRA, that it should be an army of soldiers fighting the British Army. Guerrilla warfare, yes, by necessity. But not terrorism."

"They've gone a long way from your ideal."

"Yes, we have a long way to go before we get back to where we should be. But if we do nothing, that means we've surrendered to the abuses perpetrated by the other side, given up on our objective of uniting the thirty-two counties. And in that case, all the men who died for that goal died in vain. Do you share that ideal, Brennan?"

"I do." And he did, but at what cost? That was the question with which he had always grappled. He said then, "Look ahead for a minute to a united Ireland. Pretend we're already there. What do we have? Eight hundred thousand Protestants in the North, most of whom will never, ever accept the new Republican state, particularly if it's ruled from Dublin. We're the state now; they're the rebels. It's our lads in the tanks and the armoured cars, our lads running the detention centres. Now we're the strong arm of the law, trying to put down what will be in effect a permanent insurrection."

"I'll tell you this much, Brennan. Not one of us will abandon our objective because of the difficulties that lie ahead. Not one of us will shirk from the responsibilities we'll face when we're running the country that was stolen from us all those years ago."

Silence fell on them at that point, as Brennan brooded yet again over what is right and just in war, and what is not. And over the moral implications of *not* going to war, and surrendering your people to continued oppression.

Molly sighed and put her hand on Conn's arm. "Well, we won't solve those big questions tonight. But thank God you sent me the warning to stay away from the Cromwell statue, to cancel the paint splash. Even if none of the explosives that day were primed, I still might have been charged with—"

"I didn't send you a warning."

"Of course you did. I got your note in my post box. 'Cancel Tuesday's paint job. Cancel and stay away.' And it was your—" she glanced at Brennan "—your coded signature."

Conn shook his head. "Wasn't me. I didn't even know about it, the plan to blow up the statue."

"But then who . . ." Molly's voice faltered. The whole conversation faltered. Conn was still not giving anything away.

†

Two days later, the last day of May, was moving day. Tess rang that evening to say Conn had arranged to sublet his Cricklewood flat, and they were going to a lovely place not far from Molly's in Kilburn. Tess wanted to pass along the new address. Right now they were packing Conn's things up for loading in a borrowed van. She couldn't stay on the phone and chat because Conn had been late getting home from his first day back at work, and it was getting dark, and they had to get his stuff moved. Molly immediately offered her assistance and that of her big, strapping brothers, who were doing nothing but having a few cans and debating how soon to return to New York.

So Molly, Terry, and Brennan arrived at Conn's flat ready to work. It took some persuading but the mother-to-be stood aside and let Molly and the three lads do the heavy lifting. Soon all the items and boxes were stacked on the pavement in front of the building, waiting for Conn's pal to turn up with the van. The night was cool and foggy but there was no rain. Brennan took the opportunity to have a smoke. Molly and Tess stood by the doorway of the building, chatting about Tess's plans for the new flat and the best place to buy good quality baby furniture. Conn went back inside and returned with a long narrow box.

"What have you got there, Conn? Long-stemmed roses?" Molly asked, eyeing the box. It was covered with dust and bits of what looked like fibreglass insulation. Not hard to guess what it was, and that it had been hidden between the inside and outside walls of the flat.

"Sure, it's my new golf clubs, Mol. I'm going to be a dad so I intend to act the part, dressing myself in plaid pants and embarrassing my children from day one."

There was no plaid on him now. He was wearing a dark green nylon jacket over a black T-shirt, and there appeared to be a bit of a bulge in the right-hand pocket of the jacket. Not a bunch of golf balls or tees, Brennan guessed.

The men all stood on the pavement, waiting and talking about the arrival of the twins in December, and how Conn was going to make sure they were born in the Republic of Ireland, such as it was at this moment in history; otherwise they would be citizens of the United Kingdom and that just would not do for the sons or daughters of Conchobar and Tessie Burke.

A white van pulled up in front of them, and the driver hopped out and greeted Conn in a voice that had been born and bred on the north side of Dublin; he congratulated Conn on his release from the nick and opened the rear door of the vehicle. The men began loading Conn's earthly possessions into the cargo hold.

"D'yez need some help there, boys?" Molly called from the walkway.

"You've already done enough lifting for one day, Molly," said Conn. "Now all you have to do is keep my bride from coming over here and undoing everything we do. She's an awful one for reorganizing things after I think I've got them done. Everything has to be symmetrical for Tess. They have a name for that, don't they? Some kind of psychological thing. I figure that's how she ended up with twins in her belly. I thought my job was done when I pulled out and left her with child. But no, she decided that two symmetrical children are better than one."

"Well, then, I'll not be letting you near me again, Connie, because I just might produce four next time round!"

"Yeah, I know, and then eight. What have I got myself into with this woman?"

In the next instant, Brennan heard the sound of a motor and turned to see a small, battered car coming up behind the van with its lights off. Before he could react, two young men flung the car doors open and jumped out. They both had guns in their hands, pointed at the crowd around the van. Brennan's eyes darted to Tess and Molly on the doorstep. He saw Molly's eyes widen and, before Brennan could make a move in their direction, Molly eased Tess to the ground and covered the pregnant woman's body with her own. Back behind the van Conn was bent over, picking up a box. He looked up and saw the gunmen. They recognized their target and trained their weapons on him. In the time it took for Brennan to wonder what move to make or what his cousin was going to do, Conn had his own pistol out of his jacket and had fired one shot at the man on the street side of the car. The man yelped in pain, and blood sprayed out of the wound in his arm. His gun went flying from his hand. This had barely registered when Brennan heard another shot and the second man, too, was left empty-handed. He clutched his shoulder and made a dive for the car. His accomplice followed. The doors of the car slammed shut, and Brennan heard the grinding of gears. Conn moved towards the vehicle, gun still raised, and Brennan, Terry, and the van driver followed, but the car reversed, turned, and peeled away. Conn aimed and shot out the tail lights before the would-be assassins disappeared around a corner.

Conn turned on his heel, adjusted something on his gun, and made a beeline for Tess. Molly was still covering Tess on the ground.

Conn helped Molly to her feet, embraced her, and then did the same with Tess. They clung to each other and spoke private words. Brennan could hardly imagine the conversation, following a gunfight not twenty feet away from the woman carrying Conn's children.

Conn took a deep breath, then disengaged himself from Tess. Her face was streaked with tears. Conn was dry-eyed, his face tight with fury. "Lads," he said, "would you excuse me for a moment? There's something — someone — I have to fucking straighten out here."

"Conn, you were nearly killed! How long is this going to —"

"Have to deal with this, Tessie. Why don't you get into the van where it's warm and wait for me?" He gently set her aside and walked to his neighbour's door.

Brennan saw the curtain closing in the window of the house. He imagined there had been a lot of curtains twitching in the street after the episode that had just occurred. He looked around and saw a few faces in a few windows; they all retreated after being seen.

Conn knocked on the neighbour's door and knocked louder when there was no response. Finally, a man opened the door and peered out. Conn had his gun out of sight, and his hands up in an effort to show he meant no harm. He must have reassured the man, or charmed his way in, because the door closed behind him.

The van driver scooped up the handguns that had been dropped in the street and returned to his vehicle. He stood by the cargo door, keeping watch over the street. Molly led Tess in behind him. The Burkes did their best to put a good face on and soothe the future member of the family.

It seemed like an hour but was probably no more than fifteen minutes when Conn emerged from the house. "We'll have nothing to fear from that pair again."

Brennan took him aside and asked, with as much calm as he could muster, "How do you know they won't be back to finish the job? Next time Tess might not be out of range, so they might get both of you. All of you."

"Believe me, Brennan, when I say they won't be back."

"What did you do? Put a contract out on them or what?"

Conn laughed. "Don't trouble yourself, Father. If I had wanted them dead, I'd have blown the heads off them through the rear window of the car instead of vandalizing their tail lights. The whole thing was a misunderstanding. They were given to understand that a certain person, who died suddenly, died at my hands. But rumours of my release from custody were premature, and inaccurate. What we had here was a failure to communicate. I was in fact still behind bars when that person's soul departed for its afterlife in hell, and I have the paper from Her Majesty's prison service to prove I was in there at the time. The deceased was executed by somebody else. The fellow I rang now knows that. He apologized profusely, and I'll be getting no more aggravation from that quarter. Now, where were we?"

Brennan looked at his cousin with a mixture of admiration and exasperation. If the younger Burke had the jitters, he was hiding it well. Brennan reflected on the four values prized above all by the Irish of ancient times, perhaps of all time: courage, loyalty, generosity, beauty. Conn Burke was not deficient in any of these, and most certainly not in courage. "To hear you talk, Conn, one would think you suffered nothing more than a minor interruption of a business meeting."

"You have to have nerves of steel to stay in business these days, Brennan. And sometimes you have to sink to using clichés, like 'Do you know who I am?' That sort of thing. All sorted. Let's get me and my bride over the threshold of our new home, shall we?"

Chapter XXVII

I balanced all, brought all to mind,
The years to come seemed waste of breath,
A waste of breath the years behind
In balance with this life, this death.

William Butler Yeats, "An Irish Airman Foresees His Death"

The day after the attempt on his cousin's life, Brennan found it difficult to take seriously the petty annoyances and troubles that plagued his provisional parishioners at St. Andrew's church. But he did his best to project the patience of a saint, and he put in a full day of work before returning to the flat in Kilburn. Molly was setting food out on the table when he walked in, and he didn't even bother to change out of his collar and clerical suit before sitting down with Terry to a much-needed Irish supper of bacon and cabbage, spuds, and mushy peas.

"Conn's coming over in a bit," Molly said.

"Hope he doesn't have a team of assassins trailing him this time."

"If he does, Terry, you can take up a rifle and fight by his side again for old time's sake."

They heard a knock on the door just as they picked up their forks.

"Here he is now."

Molly started to get up, but Terry said, "I'll let him in. Can't be too careful!"

Terry got up and pulled the door open and found himself facing not Conn Burke but Detective Sergeant John Chambers. Chambers was looking thin and rather pale, but well turned out in a navy sports jacket and a light blue shirt with the collar open.

"Is Molly at home?"

"Yes, she is," Terry answered, "but before I let you see my sister I want your word that your intentions are honourable."

Chambers laughed, a little uncomfortably, Brennan thought. Well, the man was in an awkward situation, to say the least.

And it dawned on Brennan then that Terry had never met the detective before. Terry had not been present at any of the encounters Brennan and Molly had had with Special Branch, though Special Branch had no doubt clocked Terry while carrying out surveillance on the family.

"Come in, John," Brennan said. "She's right here."

"John!" said Molly. Her hands flew up to her hair, and she patted it into place, then laughed at herself. "It must be innate. Male comes to door. Female engages in worried-about-hair behaviour. Would you like to join us for supper? There's plenty."

"No, no, thank you, Molly."

Brennan made the introductions. "John, this is our brother, Terry. Terry, Detective Sergeant John Chambers."

The two shook hands. The Special Branch man looked tense; this was obvious enough that Terry refrained from making a little quip about the detective's visit to Molly's flat.

Chambers looked at Molly and said, "I have to speak to you. I'll talk, and you people eat."

"All right," said Molly, "but if you change your mind about eating, I'll fill a plate for you. In the meantime, have a seat and relax for a bit."

They all sat down around the table.

"You didn't get me into any trouble after I revealed to you that your cousin was innocent of the murder of Detective Sergeant Heath, so I'm taking my chances again. May I have your assurance that anything I tell you stays in this room?"

"Of course, John. And I think I speak for my brothers as well."

"Absolutely," Terry agreed.

"Not a word from here," Brennan assured him. "And there's nobody listening through the walls or the light fixtures."

"I know." His eyes flickered over to Molly. She must have told Chambers about the ham acting that led to the exterminators coming in and eradicating the bugs.

Nobody knew what to say, with the police officer at the table. Even Terry was subdued. They all knew the Special Branch detective must have something serious to report. They also knew Conn was expected any minute. Brennan couldn't quite picture Conn Burke and Special Branch at the same table, unless it was in an interrogation room. But he put that out of his mind and listened to John Chambers.

"It goes without saying that I shouldn't be saying anything. I don't want to get myself in hot water, and I don't want you to put yourselves in danger by acting on the information I give you here today. But you've all given me your word, so I'll say no more about that."

Chambers was on edge, and everyone else caught the mood. Molly kept her eyes on him as if he were a surgeon coming out of the operating room to speak to the family.

"We in Special Branch are aware of a network of Irish Republican subversives working undercover in this country."

Brennan willed Terry not to make a wisecrack about the detective's rather stilted delivery. They needed to hear what the man had to say.

"This conspiracy was born many years ago, decades ago, over there." He jerked his head in the general direction of the west. "In Ireland. The plan was that these individuals would slip into England one by one, using false names and forged identity papers, and would establish outwardly respectable lives here so that, when it came time to act, they might avoid falling under suspicion. They are known to themselves, and now to us, as the Twelve Apostles, taking their inspiration from the assassination squad set up by Michael Collins during the Anglo-Irish War of 1919 to 1921." The war of many names: the Anglo-Irish War, the War of Independence, the Tan War, the (Old) Troubles.

"That might resonate pleasantly in the ears of some Irish but, as you can imagine, it would strike fear into the English person who knows a bit of history but is trying to get on with his daily life in the here and now. These twelve foreign agents are not necessarily tasked with assassination and murder, though I think any of them would kill, and probably have done, if they thought it would serve their cause. The Twelve Apostles have various tasks, including gathering intelligence about political, military, or police moves that might pose a threat to the Provisional IRA members living and causing mayhem here in England. Some of the Apostles are members of the IRA; some are not. But there is considerable overlapping, and the two groups communicate with one another and help each other out. The number of Apostles is intended to remain at twelve. They are usually men but currently there are two women. Over the years, if one of the group had to get out of the country, or if he became incapacitated, or if he died, he was replaced by a new recruit.

"The Apostles' biggest coup, so far, is to infiltrate the law enforcement and security apparatus of this country. I have to say that many of us—nearly all of us—at New Scotland Yard found it laughable when we first heard that claim. How could one of these Irish subversives get hired and start working on the inside without anyone catching on? But it's happened."

"Do you know who it is?" Terry could not resist asking.

"You'd be surprised what we know" was the detective's response.

Brennan glanced at Molly, who had hardly touched her food. Nobody had.

"For instance, we know a great deal about your family. Starting way back when the Fenians were throwing bombs around here in England in the late 1800s. Did you know we were originally called the Special Irish Branch? We were established to deal with the Fenian threat and the dynamiters. There were Fenian Burkes then and there are Fenian Burkes now. Five generations. And rebels in the centuries before that, I have little doubt."

Five generations. The youngest of the Burkes today. Brennan started to reach for his sister's hand, as a gesture of comfort, but he stopped himself. He didn't want to show any sign of weakness to Detective Sergeant Chambers, not that the man was unaware of the impact of his words.

"The members of this shadowy organization also help smuggle like-minded people into the country to do their dirty work and smuggle them out when it gets too hot for them here. And that's what I'm coming to, after that long introductory spiel. I'm here to warn you about young Finbarr. Do not let him come back into this country."

Molly let out a little cry and covered her mouth with her hand. Brennan was about to give Chambers a blast for upsetting the boy's mother. But one look at Chambers showed that he was not getting any enjoyment out of this at all. There was no smugness, no triumphant glint in his eye, over the knowledge Special Branch had about the activities of Molly's son. Chambers looked every bit as tense as Molly. There was no doubt that he cared very deeply about her.

"We know that Finbarr was recruited by a very dangerous individual called Kane. I believe everyone in the room met this Kane on at least one occasion."

"Is Kane one of the Twelve Apostles?" Brennan asked.

Chambers greeted that with derision. "He was beyond the pale even for an assassination squad."

"Was?" Brennan asked.

"Poor old Kane is no longer with us."

"Is that right? And what happened to him, I'm asking myself."

"Died of natural causes?" Terry inquired.

"In a sense, I suppose. He died of a condition known as lead behind the left ear. Almost always fatal. We had figured the IRA would get to Kane before we did; even *they* don't need a loose cannon like him.

And apparently that's what happened. I hear there was a botched attempt at revenge ordered by one of Kane's deputies. Turns out he sent his crew after the wrong man, an innocent man. But he was able to deflect the attempt on his life."

He paused and looked around the table. Brennan wondered whether Special Branch knew that Brennan and his two siblings had been present for that attempt. He got the impression there was little that got by this detective.

"But my point here," said Chambers, "is that Finbarr is believed to have carried out a couple of assignments in Belfast and here in England, on orders from Kane."

"What kind of assignments, John?" Molly asked. Brennan hardly recognized her voice.

Chambers put up his hand, *don't ask*. "Here is where I'm acting against my own interest. Because there's nothing we in Special Branch like better than another arrest to bolster our statistics. But, to help a friend, I'm giving you a warning."

The detective's eyes were on Molly, and everyone at the table knew the word "friend" was an exercise in British understatement.

"The Apostles' network got Finbarr out of England," he said. "So far, I don't think Garda Special Branch is aware of Finbarr's presence in the Republic. What you don't want is their Branch talking to our Branch about your son."

Molly was trembling, and Chambers looked as if he wanted nothing more than to go around the table and hold her in his arms. The Special Branch man was taking an enormous risk revealing all this information to members of the "Fenian Burke" family. But he must have convinced himself that Brennan and Terry would do nothing that would make things any worse for Finbarr or Molly.

It was then that they heard the second knock at the door. Molly got to it this time but, if she had intended to impart some words of warning, Conn did not afford her the opportunity. He burst into the room full of talk about his wedding. "Tessie is of the view that

I've been acting the maggot too long—getting myself arrested for murder, languishing in the *Sasanachs'* dungeon, generally wasting time—so I'm trying to get back in her good graces by planning the most brilliant wedding ever to be—"

He stopped in his tracks, broke off in mid-sentence, and stared at the police officer sitting at his cousin's table. The cop returned the stare. Brennan had never been in the wild but he could now visualize the moment when two fearsome animals came face to face, two alpha males, two natural enemies.

Who was going to break the silence first? It was Chambers. "You're a free man, Mr. Burke. Congratulations."

"No thanks to you lot."

Brennan was sure everyone in the room except Conn had the same gut reaction to that. Here was the man who had gone way out on a limb to give them the nod about Conn's innocence, and nobody could speak up and give him the credit that was owed him. The knowledge was too dangerous, the risk to the cop's career too great.

"What are you doing in my cousin's home?"

"Your cousin was kind enough to invite me in."

"I didn't ask you what Molly had done. I asked what you are doing here."

"Conn!" Molly said. "Detective Chambers is here as my guest. He—"

"Haven't you finished your work with us now, Chambers?"

The two men didn't take their eyes off one another. "I have, yes. I'm finished with this."

"I've got to go," Conn announced. "There's something I have to do."

"Why don't you take a break from doing things, Mr. Burke? Why not cease your activities, get married, and raise your children in peace?"

"Is that what you would do? Give up your own commitments? Retire from it all?"

"Yes. I would."

"I've got to go." And he was gone.

Chambers looked even more strained than he had when he arrived. Little wonder. But Conn's attitude was only to be expected if, as Brennan suspected, his time as an IRA prisoner in Brixton was much more harsh than he had ever let on. Brennan knew he had been belted on more than one occasion. If he had suffered even more ill treatment in there . . . but he didn't know, one way or the other.

Brennan tuned back in to the conversation, which Terry had brought around to where it had been before the interruption. "What are you going to do about the Twelve Apostles?" he asked Chambers.

"I can't tell you that. But I can tell you this. They're down to eleven now."

"What happened?" Molly asked, in a voice that indicated she knew perfectly well what had happened to the twelfth man.

"Liam O'Brien!" Brennan said.

Chambers gave a curt nod and got up from the table. He went to the sitting room window, peered out, and then returned to his seat.

Brennan thought of Rory Óg O'Brien not wanting his name overheard, claiming to have been in Dublin when in fact he was in London, making calls to Liam's home. Rory Óg was almost certainly another of the Apostles.

John Chambers looked at Molly's plate. "Eat up, my dear."

"I can't."

He smiled at her. "Ah but sure, you have to eat more than spuds and mushy peas, Máire."

"That's very good, Chambers. You've got the accent down pat," Terry said. "Talking like that, you could pass for a true Irishman. Must be all the eavesdropping you've done in Kilburn and Cricklewood over the years. Why don't you join us and have a drink. It will do you the world of good, and we won't grass on you."

"Wouldn't say no. I've a throat on me, no question."

"*Máire?*" their sister said. She was staring at Chambers.

"Of course he knows your real name, Mol," Terry said. "He

probably knows the full names and birth dates and pillow talk of every single member of our *well-known Republican family*."

"I do, sure," the Special Branch man said, still in an Irish voice. Terry got up and returned to the table with a bottle of whiskey and glasses. Chambers sat eyeing the bottle until Terry filled everyone's glass.

The cop downed his in one go, and then went back to the window. He surveyed the street below, and Brennan felt a chill, wondering what he was waiting for. Would there be a squad of Special Branch police converging on them at a signal from Chambers? Should he grab his brother and sister and make a run for it? But where? The police would find them wherever they went. And why would the three of them be a target? It didn't make sense. Brennan willed himself to stay calm and listen.

"Fuck," Chambers said, joining them at the table once again, "you put the heart crossways in Declan that day, Brennan, you running all over the streets of Wexford town and busting in to the place, when you were supposed to be up at the ruined abbey with your ma and Máire here. But I'll call you Molly, if you prefer it, pet."

"How do you *know* all this, John?"

"He knows because he was there," said Brennan, putting into words what his mind had just processed. "I'm sorry," he said to Chambers, "I don't know your name. I never did. Molly knows, though. Or she did, way back."

Molly's eyes were fixed on the policeman as if he were a ghost who had just materialized out of the mists. And, in a way, he was. "I knew there was something familiar about you," she told him, "but I couldn't place you. Not after so many years. So I thought you must have been following me as a Special Branch officer for years, and that's where I saw you. But, no, it was Wexford town, and you're a Delaney."

"Kevin Barry Delaney."

"My God!"

"I don't have much time." Tension was evident in his voice and posture.

"What do you mean?"

"So let me give you the story. Your grandfather Christy put the kibosh on a plot my father and others in Wexford were cooking up, a revival of the bombing campaign on English soil, this time to mark the three hundred years since the massacres committed by Cromwell in Wexford and Drogheda. The targets would be limited; they would be abbeys, churches, and other great buildings matched up with the kinds of places Cromwell and his men had destroyed in Ireland. And each attack would be billed as an act of revenge. That's what was being debated at the meeting in the Cape Bar you stumbled into, thanks to young Brennan here running away from the abbey. I was there with my father. I was supposed to stay out of sight with my sisters, but we all emerged from the woodwork when your crowd showed up, babies and all. I remember you well, Molly. You, too, Brennan.

"Anyway, Christy Burke said Wexford's bombing campaign was a bad idea. Pointless destruction—the murder of innocent buildings, as he put it—which would gain us nothing in the end. And the anti-Cromwell message would be lost because of all the monasteries destroyed the century before by Henry the Eighth! But he told the boys in Wexford he'd support them in something else. Whatever it was, it must never put civilians, women, or children at risk. The fact that the IRA began blowing up all kinds of non-military targets in England in 1973 was completely unrelated to the more modest Wexford plot.

"Christy asked my father and the others, 'What worked before? What got the Brits out of the Twenty-Six Counties?' And he talked about the accomplishments of Michael Collins when he was director of intelligence for the IRA during the War of Independence. Collins set up an assassination squad to put the eyes out of the British. In other words, to eliminate their spies. But more to the point for us was that he also had a network of spies and informers of his own, working in the police offices. He knew what was going to happen before it happened. Start thinking like that. Get a network of people in place who know what's happening, and who can protect our lads as we bring the war home to the seat of the British Empire. Penetrate the police and the security organizations, if possible. Christy urged the boys in Wexford to take the long view. Get to work now setting up a squad, for the future.

"The planning began that very day. It was going to be my father's role to start recruiting people to go undercover in England. We pulled up stakes and emigrated to Australia when I was still a child. We were fixed up with false papers, new names and histories. At first we were given the name Thornbury, but it was apparent immediately that me oul da, God rest him, would blow his cover the first time he pronounced it: *T'arnbury*. So we made it Chambers. Our story was that we were of English stock, living in Australia, and then moved to the mother country.

"But by the time we made all those moves, my father was too old to embark on a career as a police officer in England. So I stepped into the breach."

"You're the mole inside Special Branch!" Brennan exclaimed.

"The mole, the spy, the Apostle Kevin. I thought the most believable role for me to play was that of a striver, a fellow from a humble family trying to climb the ladder of society and class. Hence, the not-quite-there upper middle class accent. A common type in this country. *Frightfully* common, the toffs would say. I reasoned that if my betters were busy sneering at the class anxieties of a typically insecure Englishman, they would not suspect me as a bog Irish spy."

Brennan recalled the condescending attitude displayed towards Chambers by Mawdsley—MI5 spook and brilliant character actor, Cedric Mawdsley—who had lured them from Molly's flat to the great country house at Blythewich, so his colleagues could wire the flat for sound. Mawdsley was the very type that Chambers had pretended to emulate. Chambers had been utterly convincing in his role.

"You weren't just faking it when you said you admired the Irish!" Molly exclaimed.

"I was pretending to pretend. Jolly good show, eh what?"

"Yes indeed."

"How did you like my collection of bogus Irish music, *Ireland O'Rama*? I was afraid I might have gone over the top and blown it there. But it was great gas seeing the expression on your face."

"No worries there. I fell for it and thought you were trying very hard to be open-minded! And then you produced Planxty, on the advice of the man in the record shop, or so you said."

"I've always been a fan of Planxty. Had to bite my tongue so I wouldn't sing along with every note. My real collection of music is at home, secreted away in 'What to Listen for in Beethoven' covers, the sort of thing a striver like me would be expected to have. At night I would sit in my car outside Hannigan's, partly to play my role of Special Branch copper watching the shifty Irish, but mainly to listen to the craic. I'd roll my window down and listen to the music, wishing to God I was in there. I envied Conn, being able to get up there and tell his tales and get his laughs and sing his rebel songs. I longed to be able to do that myself. Conn and I went on a rip together in Glasgow once. One of the best nights of my life. I let my hair down that night. Took a huge risk."

"You're a friend of Conn!" Molly exclaimed.

"We're friends and brothers in arms."

"But when he was here just now, the way he spoke to you . . ."

"He didn't know what was happening and didn't want to blow my cover. He couldn't let on that he knew who I really was, so he had to play a role."

"We should call him, get him back here," Terry said.

"He'll be back," Delaney said quietly, "but he'll be too late."

"What do you mean?" Molly asked.

He ignored her question, and returned to his role as a spy.

"What really had me terrified was spending time with you, Molly." He fixed his eyes on her and was silent for a long time; it was as if he had forgotten everyone else in the room. "If ever I was going to blow my cover, it would have been with you. And that's what nearly happened, on the trip to Bath. We got onto the subject of children and of course I could never have brought children into the world, because I'd never be able to tell them who their father was, who they really were. So that doomed my young marriage. Which means I've spent far too much time alone, brooding and looking into the bottom of a bottle. And then I met you, and I couldn't tell you any of this even though we are both Irish patriots, and . . . fuck, I'm sorry, I don't usually do all this whinging."

"It's hardly that," Molly assured him. "I can't imagine how you avoided a nervous breakdown."

"I nearly had one the day we went to Bath! I was so tense and wound up when we were together in the bar, I forgot to keep up my English accent."

"I just thought you were making fun of me."

"Well, that's what I hoped, that you'd think exactly that. So I staged that pantomime in the call box. I figured you'd come out eventually and when I saw your reflection in the glass I started blathering into the phone. There was nobody on the other end. Made myself out to be a merciless bastard, and pretended to mock a Scottish dialect. All so you wouldn't catch on that I had let the mask slip. You know, the temptation was almost physical, to come clean and confess it all to you, so you would know I was not an oul bigot working against the Irish here in *Sasana*. So I doubled my efforts to be convincing. I thought the best way to do that was to play the role of someone who really did want to understand those confounding Irishmen."

"You were utterly believable, John. *Kevin*. And I know everyone here would agree."

It was brought back to him that there were others besides him and Molly in the flat. He looked at them all in turn. "Anyway, you can now fill in the rest of Conn's story about the shooting of Richard Heath. The third person present at the murder scene, the man Conn would never have named, was me."

This was met by a stunned silence.

"I was doing my bit for Wexford's revenge, small token though it was. We had been waiting since 1949. Since 1649 really. The message was *See what we could have done to your great abbey? But we're better than that. Cromwell showed no such restraint. Maybe we won't either, next time.* We had the support and assistance of the England Department, but just barely."

"England Department?" Brennan asked.

"The England Department of the IRA. They went along, largely thanks to Conn's persuasive abilities, but they didn't like such a big operation wasted, as they saw it, on a message other than 'Brits out, united Ireland.' They gave us a hand, though, good soldiers that they are. Anyway, one of the Twelve Apostles is an engineer. Works with the U.K. government to maintain the heritage properties. He's also a man knowledgeable about explosives. And how to keep them from exploding. He had been putting this material in place, bit by bit and ingeniously hidden, over a period of several weeks. Conn's role was to watch this man's back while he did his work."

Brennan formed an image of the engineer bent over his work in the corners of the great abbey, Conn watching from the shadows with his hand on the butt of a Browning Hi-Power pistol.

"Our man on the inside hoped to have everything ready on the twenty-fifth of April, Cromwell's birthday, but there were some snags, so we weren't sure. Conn and I agreed that I would drive into Elverton Street, and he would wait for me. If the operation was on, he would call in the warning to the Met to evacuate the abbey, then come to the corner of Elverton and Horseferry Road with a rolled-up newspaper in his hand. That would be my sign that it was on.

"Well, it was on, so Conn called in the warning. Then he came to our meeting spot. He didn't expect to see me in Richard Heath's car, but your cousin was able to spot two Special Branch men without any difficulty. What he didn't know was that there was now another, very urgent, reason for making sure the bomb plot went ahead.

Dickie Heath was going to die in the chaos, and it was going to look like an accident, or a fight with someone on the scene. Because Heath had found out about the Apostles. He didn't know all the details yet, but he was on the trail. He had beaten the information out of Liam O'Brien. It was Heath who committed the murder in Essex County."

"The Special Branch detective killed Liam O'Brien!" Molly exclaimed.

"That's right."

Brennan recalled Mairéad and Rory Óg O'Brien's description of the brutality unleashed upon Liam.

Kevin Delaney continued his grim recital. "Heath knew it would look as though Liam had been killed because he was an informant. But what looked like a police informant was really one Irish undercover agent reporting to another for the cause. Liam posed as a tourist on his trips to Colchester but the only touristy thing about him was the camera he always carried. His task was to find abbeys and other church buildings equivalent to those destroyed by Cromwell's army in Ireland, and plant hoax bombs in them, like the Westminster Abbey job. Problem was, so many of the buildings here in England had already suffered the same fate under the two Cromwells, Thomas and Oliver. Anyway, I used to go to Colchester to meet him, at St. John's Abbey Gatehouse. If anyone asked questions, he would say he was with the Heritage Buildings Preservation Society. So that was our code. One of his other roles was as gardener to various political and military grandees. He gained a lot of useful information that way. Liam O'Brien lived and died an Irish patriot.

"Detective Sergeant Dickie Heath took Liam somewhere, maybe relaxed him with drink, got behind him and handcuffed or tied him up, and beat the information out of him, then dumped his body. I don't know how much Liam said under duress. Torture, in other words. Heath took that young fellow apart with a claw hammer. I always thought Heath was a fucking psychopath. No doubt in my mind now. Not that he's the only one to resort to such methods in this conflict. Very, very few people can hold up under such hideous pain. I'm not sure I . . . not sure I would. Whatever the case, Heath came back with information about me, which I detected right away. I didn't let on I knew he was suspicious, but you can imagine the stress I was under. The double life was tearing me apart anyway. Medic tells me I have an ulcer. That's the least of it.

"So, I arranged to ride with Heath in his car. Somehow in the midst of all this plotting and scheming, Conn had got wind of the bomb at the Cromwell statue. That was real. It would have been set off by a remote device, and Cromwell's present-day admirers would have been blown to hell to join their hero."

"This one wasn't a hoax—it was going to blow up!" Terry exclaimed.

"That's right, and it was going to take the Cromwell Association with it. But you know Conn. He refused to go along with that, even though I later heard that he said it would serve the fuckers right. But he was having none of it. So he comes flying at our car in Elverton Street, pulls his gun on us, and forces us to stop. He grabs the driver's side door handle, yanks it open, and shouts across Heath at me. He wants the contact number and the code so he can call off the Cromwell bombing. Even under all the strain, Conn had the presence of mind to invent a cover story. He demanded that I give him the 'notes' I had promised him for the work with 'Ollie,' so Ollie wouldn't go off and never talk again. In other words, he tried to make it sound as if he was a tout and wanted his money; otherwise his source, Ollie, would dry up. But I had no need of pretence at that time. Because Heath was not going to live to report any of this.

"I had a crisis of conscience at that point, at least about the bombing. I had never been party to an attack on a group of civilians—even Cromwellians—and I saw the light. So now I was desperate to stop the Cromwell explosion. I handed Conn the phone number and code."

It was as if Brennan and his sister and brother had been made into statues themselves; there wasn't a movement, wasn't a sound, from any of them, as Delaney told his story.

"But Richard Heath wasn't fooled, not with what he had put together about me. He realized that Conn and I were in cahoots. So Heath had to die immediately before he could radio any of this in. I said to Conn, 'He knows everything.' Heath went for the radio but Conn refused to shoot him. So I grabbed Conn's gun and shot him. Had to. I was at war with him, just as he was at war with Liam O'Brien."

Again, he had stunned everyone into silence.

"I wanted to let Conn know that Heath had tortured and killed O'Brien but there wasn't time. Conn was off to the call box again to phone in the second warning."

Terry finally found words. "And then you had to carry on in Special Branch as usual, after killing one of your own officers."

"*My own* people, Terry, are the people of Ireland, and those in the North who are still not united with their countrymen. And I take care of my own. I sent you a coded warning, Molly, using the code Conn and I had, telling you to cancel the paint job on Cromwell. As for Conn, you can rest easy. He won't be facing any charges in connection with the bomb plot. All Special Branch will find about Conn is a doctored file attesting to his innocence."

"But," Brennan said, "if you are under suspicion, they're not going to trust anything you write in your files."

"It's not in my files. It's in Dickie Heath's files. I forged the notes in his name. The record is going to show that Detective Sergeant Richard Heath's detective work found that Conn was innocent of the conspiracy, and Detective Sergeant John Chambers tried to cover that up to deflect attention away from his own treasonous activities. That way, it's believable. Make sure Conn's solicitor knows the file is there."

"That saves Conn from a long term in prison, Kevin, but why in God's name would you let yourself be implicated?"

"Because . . ." he cleared his throat and began again, "because they're already on to me. Heath shared his suspicions with one or more of our senior men. I know they were just waiting to make their move."

"And the reason they know Conn is innocent of Heath's murder is . . ." Brennan began.

"They know I did it. I've been on the run since Conn was released."

"Oh God, Kevin," Molly whispered.

A few seconds passed and then Delaney got up again and went to the window. His eyes raked the area below. He turned and said to them, in a tone that was almost business-like, "There is also a report in Scotland Yard—a genuine report—showing that there was a 'consistent mechanical defect' in the explosives in the abbey; they could not have been detonated."

The Burkes sat quietly for a few more moments trying to take it all in. Then Terry asked, "Do the police know Heath killed Liam O'Brien?"

"They do now. And I wanted to get that information to Conn, but I had no plausible excuse for visiting him in prison. Even if I had, it would have put him in danger, talking to a peeler. And it was hardly a message I could entrust to anybody else to deliver. So he didn't have the full story about why Heath was killed.

"And the fate that befell Heath was kinder than the fate he bestowed on Liam O'Brien. Or the fate that awaits me if they manage to take me in. Our interrogators will not be gentle. And I cannot bear the thought that I might reveal the names of other patriots we've put in place over here. Give them up under torture. That's what I'll be facing if they take me . . . if they take me in."

"It's time for you to get out, John. Kevin. Get on a plane and—"

"There isn't time, Molly." His face was as white as alabaster. "Could I speak to you for a minute?"

"Of course. Would you like . . ." He nodded. Yes, he would like to speak privately.

She led him into her bedroom. Terry looked at Brennan and got up, ready to follow them into the room. Brennan shook his head. "She'll be fine," he said quietly.

A few minutes later they emerged, Kevin Delaney followed by Molly. She had something in her hand, a cassette tape. She was as pale as he was; they both looked haunted.

"Now, could I have a word with you, Brennan?"

"Certainly, Kevin." He nodded towards the bedroom and they went inside. Window blinds shut out the early evening sun; the room was dim, and the two men stood awkwardly, face to face. What was Brennan going to hear now?

Delaney took a deep breath and said, "I didn't want to tell Molly this. You can decide whether you think she should know. It's about her son. This is how the whole fucking thing began to come apart for me. The Branch got on to the fact that somebody new was bringing in components for bombs here in London. They also suspected the same person had been involved in an insurance bombing in Belfast. Do you know what I'm talking about?"

"Insurance bombing?" Brennan thought he had heard something about bombs and insurance, but he just shook his head.

"Some of the boys in the IRA would take a fee or a kickback from business owners in return for blowing up their premises, so the business owners could make a claim through their insurance companies."

"Mother of Christ!"

"I know, I know. Some of these businesses were barely hanging on, given the situation over there. All of a sudden, the solution comes in the form of a bomb and an insurance cheque. And money handed over to the IRA for the service. Call it fundraising, if you will."

Fundraising. Was this what the lads in Dundalk meant about Finbarr's activities? Was he learning at the feet of those who had blown up Tess's father's printing shop a few years back?

"Well, I heard about this," Delaney said now, "and through other information I had, I concluded Finbarr was involved. I know he had slipped over to Belfast at least once. And he was playing a part in smuggling explosives into England. Maybe for the same scheme, maybe something else. I don't know. So I arranged for Liam O'Brien to contact Finbarr, meet him, and get him over to the Republic to avoid arrest. Liam, God rest him, did his best. But he wanted to do it right. Making the contacts and the arrangements, getting some paperwork forged, all that took time, and there were some snags. Finbarr himself had the janglers and was not always cooperative with the plan. Anyway, poor Liam was murdered before he could get Finbarr out. Then Liam's father, Rory Óg, took over the job. I thought I was going to die of high blood pressure waiting for the little bollocks to get the fuck out of England! I don't know what will happen. But Richard Heath had been watching Liam O'Brien, and when this connection with Finbarr was made, this and a few other things led Heath to suspect me. He confirmed his suspicions, I know, when he extracted the information from O'Brien before killing him."

"This all happened because you tried to save young Finbarr."

"Sure, I'd do it for any promising young lad," Delaney said with an effort at light-heartedness.

"You did it for Molly."

"Take care of her, Brennan," he said and returned to the living room.

Delaney walked over to Terry and shook his hand. He did the same with Brennan and said, "Pray for me, Father."

Brennan would; if anyone was in need of prayer, it was Kevin Delaney. "The blessings of God on you, Kevin."

Without another word, without looking at Molly, Delaney walked out.

Brennan and Terry regarded their sister in silence. Finally she spoke up. "He said he was sorry for tailing us, questioning us. I said not to worry, that he was doing his job. He laughed at that, and then we both did. He said it has been extremely difficult for him, living a lie, leading a secret life, doing some of the things he's had to do. He has always been lonely but he said it was a life he chose. For the cause. He told me to look out for Conn. And . . . for Finbarr. He said he had fought down the temptation to confide in me when we were together, to spill the whole forty-year history. He gave me this." She showed them a Planxty cassette, *The Woman I Loved So Well.* "He put his arms around me and said, 'I loved you, Molly. I loved you.'"

"Loved you," Brennan said, "past tense."

"Yes," she said. She was shaking. "As if it is impossible for us ever to be together. And of course it is. I would never make things even worse for him by—"

"No," said Brennan. "Past tense as if he's already dead."

"Get him back him in here!" Terry exclaimed and crossed the room in two bounds. He yanked open the door, and they ran from the flat, down the stairs, and out to the street.

What they saw stopped them cold. Kevin Delaney was standing off to their left, at the edge of the narrow laneway between their building and the next. His hands were down by his sides. He was looking across the street, where there were three police cars with their doors open, and six men in bulletproof vests spanned out along the pavement. Six rifles were pointed at Delaney. The neighbouring buildings cast shadows over the cops; Delaney stood in the blaze of the sun.

Brennan wondered if he could ever bring himself to tell his sister that Delaney had risked arrest, imprisonment for life—even, as he suggested, torture—for her son. For her. The risk had become a reality. This was day one of his long descent into the abyss.

Before Brennan could think of anything to say in such a perilous situation, Delaney shouted, *"Tiocfaidh ár Lá!"* It was a Republican rallying cry: Our day will come! Then he raised his right hand and fired one shot from a revolver over the heads of the police. The line of officers instantly fired back. The volley of return fire was deafening. It blasted Kevin Delaney back six feet, and he landed face-up on the pavement of the laneway. Blood poured from the wounds in his neck and body.

It was then that the police spotted the three onlookers in the doorway of Molly's building. Five of the six rifles were instantly trained on Brennan and his sister and brother. Brennan tore his eyes from the barrels of the guns and looked over at Delaney. Was he still alive? He needed an ambulance; he needed a priest.

Terry said in a low, calm voice, "Mol, Bren. Raise your hands, slowly."

Brennan returned his gaze to the policeman directly across from him, then lifted his hands away from his body and up in the air. His brother and sister were doing the same.

Time had altered; everything seemed to be happening in slow motion. There was shouting from the police, but Brennan could not take in what they were saying. Two of the officers went to Delaney. Two came towards the building, and two stayed where they were, surveying the street and the rooftops. One of the cops frisked Brennan and then Terry. The cop looked at Molly, turned towards one of the police cars, and raised his hand. A female officer emerged and walked towards Molly, gave her a cursory pat-down, nodded, and returned to the car. None of the Burkes protested. Each one of them understood that, in these extreme circumstances—the police having seen the enemy agent emerging from Molly's flat, the enemy agent firing a gun—Brennan, Molly, and Terry were lucky to be still standing.

But Brennan had only one objective now: to get to Delaney and comfort him, give him the last rites. Brennan looked to the lane and saw the officers crouched beside the fallen man. One appeared to be checking his injuries and searching him for further weaponry. He had already picked up the revolver from the street. He was talking. To Delaney? Interrogating him? The other cop was speaking urgently into a radio.

"Let me go to him," Brennan implored the officer facing him. "Let him have the sacrament."

The cop eyed his Roman collar and exchanged glances with his partner, but they had other priorities. Brennan was vaguely aware of

Terry talking to the police in calm, measured tones. His experience in military and civilian aviation, in handling emergencies, stood him in good stead now. Stood them all in good stead. Brennan half-listened as his brother told the London police who the three of them were, that he was an airline pilot and former member of the U.S. Air Force; that, yes, Molly had been picked up but had been cleared of suspicion and that several other officers would verify this; that his brother was a priest; that their documents were all in order in the flat. That they had recently become acquainted with the Special Branch detective. That none of the three were members of the IRA or any other clandestine organization. Then there was talk about searching the flat, and two cops disappeared, presumably to do that.

But this was all happening at the edge of Brennan's consciousness. It was agonizing for him to see Kevin Delaney lying still on the pavement, without the comfort of a loving hand, without the comfort of the final sacrament. And it was just as heart-scalding to see Molly standing there, tearful and stricken but unmoving.

Brennan heard a siren approaching. He resolved there and then to do his duty for Kevin Delaney. There was no time to wait for permission from the armed men who controlled the scene. He slowly raised his hands again and began walking to the laneway. Images came unbidden to his mind, images of the priests he had heard about in Belfast, shot to death by British soldiers as they, the priests, ministered to people lying wounded on the ground, people who had been shot by the soldiers minutes before. But Brennan kept on walking. He felt, rather than saw, someone fall into step beside him. He knew it was Molly.

Kevin Delaney lay in a pool of blood, gasping for breath. His eyes found Brennan and then Molly, and fastened on her with a look of desperation. Molly knelt on one side of him and Brennan on the other. Brother and sister exchanged glances, and Brennan spoke first. He took the dying man's left hand in his and said, "Kevin, if you can, say an Act of Contrition with me. If you can . . ."

Delaney tried to speak, but all that came out was a rattling sound. His eyes locked on Brennan's; it seemed he was beseeching him to . . . what? Absolve him? Brennan whispered the prayer. "O my God, I am heartily sorry for having offended Thee." Brennan could not interpret the intense expression on Delaney's face, though he had seen it many times before. What goes through a man's mind *in extremis*? No one can know until the time arrives. But Brennan took it to be consent, desire for the sacrament. He made the sign of the cross over him and said, *"Ego te absolvo a peccatis tuis in nomine Patris et Filii et Spiritus Sancti. Amen."*

Molly took Kevin's right hand, leaned over, and spoke in his ear. Brennan could not hear her words and had no wish to. She bent forward and kissed his forehead.

Brennan could see the life fading from Kevin's eyes. When it was clear that his life had left him, Brennan and Molly rose, slowly, and starting walking to her home.

Brennan looked around him. He thought he saw something move in the shadow between two buildings at the end of the laneway. A man emerged from the shadow, a gunman. It was Conn. He was staring straight ahead, at Delaney. He shoved the gun out of sight under his belt. He had arrived too late to do whatever he thought he might have done.

Brennan understood now what Conn and Delaney had been trying to do back in the flat: Delaney was telling Conn he was giving up the fight. Conn knew how it would have to end, and he wanted to prevent it. But it could not have been prevented. Conn never had a chance. He looked stricken. Bereft. He fell to his knees.

An ambulance came screaming into the street. And more police arrived. The forces of the Crown closed in on what remained of Kevin Barry Delaney.

Acknowledgements

I would like to thank the following people for their kind assistance: my first readers, Joe A. Cameron, Rhea McGarva, and Joan Butcher; Bill McKillip and Bob Kroll, for their advice on military matters; law professor Steve Coughlan at Dal and barrister Stephen Mason in England; and the people at *insidetime*, the prisoners' newspaper in the U.K. Thanks as well to my insightful and sharp-eyed editors, Cat London and Crissy Calhoun. Unacknowledged by name, but appreciated all the same, are a few fellows in Belfast and in London's Kilburn High Road, who have been quoted anonymously herein.

A special word of appreciation goes out to Eric Bogle, for permission to use lyrics from his matchless song about the futility of war, "No Man's Land."

This is a work of fiction. Any liberties taken in the interests of the story, or any errors committed, are mine alone.

At ECW Press, we want you to enjoy this book in whatever format you like, wherever you like. Leave your print book at home and take the eBook to go! Purchase the print edition and receive the eBook free. Just send an email to ebook@ecwpress.com and include:

Get the
eBook free!*
proof of purchase
required

- the book title
- the name of the store where you purchased it
- your receipt number
- your preference of file type: PDF or ePub?

A real person will respond to your email with your eBook attached. And thanks for supporting an independently owned Canadian publisher with your purchase!